The BRAVEST SOLDIERS

Book 2 In The Immense Sky Saga

ELAINE AUCOIN SCHROLLER

Human Authored™, Reg #: 3079446,
   https://authorsguild.org/human

ISBN 979-8-9852616-2-2: eBook
ISBN 979-8-9852616-3-9: Paperback

Cover design: Elaine Schroller and Lewis Poore
Cover images: © Nicole Matthews/Arcangel (woman); Kyle Strauss/iStock (Sydney Harbour Bridge); Almay (Australia map)

05112025

Praise for The Bravest Soldiers,
Love and longing in
WWII Australia and the South West Pacific Area

"A rich and moving saga of bravery both at home and in the face of battle." —Kirkus Reviews

"A sweeping portrait of life on the Australian home front during the second World War."
—Publisher's Weekly BookLife Prize

"A compelling story told with insight and understanding... Schroller deftly builds a portrait of two proud women ... as courageous as the men they love."
—The Prairies Book Review

"...a tapestry intricately woven with the threads of valor, passion, and heartrending sacrifice."
—The Historical Fiction Company

"...captures the essence of a tumultuous era through deeply personal narratives ... a rich, immersive experience..."
—Chrysalis BREW Project Review

"...heartfelt and memorable... Having grown up in Queensland and Canberra, I ... was shocked at what people in Australia had to do back home while the men were away fighting."
—Readers Favorite 5-star Review

Praise for Dare Not Tell,
Romance, secrets, and redemption in
WWI France and Australia

"Fans of historical fiction romance novels will be delighted to read the arch of Sophie and Joe's love."
—Publisher's Weekly BookLife Prize

"Vividly evocative and steeped in history... Readers will be left impressed with Schroller's control over her historical atmosphere as well as her multilayered, intriguing characterizations."
—Prairies Book Review

"Dare Not Tell is heart-breaking, touching, mysterious, and thrilling."
—Feathered Quill Book Reviews

"I couldn't wait to pick up the story to immerse myself in their world... I didn't want it to end."
—Rae Blair, author of *More Than I Ever Had*

"...a beautifully written story, with a rich sense of place..."
—Kimberly Sullivan, award-winning author of *Dark Blue Waves* and *Shadows In the Apennines*

"Dare Not Tell is a poignant portrayal of the long-term impact of trauma and how visceral fears can create isolation and distance even in the best of relationships. Schroller's writing, command of history, and compassion for how relationships evolve through tragedy are superb."
—Teri Case, award-winning author of *Tiger Drive* and *In the Doghouse*

Also by Elaine Aucoin Schroller

Dare Not Tell,
a novel of romance, secrets, and redemption
set in WWI France and Australia

To Patricia and Emma, two Australian ladies who generously shared their stories of life, love, midget submarines, and General Douglas MacArthur in WWII Sydney and Brisbane with me.

To my mother Beth, who has been with me at every turn in this adventure.

Glossary and a Note on Spelling

I'm an American novelist, so expect US spelling in the text of this book: for example, check instead of cheque, recognize instead of recognise, favorite instead of favourite, and harbor instead of harbour unless Harbour is part of a proper name.

However, when you're reading letters and dialogue from the Australian and French characters, expect British spelling and Australian expressions and slang.

ACT: Australian Capital Territory, a territory within New South Wales where Canberra, the capitol of Australia, is located.

AIF: Australian Imperial Force, the Australian army.

ANZAC, Anzac: in uppercase, the WWI acronym for Australia New Zealand Army Corp; in lowercase, usually refers to a specific type of cookie/biscuit made with coconut and oats, but no butter or eggs, which meant they didn't spoil when sent to troops in WWI and WWII.

AWLA: Australian Women's Land Army; members were usually called Land Girls.

NSW: New South Wales, the state in eastern Australia where Sydney is located.

QLD: Queensland, the state in northeastern Australia where Brisbane is located.

RAAF: Royal Australian Air Force

RAF: Royal Air Force (the English one)

SWPA: South West Pacific Area, the area under the command of General Douglas MacArthur, including Australia, Papua, New Guinea, and the western Solomon Islands, plus the Philippines, Borneo, Dutch East Indies (except Sumatra), and East Timor.

VIC: Victoria, the southernmost state in mainland Australia where Melbourne, Jean-Luc's winery, and his army training grounds are located.

Please also be aware that historical fiction sometimes uses terms that can be considered offensive in the present; I have tried to counterbalance such terms by limiting their use.

Cast of Characters

THE MAJOR PLAYERS

Sophie Parker: American. Wife of Joe Parker, godmother and adoptive mother of Jean-Luc Guy, stepmother to Sam Parker. WWI nurse at the American Hospital in Paris. Now devotes her time to raising money for charitable organizations in Sydney.

Joe Parker: Australian. Husband of Sophie, father of Sam, adoptive father of Jean-Luc. WWI captain in the Australian army. Now head of Forensics for New South Wales police.

Sam Parker: Australian. Pilot for an aerial surveying company. Joins the Royal Australian Air Force (RAAF) No 4 Squadron at the onset of WWII. Trains new pilots and then flies tactical reconnaissance in New Guinea.

Jean-Luc Guy: French. Winemaker in Victoria, Australia. Joins the Australian army's 7th Division. Fights in Syria/Lebanon and the Kokoda Trail in New Guinea.

Marianne Ryan: French-Australian. Seamstress and aspiring designer. Sails to Sydney with Sophie and Joe to spend a year in her Australian father's birth country.

SUPPORTING CAST

Moira & Thomas Kelly: The Parker's housekeeper/cook and handyman.

Patricia Lawson: Marianne's flat mate in Sydney.

Lily Holt: Sophie's widowed mother.

Flora: Lily's widowed sister, Sophie's aunt.

Angel: Flora's aging mare.

Howard: The Parker's terrier mutt. Loves to play fetch and run around everyone's ankles.

Teddy, Katie, & Cora O'Brien: Children who are taken in by the Parkers during WWII.

Edmund Stone: Writes for American military publications. Friend of the Parker and Ryan families.

HONORED DEAD

Ben: Sophie's older brother. Killed by a German shell in 1916.

Robbie: Joe's younger brother. Missing, presumed killed in April 1917.

Annie: Joe's first wife. Sam's mother. Influenza in November 1918.

Michael: Sophie's first husband. Suicide in March 1927.

Natalie: Jean-Luc's mother. Sophie's best friend. Auto accident in May 1928.

AUSTRALIAN CHORUS

Fred Thompson: Joe's right-hand man in forensics.

Miss Pringle: Joe's right-hand woman in forensics.

Patrick & Catherine O'Brien: Parents of Teddy, Katie, and Cora.

Mrs. Albert: Tenement landlady.

Monsignor Sullivan & Father O'Donnell: Priests at St Mary's Cathedral in Sydney.

Ellen & Kino Mitsui: Neighbors of the Parkers.

John F. Kennedy: Commander of PT-109 and 35th president of the United States.

Alan & Neil: American pilots, friends of Edmund Stone.

Alf & Vern: Gardeners at Flora's Sydney estate.

Betty: Member of the Australian Women's Land Army. Works at Flora's country estate.

Assistant Commissioner Bobby Davies: Joe's boss. Wants Joe to remain in Sydney.

Colonel Roger Davies: Wants Joe to re-enter the army.

Franklin & Bluey: Sam's squadron leader and RAAF mate.

EUROPEAN CHORUS

Will & Hélène Ryan: Marianne's parents.

Chris Ryan: Marianne's brother.

Nick: Chris Ryan's best friend.

Monique & Georges: Nick's parents. Longtime friends of Edmund Stone and the Ryan family.

Vanni: Longtime friend of Georges, Edmund, and Will.

More than kisses, letters mingle souls.

John Donne

PART 1: 1939 - 1940

SYDNEY, AUSTRALIA

You sing of England's might and power,
In air, on land and sea,
That she is ever ready to defend
The cause of liberty.

Author Unknown,
"The Womenfolk We Left Behind"

ONE

HOME AT LAST

FRIDAY, 1 SEPTEMBER 1939

S ophie Parker could hardly contain her excitement as the steamship passed Botany Bay and then the golden crescents of Coogee, Bronte, and Bondi beaches. She braced herself against the ship's railing, scanning Sydney's sandstone cliffs until she found what she sought—a house on the highest point in Dover Heights, its white façade gleaming against spring's immense blue sky.

"There it is!" She passed the field glasses to her husband. Joe stood on her right, peering at the shore intently. The taut lines of his shoulders relaxed as he, too, found their home.

The vessel rounded Watson's Point and passed between the North and South Heads into Sydney Harbour. Rocky fingers jutted from the mainland to form bays, each with distinct personalities. Sophie reeled off their names like old friends: Rose first and then Double, Rushcutters, Elizabeth, and Woolloomooloo. Past Mrs. Macquarie's chair at the tip of the Royal Botanic Gardens and Fort Macquarie at Bennelong Point. Ferries chugged from Circular Quay to ply their routes while the ship slipped under the Harbour Bridge, glided into Darling Harbour, and slowed to a stop at Pyrmont Wharf.

After five months of traveling that had taken them around the world—from Sydney to Vancouver, across North America to England and France, through the Suez Canal, past the Arabian Peninsula, India, and around the southern coast of Australia back to Sydney—she and Joe were home.

Her favorite place in the world.

—

Sophie had a long list of second favorite places in the world, one of which was the huge, clawfoot bathtub she'd sourced when she and Joe bought this house and turned a small bedroom into an en-suite bathroom. She leaned back, luxuriated in hot water and lavender-scented bubbles, and reviewed the day so far.

Their arrival in Sydney had been considerably more complicated than their departure from Sydney had been. For one thing, they arrived with two additional people in tow. Sophie's widowed mother Lily was relocating from England to Australia to live with her sister Flora, who was also widowed. Lily had left a good portion of her possessions at the family's London townhouse, but she brought a large number of trunks. Marianne Ryan, the twenty-two-year-old French-Australian seamstress who had traveled with them as Lily's companion, was only staying in Australia for one year, but she brought a trunk, her precious dressmaker's form, and her even more precious portable sewing machine.

Luckily the purser had been able to arrange portage before they disembarked, so they didn't have to bother with trying to find someone to do it amidst the dockside clamor.

Their arrival had been exciting, joyful, and more than a little exhausting once they'd finally snagged enough porters to help Thomas, their caretaker, load their valises into the two waiting cars. The reunion at home with their housekeeper and cook Moira Kelly, had been joyful too, with the addition of Howard, the Parker's terrier mutt, yipping and racing around everyone's ankles.

The house was quiet now, had been for some time, and Sophie idly wondered where Joe had disappeared to. When he finally made it upstairs, the bathwater water was cooling and the bubbles had mostly dissipated.

She heard him calling from their bedroom. "Sophie, where *are* you?"

"I'm in the tub. Exactly where I said I'd be. Where have *you* been?"

Joe entered the bathroom and held a slip of paper so she could read it. "Here's the message I sent to Will and Hélène."

SYDNEY 1 SEP 1939
TO: H/W RYAN VILLERS-BRETONNEUX FRANCE
ARRIVED HOME THIS MORNING STOP
MARIANNE EXCITED TO BE HERE STOP
SOPHIE AND I WILL LOOK AFTER HER STOP
OUR BEST TO YOU BOTH AND CHRIS STOP
J PARKER

She scanned the message and nodded. "Thank you darling. Did you get sidetracked after that?" Joe's tie was loosened, his top two shirt buttons were undone, and his sleeves were rolled up to his elbows. Clearly, he'd been doing something more than just sending the telegram.

"Erm..."

"Let me guess. You used the phone in your study to call in the telegram, and since you were there, you couldn't resist opening the boxes with your forensics notes from our trip."

Joe gave her one of his looks that said he couldn't believe she knew exactly what he'd been doing. Silly man. Of course, she knew. She adored her husband, but she couldn't resist teasing him since he had promised to be upstairs right after he sent the telegram.

"You know as well as I do, you'll have your nose buried in your notes all day tomorrow. And on Sunday morning you'll be off to the rowing club at the crack of dawn. Am I right so far?"

He rolled his lips to suppress a grin. A dimple always appeared when he did that. Sophie loved that dimple. She didn't see it nearly often enough.

"Then after you make Sunday breakfast you'll be right back in your study where you'll probably remain until everyone arrives for your birthday dinner. If I'm very lucky…" she rose from the water and paused to let her husband appreciate the vision before him, "I'll have your full attention again in… A week? A month?"

His Adam's apple bobbed as his eyes tracked the last of the bubbles sliding down her skin.

She reached to his wrist, careful not to get his watch wet. "It's almost six. Mrs. Kelley said dinner would be ready at seven. You're running out of time to take full advantage of an opportunity that is presenting itself to you before you turn a year older."

Joe's dimple resurfaced as he yanked off his tie and started in on the rest of his buttons. "I don't know what I was thinking."

She loved this about them: the humor, the affection, the respect that had bound them together from the first moment they met. They were strong strands on their own, but together they were stronger. The fact Joe had always been her physical ideal didn't hurt either. "Neither do I darling. Neither do I."

Two

A Dream Come True

Saturday, 2 September 1939

From the covered balcony that wrapped around the Parker's hilltop home, Marianne Ryan gazed at the expanse of Sydney and the promise of the vast continent beyond.

She could hardly believe she was halfway around the world from her childhood home in Villers-Bretonneux. She had left France at the height of the European summer and now she was far below the equator on the second day of the Australian spring. Even after four weeks at sea, crossing the Mediterranean and Arabian Seas and the Indian Ocean, she knew she would never tire of the endless expanse of the Pacific Ocean and Sydney's sparkling harbor.

How could her Australian father have given up this glorious place to remain in France after the war? How was she going to leave at the end of twelve months?

Reluctantly, she turned from the views and began the letter she had promised to write upon arrival.

Sydney
2 September 1939

Dearest Maman and Papa,
I can hardly believe I am finally in Australia! We
arrived yesterday, as you know from the telegram Joe
sent as soon as we arrived at their house. It sits on a hill
with views of the Pacific Ocean from the front and the
entire city plus Sydney Harbour from the back. Sophie
was so excited when she spotted it from our ship that she
nearly dropped the field glasses overboard as she passed
them to me and her mother so that we could see too.

The views from the Parker's balcony remind me of be-
ing able to see all the horizons from the top of the tower
at the Australian memorial at home.

Except everything here is different from home. Home is willows
lining the banks of the Somme River as it meanders through fields
still rendering an iron harvest of spent shells and barbed wire. Home
is solitary lichen-pocked pillars marking conflicts from past centuries and dozens of new cemeteries—French, British, Australian,
Canadian, American, Indian, African, Irish, Chinese—bristling
with headstones under a pale northern sky. Home is battle-scarred
and sorrowful.

Here the Pacific Ocean crashes unceasingly against layered cliffs.
Here a modern city sprawls towards hazy hills leading to a massive
continent. Here the setting sun paints an immense sky with oranges
and golds so vivid she can almost believe they are fire and not light.
Here the future is eager and confident.

Today Sophie drove me around the city and then we
took a ferry across the harbor to the northern beaches
and back. The ferries here are just like busses and trams

going to different parts of Sydney.

The voyage from France was incredible. Since we had to wait several days for our turn to pass through the Suez Canal, we were in Port Said long enough to take a trip to see the pyramids and the Great Sphinx (I wish Napoleon's troops had not broken off its nose) and then to shop for fabric in the bazaar. There were so many beautiful bolts of silks that my head was spinning. But I have exciting news – when I sketched my ideas for some of the silks, Sophie bought the fabric and said she will commission me to make two dresses for her and one for her mother! Just think – I will have an international clientele when I return home. That should help considerably when I open my own dressmaking shop.

I spoke many times with Sophie and her mother Lily during the voyage from France to plan how I should best spend my time here. Since Lily has not been to Australia since Sophie and her brother were small children (almost 40 years ago!), Lily suggested that I could travel with her and her sister Flora to various places around the country before I look for a job. Next week I will visit Melbourne with them. It is a ten-hour journey, but we're going to drive so we can stop wherever we like along the way instead of taking the overnight train. After that, we will go to the Blue Mountains. Flora says there are all sorts of tours to see caves and the forest at the bottom of the canyon.

Tomorrow is Joe's birthday. Sophie says he loves apple tarts, so I will bake your tarte tatin as a surprise for him. Mrs. Kelly, the Parker's housekeeper and cook, has promised to help me. Sophie hopes their sons Sam and Jean-Luc will be able to attend the birthday dinner. She says they often fly to Sydney since Sam is a pilot. Apparently, he has his own Tiger Moth aeroplane. Perhaps one day I will ask him to take me up.

Thank you for letting me follow my dream to come to Australia. I promise to write often and tell you about my adventures.

All my love to you both and to Chris,
Marianne

THREE

BURNT APPLE TART

SUNDAY, 3 SEPTEMBER 1939

S am Parker frowned. The woman who opened the door was not who he was expecting.

He expected a short, plump, middle-aged woman with frizzy salt-and-pepper hair pulled into a tight knot atop her head. He expected a pristine apron and aromas of something mouth-watering wafting from the kitchen. The woman he expected to see was the epitome of comfort and gentle humor whose voice still bore traces of an Irish lilt even after forty years in Australia. He expected a wide smile, an affectionate hug, and a teasing, "Master Sam! You're home!"

Instead, he saw a tall young woman whose reddish-blonde hair had escaped the bonds of the ribbon meant to hold it back. Damp tendrils clung to her forehead. She pushed them away with the heel of her hand, leaving a streak of flour in their place. The apron tied around her slim waist might have been pristine once, but now it bore scorch marks.

This woman was scowling at him.

He spoke without thinking. "You're not Mrs. Kelly!"

Her eyes flashed. "And you are not Monsieur Par— Mister Park-er!"

"But—" Why was she calling him monsieur? "But I am. Mister Parker, I mean. Well, I'm one of the Mister Parkers, at least. I'm Sam, Joe Parker's son. My father…" Sam checked the number plate beside the front door. His father had definitely lived here before leaving on a journey several months ago. He turned back to the young woman. "My father lives here. With his wife Sophie. Who are you? Where's Mrs. Kelly?"

He'd babbled too long.

Something was burning.

The mystery woman swiveled and ran, leaving him and his companion standing on the front step.

Jean-Luc Guy, the young man beside him, rolled his eyes. "You must work on your technique. No wonder none of your girlfriends last more than a month."

Sam shot his adopted brother a look of disbelief. "I know how to talk to women. And anyhow, I didn't hear you jumping in to say anything helpful. Or were you playing the strong, silent type?"

A frustrated groan and a series of sharp barks echoed from the kitchen through to the entry hall.

Jean-Luc tossed the flowers he was carrying into Sam's hands and headed to the back of the house where the kitchen was located. "No, *mon ami*, I am playing the knight in shining armor who rescues the damsel in distress. You may rescue the dog."

Sam looked at the bunch of flowers, dropped them on the entry table, and followed his brother. "Something tells me she doesn't need rescuing, mate. It's more likely I'll have to rescue you."

—

Several hours later, the dining room of the Parker home hummed with voices. Sophie sat back in her chair at one end of the table, her eyes roving and ears perked to catch snippets of conversations.

Joe sat at the far end with his son Sam and her mother Lily on either side. Lily had been asking Sam about his experiences flying as a pilot for an aerial surveying company. Sophie automatically checked Joe's demeanor as Sam spoke, but Joe remained relaxed so Sam must not have mentioned any stories about airborne stunts or close calls. Father and son had exchanged more than a few terse words on previous occasions. Joe thought Sam could be reckless. Sam thought Joe worried too much.

Jean-Luc, whom Sophie had adopted over a dozen years ago, sat to Sophie's right. Sophie's Aunt Flora sat to her left.

Marianne Ryan sat between Lily and Flora, facing Sam and Jean-Luc.

Jean-Luc and Flora chatted for a few moments about the gardens at Flora's home and then drew Marianne into their conversation. Jean-Luc had plenty of ideas for what Marianne should see and do in Sydney during her first few days and then in the weeks that she would travel with Lily and Flora. Flora suggested they should consider going to the Blue Mountains first, before it got too hot. Jean-Luc recommended making the trip to Melbourne first for the same reasons. Then Jean-Luc said there was a sizeable French population in Sydney and he'd be happy to give Marianne the names and contact information for some of his friends in case she ever tired of speaking English.

"You speak English beautifully," Flora said to Marianne.

"It is thanks to my Australian father," Marianne said. "And the Australian forces who liberated my town from the Germans."

Everyone stilled as Marianne spoke.

"After the war was over the school in my town was rebuilt by donations from the state of Victoria. The playground has a large sign *inscrit*...ooh, what is the word...inscribed? No...painted...with the English words Do Not Forget Australia. My brother Chris and I learnt proper English from the first day of classes."

"Crikey," Sam said. "Jean-Luc says I barely speak English."

Jean-Luc scoffed. "Is that what you call it?"

The quiet that had descended at the mention of the Great War evaporated as Sam and Jean-Luc's banter began its usual rhythm. Sophie knew Marianne had grown up with a younger brother, and she was pleased when Marianne easily fell in with their rounds of good-natured teasing.

"It sounds like English to me," Marianne said. She shrugged and graced Sam with a mischievous smile. "But it is hard to tell with the accent."

Sophie stifled a laugh at Sam's delighted grin in reaction to Marianne's comment. "Thank you. I think," he said. "I admit my marks in English and French classes were—"

"Abominable," Jean-Luc interjected.

Undeterred, Sam threw his brother a casual side-eye. "But I'm good in mathematics and mechanical stuff, which this one—"

"Don't believe everything he says," Jean-Luc added. "My marks in math were better than passing. I let him think he was helping me. Botany is my forte."

"I am good at fixing my sewing machine, but botany to me means hours of weeding in my mother's vegetable garden."

Jean-Luc perked up. "I grow grapes and make wine for my living. Did you know that an Australian wine won first place against French wines in a competition last century? Then an insect—"

Sam groaned. "Oof. Don't let him start on bugs that eat vines. Violet has to listen to him, but you don't."

"Who is Violet?"

"His long-suffering lady friend," Sam said.

"—devasted most of the vines in Australia," Jean-Luc continued. "In Europe, too."

"*Désolé*, Jean-Luc," Marianne said, "but I would rather deal with anything than insects. Especially spiders. And before either of you rushes to tell me, I know spiders are arachnids and not insects."

Both young men grew serious. "There *are* spiders you need to watch out for," Sam said.

"Before I left France, my father told me huntsmen are huge…"

Jean-Luc nodded. "Bigger than your hand. But their venom is rarely fatal compared to redbacks."

Marianne paled and Sophie felt it was time for her to chime in. "There are no spiders in this house, Marianne."

"Mrs. Kelly won't allow them in," Sam said, exchanging smiles with Moira Kelly.

"She is our protector," Jean-Luc added.

Mrs. Kelly cleared empty plates and bowls while she looked on fondly at 'her boys' as she affectionately referred to Sam and Jean-Luc. She had known Sam for almost all of his life, having worked for a newly-widowed Joe Parker when he and Sam left Melbourne for Sydney back in 1922. She had agreed to stay on when Joe and Sophie married, bringing Jean-Luc into the new family in 1931. Moira lived with her husband Thomas in a cottage at the rear of the Parker's property.

Sophie turned her gaze from her family when Mrs. Kelly cleared her dinner plate and spoke to her in a register below the surrounding conversations.

"Mrs. P, would you like me to serve dessert now, or shall I wait a few minutes?"

"Let's wait a bit," Sophie replied. "Sam and Jean-Luc aren't flying back to Melbourne until tomorrow afternoon, so we don't have to rush through like we did last time."

Sophie rose from the table. "Would everyone like a chance to stretch their legs before we have coffee and dessert in the drawing room in..." she glanced at her wrist watch. "Twenty minutes?"

In the flurry of napkins moving from laps to tabletop, Joe said, "I think I'll take Howard out for a short walk. Anyone want to join me?"

Sam and Jean-Luc immediately nodded.

"I would, too," Marianne said. "May I have just a moment?"

"Certainly," Joe said.

As Marianne left the dining room and headed to the downstairs washroom, Sophie took her mother's arm. "Mother, Aunt Flora, let's use the facilities upstairs," she said. "I want to show Mother our glorious views."

After the older ladies finished their ablutions, Sophie beckoned them to a set of French doors that opened to the balcony surrounding the house. Sydney at night was almost magical with lights outlining its myriad bays and shorelines. The harbor shimmered on one side. The indigo Pacific Ocean met starry sky on the other side.

"This is just lovely," Lily said. "Even lovelier than the description in your letters."

Sophie pointed out landmarks visible from their vantage point: the Harbour Bridge, Garden Island, the lighthouse at Watson's Point. "It was sheer luck Joe and I found this house. The owner had gone bankrupt during the depression and fled New South Wales to escape his debts, leaving the bank with the property on its books. Sam and Jean-Luc were still in high school when we married, and we wanted enough space for the boys and their friends to spend time here instead of running around town and getting into mischief."

"They are charming young men," Lily said. "But I imagine they found mischief despite your best efforts."

"They did," Sophie agreed. "But the prospect of all the sandwiches and snacks they and their friends could eat meant they usually came here straight after school, so not nearly as much as they could have, thank heavens."

Joe and the others, with Howard trotting between them, crested the hill to the house. "I think it's time to get back downstairs before the birthday boy gets another minute older," Sophie quipped as they waved to the other half of their dinner party.

F O U R

A NEW NIGHTMARE

SUNDAY, 3 SEPTEMBER 1939

Still chatting, everyone settled in the comfortable armchairs and sofas in the drawing room. Howard patrolled the room, trying to decide which human was most likely to scratch his ears or, even better, drop crumbs. Joe tuned the radio to the classical music program and turned the volume down to simply provide a pleasant background.

Mrs. Kelly popped in with a china coffee pot and placed it on the low table beside dessert plates and cutlery. "Right. I'll be back with a lovely Victoria sponge." She returned a few minutes later with the promised cake, blazing with candles, which she set in front of Joe.

"Your cake tastes delicious, Madame Kelly," Marianne said, taking a bite after the last strains of Happy Birthday died down and Joe had blown out the candles. "Thank you for rescuing dessert."

Mrs. Kelly gave her a sympathetic smile. "It's all right, lovey. These things happen."

Everyone else looked on, questioning.

"I must explain," Marianne said. "I wanted to make a *tarte tatin*, an apple tart, one of my mother's special recipes, for Joe's birthday. But I am not as good at cooking and baking as my mother."

"Ah," Sam said. "*That's* what was burning."

Marianne arched a brow at him. The tart she had attempted to bake had not gone as expected. Working in an unfamiliar kitchen, she had done her best to translate her mother's French instructions and measurements, but Howard had been underfoot, Mrs. Kelly had excused herself for a moment, and someone was knocking on the front door. Before she knew it her efforts were burnt to a crisp and two strange men were witness to her failure.

"Sorry Marianne." Sam turned to face his parents. "Jean-Luc and I wanted to surprise Dad. We arrived at a critical moment and Mrs. Kelly was unavailable, so Marianne had to answer the door."

"Not to worry, Marianne," Sophie said, leaning over and patting the young woman's arm. "The house is always in an uproar when these two come home for a visit. If you want to try again, we'll make certain Sam and Jean-Luc are already here or they aren't expected for hours."

"We apologize for causing a disruption," Jean-Luc added.

"Righto, you've told you us all your news and we've told you ours," Sam said. "What are we to make of Herr Hitler's incursion into Poland?"

"I think it will be very bad," Jean-Luc said. "He has already invaded Austria and annexed the Sudetenland."

Lily said, "Even before I left home, the English newspapers were full of all the possible consequences."

The music wafting from the wireless fell silent. "We interrupt this broadcast," the announcer said. "To bring you a live message from the British Prime Minister, Mr. Chamberlain, from 10 Downing Street in London."

"Everyone, wait just a minute, please." Joe rose and raised the volume. "I think we need to listen to this."

The room fell silent as a crackle of long-distance static transmitted from the radio station.

"This morning," Neville Chamberlain said, "the British Ambassador in Berlin handed the German Government final notice, that unless we hear from them by 11 a.m. that they will at once withdraw their troops from Poland, a state of war would exist.

"I have to announce that no such undertaking has been received and that consequently this country is at war with Germany. I refuse to believe that there is anything more or anything different that I could have done. I know you will all play your part with calmness and courage. I have been heartened by the assurances of support we have received from all parts of the Empire."

The Australian announcer came back on the air. "Eleven a.m. is 8 p.m. Sydney time, ladies and gentlemen. It is now 8:15 p.m. and I'm told that Mr. Menzies is preparing a statement for Australian citizens, which we will broadcast shortly. Until then, we will return to our musical program."

A chorus of disbelief erupted in the drawing room. Mrs. Kelly rushed in to find out what was the matter. She then ran to get her husband Thomas, and they joined the group listening in stunned silence when Prime Minister Menzies announced the Commonwealth of Australia was also at war with Germany and that it would be 'a struggle which we must win at all costs.'

Sophie locked eyes with Joe while Menzies spoke. The struggle and cost of the last war had been almost greater than they could bear. Reliving battles at Fromelles, Bullecourt, and Villers-Bretonneux in nightmares, one of which had shaken their relationship to its core. Ben's death when his ambulance was hit by a German shell. Robbie, declared missing and presumed dead. Annie's death from influenza carried to Australia on returning troop ships. Wounded who had died in her care. Soldiers who had died under his command.

Who would they lose in this new nightmare?

FIVE

WAR, REDUX

MONDAY, 4 SEPTEMBER 1939

S ophie went to bed with a splitting headache and slept badly, her dreams a jumble of Germany's 77-millimeter gun thudding in Parisian suburbs and the very real threat of occupation. Roads outside the city had been crammed with people evacuating, heading west, although to where most hadn't known. They only knew they had to flee: possessions flung into a cart, babies crying, mothers shouting for their older children to stay close, old men guiding a few skinny cows, chickens squawking in willow baskets.

She woke in a panic that lasted until the scent of Joe's shaving soap and pomade pulled her back to the present. He tugged on an under-shirt and then his shirt, the shrapnel scars on his back disappearing under snowy white cotton. She yawned as she said, "Joe" to catch his attention.

He kneeled on his side of the bed, the mattress dipping under his weight, and kissed her cheek. "Go back to sleep love. I'll see you this evening."

"Hmmm," she replied, still drowsy. The urge to send him off properly on his first day as head of the forensics department won over her body's desire for more sleep, so when he finished dressing, she followed him downstairs, fiddled with his already-straight tie, and kissed him goodbye. "Good luck on your first day, darling."

After Joe left, Sophie immediately went back to bed, dozing fitfully until the sun had risen high enough over the cliffs to flood the bedroom with morning light. She stretched, threw off the bedclothes, and rose. Pulling on her dressing gown, she opened the curtains and gazed out. Thin lines of clouds split the rising sun's rays into shafts of light reflecting on the ocean. A perfectly beautiful spring day made perfectly awful by the radio announcements last night.

Voices and laughter sounded from downstairs so she went to investigate.

Sam, Jean-Luc, and Marianne were gathered in the entry hall, pulling on light jackets. "Good morning," she called from the landing. "You look like you're off somewhere."

The trio of young people turned their faces up to her.

"Jean-Luc is going into town to meet up with his French friends. Marianne and I are going to walk to the lighthouse," Sam said. "It's late in the season, but Thomas said he has seen whales heading south in the last few days. We thought we'd try our luck since the sea is so calm this morning. Do you want to come with us?"

Searching their faces, she knew they had no idea how Prime Minister Menzies' words would affect them. They would discover it soon enough. Let them enjoy moments like this one while they could. "Thank you, Sam, but no. I need coffee more than whales at the moment and I don't want to hold you up. What time are you flying back to Melbourne?"

"Not until three o'clock. We'll be back here in time for an early lunch."

"I'll see you later then," Sophie said. "Don't forget the binoculars."

With the young people out of pocket, Sophie choked down a bit of breakfast and started on a second cup of coffee, flipping distractedly through the Women's Supplement to the day's *Sydney Morning Herald* in an effort to take her mind off the gut-wrenching news that the world was once again at war.

She scowled at the advertisements. Did anyone really need stockings like HRH the Duchess of Kent? Why was there a half-page ad for 'Charming Additions to Your Wardrobe'? Didn't these people understand there was a war on? Again? She tossed the supplement aside and went back to the newspaper, turning to the inside pages where the real news appeared.

A large map of Europe caught her eye, so she pushed her breakfast dishes aside to open the paper fully on the dining table. Had she and Joe really been in France only a few weeks ago? She traced their route from Paris to Villers-Bretonneux, then on to Chamonix in the French Alps, and finally to Lyon, Arles, and Marseille.

There had been undercurrents of war they'd been warned about: Edmund Stone, an American journalist friend, had been certain Germany would invade Poland. French friends in Chamonix had been certain the Germans and Italians would invade France via the Alps.

Now, mere weeks later she faced reality rather than possibility, and dread draped her like a shroud. She had been a nurse at the American Hospital in Paris during the Great War and had seen firsthand the ravages that men could inflict on one another. But the men she nursed then had been other women's sons. She had no doubt that soon she would have to face sending her own sons off to war. She knew them too well to think they would stay at home and leave the fight to other men. She knew too well what they would face.

And there would be absolutely nothing she could do to keep them safe.

—

Marianne peppered Sam with questions about migrating whales as they walked the half mile to Macquarie Lighthouse.

Sam pointed to the south and swept his arm in an arc to the north. "In May, June, and July they migrate north from the waters around Antarctica all the way up to Queensland, where the water is warm. They give birth up there. Now they're migrating back south with their calves."

They reached the grassy park surrounding the lighthouse and found a bench. "And we'll be able to see them?"

"I hope so," Sam replied. "On their way south, they stay further from shore to avoid the Australian current, which flows north. But the ocean is so calm this morning that any disturbance out there is probably a whale. We might even see one of them breach. If nothing else, look for sprays of water above the surface."

She took the binoculars he offered. "You know a lot about this."

"Dad and I used to come out here when I was a nipper," Sam said. "Every Sunday we explored a different part the coast. Cliffs, beaches, bays. What about you? I imagine there aren't any whales in your part of France."

"My part of France is a tiny town in the Somme valley on the Roman road between Amiens and Saint Quentin. My parents met during the war when he was a soldier and she was cooking eggs and chips for homesick Diggers and Tommies at the family's *estimanet*."

"What's an *estimanet*?"

"It's like a café, only smaller. The men of my mother's family were killed in the war. To survive, my mother, grandmother, and aunt turned the front room of their house into a dining room. Papa and maman married after the armistice. He wanted to remain in France to search for his countrymen who had died in battle."

"No offense, but that sounds like grisly work," Sam said.

Marianne nodded. "I agree, but for him it was important to move their remains from mass graves and honor them in proper cemeteries and memorials. Now Papa is in charge of the Australian National Memorial in Villers-Bretonneux."

"And that's where my dad met your dad?"

"Yes. At the memorial in July. There are huge walls carved with the names of soldiers whose bodies were never found. He helped your father find your uncle's name."

She stared at the sea for a few moments before she returned the binoculars to Sam. "Our fathers fought in the battle that liberated my town on the 25th of April in 1918."

"I had no idea. That might be why Dad is always so broken up on Anzac Day."

"It is possible. So, no, there are no whales in my part of France. Only more cemeteries than you can count." She turned back to Sam. "And you? How did you come to fly aeroplanes?"

"A friend of a friend was working as a mechanic at Mascot Airfield. I gave him a hand a few times and fell in love with the idea of flying so I learnt how. Long story short, now I fly for a company that does aerial surveys for maps and such."

"Is it exciting?"

Sam nodded. "I love flying and seeing the land from above and how it changes. The actual work is interesting. Plus, the wages are good enough that I was able to buy and restore an old Tiger Moth. That's how Jean-Luc and I can get to Sydney so often. I'm based in Melbourne so I fly up to the winery in central Victoria, we fuel up at Wangaratta, and then we head here. It's half the amount of time we would spend taking the train or driving. I've even taught a few people to fly. Have you ever flown anywhere?"

"No, *jamais*. Never. The closest I have been to the clouds is the top of the memorial tower at home."

"I'll take you up one day if you like. You'll see things you'd never be able to see from the ground. My absolute favorite thing is flying at night, though. The stars seem close enough that you can reach up and touch them. It's like the best dream I've ever had."

He checked his watch and then scanned the horizon one last time. "I'm afraid we aren't going to see any whales today."

Marianne lifted her face to the sun and breathed in fresh scents of salt and sea. She had felt very alone last night, the odd one out with everyone else all paired off, while they listened to the wireless announcements. Spending the morning with Sam on windswept cliffs had been a lovely respite from the wartime thoughts that had troubled her sleep the night before. "Can we try again another time?"

SIX

THE CALM BEFORE THE STORM

MAY 1940

Nothing happened for months after Germany's blitzkrieg attack on Poland in September 1939.

Sophie fumed when the newspapers called it the Phony War. Letters to the editor asked why Britain and France had even bothered to declare war on Germany. Clearly the Germans only wanted Poland for the same reason it had invaded Austria and annexed the Sudetenland. Germany was only giving itself space to grow. To live freely. It only made sense, didn't it? It was nothing to do with France or England, and especially not Australia, twelve thousand miles away. Those Europeans were always squabbling amongst themselves, had been for centuries. And the Great War had been the war to end all wars, hadn't it?

"Some of these letters to the editor are..." Sophie declared when Joe arrived home.

"Are?"

"So insular and short-sighted that I want to track down every one of them and shake them until they get it through the lump between their ears that Germany will not stop."

"And we know that how?"

"Joe. Seriously. Germany is building up its strength and preparing for further outrages. Why can't anyone understand that?"

"Perhaps the letter writers are right. Perhaps there won't be any more acts of aggression on Germany's part."

She usually admired Joe's ability to see both sides of a question, but his skill at playing devil's advocate was not appreciated today. "Do you think I'm wrong?"

"No. I don't. You and I both know Germany won't stop. We're in it and it will be a long, hard fight. This is only the calm before the storm. Unfortunately, you being right isn't going to stop the naysayers and unbelievers."

"Oh God. What are we going to do?"

"What we can't do is panic. We have to carry on as best we can. We can't allow ourselves to become overwhelmed or—"

"Or we'll drive ourselves crazy. But the boys—"

"Are adults, fully capable of making their own decisions. We hope for the best, but prepare for the worst."

Then, on 10 May 1940, eight months after Britain and France declared war on Germany, German troops invaded Belgium, the Netherlands, and Luxembourg. Nightmares, originally a slow wave, now roared to life. Sophie knew France was next. The only question was when.

SEVEN

THE SOLDIER

MAY 1940

Taking a well-earned break, Jean-Luc sat to rest in a sheltered spot with a view of vines under an autumn sun spread before him.

He rifled through the latest issue of Sydney's French language newspaper Sophie had sent to him. Stories in *Le Courrier Australien* reflected the sentiments of most French people living in Sydney: that the Germans would soon barrel their way into France, just as they had over twenty years ago. The only question was what could, or would, the French expatriates in Australia do about it. On his last visit to Sydney, his friends hadn't decided whether to join the Free French armies that were forming in French colonies and protectorates like Noumea and New Caledonia in the Pacific, and Syria/Lebanon in the Middle East, or to stay at home to rally support and funds for it.

Jean-Luc knew he wasn't a hero. He knew he wasn't even particularly brave. But he knew he had to join the fight. The only question was with which army. He could join the Free French who were making their way to Europe from Australia. He could probably get to England and join the British army there. Or he could follow his first impulse and enlist with the AIF—the Australian Imperial Force. He had heard enough stories about Australian exploits and camaraderie during the Great War to know they didn't give up, even in the direst conditions, and only then if they had exhausted every possible solution to come out on top. When he looked at his choices that way, the answer was obvious.

A cool wind ruffled the newspaper. Jean-Luc snatched the pages before they could be blown into the vineyard where the last of the grapes waited to be picked.

12 May 1940

Dear Sophie and Joe,

I am writing to tell you I've enlisted in the AIF. I started life French and I want to do what I can so that those in France can remain French, but if I'm honest I have more faith in the Australians to achieve that.

I will be in the 21st Battalion, which was raised at Puckapunyal last month. It's only a few miles from the winery, on the west side of the Goulburn River. After training, they'll ship us wherever they need us, as I'm sure you can guess. I want to help finish up the harvest here and at least get the juice in the barrels before I report to training next month.

I'll do my best to get to Sydney in between the two.

Yours affectionately,
Jean-Luc

Eight

The Pilot

May 1940

S am Parker poked his head into his father's study. The big table was covered in file folders. His father sat, hunched forward over his table, in the old oak swivel chair Sophie had found at an auction. Joe's reading glasses had slipped down his nose, but he was so intent on the sheaf of papers he held he seemed not to have noticed.

Perhaps now wasn't the best time after all for the conversation he needed to have with his father. He turned to leave but the movement caught Joe's attention and he looked up.

"Sorry, Dad," Sam said. "Didn't mean to disturb you."

Joe let the pages drop onto the tabletop, removed his glasses, and pinched the bridge of his nose. "No worries. I was beginning to go blind. Have a seat." He gestured to the armchairs in front of the table. "What's on your mind?"

Sam shoved his hands in his pockets and toed the edge of the rug, just as he had done when he was a boy and didn't want to admit he'd done something wrong or had a secret that was just too big to keep. He nudged the edge of the rug once again for luck before he met his father's gaze.

"I've enlisted."

His father opened his mouth twice before the words actually came out. "You've enlisted."

"Yep. Air Force." He braced himself for the objections that were sure to come—not to enlisting, but flying. Several years ago, his father had observed him doing a tricky maneuver that could have ended in disaster. It hadn't. He'd landed safely, but Sam knew his father hadn't forgotten the incident.

Joe swiveled in his chair, opened a file drawer, and withdrew two glasses and a bottle of whisky. He poured one for Sam and one for himself, then pushed Sam's glass across the papers.

Sam and his father silently toasted each other, and they each took a sip.

—

Joe gazed at his son. Twenty-five years old. Tall, fair, and good-looking, just like Annie. He'd always said that Sam got his height and looks from her side of the family. But at that moment he could hardly believe Sam had been so shy that he couldn't speak when Joe stepped off a troop ship in Port Phillip more than twenty years ago.

"Say hello to your dad," Joe's mother had said, but Sam had shaken his head and shuffled back, hiding behind her skirts. "He's just shy," she explained. "I've shown him all your pictures so he'd recognize you." She turned to Sam. "Don't you remember lovey? It's your dad, in the flesh, looking just like his photograph. Say hello."

Joe had dropped to a crouch, desperate to not have his son be afraid of him. He took off his hat and wiggled his ears.

Sam had either remembered his father doing that or he simply found it funny because he'd burst into giggles. Joe's heart had leapt at the sound of his boy laughing.

Since then, they'd had twenty-one years together. Joe forced down another sip of his whisky. "Tell me," he said, just as had dozens of times before, forcing his voice to remain calm and quiet, not judging or correcting, simply waiting to hear what his son had to say.

"There's not much to say, I s'pose," Sam began. "I've been flying for work and pleasure for almost six years now." He sat in one of the armchairs. "For me, the air force makes more sense than the army."

"Hmmm."

"Yeah. There aren't that many people who know how to fly, all things considered. The air force will need all of us."

"Have you told Sophie yet?"

"No. I wanted to tell you first." Sam slung one ankle over his knee, relaxing now, Joe guessed, that the first announcement had been made. "She isn't going to be happy about it after Jean-Luc's news. I was hoping you'd be there when I break it to her."

Joe nodded. "When do you need to report for duty?" He immediately regretted asking because the woman in question had arrived at his door.

Both men automatically rose when they saw Sophie standing on the threshold.

Sophie looked at him first and then Sam. "Am I interrupting?"

Joe walked over to her and kissed her cheek. "Erm... You're home earlier than I expected."

"The exhibition wasn't nearly as interesting as I'd hoped it would be," she said. "Aunt Flora and Mother liked it far more than I did. Marianne and I managed to slip away after I found a docent to guide them. Flora and Mother then proceeded to lecture the docent when they realized they knew more about the artist than he did."

Joe shook his head. His mother-in-law and her sister were well-read, well-traveled, and neither suffered fools. "Poor bloke."

"Well, really, you'd think the museum would actually train their people on the material before setting them loose on the public.' Sophie looked longingly at Joe's glass. "Pour me one, would you darling? I've had a long day."

While Joe poured, Sam bent to greet her with a kiss on the other cheek. "You're not interrupting," he said. "You're just in time, in fact. There's something I need to tell you."

Sophie turned from Sam to Joe and back again. Sam wasn't quite meeting her eye, which experience told her meant he had done something she might not approve of. Joe wasn't quite meeting her eye either. That was not a good sign.

She'd rather stand if they were going to tell her something distressing, but she'd been on her feet for hours at the museum, so she compromised and perched on the arm of the other chair. "What is it?"

Sam hesitated, glanced at her, and then studied his drink as though it was the most interesting thing in the world. He knew better than to do that, and she caught Joe looking worried as he watched for her reactions, as if he was waiting to see how she would take Sam's news. Whatever it was, she wasn't going to like it.

"Sam?" she prompted.

"I've signed up. Volunteered. You're looking at one of the newest members of the RAAF."

"RAAF," she repeated. She grabbed the back of the chair for support, her knuckles going white and her lips parting in a silent O as Sam's news sank in. Oh God. First Jean-Luc, probably already snatched by Army Intelligence because he was a native French speaker. Now Sam. "You're going to fly."

Sam nodded. "I report to No 4 Squadron for training in three weeks. Good news though. I'll be stationed at Richmond, so I'll be able to get into Sydney fairly often."

"Training? But you already know how to fly. You've had your pilot's license for years."

"True enough," Sam said, swirling the liquor in his glass. "And the trainers are Moths, which I'm already rated on. But I have to get rated on Wirraways once we get them."

"Wirra what?"

"They're Australian-built planes," Sam said. "We've been told our squadron will train in army cooperation tactics."

"So..." She shot a confused glance at Joe. "I don't know what any of that means. You're not going to join that Empire training program in England? Or is it Canada?"

"Nope. Believe it or not, I'm not the sort of brash young pilot they want in Europe right now. They need experienced pilots like me to train recruits here to replace the ones they lose over there."

Sophie's shoulders relaxed. "Oh. Well. Good. You'll be close to home, at least. But what is a Wirraway?"

"The name is an Aboriginal word meaning challenge. They're a sort of all-purpose aircraft. My squadron will provide ground forces with artillery observation, reconnaissance, and close air support. That kind of thing. Two-man crew. A pilot and an observer. It'll be a lot like the aerial mapping flights I've been doing, only in an RAAF plane. With guns." Sam downed the last of his whisky. "And the wings have been strengthened for dive-bombing runs."

Her shoulders immediately tensed again. The room became unbearably cramped.

"Sorry, darlings," she stammered. "I just need to..." She fled to the quiet of her own study where she lifted a framed photo of her brother. Ben, like thousands of other young American men, left colleges and universities in the United States to volunteer for the French in the years before the US joined the Great War in 1917. Most, like Ben, drove ambulances in the French sectors. Those who had flying experience flew for the French. The first of them formed the Lafayette Escadrille, piloting impossibly fragile single-engine bi-planes crafted of wood, wire, and fabric over the same French battlefields Ben patrolled with this ambulance.

She had met several Lafayette Escadrille pilots when they visited chums at the American Hospital in Paris. They had greeted her exuberantly while she grasped Jean-Luc's little hand tightly and rushed to meet Joe, who had come to Paris on rest.

On a rare leave in Paris, Ben had recounted an aerial battle. The plane spiraled to earth, engine sputtering, smoke trailing. A noxious black plume shot upward when the remaining fuel exploded on impact. Her brother's face had crumpled as he spoke of hope dying when his pilot friend didn't bail out. "He went down behind the German lines, Soph. There was no way to retrieve his body. And even if we could have..."

She had wrapped her arms around Ben while he sobbed as she'd never seen him sob during their childhood scrapes and sorrows. "What's left of his body will probably never be found. We'll never be able to bury him. His family will never be able to visit his grave. He's just...gone. Disappeared from the face of the earth."

At the time they hadn't known that combatants on both sides buried downed pilots with full military honors and did everything in their power to let the other side know the location. She suspected knowing wouldn't have eased Ben's grief one jot.

Nothing would ease Joe's grief or hers if something happened to Sam.

NINE

LOOK AFTER THEM FOR ME

MAY 1940

Marianne looked up from the newspaper spread out on the dining table, where she had been circling likely 'Flat Mate Wanted' entries in the long columns of advertisements.

Hands in his pockets, Sam sauntered in to the dining room and peered over the table. "Are you leaving?"

"Sam! Hello. Sophie helped me to find a job at David Jones department store and I'm looking for a flat. Since I cannot travel back to France because of the war, I don't want to impose on your parent's hospitality forever. When did you arrive?"

"Just flew into town for the weekend. I had something to tell Dad and Sophie and I didn't want to do it over the phone. I joined the air force."

"Oh." The pen slipped from her fingers, hitting the table with a soft thud. "How did they take your news?"

"Dad went even quieter than usual. Then Sophie arrived and she went quiet too after I told her my plans." He huffed a laugh. "You know something has affected Sophie when she goes quiet."

Marianne watched as Sam pulled out a chair and sat, fingers drumming the table top, as if he wasn't sure how to broach something.

"What is it?"

"Listen, would you look after them for me?" He looked around the room for a few moments, and then walked over to the big windows looking out to the ocean crashing on the rocks below. "Don't let them worry too much. When they do that, they start withdrawing from each other. I don't want worrying about me and Jean-Luc to cause any problems between them."

"But... Your father and Sophie are two of the happiest married people I've ever met. They were like newlyweds on the journey from Marseilles." She rose and joined Sam by the window, thinking back to last July. "Of course, I didn't know them until they arrived at my family's house." She had watched them, Sophie in a summery frock and Joe in a linen suit, making their way up the front path and pausing to take in the open fields of wheat mingled with poppies and cornflowers surrounding her home.

The Parkers had been friendly on arrival, Sophie offering an armful of gladioli wrapped in tissue and Joe with a box of chocolates from Amiens' finest chocolatier, but her father must have sensed an underlying tension when he met them at the Australian memorial earlier that day. He'd often said that he only invited home those who seemed to harbor some deeply entrenched pain that they couldn't shake, even twenty years after the war. Her mother had never complained when her father brought someone home without warning. She knew the person really needed someone like Will who understood what the war had been like.

"They went to the memorial to find my uncle Robbie's name on the wall," Sam said. "Apparently, he was a real hell raiser. Dad was always in trouble with his dad because of things Robbie did. Anyhow, I know Dad thinks I'm like his brother. I've heard him say it more than once, especially when I started flying. I think he was afraid something would happen to me and my body would never be found either. But I'm not like my uncle. I've never been in any trouble. I couldn't chance it. Someone had to look after Dad, and after my nan died when I was six, I was all he had left."

"Didn't he ever think to remarry when you were so young?"

"Once. Maybe. There was a woman he stepped out with for a time. Alicia. She was a widow and nice enough but her two daughters were the silliest girls I'd ever met. He seemed happier after they broke things off than he ever did while they were courting. When Sophie and Jean-Luc arrived in Sydney, he just brightened up."

He finally stopped gazing at the ocean and turned to her. He was so close that she could see the flecks in his blue eyes. She liked eye colors, always had. Sam's were lighter than his father's—Sydney sky versus Pacific Ocean. "Anyway. I would appreciate it if you would.... I know they're going to worry about losing me and Jean-Luc. It's what parents do, isn't it?"

Marianne nodded. "Just like my parents must be worried sick about my brother Chris. He always wanted to join the alpine troops. I imagine he has already enlisted." She took Sam's hands in hers and squeezed. "I will be happy to do it. In fact, I will write to you with regular updates. My only condition is you must write to me too."

Sam looked so relieved that Marianne wasn't sure if he was going to hug her or kiss her or shake her hand. In the end he simply nodded.

She took refuge in the most comforting thing she could think to offer. "Cup of tea? I'm sure Mrs. Kelly will let us invade her kitchen."

"Only if you promise not to burn the water," he teased.

"For that, Sam Parker, you may make the toast and we will see how well you do."

As the tea steeped and Sam, much to her surprise, expertly toasted slices of bread, Marianne tried to think of something that might take Sam's mind off worrying about his parents. "Would you like to look for whales again in the morning?"

She waited patiently while Sam buttered their toast. "I have a better idea. Why don't I take you up in the Moth?"

"Really?"

"Why not? I promised you I would and we may not have another chance for a long time."

"I would love to go flying! What do I need to do?"

"Stand up, please."

While he munched his piece of toast, Sam looked her up and down, from her hair waving to her shoulders, to her dress and cardigan, to the low-heeled brown oxfords that were so comfortable she could walk anywhere in them.

"You're about as tall as…"

There it was. She had always been the tallest in her classes. The boys had nicknamed her *la girafe*. For a moment, she felt as if she was back in school, readying a furious retort to their mocking, until Sam nodded his approval.

"Perfect."

What? No one had ever said *that* about her height.

"You can wear the gear Jean-Luc uses when he flies with me, but you'll need to dress warmly underneath. Moths have open cockpits and it'll be cold and windy up there. Do you have a pair of trousers and a heavy jumper? Boots would be good too."

She did a mental inventory of the clothes she'd brought from France and the items she'd purchased while in Sydney. Her face fell. "I don't have any boots."

"Ask Sophie if she'll lend you a pair of hers. Thick socks, too."

The prospect of actually flying was becoming real. She wouldn't give up this chance even if Sophie's boots were too small and rubbed blisters all over her feet. She beamed at Sam, who grinned at her obvious excitement.

"What time will we go?"

"I'm meeting a friend in the afternoon, so early. Before breakfast. I don't want to chance you losing yours. It takes forever to clean up afterwards."

TEN

POST-FLIGHT CHECKLIST

MAY 1940

Sunrise hadn't yet lightened the Pacific side of the sky when Marianne settled on the back of the battered BSA motorbike Sam was fixing up and they headed to Mascot Airfield. She kept her arms firmly around his waist for the entire ride. She had no intention of bouncing off when what awaited her at Mascot was finally possible. The fact that holding Sam was incredibly pleasant was an added bonus. She'd never held a man that way before, and feeling the muscles in his body respond to the curves, stops, and starts of the ride had been instructive to the point that she wondered how the rest of him...

No, she was *not* going to write that to her parents. Besides, the young woman who had come to the house to collect Sam after breakfast seemed to have claimed him already. Not that he was a coat or a hat to be... Never mind. She had things she wanted to accomplish while she was in Australia, and they didn't include looking for a man or even having a fling.

Sydney
25 May 1940

*Dearest Maman and Papa (and Chris if you are still
at home),*
*I had the most wonderful adventure earlier today. My
first aeroplane ride! Sam Parker offered to take me up
in his Tiger Moth so I could see Sydney and everything
around the city from the air.*

*It was amazing. I know Mlle Jaubert taught us in
school to avoid hyperbole, but obviously she has never
been flying. There are times when words like amazing,
incredible, and unbelievable are still not enough.*

*When we arrived at the airfield, Sam's plane was
ready to go. He had called yesterday afternoon to file
something called a flight plan. All pilots have to do that
so the people on the ground know who is in the air and
when and where to start looking if they don't return on
time.*

*One of the ground crew helped Sam tow the plane from
its shed to the grass taxiway reserved for small planes.
The passenger seat is in the front of the plane, and Sam
helped me up after I donned the heavy flight jacket,
helmet, and goggles that his brother Jean-Luc wears.
Then he showed me the parachute I would sit on and
pulled the straps over my shoulders.*

She also wouldn't write that Sam's hands on her waist when
he guided her up had sent a shiver through her body or that Sam
stroking the side of his plane like a lover before he climbed in had
added heat to the shivers...

No. Back to the safe things.

The man spun the propeller when Sam told him to and before I knew what was happening, we were rolling down the grass. Sam tapped my shoulder to let me know when it was time to lift off. I felt my stomach fall when I realized we were no longer on the ground, which seemed to be moving very fast below us. Thank heavens Sam warned me not to eat any breakfast, not even a cup of tea, or I might have embarrassed myself.

Then, and I know I am veering to hyperbole again, I experienced the most incredible thirty minutes of my life. Sam flew over land first so I could see Sydney and Cooks River and the Paramatta River winding their way through the suburbs. Past that are farms and then bushland. Then we flew over Sydney Harbour and the bridge and up to the northern beaches. I forgot to ask how high we flew, but the ferries and houses looked like those miniatures in the toy shop in Amiens.

She'd looked back once when Sam tapped her shoulder again and mouthed OK? at her. She had responded with rapid nod and he motioned that he would be turning right.

Then Sam flew out over the ocean for a several minutes. The sun had risen high enough to make the water sparkle and houses and buildings along the coast glow. He turned to the coast and flew over the bays, tapped my shoulder again, and pointed down, but I had already spied Sophie and Joe's house. I could see a tiny figure towards the back of the property. It must have been Mrs. Kelly. Sundays are her day off, but she always

*feeds the chickens and gathers eggs before she and her
husband Thomas go to Mass.*

By that time the thought of breakfast had been more than welcome. In the distance, she could see the grassy fields at Mascot. Sam
took the plane lower and lower, turning into the wind and lining
up with the small taxiway they had departed from. It had seemed
impossibly short. There was no way they could possibly land safely.
She'd screwed her eyes shut and braced herself for the inevitable
crash. But then...

*Sam must be a very good pilot because I barely noticed
the wheels touching down, just a couple of little bumps
when we landed. The RAAF planes will be in good
hands with him.*

She'd been so giddy from the experience that she laughed at all of
Sam's teasing when they returned home in time for the big breakfast
Joe cooked every Sunday morning after he came home from rowing.
Joe had seemed less than pleased with Sam for taking her up, and she
remembered Sam saying flying worried his father, but the tight lines
around Joe's mouth gradually eased the longer she and Sam teased
and laughed.

*I spent the rest of the day working on one of the dresses
I am making for Sophie.*

*I will close for now since it is already 10 pm and I have
to be at work at 8 tomorrow morning. Please write back
soon and tell me all your news.*

*All my love,
Marianne*

Cutting, pinning, and basting the fabric had only occupied one part of her mind, leaving her free to ponder Sam's relationship with Isobel, the young woman who had arrived as they finished breakfast. Sophie and Joe hadn't met her before, but they welcomed her warmly enough. Isobel had been perfectly coiffed, a silk scarf protecting her hairdo while driving an expensive car with the top down. It was obvious that she was smitten with Sam, but it was harder to gauge his feelings for her as she watched them leave the house and walk to Isobel's car. Her arm linked possessively in his. Her face turned up to him. His effortless acceptance of her car keys, and perfect ease opening the passenger door for her. It all hinted at a certain intimacy between them, but Sam hadn't seemed to be giving nearly as much as he was receiving. Interesting.

Ouch! She'd been so deep in thought that she hadn't noticed the pin she'd placed at right angles to the seam she'd been basting.

ELEVEN

CALL TO ARMS

JUNE 1940

S ophie woke early the day after the news reported the fall of France.

Jumbled snippets of news swirled in her mind. The tremendous losses the British had suffered at Dunkirk. The Germans marching into Paris. The Battle of France had begun several weeks after Sam's announcement that he had joined the RAAF. She feared it was only a matter of time before the Australians would be called to Britain's side in Europe.

Sunlight had only just begun to bounce off the mirrors and the glass in the picture frames on the mantelpiece and the face of the little clock on the nightstand, but Joe was nearly dressed, checking his tie in the mirror over his dresser. How many times had she been witness to that mesmerizing tie tying ritual? Collar up, top button buttoned, a length of silk—usually some shade of blue, sometimes with a foulard pattern, more often with a darker blue or grey stripe—slipped around his neck. He'd hold each end in a hand and slide it back and forth to get the ends in the right place before he began. One wrap over, then another, then the broad end tucked under the top loop, then a gentle tug down while his other hand maneuvered the knot up so it met the top shirt button. His chin lifted, Joe would wiggle the knot back and forth until it was in just the right place, where it would stay knotted until he tugged it back down eight, ten, sometimes even twelve or fourteen hours later. His chin always waggled back and forth during the crucial knot-placement period.

Then, when he was satisfied with the results of his efforts, his chin lowered to its normal height and his eyes flickered over his reflection, a quick double-check to make sure his automatic movements had borne the same correct result as every other time.

Sophie had seen Joe tie his tie hundreds of times—when he was fully awake, when he'd been roused out of sleep and called to the station or the scene of a crime long after they'd gone to bed, when he was angry, frustrated, sad, happy.

Today was different though. An open letter lay on the foot of their bed.

Your commission in the Australian Imperial Force may be reinstated, the letter said. Report to the commanding officer in Sydney on this date at this time, the letter said. Joe had been an officer, and a good one, and his country had summoned him back. He would answer the summons, of course he would. Service was in his bones. He'd been a police constable before the war and had returned to the police force when he came home and had climbed the ladder to Inspector First Class and then to head of Sydney's forensics department.

Yes, service was his lifeblood. Sophie loved him for it. She admired him for it. She understood how important service was to him and only rarely grumbled when he frequently bowed out of social engagements at the last minute or didn't arrive home until the wee hours.

Surely, the army had made a mistake. Surely, Joe was needed at home more than in France. She was already giving their sons to the effort. How on earth could she give her husband too?

Never in a million years would she say those words aloud though. Joe and her boys wouldn't be the men she loved if they hadn't answered the call.

She made her way to Joe's side. Thank God he wasn't in his AIF uniform from the last war: 57th Battalion, 15th Brigade, 5th Division. Recruited in Melbourne in January 1916 to bolster the numbers of the first ANZAC Corps after it was decimated at Gallipoli and evacuated to Egypt.

Joe turned to her and she fiddled with his tie, brushed a bit of lint off his shoulder, smoothed his lapels. Anything to keep him close for just a little longer before he ventured into the unknown this meeting held. "All present and correct," she said.

He caught her fingers, gently stilled them under his broad palm, and rested his forehead against hers. "We'll get through this." he said quietly.

TWELVE

SOCKS AND SUPPLIES

JUNE 1940

After Joe left, Sophie rolled and tucked yet another pair of woolen socks and placed them in a box that was nearly full of socks. Some boxes in the drawing room held jars of Vaseline and bars of Lux soap. Knitted caps and scarves would fill other boxes.

She checked her list and drew a line through ten pairs of socks. She had no idea yet who would be collecting supplies for the troops, the Red Cross or another group, but she knew the drill from the last war. Endless quantities of supplies would be needed. She was simply getting a head start.

Then she started in on the next ten pairs, laying a sock flat, carefully positioning its mate over it—heel to heel and toe to toe. She made the first fold over at the heel so the top of the sock touched the toe, then, in a flip made smooth by practice, picked up the pair, rolled from the fold until she reached the top, pulled back the outermost top, and pushed the rolled wool into itself.

She fell into the rhythm of her task, align, fold, roll, tuck, place in box—until she finished the next ten pairs and crossed through another line on her list. She had ten more pairs to fold, one more box to fill.

They were the best socks available at Myer's department store, one hundred percent Australian merino wool. The curves of the heels and toes were finished without a flaw, no lumps or bumps to rub blisters or sore spots. She'd given up trying to knit them herself. As much as she would have loved to give her men a part of her to take with them, knitting was not her forte. Her scarves got wider and wider the longer she knitted.

The pattern for the caps had promised it was suitable for beginners, but an afternoon later and halfway into it, Sophie was certain the instructions had been misprinted. She knew when she was defeated, and she handed the tube-like thing emerging from her knitting needles to Moira Kelly.

"Mrs. Kelly, this is impossible."

"Ah, Mrs. P, you just need to slow down a little." Moira pulled the needles out of the knitting, and began to unravel the misshapen cap. "I'll get you back to the beginning."

Yes, Sophie thought, get me back to the beginning, before Hitler became a megalomaniac and began conquering Europe for his own gain. Take me back to Sam and Jean-Luc first meeting when they were barely teenagers, still fresh-faced and gangly-limbed, devouring after school sandwiches. They'd covered her dining table with school books and papers, alternating between quiet and boisterous as they did their homework and teased each other about their biology lesson or the French exam.

Then, when the aromas of roast chicken or beef stew or, if they were lucky, their favorite cottage pie, began wafting from the kitchen to the dining room, the boys would hurry to pack everything away in their schoolbags, ready for the next day, and set the table.

Every afternoon was the same then, her dining room full of boys and books and she'd loved it. She loved that Jean-Luc had found such a good friend. She loved that Sam was such a nice young man—a little cocky and loud at times, but her brother Ben had been the same kind of boy.

On evenings when she didn't have plans, she'd eat with them, and grill them on their lessons or let them regale her with one of their tales of googlies and silly midoffs in their last cricket match. And the evenings when Joe joined them were the most pleasant of all.

Those nights, with Joe and their boys laughing and eating and talking about everything under the sun, had been golden and lovely. Those were the nights when she and Joe deepened their friendship and fallen in love. They married, weathered the trials and tribulations of raising the boys to adulthood, seen them launched into life as their own men, and relished the joys of a quieter house.

But now. Now their lives had been upended. The war headlines were summarized every day on the front page of the *Sydney Morning Herald*. The wireless never stopped broadcasting it. People never stopped talking about it, or, like Joe, they went quiet while memories of the last war haunted their thoughts.

Her heart sank into her stomach every time she heard or read the news. Millions of mothers and fathers and sisters and brothers and wives had lost loved ones. And now she and Joe faced the very real possibility that they could lose the sons who were dearest to them. She blinked back the tears that were threatening to fall. No. She was not going to think that way. She couldn't. She would go mad.

The solution was simple. If she had to give her husband and her boys to this godawful effort then she was going with them. Her nursing skills were rusty, and she might have to think of another way to contribute, but she was not going to stay at home, twelve thousand miles away from them.

She picked up a sock and placed its mate on top. She folded, rolled, tucked, and started to plan.

THIRTEEN

COLONEL AND COMMISSIONER

JUNE 1940

Feeling thoroughly annoyed at having to wait, but resisting the urge to tap his foot or pace, Joe sat on the hard wooden bench outside the office of the man who had summoned him.

While he waited several junior officers came and went from the colonel's office. All of them carried files. Personnel files, Joe guessed, some carrying cardboard boxes big enough to hold dozens of files, while others carried only a few files.

The steady stream of deliveries continued until Joe checked his watch and realized he'd been cooling his heels for nearly thirty minutes. Maybe he could reschedule this meeting. A woman in a dark suit, steel-rimmed spectacles, with her iron-grey hair pulled back in a severe bun, typed steadily away at a desk positioned at a ninety-degree angle to the office door.

Occasionally a young man with second lieutenant pips on this uniform opened the door and handed her a sheaf of papers. They spoke in hushed tones, the woman nodding and the young lieutenant pointing something out on a page or two. Then the lieutenant went back in the office.

They never once looked at him.

When the heavy wooden door closed, Joe rose from the bench and approached the woman at the desk. Her typing speed was admirable and she didn't need to look at the keys on the typewriter, instead reading from pages of shorthand notes as she typed.

Joe cleared his throat to get her attention. She didn't look up.

"Pardon me," he ventured. "I wonder if you can tell when I can expect to be called in."

The woman pressed the dot key on her typewriter a little harder than Joe thought was necessary and shoved the carriage over to the right.

"I was told to be here at eight sharp," he added. "It's now eight-thirty."

"He's a very busy man," the woman replied. "There's a war to organize."

Joe resisted the urge to roll his eyes. She was one of those people who volunteered absolutely no information and managed to make you feel like a dolt for asking a question.

"Yes, I understand," Joe said. What could he say to get her to at least give him an idea when he'd be seen? "But I have a court case to prepare for and I'm short-staffed at the moment."

"Hmmm." The woman never wavering in her typing.

Joe tried again. "My lab technician is out sick and I need to get over to the university for a meeting with a man who could help me with evidence."

"Yes, he knows all about it, Inspector Parker."

Was that the tiniest glimmer of amusement in her demeanor? She obviously knew who he was. "All I'd like to know is when I can expect to be seen. If you can't give me any idea of that, then I need to either reschedule this meeting or I—"

The woman stopped typing and fixed him with a raised-brow stare that reminded Joe of his headmaster when he was in school.

"Joe," a man's voice said.

Joe immediately looked away from the woman and saw his boss, Assistant Commissioner Bobby Davies of the New South Wales police, gesturing to him from the open office door.

Joe kept his jaw from dropping, but only just. Why was the assistant commissioner here at the same time he was supposed to be talking with a colonel about his possible re-entry into the army?

He glanced at the woman. There it was again, that glimmer of amusement. She performed a slow blink while looking at him. "I believe they're ready to see you now," she said, and, turning back to the page of shorthand notes on her desk, she began typing again.

"Assistant Commissioner," Joe said, extending his hand to his superior officer. The two men weren't close friends, but they were more than mere colleagues and had a cordial relationship both in and out of the office. They'd met on numerous occasions at social gatherings. Sophie and the Assistant's wife...what was her name again? She'd told Joe to call her by her Christian name last time they met. It didn't matter, he wasn't going to use it. Strict formality was his best bet today since he had no clue what he was in for once he entered that office.

"How's Mrs. Davies?"

"She's well. And how's that delightful wife of yours? Clara told me she's going to have Sophie for luncheon soon. Something about organizing the next Firemen and Policemen's Ball. She wants to make use of Sophie's fundraising skills again."

All the while Assistant Commissioner Davies was talking, he was also leading Joe deep into a huge room. Banks of file cabinets lined the walls, obscuring fine old wood paneling.

An ornately carved desk faced the door. A man in full colonel's uniform sat behind it, and Joe looked into the eyes of a man who looked remarkably like the assistant commissioner.

"At ease, Captain Parker," the colonel said, "and have a seat."

Joe started at the use of his army rank, but automatically saluted even though no one had called him captain for years. "Sir."

He wasn't sure which man to look to first, assistant commissioner or colonel. He chose assistant commissioner. "Sir? Are you two related by any chance?"

"Got it in one, Joe." Bobby Davies gestured to the colonel. "Joe, my baby brother, Roger. Roger, this is Detective First Class Joe Parker, now heading up Sydney's forensics department."

Colonel Davies shook his head. "I'm only younger than him by about five minutes, Parker."

He'd walked into this office confused as it was when his superior opened the door, but where on earth was this going? Take refuge in social niceties again. "I had no idea you were a twin, sir."

"I am," Assistant Commissioner Davies said. "And as the elder brother, I've come to negotiate for you with Davies the Younger."

What? Joe was thoroughly confused. There was a war on. He had come in here fully expecting to be told the Australian Imperial Forces needed him back in France. He and Sophie had already started coming to terms with it. They didn't like it, but like didn't come into the equation, did it?

"Parker," Colonel Davies began, "let me fill you in. My brother says you're needed more in Sydney than you are in the Mediterranean."

"The Mediterranean? Not France?" Joe struggled to understand.

"The Australian army won't be going to France this time," the colonel said. "They're needed in Egypt and North Africa, especially since the Italians have sided with the Germans. You're not to mention a word of that. It isn't common knowledge yet. My brother says the people of Sydney need you more than the army needs experienced officers like you."

Joe looked from one man to the other. Was this how the baby in the Bible felt? Tugged on by two women, both of whom were claiming to be its mother?

"So, you want me to make a choice between fighting and... What? Continuing on as the head of the Forensics department?"

"Something like that," Colonel Davies said. "My brother thinks you will find it difficult to choose. We're going to run through the pros and cons and the three of us will make the decision."

"This is highly irregular," Assistant Commissioner Davies said. "Normally you wouldn't be called upon since the police are a reserved occupation and that would be the end of it. We'd prefer it if you don't speak of this meeting. You'll understand more before you walk out of here."

"May I discuss this," whatever *this* is, "with my wife?"

"You may tell her what, but not where," Colonel Davies said. "And I need your word on that. I know you'll want to tell her. But then you'd have to swear her to secrecy, and she might inadvertently let something slip."

"Right." Colonel Davies continued, looking between his older brother and Joe. "Are we ready to begin?"

FOURTEEN

STAYING IN SYDNEY AFTER ALL

JUNE 1940

Joe walked out of Colonel Davies' office an hour later, tipped his hat to the formidable woman who was still typing steadily, and headed home to tell Sophie his news.

When he arrived, he found Sophie in her study, and a pile of receipts beside an open ledger book on her desk. She took one look at him and the usual smile she greeted him with turned to a look of alarm.

"What is it? What's happened?"

Joe blew out a breath, fiddled with the curtains, and gazed out at the rose bushes in the back garden.

"I've just had one of the strangest meetings I've ever been a part of." He turned to his wife. "I'm not going back in the army."

Sophie's jaw dropped. "What?"

"Bobby Davies was there too. It turns out he's the twin brother of the colonel I had the appointment with. They…" Joe shook his head. "I'm not entirely sure. I think they bartered for me."

Sophie's mouth closed. It opened again but no words came out. He couldn't blame her for her shock and confusion. His head was still reeling.

"The upshot is they decided I'm more useful to the war effort by staying here in Sydney."

Sophie closed the ledger book and moved it aside. She leaned forward, elbows on her desk and covered her mouth with her hands. He could see her blinking back tears and trying to compose herself before she spoke.

"I'm so relieved," she said, finally. "I didn't want to say it before, but I was scared. I know you were a good officer, darling, but..." She sniffled. "Sorry. I'm being selfish."

"Between them, they knew everything about us," Joe said. "They know about your work as a nurse, your marriage to Michael, mine to Annie. Their deaths. What happened to Ben and Robbie." He paused. "They know Sam is in the RAAF and Jean-Luc is in the army. They even know we brought Marianne here with us to get her out of France."

Sophie frowned. "That all seems a little intrusive, doesn't it? What else did they have to say? Did they explain why they needed to know everything about us?"

"Apparently they went through the entire cadre of senior police officers and did the same thing," Joe answered. "The argument is exactly the same as it was twenty-five years ago. Some need to stay behind and safeguard the peace at home. What's the point of fighting the enemy if the home front falls to lawlessness? They want to keep the most experienced officers here. We'll be called upon to do extra things to keep everyone here safe."

"I suppose I see their point," Sophie said. "Well, what are you going to do now?"

"I'm going to eat some lunch and then go to the office and try to get some work done."

—

Several hours later footsteps in the entrance hall alerted Sophie to Joe's return. She left her ledger and receipts—she hadn't made much progress—too relieved that Joe would be staying in Australia and not shipping off to Europe. She'd given up going to church decades ago, but she breathed a little prayer of thanks nonetheless. Given how reduced the police department would be with so many men who were sure to enlist, staying in Sydney could be dangerous too.

Over dinner, she grilled him about his added duties since he would be staying in Sydney.

"Did Bobby give you any indication of what roles you'll be assuming?"

Joe finished chewing the first bite he'd taken of Mrs. Kelly's steak and kidney pie and washed it down with a sip of the red wine produced by the Hunter Valley vineyard where Jean-Luc worked several years ago.

"He didn't give me any specifics." Joe took another sip and patted his lips with his napkin. "He spoke mainly in generalities. Since the militia can't send men on overseas duty, they're responsible for home front defenses. Neighborhood patrols, enforcing blackouts if they're ordered, that sort of thing. They'll liaise with the police so the right hand always knows what the left hand is doing."

"And what about you specifically? Any idea?"

"As far as I can tell, I'll be sort of a reserve detective," Joe answered. "If something comes up and a local station doesn't have the resources to investigate, Central Station will call me to assist."

"All the while doing the job you have now?"

Joe chewed thoughtfully. "It could be nice, being back on cases as they're happening, instead of after the fact."

Sophie wasn't sure what to make of that statement. Two bullet wounds in his shoulder and one that grazed his temple in February 1939 had been unbelievably frightening. She'd done everything she could to come up with a solution that kept him in the profession he loved but not in the line of lethal fire. Joe had agreed that taking on the job of head of the Forensics department was a good alternative to actively being in harm's way.

"Are you regretting your move to Forensics?"

Joe shook his head. "No, love. Not at all. I doubt I'll be needed very often. It's just a contingency plan Bobby came up with."

"Out of curiosity, how did the colonel take these plans?"

"From what I could tell, he may have been the one who had the original idea. You know Bobby. Well, his brother seems to have been cut from exactly the same cloth. Practical, conscientious, looking for the best solution to a problem. It's a wonder Bobby has managed so well with a boss like McKay."

"If only McKay wasn't such a dubious character," Sophie said. "We'll have to invite the brothers and their wives for dinner. I can't imagine two of them. Bobby is a handful all on his own."

"To tell you the truth," Joe said, "I think one of the reasons I get to stay home is that I don't speak German. I saw the list of police officers they're divvying up. Age, rank, strengths, weaknesses, languages spoken."

Joe had done Latin in school. He'd picked up a smattering of French during the war, and had added to his repertoire when they were in France last year. "And Latin isn't spoken anywhere," she said, venturing a small joke. The situation was grim, but she'd go crazy if she had to be serious all the time. "Are you glad you were so diligent about conjugating Latin verbs in school all those years ago?"

"Bobby made a crack about my Latin vocabulary coming in very handy in forensics work. Chemicals, poisons, botanicals," Joe said. "His brother gave up trying to put me on his army list after that."

Sophie gazed at her husband, sitting across the dining table from her. "And how do you feel about it? Being asked to stay at home instead of rejoining the army?"

Joe met her gaze, and then looked down. "I'm a good officer. I do what I'm ordered to do. But I wish I'd been given the chance to make my own decision."

—

Truth be told, Joe was conflicted. He had assumed his country would need him to lead again. He'd done a good job of it in the last war. Why hadn't he been chosen to lead in this war? Or been offered a position in the army doing something useful here at home? He understood the situation the brothers were in, but to be bargained over, like he was chattel, didn't sit well. He was forty-eight years old, for God's sake, old enough and experienced enough to decide for himself. It rankled. But he couldn't honestly say he wouldn't have done the same thing if he were in Bobby's position.

He'd known Bobby since Sam and he first moved to Sydney from Melbourne in 1922. Bobby had been the ranking detective at the station Joe was assigned to. He'd taken Joe under his wing, helped him learn a new city, didn't think it was crazy of him to have moved nine hundred miles away before Melbourne's police strike in 1923 decimated the force there. Joe had had a young son to raise on his own and no matter how much he agreed with the striker's demands for better pensions, wages, and working conditions, he had to get away from Melbourne. The city had too many ghosts. He had plans, plans that he and Annie had agreed on, to sit for the detective exams and do what he loved to do—solve crimes. He hadn't wanted to follow the administrative ladder, even though senior sergeants had a lot of clout in their own stations. He liked being out on the street, finding clues, interviewing people, delving into their minds to figure out what made them tick—and—what made them break the law.

Sophie said something Joe didn't catch and he forced his mind back to the present. "Sorry. What did you say?"

"I said I need to call Annabelle and let her know I'll be staying home after all."

He eyed her warily. Annabelle was the head of the Red Cross in Sydney. "What do you mean, you'll be staying home after all?"

"Oh, nothing in particular. I thought I might take a refresher course on the latest nursing techniques."

A clench began in Joe's gut. "Please tell me you weren't thinking of going back to the hospital in Paris."

Sophie's lips pursed. Her eyes dropped.

Bloody hell. She had been thinking exactly that. "The Australian army won't be sent to France this time," he said. "I can't say anything more about it and you mustn't let it slip that I told you."

"Oh." He could practically see the thoughts coursing through her brain. "So they're going wherever the Germans are that isn't France. North Africa. Or somewhere else in the Mediterranean."

"Sophie, I've given my word. Please don't ask me to confirm or deny. I admire your determination to be involved." He wouldn't stop her if that's what she felt strongly she should do, but staying at home while she and their sons were in harm's way was more than he could imagine. "Could you think of another way to help?"

FIFTEEN

ONE LAST TRIP TO THE BEACH

JUNE 1940

On the Sunday afternoon before Sam reported to No 4 Squadron for duty, Joe and Sam took the ferry from Circular Quay across Sydney Harbor to Manly on the northern side of Sydney. Manly was their favorite beach and they headed there for one last Sunday afternoon before Sam had to leave to join his squadron.

They sat at the bow of the boat, just as they always had. Sam loved to see where he was going rather than looking back at where they'd been. "How many times do you reckon we've made this crossing, Dad? A hundred?"

"At least that," Joe said. When Sam and he first moved from Melbourne to Sydney, they spent Sunday afternoons exploring the shorelines of their new city. On cold winter days they bundled up and explored the cliffs. On warm days they went where they could swim. Sam had loved being in the water since he was a little boy. The water had been their way of bonding when Joe returned from France and Sam barely knew him. Still in Melbourne at the time, they'd spent so many Sunday afternoons at Brighton Beach that Sam knew every bathing shed by heart. Then he'd beg to go into the water, content for the first few minutes to paddle where the water came up to his ankles. When he lost interest watching his toes disappear in the foam, he'd take his father's hand and tug him towards the deeper water.

Joe couldn't really remember learning to swim; his father had led Robbie and him to the water and told them to work it out on their own. From the north of England originally, the ocean was foreign to Parker the elder, and, now that Joe thought about it, it probably scared him. That's why he had treated his sons so cavalierly—he couldn't show weakness. The result was that although Joe had learned to swim, and could do it fairly well, he much preferred being on the water rather than in it.

Joe remembered the moment he decided he was not going to be the same kind of father as clearly as if it had happened yesterday. He'd been holding Sam's slippery little body, marveling at how sturdy yet fragile it was, while Sam learned to hold his breath. Sam had gotten a mouthful of salty water and flailed, coughing and sputtering. Joe's heart had been in his throat, a split second of panic, as he grabbed Sam from the water and patted his back while he coughed. Somehow, he had to make a game of it so Sam wouldn't be afraid.

"Did you forget you aren't a fish?"

Sam had wiggled and laughed. "I want to do it again!" he'd shouted.

"Ready?" He continued the game, supporting Sam's body in the water while he kicked and stroked. He was rewarded with Sam's huge smile after he kept himself afloat for two seconds. Sam's eyes, ringed with spiky wet lashes, were so bright and happy that he repeated the process as many times as his boy wanted.

By the time the sun was setting Sam could swim and he'd never looked back.

Now they were going for one last swim before Sam left. Sophie, who sometimes accompanied them, had opted to stay at home. "You two need this time," she'd whispered to Joe, and he'd known she meant it might be the last chance they had to be father and son together.

They'd spent a fair amount of time in the water, even though the day was cool and the water was cold, swimming out past the breakers and body surfing back to shore. They talked of nothing consequential while they dried in the sun and brushed the sand off their bodies and dressed. Logistical matters took up the ferry ride back to Circular Quay—what time Sam needed to leave in the morning, whether he'd informed his bank of his changed mailing address.

"Dad," Sam said when they were in the car and driving back home in the twilight, "how do you get past..."

Joe let the question hang in the air between them for a few moments. "Are you worried about what you're going to be asked to do?"

"Yeah, I suppose I am," Sam admitted. "I'm glad I enlisted. I want to do my bit. But you've always taught me that it's wrong to take a life. That's there's almost always another way."

Joe sighed. "Not in war, there isn't, I'm afraid. Your first time..." His first time had been at Fromelles in 1916. The German aiming at him may have been just as scared as he'd been, but he couldn't take that chance. Despite the dust and fug of smoke he had seen the German stagger, his mouth forming an O and scarlet staining his grey uniform as he fell. "Your first time will be a shock. But you're so busy trying to keep yourself alive that you won't have time to think about it until after."

"Hmmm."

Joe glanced over at his son. Sam was staring out his window. "It might sound simplistic, and it may be different for you since you'll be in the air and not on the ground, but you have to believe you'll get through it. Don't try to drink it away."

Sam said, "Is that what you tried to do?"

Joe felt his body stiffening, as if to better absorb a blow. Drinking too much had been his preferred method of coping when the demons he'd brought home from France wouldn't stay tamped down. He'd come home to no wife and a child who didn't know him. He had hoped to be able to pick up his duties as a police officer without a bump, but coping with the sheer viciousness of most murders, the pettiness of most squabbles, and Sam's rowdiness in his off hours had been far harder than he expected.

"I remember you and Nan arguing when I was a kid. I was supposed to be asleep, but I overheard the two of you."

"With your mother gone…" He'd been utterly lost the first time he set foot in the little bungalow where Annie and he had spent their brief married life. The devastation of war had paled in comparison. "I wasn't coping well. Too many memories of your mother and all our plans in that house. Your nan thought it would be better for us if you went back to living with her instead of living with me. That's when I decided we had to make a new start away from Melbourne."

Arriving home, Joe downshifted and pulled the car into the drive. "Talk it through with a mate or me or even Sophie. She knows a lot more than you might think. And she understands."

"Right. Well. Listen, Dad." Sam paused and Joe couldn't image what else there was to say. "Don't worry. I know there've been times you thought I was careless in the air, but I never have been. I'm careful. And I'll continue to be careful."

As much as Joe hated the thought that Sam would be going to war, perhaps flying would be less dangerous than… No, it wouldn't be. Sam would be flying bigger, safer planes, but the game would be the same as the dog fights over the Somme where young men desperately tried to kill each other thousands of feet in the air instead of on solid ground. This time the crashes would be bigger and the fireballs would be hotter. It was possible his days with his son were numbered.

SIXTEEN

LETTER FROM MAMAN

JULY 1940

Marianne surveyed the chaos of her bedroom in her new flat. She had grown very fond of the Parkers, but when they offered to let her stay with them indefinitely, she had decided against it. It was time for her to be on her own. She'd been pleasantly surprised when she found Patricia Lawson's ad for a flat mate in the newspaper. Patricia's sister Emma had joined the Women's Auxiliary of the RAAF and moved to Brisbane, and Patricia needed someone to help pay the rent.

They had four rooms total with a shared bathroom on the hallway. She and Patricia each had a bedroom, and their living room was furnished with a jumble of items given to them by friends and family. They planned to cover the mismatched chairs with lengths of fabric that matched the sofa to bring a sense of order.

Sophie had said it was unusual to find a flat with such large rooms and Marianne was grateful she didn't have to share a bedroom with Patricia. She liked the young woman very much but Pat, as she liked to be called, was messy. Marianne liked to come home to an orderly room with the bed made and clothes and shoes in their proper places.

At the moment, her bedroom still needed organizing, but instead she delved into her steamer trunk and pulled out the envelope peeking from a pocket inside the trunk.

A wave of nostalgia for France, the country of her birth and childhood, engulfed her when she re-read the letter from her mother that she had received several months ago.

> *Villers-Bretonneux*
> *16 April 1940*
>
> *Ma chère fille,*
> *No doubt you've guessed that your father and I wanted*
> *you far away from home when – if – Villers-Breton-*
> *neux is occupied by the Germans again. If that hap-*
> *pens, we will close the house and the memorial and go*
> *to England for the duration. Your papa has friends*
> *everywhere, and has been promised work at one of the*
> *cemeteries if he wants it. He says he'll do that until the*
> *Australians arrive and then he'll try to join one of the*
> *battalions.*
>
> *Christophe told your father that he intends to join the*
> *Chasseurs Alpins in Chamonix with Nick. I pray that*
> *he will be safe there, that they will not be sent to fight*
> *elsewhere in France.*

Marianne automatically clutched the letter tighter. Her brother Chris was only eighteen—four years younger than her. How would her poor mother cope with both her children parted from her? A single tear dropped, blurring the next neat line of her mother's handwriting.

> *Your father and I are very glad, and relieved, that you*
> *are far, far away from this war. War is no place for*

a lovely young woman. I know this because I lived it myself. I was so lucky to meet your father but it was so hard not knowing if he would survive the war. I've never told you this (although I'm sure you guessed) but we loved each other too much to wait for the war to be over. I'll never be ashamed of the circumstances of your birth, but I know you don't wish the same for your future.

I will write again as soon as I know more. Please take care of yourself my precious girl.

Je t'embrasse très fort,
Maman

Her adventure to Australia had taken a very strange turn. Perhaps she should have listened more closely to her father and his friends when they endlessly discussed the probability of another war. She had settled in to life in Sydney, and had even begun to think of it as home, but the truth was she was stuck halfway around the world and there was no way of knowing when she could get back to her family.

Feeling pensive and unsettled, Marianne rifled through her trunk until she found the precious supply of lace she'd brought with her from France.

The packages of lace were wrapped in the tissue paper she'd used when she packed her trunk after her father and mother agreed to let her sail to Sydney with the Parkers. Ten packets of lace, five yards each. She was saving them for a special project, a special client, someone who had the taste for something fine and beautiful and who would appreciate the history of the lace.

A bride, perhaps, who had traveled the world and wanted only the best. Or a mother who, after years of trying, had finally been blessed with a daughter after sons.

One packet was enough to trim the bodice of a nightgown and the edges and sleeves of a matching robe. She would use silk charmeuse, cut on the bias so the fabric would cling and suggest and float around the beautiful bride. One packet was enough for several pairs of tap pants and bras, also silk charmeuse, in ivory or blush or the palest dove grey.

But first she had to earn enough money to pay her rent, her meals, and buy fabrics to support herself as a seamstress in a new land. The women of Sydney were stylish, the wealthy ones often extravagantly so, but even the young women who rushed to board the trams and busses that took them to and from their jobs in offices and shops were stylish as well. She liked the sense of importance many of them had, that they were making their own way in the world, just like she wanted to.

During the voyage to Australia, she had listened eagerly to Sophie's descriptions of Sydney and the different social strata of the city's population. She couldn't cater to everyone, Sophie said, she needed to get her foot in the door, gain some local experience and make something of a name for herself. Then she could choose a niche and fill it.

Marianne originally wanted to make clothes for young women, day dresses and simple evening frocks that were affordable. She could turn them out quickly, keeping the construction of the clothes simple but with a dressmaker's flourish: a large decorative button at an asymmetrical neckline of a coat, or a tiny, perfect, flat bow at the top of a kick-pleat.

She'd spent hours on her designs during the voyage sailing from Marseille to Sydney. Sophie and her mother, Lily Holt, had been so helpful. They were both wealthy enough to appreciate fine tailoring, but so down to earth that they could imagine themselves as working women. Sophie had been a working woman once, a nurse during the war, who craved pretty clothes as a respite from her nurse's uniforms. Lily Holt was English, with that sense of impeccable taste in tweeds and cashmere that English women could carry off so beautifully. Lily thought a line of trousers might be just the thing, but it had been Sophie who inspired Marianne's desire to create exquisite underthings from luscious fabrics and lace after she showed her the gorgeous lingerie she had acquired in Paris.

Being able to travel as Lily's companion had been a special boon. She was as indefatigable as her daughter, and one afternoon in Port Said, after Joe had gone back to the ship to do some work, the three women had gone to the bazaar and shopped for fabrics. Sophie's striking coloring—lustrous dark curls and flashing eyes the color of coffee beans—cried out for rich, jewel-toned colors. Sophie had fallen in love with a bolt of silk the color of violets, and another bolt of silk that looked like molten copper. Marianne had never seen anything like quite like it. The weft thread was a several shades darker than the warp thread. When the fabric caught the light and moved under it, the effect was mesmerizing. She immediately envisioned a smart, perfectly tailored suit for the violet and an evening gown for the copper. An evening gown for the winter, floor length skirt, full but with pleats at the waist to handle the fabric, with a short train at the back, long sleeves, and a dramatic neckline that bared the shoulders. Sophie had lovely shoulders—Marianne had noticed them in the evening gowns she wore on board the ship and she thought Joe might be partial to them, if the gentle touches she'd seen him give was any indication. The effect would be very elegant. The fabric would catch the light from all angles and Sophie would look like a medieval queen. Sophie had asked her opinion when she saw her fingering the fabric and unfurling a few yards from each bolt to get the feel of the material and how it moved.

Marianne told Sophie about her ideas, while the merchant hung back watching intently while she spoke. He slipped into the back and retrieved one of his prized offerings, crimson silk edged with a deep border of gold woven in a filigree. Sophie's jaw had dropped as he brought it out to them. All he'd said was "beautiful silk for beautiful lady" and unfurled the glorious cloth. Sophie had practically swooned. Marianne had immediately gone into designing mode. He must have understood understand her intent when she began sketching in the notebook she always carried.

"A sheath, cut close to show off your figure, of course. The bold border for the hem. Sleeveless, with a high neckline edged with the border. Then a jacket, also cut close, edged all around with the gold. It would be perfect for dinner out at a nice restaurant or for one of your fundraising luncheons. Very, how do you say...modern, and very chic!"

The merchant must have had a sixth sense that he was about to make a sizeable sale, and it stood in him good stead. He returned to the back and came out with a bolt of silk the color of a ripe cantaloupe that matched the coral stones in Lily's necklace. He unfurled the bolt on a second table, away from the jewel toned fabrics. Marianne approved. Lily could not wear those colors with her typically English peaches and cream coloring. He patted his neck and pointed to Lily's necklace. "Is same," he said in halting English. "Is same color."

"Oh, Madame Holt," Marianne said excitedly. "A dress and jacket for you, too. Only this one I would make less severe than the crimson."

"No dear, I'm not slim like Sophie anymore."

"But not fussy," Marianne continued, eyeing Lily up and down and seeing it all in her imagination. "Because you are not fussy, *non*? But you are feminine like Sophie, just in a different way." She thought for a minute. "Trim made from the same fabric, a long bias strip, sewn on in loops and whorls, on the jacket's lapels and sleeves. Perfect for luncheon or church services in the springtime."

Marianne had dreamed of making a name for herself, of her opening her own shop, Atelier Marianne, ever since she was a little girl making clothes for her dolls when she was supposed to be weeding the vegetable garden or feeding the chickens. Her dream had shifted a bit—she would offer a line of stylish prêt-a-porter designs for the younger crowd and custom lingerie for those who appreciated meticulous handiwork and sensuous fabrics. What if the worst happened and she could never return home? Could her dream come true in Australia instead?

SEVENTEEN

LETTER FROM WILL

AUGUST 1940

Several weeks after Marianne moved to her flat, Sophie's brows furrowed as she went through the stack of post on the table in the entry hall.

Sorting it into piles for her, Joe, and household accounts, she encountered handwriting she didn't recognize. English stamps. She didn't recognize the return address on the back flap of the envelope either.

Joe had asked her to be wary of letters from unknown persons. A spate of prank mail had been sent to police officers by a man with an unfortunate sense of humor that bordered on criminal and Joe would want to get fingerprints off the envelope and paper. But this had English stamps. Surely it couldn't have come from the Sydney sender.

Joe wasn't home. He wouldn't be home for hours. She retrieved her gloves from her handbag and took the letter to her study. Then she carefully slit the envelope with her letter opener and peered in.

Nothing appeared to be untoward. She saw two pieces of paper, covered with writing on both sides. Rummaging in her desk drawer,

Sophie eventually found the large tweezers she kept in there, tucked in between her pencils and pens.

Taking hold of the pages with the tweezers, she withdrew them from the envelope, laid them on her desk, and unfolded them, turning the paper so she could see the signature at the end.

Will Ryan. The letter wasn't from the crazy man. It was from Marianne's father.

She dropped the tweezers back into her drawer and tossed her gloves aside.

> *London*
> *15 July 1940*
>
> *Dear Joe and Sophie,*
> *I'm writing to update you on the situation Hélène and I find ourselves in and to ask that you share what I'm going to tell you with Marianne. She will need someone to talk to once she knows too.*
>
> *Hélène and I are in England now. Some friends in Villers-Bret knew someone who put us in touch with someone in Cherbourg who was willing to risk a night-time channel crossing. It was harrowing and expensive and I hope to God we never have to do anything like that again, especially since I got horribly seasick. I'm not sure either one of us breathed until we set foot on the English coast.*
>
> *We left France because I didn't want Hélène to have to face another occupation of Villers-Bret. It's by no means certain the Germans will do anything destructive to the town this time around, but I wasn't willing to risk her being there if they do.*

While she packed our belongings, I went over to the memorial and gathered the records and important papers. I thought about taking them with us, but surely the Germans wouldn't desecrate a cemetery, would they? God, I hope not. The records are hidden in a safe place that the local councillor and I agreed on. We made sure the memorial was in perfect condition, paid our respects, shook hands, and locked the gates. We each had a key. I've handed mine over to the head of the Graves Commission in London.

At any rate, we're safe and well. The folks at the Graves Commission have been very helpful. They helped us find temporary lodgings and set to work finding something for me to do. I'm not the only one in this situation. There are two blokes from the English memorial at Thievpal.

I'd been hoping to join the Australian regiment that's forming here in England, but the brass aren't sure what to do with a 46-year-old corporal who has spent the last twenty years tending a memorial to the dead from the last war. I'd rather be fighting, but I suspect they'll assign me to whatever group they form to deal with the dead from this war.

Hélène misses home terribly, but at least her English is very good so she can communicate with the locals, even though some of the accents are tough for me to understand.

We left Villers-Bret with the clothes on our backs and a small suitcase each. I left Rex with a neighbor. It broke my heart to leave him even more than leaving our home.

And now I come to the real point of my letter. If the worst should happen, and we can't ever get back to France, or something happens to me and Hélène, I need to ask you a huge favour. Marianne is safe in Australia, thank God, and I know you've taken her under your proverbial wing. Hélène and I are so grateful to you for that. But, if, well, would you continue to look after her? Stand in for us if she needs you to? There are some days when I'm afraid we'll never see her again and I need to know she has friends she can turn to if...

Sophie read quickly, her breath catching at the enormity of the tumult in Will's and Hélène's life. Of course, she and Joe would continue to look after Marianne—they'd assured Will of that when he and Hélène and Christophe farewelled them in Marseille. Back then this war was only a vague threat. Now it was upon them in full force. Blinking rapidly to clear her eyes, Sophie went back to Will's letter.

...the worst happens. I don't know exactly what kind of relationship she has with you now – she wrote that she's happy there in Sydney and that you've been very kind to her, helping her get settled in and finding customers for her dressmaking and such. I don't have any family to speak of left in Australia. I'm begging you to do more if you can and if it's necessary.

I wish now I had made Christophe and Hélène go with Marianne. Christophe has traveled down to Chamonix, to join the Chasseurs Alpins with Nick. Chris is convinced he can serve France best by helping to defend the Chamonix valley. I hoped he might fight with the Australians, but of my children, Chris is French through and through. We haven't heard from him in several months, but he hasn't showed up on any lists of dead, missing, or prisoners, so we keep hope he's alive. I wrote to tell him we were leaving and gave him the Graves Commission address in London as the place to contact us.

Before we left, I withdrew all of our money from the local bank. We had to spend a good chunk of it on our passage to England...

She put the letter down again and cursed the boatman. How could people be so greedy when lives were at stake! Poor Will! Poor Hélène! And Christophe! Their lines of communication were so tortuous that it could be months before they knew of the other's whereabouts. At least Sam and Jean-Luc knew where they could always find Joe and her—there was no reason why they would leave their home here in Sydney. The roads in France would be packed with people fleeing the countryside, trying to head west away from the Germans. What would they do if they reached the Atlantic and the Germans were there too? She'd seen too many evacuees during the first war, old men and women struggling to keep up. Children barefoot and in ragged clothes. Babies growing thin and fussy because their mothers couldn't feed themselves, much less produce enough milk.

It wasn't right. Why should a few countries have to suffer so much because another country was ruled by a megalomaniac who wasn't satisfied with the borders as they were?

She could barely read the rest of Will's letter she was so busy planning how she and Joe could draw Marianne deeper into their family circle. How could she discreetly find out about Marianne's finances? Did she need help or was she able to support herself? Should Marianne move back here? Perhaps the best course of action was to invite Marianne to dinner, and be perfectly frank and get all of this out in the open.

When Joe arrived home from the office, Sophie followed him into his study and waited until he'd unloaded a sheaf of folders from his briefcase before she showed him the letter from Will.

"Hmmm," was the first thing he said when he finished reading and handed the pages back to her.

Sophie sat back and waited, letting him process Will's news and think it through for a few minutes before she spoke.

"I know it goes without saying that you and I will look out for Marianne's well-being," Sophie said. "It's what we've been doing since she traveled with us from France."

Joe nodded. "But you're thinking we need to do more?"

"Not more, per se," she said. "She values her independence very much and she's made a good start at establishing herself at work as a fabulous seamstress. She has a fledgling side business designing dresses and lingerie..." She waited to see if the tops of Joe's ears would turn pink. Maybe she shouldn't tell him the lace and silk confection he liked so much was the result of Marianne's talented fingers.

If he'd made the connection, he didn't let on, so Sophie carried on.

"What I'd like to do is have her read her father's letter and suggest that she think of us as her Sydney family. We haven't really stressed that enough, I don't think.

"It's not as though we abandoned her when she arrived here," Joe said.

"No, of course we didn't. But she might feel very alone, and fragile, when the enormity of what her parents have done sinks in. Leaving their home, their town, Will's work. I just want her to know that she can count on us if there's anything she needs."

"Agreed," Joe said.

"Good," Sophie said. "I think I'll invite her to come for dinner at least one night every week. Her family's changed circumstances may take some time to get used to. I don't want her to have to try to process it all by herself."

Joe blew out a breath. "I just wish I knew someone in London who could help Will find work. Unfortunately, the only people I do know are police officers."

"Well, he sounds hopeful that the Graves Commission will have a place for him. Surely there's something he can do that could keep him out of the line of fire," Sophie said. "They're already worrying their heads off about Christophe fighting with the Chasseurs Alpins."

Joe said nothing for a several moments. Sophie figured he must be thinking much the same thing she was—that they were all worried about all their sons and feeling helpless and angry that what they'd gone through in the last war somehow hadn't been enough to keep this war from happening.

His eyes ranged over the stack of files on his desk. "I'll leave it in your capable hands, if that's all right."

"It's perfectly all right, darling. I just wanted to discuss it with you before I got in touch with Marianne." She rose from her chair. "I'll leave you to get started."

The clock in the drawing room chimed seven times. "Mrs. Kelly says dinner will be ready at 7:30, so I'll see you then and you can tell me all about whatever it is you're working on."

With that, Sophie blew a kiss to Joe and left him to his files and paperwork.

Eighteen

A Frenchman in An Australian Uniform

October 1940

On October 18, all the family went to see Jean-Luc off. Despite training in the state of Victoria, the 14th Battalion of the 21st Brigade of the 7th Division embarked for Egypt in Sydney, but Sophie would have insisted they go to Melbourne or Brisbane or even Adelaide to farewell him.

Civilians weren't allowed on the dock where RMS *Aquitania* was moored, so she and Joe, plus Marianne, the Kellys, and even her mother and her aunt Flora lined the ropes marking the boundary.

The last time they were together, she told Jean-Luc that his parents Natalie and Louis would be proud of him. She overheard Joe telling him to carve his initials or some other symbol in the stock of his rifle so he could identify it in the dark if necessary. Then, bless him, Joe had tried to lighten the somber conversation by advising Jean-Luc to always take care of his feet—you can't march or rest if your feet are bothering you—as well as his weapons.

Now, as she watched the orderly lines of khaki-clad young men filing up the gangplank, Sophie couldn't help remembering Jean-Luc as a toddler she helped care for, then as an adolescent she

saw every couple of years on quick trips to Paris, then on the brink
of his teenaged years when his mother's life had been cut short. She
had loved him since he was tiny, throughout the nappy changes and
the splashing baths, soothed his hurts and shared his joys, grieved
with him when Natalie was taken from them far too soon. He in
turn had raised her spirits after grueling shifts caring for wounded
soldiers and, later, filled the empty place of the children she couldn't
bear, and been her co-conspirator in fleeing from grief. Throughout
it all she had loved him as if he was her own.

The enormity of what the young man was about to do, and what
he was prepared to do, descended like a thick fog obscuring her
vision. Only Joe's hand on the small of her back kept her steady
until the ship slipped into the distance. All she could think of was
the photograph of Jean-Luc dressed as a miniature French soldier,
complete with a realistic looking wooden rifle, that his parents had
taken before Louis left for the front. Sophie had shown that photo
to Joe when he unexpectedly came to Paris on rest in July 1917,
saying it was equal parts disturbing and adorable. In turn, Joe had
shown her a photo of two-year-old Sam saluting him, admitting he'd
been so surprised by Sam's action that he had saluted back. Later
that day Joe said he hoped Jean-Luc never had to wear a uniform.
She'd said she hoped Sam never had to salute anyone.

Now Sam and Jean-Luc were gone to fly and fight. Both in uniforms. Both saluting.

She and Joe should have known never to say never.

———

Sydney
19 October 1940

Dear Sam,
We waved good-bye to Jean-Luc yesterday when his

battalion boarded the ship. I have never seen so many soldiers in one place at one time. It is hard to believe he will be sailing the same route to Europe that I sailed to Australia. Your parents are well, but a little sad and worried he is gone.

I finally received a letter from my parents. They left our home in France and are now in England. As I suspected, my brother Chris and his friend Nick enlisted with an alpine battalion and are stationed close to Chamonix. I worry about them. They are only eighteen. That is far too young to go to war.

Have you settled in to life training cadets? Mrs. Kelly told me she will send you a fruit cake to share with your fellow pilots.

Fly safely,
Marianne

P.S. I have not written anything in English in a long time, so writing to you is good practice for me. Please tell me if I have made any mistakes!

Richmond
29 October 1940

Dear Marianne,
Good to hear Jean-Luc had the full family send-off. I've always felt lucky that Sophie adopted such a decent bloke. He's a good mate and a good brother.

Also good that you've had news from your family.

My fellow pilots are an interesting lot. Many are barely older than the cadets. I'm only twenty-five, but sometimes I feel like the dad amongst them.

Thanks for the news from home,
Sam

P.S. No mistakes that I could see. Well done!

NINETEEN

BOXES OF MEMORIES

OCTOBER 1940

The next day, after Joe headed to his office, Sophie wandered the house as if it might be the last time she saw it, until she came to the smallest bedroom in the house. Boxes of books and clothes and the possessions of two lifetimes had been stacked neatly against the walls. The names of their owners and the contents of each box were marked on the sides, the handwriting as distinct and different as their owners. Sam, sprawled in large upper-case letters. Jean-Luc, in the young man's tight, neat script.

They'd each given up their lodgings and packed up their possessions when they enlisted. Since Joe and she had an unused, mostly unfurnished room to spare, she had suggested they store their belongings here for the duration.

Sophie sank into one of the two armchairs in the room—they'd been in Sam's flat in Melbourne—and surveyed her surroundings.

It had seemed like such a good idea at the time, but seeing her sons' belongings, and lives, condensed into a dozen boxes each made her feel utterly bereft. She let the tears come, feeling them sting and well until hot, fat drops rolled down her cheeks faster than she could blink them back. Then she decided she wasn't going to blink back, and gave herself permission to cry her heart out. It wasn't fair. Their fathers had already given up so much—Joe had given nearly three years of his life. Louis had had his life cut short in a godforsaken charge at Verdun.

She had saved Jean-Luc from an orphanage after his mother, and her dearest friend, Natalie was killed in a motor car accident ten years after the war was over. There was no one else who could take him because neither Natalie nor Louis had any family still alive. Sophie had rushed to Paris from England, and as soon as she'd seen the boy she'd promised him she would always look after him. He'd looked at her, his eyes too solemn for his twelve years, and asked her how she knew.

She hadn't had a good answer for him. It was all she could do to not burst into tears. She had forced herself to use her calmest voice and answer as truthfully as she could. "I don't know," she admitted, "but I will do my very best."

Sad, serious Jean-Luc had nodded gravely and taken her hand as he had so many times when he was still a tiny boy.

She had hired an attorney to handle the paperwork to formally adopt Jean-Luc, and packed all of the boy's clothes, books, and toys into steamer trunks.

Sophie had cried until she couldn't cry any more at the sight of the beautiful Paris flat reduced to empty, lifeless rooms, at the ruin of her friends' lives, at the unfairness of it all. She had cried at the memory of Joe standing beside her at Jean-Luc's cot, when he was in Paris on leave in June 1917.

She and Jean-Luc sailed to Sydney two months after Natalie's death. They needed an adventure, something to look forward to, somewhere far away from the sorrows of England and France. She hadn't known Joe and Sam had moved there from Melbourne. Sheer luck had brought them back into each other's lives.

Sophie picked up a children's book about stars from the top of one of Sam's boxes. The inscription on the flyleaf read *To Sam, with all our love from Mummy and Daddy, Christmas 1917* in Annie's handwriting. She hadn't known Sam until he was thirteen, a year younger than Jean-Luc. What a wrench it must have been for Sam to lose his mother so young. She hoped he could remember his mother reading to him at bedtime.

Joe was still in France then. Annie would have bought this book by herself, wrapped it and placed it under the Christmas tree, and tried to explain to her little son why his father couldn't be there with them. Sam couldn't have understood, any more than Jean-Luc had, that events far beyond their control were the reason for their fathers' absence from their lives.

She'd done all she could to be a mother to Jean-Luc and, later, to Sam, and she loved them as if they were her own. Fresh tears swelled, and Sophie let them fall. The house was empty and she could cry as long and as hard as she needed to without having to pretend she was all right. Mrs. Kelly was off at the market. Joe was at work. She had nowhere she needed to be and she was right where she wanted to be, surrounded by Sam's and Jean-Luc's things.

Joe had come home early; his position at the Forensics department plus his new duties liaising with the militia, who guarded the home front, meant his hours had become somewhat irregular. He had missed lunch, and had an early evening meeting with Bobby Davies, so he'd come home for a pot of tea and, if there wasn't anything left from last night's supper, a plate of sandwiches.

The house was quiet when he unlocked the front door. Usually he could hear activity—Sophie on the phone in the little nook by the stairs, or Mrs. Kelly in the kitchen and Thomas bringing a basketful of flowers and vegetables in from the garden. Once he had come home to Sam and Jean-Luc playing tunes on the gramophone that Joe wasn't sure anyone could dance to until he saw Jean-Luc teaching Sophie the steps while Sam encouraged from the sidelines. Sam trying to convince plump, iron-haired Mrs. Kelly to give it a go had been thoroughly amusing. Mrs. Kelly was willing to put up with a lot from Master Sam, as she affectionately called him, but she had requested a waltz instead, and Sam had obliged.

Today, though, the house was quiet, and Joe quickly went from room to room trying to ascertain if anything was wrong.

When no one was to be found in the downstairs rooms, he headed upstairs. Sophie's coat and handbag lay at the foot of their bed, so she was here, somewhere. The other bedrooms were empty, their beds neatly made since Sophie insisted the boys look after themselves if they wanted Mrs. Kelly to spend her time cooking and baking their favorite dinners and cakes.

That left the spare room. Sophie was asleep in one of the armchairs, shoes kicked off and legs tucked under her. Her hanky was crumpled in one hand and a children's book lay in her lap.

Joe sat in the other chair and looked around the room.

From the looks of things, Sophie had been crying. He had a feeling she'd been holding back tears ever since the boys—boys!—they were grown men in their mid-twenties—had announced they were going off to war. And if she'd fallen asleep, she must have cried so much she was exhausted. The only time Joe had seen her cry that much was when she received news her father was dying. That had been before they were married, before they'd realized they were in love with each other. He had stopped by to pick up Sam, and Sophie had insisted they stay for dinner. Afterwards they'd had a drink in the drawing room and she told him she was leaving Sydney for England. She'd begun to cry as she spoke of her plans and he'd gathered her in his arms and held her until she stopped. They'd shared so much grief during the war—his brother Robbie, her brother Ben, the men he commanded, the men she nursed—and so much joy since they'd been reunited, that it had seemed perfectly natural to hold her and comfort her. In that moment he had known he wanted to be by her side always, through bad times and good, and everything in-between.

Sophie stirred and stretched. She blinked and opened her eyes, yawning first, then a sleepy smile brightened her features. "Joe!" She looked around the room; it was still light outside. "What time is it? You're home early, aren't you?"

"It's only around four. I could come home later, if you like," he said, a note of fun creeping into his voice.

"I'm just surprised to see you, that's all. Has something happened?"

"No, I missed lunch and I have a meeting with Bobby at seven. We have a problem brewing with sly grog."

Sophie had become well-versed in Australian slang. "Let me guess. With all the service personnel amassing in the city, the market for illegal booze has grown by leaps and bounds?"

"Correct. Bobby wants to set up a plan of attack, hence the meeting tonight, so I'll miss supper too. I thought I'd come home and get a bite to eat and relax a bit before I head to his office. What have you been up to?" He kept his tone light; he didn't want to make her feel like she needed to shed her mood on his account.

The left corner of Sophie's mouth turned down. "I just wandered in here a little while ago. I don't know why, exactly. Boxes piled on top of each other isn't a particularly grand view."

Joe huffed a laugh. "At least they got them upstairs, and didn't leave them downstairs for Thomas and me to carry."

"True. They do have a habit of leaving things until the last minute, don't they?"

"Sam certainly does," Joe said. "I'm afraid his bad habit has rubbed off on Jean-Luc. What kind of specimens do you supposed he has squirreled away?"

"Probably jars of different bugs that attack grape vines," Sophie said. "Or, I don't know, soil samples or…"

"I just hope Sam sent everything to the laundry before he tossed it all in that box labeled 'Sports clothes'," Joe countered. "Can you imagine coming home four years later—" He stopped short. His brows knit. Sam and Jean-Luc would be away for an indefinite amount of time.

Jean-Luc was on his way to Egypt following the same route he himself had taken more than twenty years earlier: around the southern coast of Australia across the Indian Ocean, up to the Arabian Peninsula, through the Suez Canal. But instead of crossing the Mediterranean to disembark in France, Jean-Luc would either travel west to Libya or north to Palestine. Only time would tell which.

Both boys were fairly well-traveled. Sophie's careful management of their finances meant they could indulge themselves and the boys with travel and books and experiences. Sam loved flying and the stars. Jean-Luc loved traveling and making wine. The boys sailed to Los Angeles two years ago—Sam to have some telescope time at the new Griffiths Observatory there, and Jean-Luc to make his way north to Davis, where the University of California had reinstated their viticulture program after Prohibition in the United States ended. Happier times.... Now war was upon them, only this time he and Sophie would be watching and waiting from the sidelines while their sons were in the thick of it. Just let them come home, Joe prayed. Keep them safe.

He must have looked as pensive as he felt because when he tore his eyes away from a box labeled 'Uni textbooks' Sophie was standing behind him, massaging his shoulders. "Ah, right there," he moaned when she found a particularly tight spot.

"If you're going to leave before supper, let's go downstairs and get some food in you," she said. "I could do with a cup of tea, and Mrs. Kelly won't mind if I heat up the rest of the stew from the other night."

"Don't tell her I said so, but I think it's even better reheated than it is on the first night," Joe said.

"Darling, haven't you realized she always makes enough so you can have something substantial to eat when you come in after a late night?"

"Mrs. Kelly may be an angel incarnate," Joe said, smiling as Sophie tugged him up from his chair and held his hand as they made their way downstairs and to the kitchen.

PART 2: 1941

AUSTRALIA, LEBANON

You sing about her soldiers brave,
But a thought comes to my mind,
That the bravest soldiers of us all,
Are the womenfolk we left behind.

Author Unknown,
"The Womenfolk We Left Behind"

TWENTY

MISSING DIAMONDS

JANUARY 1941

Sophie's original plan for Monday morning was nothing. She'd been busy all week with gathering provisions for Sam and Jean-Luc and meetings for the Red Cross fund-raising gala last night. Joe had actually been able to attend with her, for most of the evening. As co-chair, she needed to stay until the bitter end, which didn't come until well past midnight. Joe had gone home around 10:30 since he'd been up early for the police rowing team's usual training on Sunday mornings.

The gala had been held at her Aunt Flora's lovely home in Vaucluse, high on one of Sydney's hills. Sophie adored the sweeping views of the ocean from the veranda and a fresh sea breeze ruffling the shrubbery and formal plantings in the extensive gardens. She and Joe had managed a few minutes to themselves after the speeches appealing for funds were finished and the silent auction winners were announced. Joe and stars were a heady combination. They'd declared their love for each other the first time under the stars and last night she'd had another declaration from him. After nearly eleven years of marriage, it was a lovely and unexpected moment. Joe wasn't prone to public displays of affection or open declarations of undying love, but put them in a quiet garden with an astonishingly clear sky over their heads and he became remarkably forthcoming. And demonstrative.

Of course, he could have been encouraged by the gown she'd worn, silk charmeuse draped to dip low so that every time he touched her back his fingers encountered warm, bare skin. Or it could have been that she'd worn his favorite perfume, dabbed just above the curve of her neck that was his favorite place to nuzzle. No, it must have been her hair, which he had confessed he'd loved when he saw it come unpinned in Paris and had wanted to gather it in his hands and twist tendrils around his fingers. She'd made sure her hairdresser left a tendril or two loose enough to fall free under the gentle ministrations of an affectionate husband.

Yes, that was it, that tendril that he'd touched and twined as she tilted her head and invited his lips to her neck.

Sophie stretched under the soft cotton sheets and snuggled into Joe's pillow. He was long gone for the day but she'd awakened with him and they'd had a lovely, drowsy, early morning interlude. In their first marriages to other people, they had learned the basics of human bodies fitting together. In their marriage together, they had eagerly set to improving on the basics with results that were occasionally silly and sometimes sublime. She stretched again and filled her senses with Joe's scent embedded in the down and cotton of their bedclothes. Bliss.

Mrs. Kelly's light knocks on the bedroom door pulled her out of her reverie. "Come in," she called.

Her housekeeper entered bearing a tray laden with morning tea things, her glance taking in Sophie's bare shoulders and bedcovers that were more rumpled than usual. Her lips lifted in a knowing little smile as she put the tray on Sophie's bedside table.

Sophie grinned back at her.

Mrs. Kelly opened the drapes wide and morning sun brightened the bedroom. The breeze lifted the sheer curtains and their hems fluttered to the edge of the rug covering polished wooden floorboards. "What are the plans for today? I'm guessing you and the inspector will be home early today since you had a late night."

"You're right. Something simple this evening, please, since we had such a rich dinner last night. Joe loves your roast chicken with vegetables and potatoes. Or perhaps a cottage pie? He loves that too, especially when you add extra peas and carrots to the mince."

"I'll check the larder, but we should be able to manage that. And lunch? Will you be here or will you be out?"

"I'll be here. Being as lazy as I can be for a while. I have to go over the numbers from the gala and figure out how much we raised."

"Was it a good party?" She could have sworn Mrs. Kelly's eyes were twinkling at her. The woman was devoted to Joe. She hadn't been sure Sophie was the right one for him at first – wealthy society ladies didn't usually choose to spend their lives with middle-class detective inspectors – but Sophie had won her over early. Now Mrs. Kelly loved to hear about the parties and galas. Her culinary skills had graced the Parker dining table for many a luncheon when Sophie gathered her friends together to work out a solution for a problem that needed solving.

"It was marvelous. I snagged a menu for you from Aunt Flora's cook."

Sophie sat up in bed, carefully holding the sheet to her breasts. Mrs. Kelly might thoroughly approve of her and Joe having a loving marriage, but modesty won out as she reached for her evening clutch on the dressing table and extracted an embossed card.

Mrs. Kelly scanned it quickly. "Seven courses! And my word, all that butter and cream!"

Sophie nodded. "If this war drags on, the government will have to introduce food rationing and that'll be the last of seven courses with butter and cream. I hardly ate a bite of it, though. I spent most of my time trying to charm the mayor into letting us host our next function at Town Hall without paying the usual rental fee."

"Something filling and nutritious for lunch then. An egg pie and salad?"

"Sounds perfect, Mrs. Kelly."

Sophie's plan to do as little as possible that morning went awry less than ten minutes after Mrs. Kelly left her to the pot of tea and rack of toast.

She could hear car doors opening and closing. The excited voices sounded a lot like her mother and aunt, but they weren't supposed to arrive until the afternoon to discuss the results and take the checks to deposit them at the bank.

Pulling on her dressing gown, she peered out the bedroom window. The visitors were her mother and aunt. "Mother," she called from the open window.

Lily Holt looked around in surprise.

"Mother! Up here!" Sophie called.

"Oh! There you are! Good morning, dear. We're sorry to barge in on you so early, but Flora and I simply must speak with you!" Lily quickly looked to her right and then to her left. "Something has happened!"

"I'll be right down," Sophie said. "Ring the bell and tell Mrs. Kelly I'm getting dressed."

Sophie glanced longingly at her bed, pulled the covers up so it wasn't a complete disaster when Mrs. Kelly came up to make it, and selected trousers and a blouse from the wardrobe. She splashed some water on her face, and gave her hair a quick brush.

She found her mother and aunt in the dining room. Mrs. Kelly had already laid the table with cups, saucers, and spoons.

"Mother," Sophie said, kissing her cheek and then moving to kiss her aunt too. "Aunt Flora. What on earth is going on?"

"My dear, we have the most dreadful news," Flora said. Flora's large bosom rose and fell and rose again as she took a big breath. "Marjorie's diamond earrings have gone missing!"

Marjorie Turner was a longtime family friend. She'd married well, been widowed, and married well again. Marjorie loved diamonds, loved receiving them from her wealthy husbands, and loved wearing them as often as possible. She was also one of the most generous attendees at the gala last night. Sophie knew a check for five hundred pounds, an incredible amount, was in the envelope of checks she had placed in the safe when she arrived home last night.

"No! How? And when?"

Lily and Flora began talking at once, so excitedly that Sophie couldn't untangle the tale. "Stop, please. Let's sit down, let Mrs. Kelly serve the tea, and tell me one at a time."

The two older women sat and fiddled impatiently with their spoons while tea was poured. They were so shaken that their normally impeccable manners disappeared. For that to happen, they had to be rattled to the core. Or if not the core, close to it.

Sophie took charge. "One of you speak first, please," she said gently, "and tell me what all the fuss is about."

Lilly looked to her sister. "You tell the story, Flora."

Flora's bosom rose again. "As you know, several people were guests in my home overnight. Marjorie and Enid, her companion, were among them."

That sounded reasonable so far. Sophie nodded. "Go on."

"Well, when Marjorie woke this morning the first thing she did was open her jewelry box to check her diamonds were in it. You know how attached she is to them." Flora took a quick sip of tea. "But Sophie, her diamond drop earrings weren't there! She and Enid searched her room but they were nowhere to be found!"

At that point Flora, who was not prone to hysterics, rattled her tea cup in its saucer.

Lily patted her sister's hand. "It's alright, Flora. Tell her the rest of it."

"She accused me of having thieves for servants and is threatening to ruin our good names if her earrings aren't found!"

"Did you call the police?"

"Of course," Flora said. "But Marjorie didn't like the constable who came to the house. She said he was a bumbling nincompoop if he didn't question all of my servants immediately. She said it was obvious one of my servants was responsible."

"But..." Sophie began.

"The difficulty is," Lily said, "the policeman as much as accused Nell of stealing the diamonds."

Flora shook her head. "I trust Nell. She's been working for me since before Randolph died. For her to steal is unheard of."

Sophie sat back in her chair. Her aunt really was shaken. Randolph, her husband, had died several years ago, so that meant Nell had been in her employ for at least that long.

"To make matters worse," Flora added, "Enid..."

"Marjorie's companion," Lily reminded Sophie.

"Enid is the only other person besides Marjorie who knows the combination lock on Marjorie's jewelry box. It's a stout thing, wooden, with a latch that can be locked with a little padlock."

Sophie let out a big breath. This story wasn't making sense. Why on earth would a mere constable be sent out to a wealthy home on his own? Wouldn't a sergeant or a detective constable have been assigned to do the initial interviews at the house?

"And to add insult to injury," Flora fumed, "Marjorie told me that unless I find her jewels within the day, she would contact everyone who wrote a check last night and tell them to demand their money back. That Lily and I, and you too Sophie, couldn't be trusted with their money. All of the good works I've done for so many years will be tainted by this horrible accusation! My reputation will be ruined. Your mother's. And yours and Joe's will be too!"

"Joe's? But he—"

"Just think, Sophie," Lily said. "A high-ranking police official was in attendance at a party where hundreds of pounds worth of diamonds were stolen."

"But Joe wasn't even there when the earrings disappeared. He left early – just after ten. He certainly didn't steal them because she was wearing them when he left the party. You know that."

"Of course, we know it," Lily said. "But that doesn't mean the press won't have a field day twisting together a major theft and Joe's reputation."

"Where is Marjorie now?"

Flora spoke up. "She said she was going straight to her insurance company's office to make a claim for the diamonds."

Sophie ran through everything she'd heard so far. None of it was making any sense. Why was Marjorie so intent on sullying her family's—and her husband's—reputation?

"Something about this just doesn't sound right to me," she declared. "We are going to figure out what Marjorie is playing at because she is protesting far too much."

She fetched a pad of paper and a pen. "First, we're going to note down everything we know about Marjorie. What if she has something to hide? Something that would ruin *her* reputation in society. Someone could be blackmailing her. Is her husband carrying on? What if the diamonds aren't real? Are her sons secretly fifth columnists?"

Twenty-One

Sophie Investigates

February, 1941

Sydney
4 February 1941

Dear Sam,
Sophie may be the most amazing woman I have ever met. A friend (supposedly a very good friend) of her Aunt Flora accused Flora's maid of stealing her diamond earrings during a party at Flora's house and then threatened to go to the papers and tell them that a high-ranking police official (your father) was at the party and the theft happened right under his nose.

Well. Lily and Flora were extremely upset and immediately told Sophie what was happening. Sophie spent a couple of weeks "poking around" as she put it, and discovered the woman sold her diamonds because she did not want her sons to join the army or to be conscripted into the militia. She used the money to pay a doctor to attest that the sons were both physically unfit for any kind of service.

Sophie is involved in so many charitable groups and boards that she must have friends in every corner of Sydney society to have uncovered that information. Needless to say, she was livid this woman would do such a thing and told her unless she apologized to Flora and Lily, she would divulge her proof to someone who could make her life and her sons' lives very difficult.

Fly safely,
Marianne
P.S. I am still not certain I understand the difference between the army and the militia.

Richmond
11 February 1941

Dear Marianne,
Crikey. I've witnessed Sophie taking on many worthy causes, but this one was certainly outside her usual realm. Perhaps the NSW police should make her an honourary detective.

Sew straight,
Sam
P.S. The army can't conscript anyone, but once you volunteer you can be sent anywhere in the world to fight. The militia can conscript men who haven't volunteered for one of the forces, but it can't send them to fight overseas, so they're limited to defending the home front and New Guinea, which is an Australian protectorate.

Twenty-Two

From Dresses to Parachutes

April 1941

Marianne unlocked the door to her flat, her bags thudding to the floor and her keys clinking in the bowl on the little hallway table.

"It's me, Patricia," she called, unsure whether Patricia was home or not.

"In the kitchen," Patricia replied. "I've just put the kettle on."

Marianne pulled off her gloves and headed to the back of the flat.

"You made good time," Marianne said from the kitchen doorway.

"For once the tram was on time, so I didn't have to wait for it. If you hadn't decided to work late you would've been home an hour ago too." Patricia set their cups and a plate of biscuits on a tray. "There's a newspaper in the sitting room. I'll bring the tea things in there and you can read it to me."

Marianne smiled at her friend. Patricia claimed the print was too tiny and she wasn't going to ruin her eyesight and need glasses because of deciphering her boss' execrable handwriting *and* reading the newspaper, but she loved being read to in Marianne's French-accented English.

"All right," she said. "Meet you there in ten minutes. I'll put my things away and wash up."

Settled in their mismatched chairs, which were surprisingly comfortable for being cast-offs, Marianne waited while Patricia filled their teacups. A good cup of tea was as thirst-quenching as anything, as her Australian father put it. She quickly downed half the cup, while Patricia rifled through the newspaper until she found an article with the most absurd headline on the page.

"This one."

"Are you ready?"

Patricia unbuckled her t-straps, kicked them off, and raised her feet to the ottoman. "I am now."

"Comedian made a colonel," Marianne read aloud. "Jim Gerald's New Role. AIF entertainment organiser. Jim Gerald, the comedian whose most famous burlesque act for the last 20 years has been to impersonate an untidy, half-witted private, yesterday became a genuine, immaculately dressed honorary Lieutenant-Colonel. The War Cabinet has put him in charge of all AIF entertainment overseas."

She lowered the newspaper and stared at her friend. "Really?"

"Really," Patricia said. "He does this brilliant bit as a private whose puttees are wrapped all wrong and his suspenders are hardly holding his breeches up. My dad said Private Jitters would have been a sergeant-major's nightmare."

"Hmph."

"It's hilarious, I tell you. What does the rest of it say?"

"Yesterday, senior officers were saluting him, and Colonel Gerald admitted that he could not quite believe that it was all real. "It is funny, I know," he said, "and a lot of people will laugh. But I am going to take this seriously. When I came back from the last war I started to appear as Private Jitters, and on the stage I've always been a hopeless recruit, or one of those runny privates. The things I've said about Colonels—my gosh, I wouldn't like to repeat them now."

While Patricia giggled at her memories of Private Jitters, Marianne scanned the rest of the page. "Airman rescued from bush," she read. "Parachuted, fell into tree on precipice. Lismore, Thursday."

Patricia grimaced. "Ouch! How on earth did he manage that?"

"After he had jumped from an RAAF training plane, Aircraftman J. S. McG. Ross landed by parachute yesterday in the branches of a tree on the side of a precipice in the McPherson Range. Although his right leg was broken, Ross lowered himself by a creeper to a narrow ledge on the cliff face, where a rescue party found him."

Marianne lowered the paper. "Where's the McPherson Range?"

"Somewhere in Queensland, I think," Patricia said. "Geography was never my strong suit."

Marianne returned to reading. "Ross came down only a few miles from the spot where a Stinson plane crashed some years ago, and the rescue party had to face the same difficulties as then—deep gorges, rugged mountain sides, and dense scrub and vines.

"The plane—of which Ross had been the only occupant—crashed about five miles away. Ross was on a cross-country flight from No. 3 Service Flying Training School, Amberley, QLD. The engine failed and he lost control of the plane shortly before 11 a.m. As he bailed out the plane's tail struck him.

"Mrs. James Grayson, a farmer's wife, saw him jump from the machine, and telephoned for aid. The rescuers reached Ross and treated his injuries about 2.30 p.m. They strapped him to a stretcher. In many places, on the way back, this had to be lowered over ledges with ropes. Ross reached the Tyalgum Hospital about 8 p.m."

Marianne rose and crossed the room to the map of Australia they'd pinned on the wall. Amberley to the McPherson Range to Tyalgum. Sam's No 4 Squadron was in Richmond, nowhere near those places. But still, there had been too many articles about crashes, often fatal, in the past few months. Then there was the article she'd read last month about a parachute shortage leading to the death of an aircraftman.

Patricia's hopeful "Do you want the last biscuit?" broke into her reverie.

"No, you can have it."

"You've gone awfully quiet," Patricia said after she bit into the thin biscuit and carefully picked the crumbs from her skirt. "Thinking about your handsome RAAF pilot?"

Why had she placed the photo of the Parker family, complete with her, Sam, and Jean-Luc on the mantle? "What? No!"

"Why ever not? You deserve to have a bit of fun. It's not like you have to marry him."

"Patricia, he isn't my pilot."

"What was his name? Jack? Tom?"

"His name is Sam, and he is only a friend." Now she knew there was far more to Sam, but it seemed best not to give Patricia any ammunition.

Patricia gave up the pretense of eating the rest of the biscuit daintily, downed it in one go, and flicked the last crumbs onto the tea tray. "What about his French brother? Aren't Frenchmen famous for being incredibly romantic?"

"Jean-Luc has a girlfriend, but he doesn't seem particularly romantic." Marianne thought back to the French boys she'd known at home. "If any Frenchmen are, I have never met them."

"Come out with me and Rosemary tonight," Pat said, flipping to the Amusements page of the newspaper. "We're going to the pictures. There's Gary Cooper and Paulette Goddard in North West Mounted Police. He's dreamy and she's beautiful. Or... Oooh. Listen to this. The Power and The Glory, thrilling romantic drama featuring the Royal Australian Air Force in action. Dive bombing thrills in the Australian airways. Australian men. Australian machines." She lowered the newspaper and waggled her brows at Marianne. "You could see for yourself what your dashing pilot is like in action."

Marianne stifled the "Sam is not my pilot" that automatically rose to her lips in favor of "You know I must work late to finish that trousseau for Miss Smythe-Adams."

"You're no fun." Patricia's words were without rancor. She knew Marianne dreamed of owning her own dressmaking business one day. That she was entrusted with the bridal lingerie of one of Sydney's wealthiest young women was a testament to her skill. She checked her wristwatch and jumped up from her chair. "Uh-oh. I'm late. I need to change before I leave."

"Go on. I will clean up the tea things," Marianne said.

—

As Marianne rinsed and stacked the teacups and biscuit plate, an idea how she could help the war effort began to take shape. Miss Smythe-Adams' need for a lavish wedding wardrobe seemed to fly in the face of what was happening in the world. The problem was, Marianne didn't have any other skills. Not like Patricia and her friend Rosemary who were shorthand typists for an insurance company. Their skills could easily transfer to war work if they needed to. Could she learn to type? Did she even want to? She had learned how to operate a sewing machine years ago at Madame Delphine's dress shop back in Amiens. She could put off fine hand sewing for a while and sew parachutes instead. Sam and his fellow pilots needed parachutes...

Sam. Sam Parker. She thought about him more than she should, wondered how he was doing, what the new air cadets were learning under his tutelage, whether he was a good teacher.

And why were there so many crashes? Should she ask or wait to see if he mentioned them?

But first, she needed to find out which company was responsible for making parachutes and apply for a job there. That was the best thing she could do to help the war effort. That could be her way to help Chris and Jean-Luc. And Sam.

TWENTY-THREE

'CHUTE NOTES

MAY 1941

Sydney
4 May 1941

Dear Sam,
I thought you would like to know I now spend my days
sewing parachutes instead of tailoring ladies' dresses at
David Jones.

I do not know whether you receive a new parachute
every time you fly or if you keep the same one, but look
in the outside pocket. The girls sometimes attach little
notes of encouragement.

Fly safely,
Marianne

Somewhere in NSW
11 May 1941

Dear Miss Parachute Maker,
Usually we keep the same 'chute but sometimes we're is-
sued new ones. Is your note of encouragement in English
or in French?

Sew straight,
Sam

Sydney
16 May 1941

Dear Sam,
If my note was in French could you read it? I thought
you said your French was abominable.

Fly safely,
Marianne

Somewhere in NSW
21 May 1941

Dear Miss Parachute Maker,
Jean-Luc says my French is abominable. I can still read
it though.

Sew straight,
Sam

Sydney (where else?)
25 May 1941

Dear Sam,
Tu es certain que tu peux lire le français?

Fly safely,
Marianne

Somewhere in you know where
29 May 1941

Dear Mlle Parachute Maker,
Oui, je peux lire le français. Could you send a French-English dictionary though? On the off chance you throw a new word at me.

Sew straight,
Sam

Sydney
31 May 1941

Cher Sam,
Tout le monde ici pense à toi, et nous espérons que tu n'aura jamais à utiliser ce parachute.

Soyez prudent lorsque tu pilote ton avion,
Marianne
P.S. Bonne chance pour traduire cette note!

How good was Sam's mastery of French verb tenses? No matter. She was sending a dictionary so he could decipher everything: *Dear Sam, Everyone here is thinking of you, and we hope you never have to use this parachute. Be careful when you fly your plane. P.S. Good luck translating this note!*

TWENTY-FOUR

THE CEDARS OF LEBANON

JUNE – JULY 1941

J ean-Luc chewed the end of his pencil, wondering how much to tell his parents and deciding that since they had both experienced war, there was no reason to shield them from his war.

Somewhere in Syria-Lebanon
27 June 1941

Dear Sophie and Joe,
I don't know what the newspapers at home have report-ed, but the Vichy French troops we're fighting here are a combination of colonials, mercenary troops, foreign legionaries, and native regiments who don't care about politics, only maintaining their professional reputa-tion. We've learnt more about hand-to-hand fighting and rigid discipline from them than we ever imag-ined.

In short, they are formidable.

They also know this countryside like the backs of their hands. They had good artillery, and a great number of mortars and machine-guns, plus heavily armoured medium Renault tanks which caused a lot of trouble to my division, which was the Australian coastal column. In the hills, their cavalry was superb.

They had bomber and fighter squadrons too, and once or twice our column was shelled by Vichy naval units, but we had RAF and RAAF bombers protecting us and our captain tells us we are progressing as planned.

My company has stayed remarkably safe and I've escaped injury, with the exception of the usual cuts, scrapes, and bruises. Joe, you'll be happy to know I passed on your advice about taking care of our feet. We had the good luck to come across a deep, stone-lined irrigation canal originally built by the Romans and we all took the opportunity to pull off our boots and socks and have a nice long soak in the water. We're all either sunburnt or brown as berries, as Sophie would say.

I'll write again when I can.

Yours affectionately,
Jean-Luc

Somewhere in Lebanon
17 July 1941

Dear Sophie and Joe,
You may not have received the letter I sent two weeks

ago, but you've probably seen the news that Beirut fell and an armistice has been struck. As a lucky result, my division has garrison duties along the coastal zone. It's far more comfortable work than tramping up and down rocky hills and through gullies, looking out for snipers and surprise attacks all the while.

This country is beautiful though. The Mediterranean is as blue as blue can be, and in peacetime you could probably ski in the mountains in the morning and spend the afternoon swimming at the beach. Sophie, it reminds me very much of Menton in the south of France, only substitute cedar trees for the umbrella pines in France.

It's a good climate and landscape for growing olives and grapes, too. It's no wonder the Phoenicians became so wealthy exporting oil and wine. We've seen a lot of vineyards and the locals don't seem to mind letting us sample their wares. There's even a winery that has been run by monks for decades. I've picked up a little bit of Arabic, mostly the polite words and some not so polite ones too, but the French have been here so long that many people speak French fluently.

My division has been on rest for a few days before we head north to HQ in Tripoli, which is about 100 miles north of Beirut. We hope to get permission to play tourist at some point and make the trek to Baalbek, the site of a temple complex which includes two of the largest and grandest Roman temples anywhere, the Temple of Bacchus and the Temple of Jupiter. Apparently, we have the Germans to thank for excavating the temples at the beginning of the century. It was once called Heliopolis. Joe, I know how much you like the Romans, so

I'll be sure to take photos.

I must close for now. I need to get some food and coffee before I go on duty in an hour. What have you heard from Sam? Let me know all your news and please give my best regards to Mrs. Kelly and Thomas, as well as Marianne when you see her next.

Yours affectionately,
Jean-Luc

TWENTY-FIVE

TARTE TATIN, NOT BURNT

SEPTEMBER 1941

Marianne grinned as she began writing a new note to Sam. It was hard to believe it had been two years since she arrived in Sydney and her first, ill-fated attempt at baking.

Sydney
4 September 1941

Dear Sam,
Your father had a nice birthday yesterday. Without you and Jean-Luc knocking on the front door in the middle of everything, I was able to bake him a delicious, unburnt tarte tatin.

Fly safely,
Marianne

Somewhere in NSW
6 September 1941

Dear Marianne,
I'm sorry I missed that. The apple tart, not interrupt-
ing your baking efforts. I don't suppose you could send
a slice so I can taste for myself? On second thought,
perhaps I can find an excuse to get to Sydney for a few
hours. Is there any left?

Sew straight,
Sam

Sydney
8 September 1941

Dear Sam,
The post is very quick between your air base and Syd-
ney, but I am sorry to say you are too late. The tart is
long gone.

Fly safely,
Marianne

Somewhere in NSW
10 September 1941

Dear Marianne,
I was afraid of that. Would you give me some advance
warning next time you make one?

Sew straight,
Sam

Sydney
12 September 1941

Dear Sam,
I will do what I can, but I think you will have to nego-
tiate with your father for a slice. It is his favourite after
all.

Fly safely,
Marianne

Somewhere in NSW
14 September 1941

Dear Marianne,
Or you could send the whole thing here. I won't tell Dad
if you don't.

Sew straight,
Sam

Sydney
17 September 1941

Dear Sam,
How do you propose I bake a tarte tatin and send it
to you without anyone knowing? My flat has a tiny
kitchen, so I could not make it there. I would have to
use your parents' kitchen and either swear Mrs. Kelly to
secrecy or wait until she was out of the house for several
hours. I know Mrs. Kelly's allegiance to you is strong,

but I suspect it is stronger for your father.

Fly safely,
Marianne
P.S. Sophie would be a problem, too, since she is in and
out of the house so many times during the day.

Somewhere in NSW
25 September 1941

Dear Marianne,
So... Does this mean you're thinking about it?

Sew straight,
Sam

Sydney
28 September 1941

Dear Sam,
I could probably summon the required levels of devi-
ousness, but I do not believe a tart would survive the
post.

Fly safely,
Marianne

Oh, this exchange had been fun, Marianne thought as she folded her letter, something that had been sorely missing from her life. She was sorry this round of correspondence had reached its logical conclusion. Sam had certainly seemed willing to play. Perhaps he would again.

TWENTY-SIX

JAPANESE NEIGHBORS

EARLY DECEMBER 1941

Sophie hurried to the front door. The knocking, which had been insistent, continued with the addition of a woman's voice.

"Sophie, are you there?"

Sophie flung open the door. Ellen Mitsui, their neighbor from three houses down the road, had been crying. Tears streaked Ellen's usually perfectly powdered cheeks.

"Ellen! Come in. Whatever is the matter?"

Ellen's tears started again so Sophie helped her into the house and guided her into the big sunny drawing room.

"Please, sit down," she said, and poured her friend a glass of brandy. "Sip this and tell me what has happened. Are you all right? Are the children all right?"

"It's Kino. He's been attacked. Someone threw a rock through the shop window and then..."

Oh Lord. She'd been afraid something like this would happen. Japan had had a long and friendly relationship with Australia. Kino Mitsui had been born in Japan but had emigrated with his family when he was still a young boy. He was one of thousands of young Japanese who had married Australian girls, started families, owned thriving businesses, and been upstanding members of the community. But ever since Japan became part of the Axis powers the Japanese in Sydney had been subject to increasingly violent attacks and acts of vandalism. These only increased in frequency and violence after Japan bombed Pearl Harbor, destroying the American naval fleet stationed there. The United States and Britain had immediately declared war on Japan, which meant Australia was at war on two fronts.

She handed Ellen her handkerchief. "Is he badly hurt?

"I don't know…" Ellen sobbed. "Nobody will tell me anything except he's been taken to hospital."

"Where are the children?" The Mitsuis had three daughters ranging in age from six to ten.

"They're at school. They don't know about this. What am I going to tell them?" Ellen wiped her eyes and nose. "Sophie, can you call Joe? Can you ask him to find who did this?"

"I will. Here," she said, tipping another half inch of brandy into Ellen's glass. "Drink this. I'll call Joe's office and have Mrs. Kelly put the kettle on.

When Mrs. Kelly brought in the tea things and poured a cup for Ellen, Sophie asked her to stay in the drawing room with their neighbor while she called Joe.

"He's only just arrived, Mrs. Parker," Miss Pringle said after pleasantries had been exchanged. "Please wait one moment while I fetch him."

The older woman's heels tapped through the lab's reception office to Joe's office. "It's your wife, sir."

She didn't often call Joe at work, and concern automatically edged his greeting whenever she did. "Sophie? Has something happened?"

"Joe, Ellen Mitsui is here. There's been some sort of altercation at Kino's shop. The hospital phoned to tell her he's there and she came here to ask for your help. Can you find out what's happened?"

"Of course. Let me speak with Ellen for a moment, would you?"

"This is going to be tricky, isn't it, darling?" Public opinion towards the Japanese in Australia plummeted the day after the Americans were attacked early in December. The government's reaction had been to seize the records of Japanese businesses, probably to determine who could have been spying so something similar could be wreaked on Australia.

Within days, some very nasty attacks had begun—bottles thrown at Japanese men, slurs, ugly things said to Australian women who'd married them. Almost overnight many citizens had turned from acceptance of Japanese, many of whom had lived and worked in Sydney for decades, to distrust and outright hatred. It was a frightening thing to witness.

Sophie lay the telephone receiver on the table and crossed the entry hall to the drawing room doors. "Ellen, Joe needs to speak with you."

She stayed close to her friend while she answered Joe's questions and gave him the exact address of Kino's jewelry shop. Ellen fidgeted the pearls on the necklace she wore while she spoke. Kino's family had been in the pearl business for years, beginning before the first war. The sons of the family had worked their way up in the world, becoming educated and moving from physical labor to selling pearls to branching out to high end jewelry shops.

Ellen's voice wavered when said good bye to Joe. She held the receiver to Sophie.

"Yes, darling?"

Joe's voice on the other end of the line was businesslike. "I'm going over there now."

"What about the children? They're at school now, but classes will be ending in a couple of hours. Shall I pick them up?"

"Ask Thomas to do the school run. Tell him to bring the kids to ours and then keep an eye on their house." He blew out a breath. "I don't know what we're facing yet. Whoever did this to the shop may know where they live. I don't want Ellen and the children there if they do. Keep them at our house until you hear from me again."

"All right, darling. Be careful, please."

"I will. I'll ring you when I can."

Sophie replaced the receiver and turned to her friend. "Let's have that cup of tea now, shall we? I'll tell you what Joe has asked us to do."

Ellen sank into the sofa cushions. "You know Kino wouldn't do anything against Australia, don't you? He's lived here all his life. This is his home." Her voice rose as she spoke and ended in a sob. "This is his home. Not Japan."

Sophie wrapped her arms around Ellen while she cried.

Joe's voice was somber when he telephoned several hours later. "It was a mess, Sophie. The shop's windows were smashed, all the jewelry cases broken, and most of Kino's inventory is gone."

"What about Kino? How badly was he hurt?"

"Broken nose, several cracked ribs. He may have some internal injuries, too. They worked him over. Not enough to kill him but he's going to be in hospital for at least a couple of weeks."

Sophie sank into to the needlepoint seat of the chair in the telephone nook. Ellen's three children were playing upstairs in Sam's room. Ellen had gone up with them and was resting in Jean-Luc's room. "Have you been able to speak with him?"

He blew out a breath. "Only for a minute before the doctor gave him something to help him sleep. There were two men Kino didn't recognize. Apparently, this wasn't just a robbery, it was done because he's Japanese. They called him some really hateful names, and when he tried to explain he's lived here most of his life, they accused him of being a spy. That Japan was planning to do the same thing to Australia that they did to America and he was helping them. Quite frankly, he's lucky to be alive. Someone next door heard the racket and called the police. The local coppers were already on the scene when I arrived."

"When can Ellen see him? She'll be worried sick when I tell her."

"Well, he's asleep now and probably won't be awake again until the morning."

When Joe had been shot in the New Year's Eve drug raid, she'd been frantic with worry. She had camped outside his hospital room until she was able to convince the duty nurse to let her in to see him. Ellen hadn't been a wartime nurse, so she wouldn't have that to lend credence to her request. And tensions were already running high towards Australian women who had married Japanese men. "She's going to want to see him tonight."

"Call a taxi and bring her then," Joe said. "I have a constable stationed here at the hospital. I'll wait here for the two of you to arrive."

When Sophie and Ellen arrived half an hour later, Joe led Ellen to the bench in the waiting area and sat beside her. "You need to prepare yourself," he said gently. "Kino was badly beaten and looks very rough right now. The doctor says he should pull through, but they need to be cautious."

"But Joe, who did this to him?"

He shook his head. "We don't know. Can you think of anyone who he had problems with? A colleague? Landlord?"

"No of course not. Everyone who knew Kino loved him. It must've been..." Ellen's tears threatened to fall. She fumbled with the clasp on her handbag, teardrops coursing down her cheeks while she extracted a lace-trimmed hanky and dabbed at her eyes.

Joe retrieved his notepad and pencil from his breast pocket. "Must've been whom?"

Ellen sighed. "He'd been receiving letters. Poison pen sort of letters that called him hateful names just because he's Japanese."

"These letters. How did they arrive? Where were they delivered? To the house or the shop?" He already had a problem on his hands. If the letters had been delivered to the Mitsui home, that meant the perpetrators knew where Kino and his family lived. He'd need to keep an eye on the house too.

"The shop. But I was there when he opened one of them. He didn't want me to read it, but I knew something was dreadfully wrong. I was so shocked. And angry. I made him show me the others."

"How many others?"

"There must have been five or six of them. Threatening the shop, him, demanding that he go back to Japan where he belonged." A broken sob escaped her lips. "He never wanted to go back. He had no family there anymore..."

The doctor emerged from Kino's room. Tucking his clipboard under his arm, he crossed the hall to where they were sitting.

"Mrs. Mitsui, you can see him for five minutes, that's all. Your husband needs his rest."

Sophie walked Ellen to Kino's room and closed the door behind her friend. Joe stood by the room's door, speaking with the constable.

Joe motioned Sophie aside. His expression was so grim that she feared he was going to tell her the worst.

Fully expecting to hear that Kino wasn't expected to survive the night, she was completely unprepared for Joe's next words.

"As soon as the doctors determine he's well enough to leave hospital, he's going to be interned."

"What? Interned? What does that even mean?"

Joe scrubbed a hand over his chin. "He and every other Japanese national have been ordered to detention centers."

Sophie struggled to comprehend what she'd just heard. "Detention centers? But he hasn't done anything. Why should he be punished? He was the victim here."

"It doesn't have anything to do with the attack. When the Americans declared war on Japan, Britain and Australia did as well. Japan is now our enemy. Every Japanese in Australia is now our enemy too."

"But he's been in this country for years!"

"Doesn't matter. The government says that any and all of them could be spies, that despite outward appearances of living here for years, owning businesses, contributing to our economy, that they've actually been laying the groundwork for Japan to attack here and invade us the same way they've attacked and invaded their way through Southeast Asia."

"But what about his family? What will Ellen and the girls do? What about all the other families?"

"I don't know anything more than what I've just told you. This isn't common knowledge yet so please, you can't say anything to Ellen. We have to act as though we know nothing."

"She'll find out soon enough, won't she?"

"I was able to get the powers that be to agree to let me place a constable to guard his room and not someone from the army or the government."

"Joe! This is outrageous! He's not a spy. You and I both know he isn't!" She stopped abruptly, her lips set in a firm line. "I'll get Aunt Flora to call—"

Joe shook his head. "It won't help. The decision has already been made. The best way you can help them now is to encourage Ellen to get some rest. She's going to have a hard enough time dealing with it all when she's officially informed."

"But—"

They turned abruptly at the sound of the door to Kino's room opening. Ellen rushed to Sophie, who extended her arms to envelop her friend. She let Ellen cry against her shoulder for a few moments and then led her to a chair.

Ellen fumbled in her handbag. "My handkerchief. I can't think what I've done with it."

Joe pulled the spare he always carried from his inside jacket pocket and handed it to her. Early in their marriage, and amazed by the number of times he seemed to give them away or use them to bind cuts and scrapes, not always his, Sophie had ordered two dozen men's handkerchiefs and convinced him to always carry one for himself and one for whomever needed one.

Their friend wiped her eyes and her nose. "Keep it," Joe said. "I have plenty more at home."

"My God, Kino looks horrible. Joe, please find whoever did this to him!" she said, and a fresh wave of tears began.

Sophie glanced up at Joe who signaled with an almost imperceptible shake of his head that she shouldn't make promises he wouldn't be able to keep. She placed an arm around Ellen's shoulder. "You know he'll do everything he can to get to the bottom of this."

"Let's get you home," Joe said. "I'll go bring the car around."

"But I want to stay here with him. Could the girls spend the night at your house?"

Sophie rose. "Ellen, of course they can stay with us. But you need to rest just as much as Kino does and you can't do that sitting in a hard chair in a hospital corridor. You'll need to be strong for him."

—

While Joe drove up to the hospital's front entrance to collect Sophie and Ellen, his mind raced through everything that needed to happen. He had stationed a constable outside the hospital room, two constables at the shop. Assuming Ellen and her daughters spent the night at his and Sophie's home, he probably didn't need to station anyone at the Mitsui home, not that he had a surplus of constables anyhow.

He could ask Thomas to keep an eye on the place. That would work. He checked his watch. Already half ten.

"Ellen," he began as he turned out of the hospital grounds, "I'm sure the girls are already asleep. Why wake them? Stay with us tonight."

"Wonderful idea, darling," Sophie said before Ellen had a chance to protest.

Ellen roused herself from staring blankly out the car window. "But—"

"The girls will think it's a big adventure," Sophie continued, patting Ellen's hand. "And I'm prescribing a nice relaxing soak for you as soon as we get home."

With Ellen safely ensconced in the tub, Joe told Sophie, Mrs. Kelly, and Thomas what little he knew and his plans for the next day. "First thing the shop window will have to be fixed. I'll need Ellen to do an inventory of the shop to see what has been taken. I was able to speak with Kino for a moment before the sleeping draught kicked in. He said he'd already locked up almost everything for the night just before the attack."

"Is there a way to spare Ellen from that task? Isn't there someone, a clerk or an assistant, who could help instead?"

"Normally, yes," Joe said. "But they could be responsible for the attack." Most likely this was similar to the attacks on Germans that had occurred after HMAS *Sydney* was sunk by the Germans off the coast of Western Australia last month. All six hundred and forty-five hands on board had been lost. Attacks on locals of German heritage had begun almost immediately afterward. This was exactly the same sort of situation. "I'll have to question them."

TWENTY-SEVEN

INTERNED INDEFINITELY

MID-DECEMBER 1941

Two weeks later, Joe and Sophie accompanied Ellen and her three young daughters to the hospital to say good-bye to Kino before he was discharged and sent to an internment camp in Cowra.

Ellen's reaction to the location was vehement and vocal. "That's two hundred miles from Sydney! How are we supposed to visit him when he's so far away?"

Sophie doubted detainees had visitation privileges, but she had helped Ellen lodge a formal protest with the Aliens Appeals Tribunal in Kino's defense. Sophie had a feeling the process would be long, frustrating, and ultimately, unsuccessful. Still, the fact that an actual process existed gave Ellen a shred of hope, which Sophie worried might be crueler than an outright denial. It was a lot like reporting a man missing in action: the chances were nearly nil he was alive somewhere, but since his body hadn't been found his family refused to give up hope. However, Ellen had asked for her assistance and Sophie did what she could to help.

"I have a bad feeling about this," Sophie whispered to Joe as they entered the hospital. "Those poor children should not see their father marched out in handcuffs by armed guards."

"What do you suggest? Have the guards hide until Ellen and the girls leave?"

"I—" Sophie beamed at her husband. "You are a brilliant man, Joe Parker. That's exactly what should happen." She turned to her friend. "Ellen, why don't you and the girls wait here in reception while Joe and I go make sure Kino is ready to leave?"

Ellen, who had been informed of how Kino's departure would transpire, seemed to relax. "That's a wonderful idea. Girls, let's sit here for a bit. Mrs. Parker will let us know when your father is ready for us." She mouthed, "thank you" above her daughters' heads as the girls chose chairs.

Sophie and Joe immediately marched to Kino's room and addressed the two guards posted on either side of the door.

"Gentlemen, I'm going to rely on your consciences as fathers and sons and ask that you allow Mrs. Mitsui and her daughters to say their good-byes without having even more distress caused by your presence," Joe said.

"But sir—"

Undeterred, Sophie took up their argument. "My husband is a high-ranking officer in the New South Wales police. You can trust that he will not allow Mr. Mitsui to flee or otherwise try to escape."

"But missus—"

"Joe, would you please show them your warrant card?"

Joe presented his warrant card to the nearest guard, who examined it closely. "Detective First Class Joseph Henry Parker," he read aloud before he passed Joe's credentials to his fellow guard.

"I'm also chief of the forensics lab," Joe said, handing a business card to the guard.

"Please? The situation is difficult enough without traumatizing three little girls," Sophie said. "Can you simply move around the corner? Or wait in an empty room? My husband will take your place outside the door."

The first guard considered her request. "How will we know when they're finished?"

Sophie resisted the urge to shake her head in disbelief, instead opting for a more sympathetic approach. "Can you imagine how your children would react to telling you good-bye for an unknown period of time? I think the crying in the hallway when they leave will probably be a dead giveaway."

The two guards held an unspoken conversation across the closed door to Kino's room. Then the first guard shrugged, handed Joe's cards back to him, and nodded. "All right. We'll wait around the corner. Ten minutes and not a second more."

Similar attacks occurred against other Japanese owned businesses. Some attacks happened in broad daylight, but most took place at the end of the workday, as shopkeepers were closing for the night.

Joe huffed a frustrated breath. "No one ever sees anything," he told Sophie during dinner several days after Kino's internment. "Or if they do, they aren't willing to say anything to the coppers who investigate afterwards."

"I've seen several articles about anti-Japanese sentiment in the newspaper," Sophie said. "It seems to have grown by leaps and bounds. Are you certain it's the same group of hoodlums?"

"We just don't know yet. We could be dealing with a gang since the attacks are so similar. They throw bricks or rocks through the shop windows and then rush inside and attack the Japanese owner. It's just like what happened with the local Italians and Germans a couple of years ago."

The doorbell sounded and Joe got up to answer the door. He led Fred Thompson into the dining room.

"Fred!" Sophie exclaimed. "Is everything all right?"

"Evening, Mrs. Parker. I thought I'd stop by on my way home. I have some news."

"We're a bit out of your way. Your news must be important," Joe said.

Fred nodded. "It is, sir."

"Joe, take Fred into your study. I'll put the kettle on."

Joe led Fred out of the dining room and turning down the back hallway to his study. "Or would you like something stronger?"

When Sophie brought in a tray with teacups and slices of Mrs. Kelly's apple cake, Joe and Fred were adding three new pins to the map of Sydney's Central Business District on the wall. The map was exactly the same as the one that hung in Joe's office. The pins were the same, too.

Sophie studied the location of the most recent attacks. "They're working their way across the city, aren't they?" she observed. "If that's the case, then the next targets could be the shops on George Street. You could station some men in the general area and wait until someone throws the next brick. They should be in mufti, though, so they blend in with the crowds."

"You'll have your sergeant's stripes any day now, Mrs. Parker," Fred said. "That's exactly what I was suggesting to the inspector."

"Set it up first thing in the morning," Joe said as he massaged his temples. "This has to stop. If the latest victim doesn't pull through, it'll be murder." Not that a staggering number of his fellow citizens would find anything wrong with killing Japanese shopkeepers. They'd had no qualms about killing an Italian grocer in Newtown last year. It hadn't mattered that the man had been in Australia for twenty-five years and had become a naturalized citizen.

There were times Joe despaired of the human race.

HOME FRONT PRECAUTIONS

LATE DECEMBER 1941

As December dragged on, the government ordered lights be dimmed at night and air raid trenches be dug. Rumors and whispers that Australia could be next in Japan's plans, that the government was prepared to cede all territory north of the Brisbane Line, held an edge of panic. The blackout and air raid trench orders had only fueled hysteria.

Sewing dark curtains for every window of the house and making sure they blocked light at night was easy enough. Digging an air raid trench was another thing entirely.

Sophie and Joe, plus Thomas and Moira Kelly, stood around the dining table. Moira had moved the console bowl of flowers and the candlesticks that usually flanked it to the sideboard. In their place, Sophie unrolled house plans and plot surveys showing the boundaries of their land. The large sheets obscured the polished mahogany tabletop.

All four looked over the pages with pursed lips.

"It's too bad a cellar wasn't dug when this house was built," Joe said.

"I think the best place would be to run it close to the back door of the house and the front door of the cottage," Sophie said. "That way all four of us can get to it quickly."

"That would take it straight through the kitchen garden," Moira said.

"Well, if this war is anything like the last one, we're going to face food shortages and rationing sooner or later," Sophie mused. "Expanding the garden is probably something we should plan to do anyhow. The best time to do that is when we're digging the trench."

She glanced at Joe and Thomas. Aside from Joe's earlier comment, both had been quiet. Joe's expression was grim.

"This is the first time I wished we didn't live on this hill," he said. "Unless we and the neighbors can keep a complete blackout, we could be a prime target."

Sophie looked around the table. "Perhaps it's best if you leave Sydney and move inland," she said to the Kellys. "My mother and Aunt Flora are decamping to Leura in the Blue Mountains for the foreseeable future. You could join them there, and—"

"Mrs. P, we're not leaving you and Inspector Parker," Moira declared. "So don't even think about asking us."

Joe smiled wryly at Thomas. "Do you still have your entrenching tool, Private Kelly?"

"Can't say I do, Captain Parker," Thomas answered.

"Nor do I. Let's see about hiring a couple of men to help us do the work once you all have decided what should go where."

Sydney
25 December 1941

Dear Sam,
I am writing this from your parent's home. Christmas here was very subdued, but Mrs. Kelly prepared a nice dinner and we toasted your health and Jean-Luc's.

Your father told a funny story about you trying to stay awake all night to catch Saint Nicholas putting presents under the Christmas tree.

Earlier this month one of the neighbors was interned because of his heritage. I am certain you can guess who if I say he and his wife have three daughters and he sells a great deal of pearl jewelry. The husband was beaten very badly and his shop was damaged and burgled. There have been several similar crimes in the city. The police are still trying to discover the perpetrators (I learnt a new English word).

I helped Sophie and Mrs. Kelly sew blackout curtains and your father and Thomas hired some men to dig an air raid trench between the house and the Kelly's cottage. The cellar is the shelter in the building where Patricia and I live. We fixed it up with cushions, lanterns, and magazines. I pray we never have it use it.

That is all the news from the home front. Did you have a Joyeux Noël in spite of the circumstances?

Fly safely,
Marianne

Richmond
30 December 1941

Dear Marianne,
I pray none of you have to use your shelters too.

In my defence, I was seven years old, a prime age for

*still wanting to believe in Father Christmas but need-
ing to see him for myself. I remember being very happy
when I learnt Christmas comes to Australia before the
rest of the world, because that meant he wouldn't run
out of presents, mainly because I was hoping for a bicy-
cle. Dad had a heck of a time trying to explain how it
got down the chimney.*

*We had a decent meal in the mess – not nearly as good
as Mrs. Kelly's cooking, but not bad, considering.*

*Sorry to hear about the neighbors. Dad and Sophie
always liked them. C'est la guerre, I suppose. I wish it
wasn't.*

*Merci for the Noël greetings. Here's hoping for a Bonne
Année.*

Sew straight,
Sam

*P.S. See? I am using the French-English dictionary you
sent to me.*

PART 3: 1942

AUSTRALIA, EGYPT, NEW GUINEA

Theirs is a lonely sorrow,
their hearts are filled with pain,
Nothing can ease their torment,
'Till we come home again.

Author Unknown,
"The Womenfolk We Left Behind"

TWENTY-NINE

RADIO SILENCE

JANUARY 1942

Unbeknownst to Patricia, Marianne went by herself to see The Power and The Glory, the film about the RAAF in action. The dive-bombing scenes terrified her, but she was horrified by the storyline that fifth columnists, locals who disagreed with the Allied war effort and worked to undermine it, were actively sabotaging Australian planes.

Sydney
9 January 1942

Dear Sam,
I read about a crash where an officer and an airman
were killed when an aircraft from the RAAF station
at Canberra crashed near Williamstown. Is that your
station? Please tell me you are all right.

Marianne

Reminding herself the film was only fiction, she tried to tamp down panic over too many newspaper articles about RAAF crashes until Sam didn't respond as quickly as usual to her last letter.

Sydney
28 January 1942

Dear Sam,
Are you safe and well? Please let me know. I am getting
worried.

Marianne

THIRTY

ONE COMES HOME

JANUARY 1942

Sophie handed Jean-Luc's letter over to Joe after she finished reading it. "He's a man of few words, isn't he?"

Somewhere in Egypt
29 January 1942

Dear Sophie and Joe,
I'm a French bloke wearing an Australian uniform who's waiting to board an American ship docked in an Egyptian port.

We leave Suez tomorrow on the USS Mount Vernon. They tell us we should arrive in Adelaide sometime in mid-March, but they haven't told where we'll be sent once we get there. I'll let you know as soon as I can after we arrive.

Yours affectionately,
Jean-Luc

Joe scanned the flimsy sheet of paper. When he looked up from it, Sophie's eyes were bright with unshed tears. He rounded his desk and crouched beside the armchair she was sitting in. She leaned into him and let out a soft sigh.

"He's coming home, Joe. He made it through. He's coming home."

THIRTY-ONE

STAKEOUT AT VICTORIA BARRACKS

FEBRUARY 1942

Joe Parker, former captain in the Australian Imperial Force, former Inspector First Class, now head of the Forensics department in the New South Wales Police Force, and currently a liaison between the police and the militia charged with defending Australia and her protectorates, tried to find a more comfortable section of the wall to lean against. The late summer sun must have shone on this wall all day, because the bricks still radiated warmth.

As part of the deal his superiors had made with the army to keep him firmly tethered in Sydney, the army had requested his assistance in figuring out how illegal booze was making its way into Victoria Barracks, the training ground in Sydney for newly-enlisted troops.

He stayed still in the dark. Watching. Waiting. It had been a very long time since he'd done something like this. Past stakeouts slid through his mind like a film, the images flashing unheeded. Until...he and Davy, Frankie, and Sid, slinking through a copse of trees—how had those trees escaped the shelling? Close enough to hear the enemy's whispers, the rub of uniforms against earth. He'd lifted a hand just enough for the others in his party to stop, and they had. Except Davy, who had inadvertently stepped on a twig and the snap was as loud as a shot in the freezing, still night. Then chaos as the two groups rushed together, knives, clubs, guns primed and ready for battle on an intimate scale. The Australians emerged victorious, but Davy hadn't survived. A German trench knife had pierced his back, kidney, liver. Joe had helped carry him to the battalion aid station, willing the lad to stay awake, stay alive, not bloody die, not be reduced to another dreadful letter to write to a family who had no clue what their son had faced in the long months in France.

He'd been standing in the same spot for what felt like hours, but when he checked his WWI-era trench watch, its faintly luminous hands showed 10:30. He and his men had been in place for only thirty minutes.

They would be out here all night if they had to, but Joe hoped it wouldn't take that long. Tonight was the first night the police were watching the camp. Victoria Barracks stood on several acres of prime land west of Sydney's central business district. The normally pristine lawns surrounding the long, three-story building were covered in tents. Lights had been extinguished at 10 pm and the light fabric of the tents were pale geometric shapes in wan moonlight. Voices that had filled the air—snatches of laughter, raucous conversations, a curse or two, quieted. Someone's particularly loud snores might keep a few of the recruits awake, but most were probably exhausted from the training they'd done all day.

Every so often a dark form slipped out of a tent and walked in the direction of the row of latrines at the edge of the fence. An undercurrent of urine and feces wafted in Joe's direction. He wrinkled his nose and waited for the smell to dissipate.

Joe's eyelids drifted down. He'd purposely chosen an uncomfortable spot to hide and watch from the shadows to help keep himself awake enough to hear, or sense, when something out of the ordinary occurred. He and his men could be waiting for one man, or several; he had no idea yet how illegal spirits were making their way inside the camp. They would study the ways of the camp and figure out how sly grog was smuggled in and who was responsible for it. Then they'd swoop in, arrest the suppliers, and the cycle would begin again. Because the cycle always began again.

Normally an officer far less senior than him would be leading this nocturnal activity, but Joe wanted to get a feel for the location, the sounds and sights of the camp at night, when everyone inside its walls was supposed to be sound asleep to face the rigors of the next day: training, drilling, rifle practice, bayonet practice. Practice, practice, practice, until the movements all became automatic, until each man's muscles were so used to making the proper movements, twisting and slicing after the first thrust of the bayonets at the ends of their rifles, preparing their bodies to march for miles on end, kicking up dust or sinking in mud all the while.

Training camp was the first place the men began their bonds with each other, learned who they could trust and who they disliked. It was where they became a cohesive team despite their personal feelings, all with the end result of staying alive on a field of battle while inflicting as much death and destruction as possible on their enemy.

It was also the place where they discovered how many of the normal activities of their lives were curtailed. No women, no booze, and no fun. For some those deprivations were too much. Others of an entrepreneurial bent found ways to get around the rules and regulations and make a little—or a lot—of money to boot. The past decade had been tough economically, and Joe wondered how many men had enlisted simply for the regular paycheck and three meals a day.

Joe checked his watch again. Eleven pm. He and his men had been in place outside the barracks for an hour. No one was stirring. Rest and repose had settled over the camp and hundreds of men slept the sleep of the truly exhausted. He needed to double-check when this lot had arrived for training—a week ago he thought, but wasn't certain. A week was probably long enough for whomever was working on the inside to size up the new recruits, choose two or three likely candidates who'd want to make a quid or two extra on a regular basis to receive the illegal booze.

Staying in the shadows, Thompson sidled over to him. "Sir, what if it's an inside job? Coming into the camp in broad daylight, hidden among the regular supplies?"

"You may be right."

Whomever was working the inside still needed to make contacts every time a new group came in for training. The contacts would pass the word around the newcomers that booze could be had, for a price, but other than that, as long as incoming supplies were never checked the system could go on working indefinitely. Yes, the police and home guard would need to keep an eye on the camp at night, but a full complement of them weren't needed. A pair of men, patrolling would probably be enough. What he needed was someone of his own on the inside who could discover who had contacts with suppliers on the outside.

"I'm heading home, Thompson. Wait a few minutes and spread the word everyone else can go back to their usual duties tonight. We'll regroup tomorrow after I've had a chance to ask a few questions of the camp commander."

"Right, sir." Thompson had chosen the administrative path in policing but occasionally Joe brought him along on missions, like this one, that weren't particularly dangerous. Thompson often said he liked the chance to work alongside his boss in a different capacity than usual, and Joe liked Thompson's ability to work out how an operation like this one could be carried out. If Thompson wasn't a copper, Joe had the distinct impression the man could have headed up a crime boss' administrative team.

By the time Joe arrived home the clock on the drawing room mantle was just finishing its midnight chimes. When Sophie and he first married, he'd had trouble adjusting to the noise, especially since their bedroom was above the drawing room and the sound carried through the ceiling and floorboards. He was a light sleeper—years of police work plus two years of soldiering would have that effect on a man—but he'd grown used to the sound over the eight years they'd been married. Now he hardly heard it any more, even though he liked the sound. There was something pleasing in knowing every hour would start with the same longer sequence of tones, and the quarter and half hours would be marked with a shorter sequence. It all appealed to his innate sense of order, he supposed. Not that he thought about the clock much, unless it was a reminder that he was up later than usual and was usually more than ready for a few minutes reading in bed before he turned off his light and fell asleep.

Tonight was a little different. Joe was keyed up with the new assignment involving the barracks. He pulled off his suit jacket, hung it on the newel post at the foot of the staircase, and went to the kitchen to put the kettle on. A hot toddy would go well with a few minutes of making notes about his thoughts while he'd stood against that brick wall in the shadows beyond the barracks fence.

"Hello, darling." Sophie's voice drifted in from the dining room as she made her way into the kitchen. She gave him a kiss, and they stood, arms around each other's waists and waited for the kettle to boil.

Sophie yawned and leaned on his arm. "How did it go? Any luck?"

Joe shook his head. "No. I wasn't really expecting to see any action tonight. But Thompson and I got a good idea of the nighttime rhythm of the camp. We'll discuss it tomorrow, but I don't see how anyone could sneak in at night. That's not to say it isn't possible, but…"

The kettle whistled and he moved to turn the stove off. He tilted his head towards the mug on the table. "Do you want a toddy too?"

"Erm…no thanks. I'll just have a sip or two of yours."

Joe stifled the snort he felt coming. He would end up sharing more than a sip or two, but he could always make a second mug if the first one wasn't enough. Besides, it was nice to have someone to talk things through with. Sophie often asked a question or had an idea that he hadn't thought of yet, or made him think about things in a different way.

The woman with whom he shared damned near everything sat at the table. "Are you thinking there's someone on the inside who brings the stuff in?"

"I think that's more likely." He mixed lemon and honey in the steaming mug and rummaged in the cupboard for the bottle of rum Mrs. Kelly kept in the kitchen for toddies. "It's probably a better use of our resources to concentrate on the clubs in the general vicinity of the camp first."

He sat too, took the first couple of sips, and slid the drink across the table to Sophie. She gazed at the contents for a few moments. "Joe, if there's a problem with sly grog around the camp, what about other problems? Are you seeing an increase in the number of prostitutes in the area?"

"We haven't gotten that far, but it's definitely on my list of things to speak with Thompson about in the morn—" He stopped short and grasped the foot on his thigh. Sophie had kicked off her slipper and was wiggling her cool toes in his hand. He squeezed the ball of her foot. She hummed appreciatively. "How is it I was the one of my feet for hours and you're getting the foot rub?" he teased.

"You know as well as I do that I'll rub your feet when you get in bed."

"In that case..." He downed the remainder of the drink, lifted Sophie's foot from his thigh, and rinsed the mug. "C'mon. I'm going to have a quick shower and then I'm going to take you up on that offer."

Twenty minutes later, clean and pajama'd and feet rubbed, Joe barely made it through two pages of his book before the yawns began. He marked his place, turned off his light, and was asleep before Sophie finished saying, "Sleep well, darling."

Several evenings later, Joe hadn't been home for more than five minutes before the phone on his desk rang. Sophie had an extension installed in his study so that he could take work-related calls in private, away from the general hubbub of their household. At the time Sam had already moved to Melbourne and Jean-Luc was working at a vineyard in the Hunter Valley a couple of hours to the north of Sydney, but both boys were in and out of town on a regular basis and, by extension, in and out of the house on a regular basis. And when the boys were in town, they saw their friends, and Sophie had always insisted that their friends were just as welcome as they were.

Joe sighed and picked up the receiver. "Parker," he said.

It was Fred Thompson. "Sorry to disturb you at home, sir, but we might have a break in that sly grog case."

"It's not a problem," Joe replied. "You're saving me from a stack of requisition forms I need to fill out for the lab. How're you going?"

"Two of our men spent part of the evening in mufti hanging around the known sly grog shops close to the Barracks." It seemed to Joe that as soon as war was declared and men began pouring into the Barracks to train, that the number of drinking establishments had doubled or tripled nearly overnight. The numbers of ladies of the night who worked the area seemed to have increased, just as Sophie had speculated.

"They heard something said in passing, sir," Thompson continued. "Something about moving product into place under the veg deliveries. They'd like your permission to stay on for a couple of hours after their replacements arrive."

Joe didn't have any objections to the plan, although he'd have to approve the overtime and that meant yet another set of forms to fill out.

"That's fine with me," Joe said. "Will you be at the station when they come off duty?"

"Depends, sir, what time they come in. My shift ends at eight tonight, and I promised Mary I'd be home in time to tuck the kiddies in for bed. It'll be the first time this week..."

"No worries," Joe said. "Let everyone know they need to fill in their time sheets tonight. I don't want them complaining that their pay packets aren't full enough. And have them write up their reports too. I'll want to read them in the morning."

"Righto, boss." Fred Thompson's voice drifted from the phone and Joe heard a ruckus somewhere in the distance. "Got to go, sir. Someone's just come in with a complaint of some sort. Give my regards to Mrs. Parker, sir."

"And mine to Mary."

"Will do. Night, sir."

Joe replaced the receiver. The clock struck the quarter hour. If he hurried, he could make a little headway on the lab requisition forms before dinner. Maybe he could convince Sophie to help him finish filling them out after dinner.

THIRTY-TWO

IT'S FIGHT, WORK, OR PERISH

FEBRUARY 1942

By the first half of February 1942, Joe was beginning to think this war felt like a slog through muddy trenches just like the last one. None of the news was good, especially the fall of Singapore to the Japanese on February 15. The 15,000 Australian troops stationed there had been taken prisoner. In one swoop, a huge portion of the army's strength had simply been eliminated from combat use. The event was made even more horrific by the rumor that Australian nurses had been killed.

Prime Minister Curtin said the disaster was "Australia's Dunkirk" and that it opened the battle for the Australian continent just as the debacle at Dunkirk in France had opened the battle for Britain.

Four days later, news of waves of Japanese planes dive-bombing and obliterating huge swathes of Darwin, warships, and planes—the first attack on Australian soil—sent a shockwave of terror through the country. Barbed wire was strung along the beaches, bisecting golden sand and turquoise water with menacing coils that brought back even more memories of the last war for those who had fought.

This war had become very real and far too close to home.

Several days after the terrifying Japanese attack on Darwin, Joe handed the newspaper to Sophie. "Read this," he said. "I think we can probably guess where Jean-Luc will be sent eventually."

"Japanese capture Rabaul," Sophie read. "Rabaul is in New Britain. And New Britain is just north of New Guinea…"

Joe nodded. "Which is just north of Australia." He leaned back in his chair, pushed his reading glasses to the top of his head, and rubbed his eyes to alleviate the beginnings of a headache. Bombardments. Barbed wire. Blood-soaked ground. It was one thing to go off to fight in a country that had been invaded. The Japanese attack on Darwin had just proven they could attack Australia with impunity. What if the unthinkable happened and invasion came to Australia?

"We need to get that trench finished," he said.

—

Joe finished his breakfast and went into his study to place a call.

"Assistant Commissioner Bobby Davies' office," was the clipped response, but Joe knew Bobby's efficient secretary well enough to call her by her Christian name.

"Maggie, it's Joe Parker. Is he available?"

"Joe! How nice to hear from you. He just arrived in the office. Let me transfer you."

He didn't have to wait long for Bobby Davies to pick up and deliver his typical greeting. "Joe, how are you going? And how is the lovely Sophie?"

"She's well. Sir, I'll get right to the point. I want to have my commission reinstated. I can't sit here while—"

"Joe. I understand. We all want to storm up north and give the Nips what-for. I do too. But you're needed here in Sydney, not in Darwin or God forbid, New Guinea. Leave that to the militia. They can hold out until the AIF gets there."

"Then find something else for me to do to help the effort. Forensics just isn't that important right now."

"How's the sly grog case shaping up?"

"We think we know how the booze is getting into the camp and who's responsible inside. Now it's just a question of catching—"

"Good, good. Glad to hear it. Put on your old uniform and go in there. Pretend you're doing an inspection."

"Sir, I'm fairly certain my constable uniform doesn't fit anymore."

"Good one, Joe. I meant your AIF uniform."

"But wouldn't I be guilty of impersonating an officer since I'm no longer in the army?"

"Damn it, Joe. You're splitting hairs. I'll call my brother and get you some official looking paperwork. No one will question your presence. Or your uniform. Just catch the bastards. Red-handed if you can. The force could use some favorable publicity for a change."

The headache Joe had tried to tamp down came roaring back with a vengeance. "Sir—"

"It's no good 'sir'-ing me, Joe. We can't have training at the Barracks disrupted. Those men will help stop the Nips on the Kokoda Track. Because if we can't stop them on the Track, and they get through to Port Moresby, then Australia is next."

"Sir."

"Good man. Let me know if you need anything to get that case wrapped up. Give my regards to Sophie."

"I will. Thank you, sir."

Joe replaced the receiver in its cradle with exaggerated care, just as he always did when he would prefer to hurl the thing across the room in frustration. Damn it. He would try again after the sly grog case was closed. In the interim, he was going to make sure the Webley he'd brought home in 1919 was clean and loaded. Unfortunately, he didn't have his wartime Lee-Enfield .303 rifle, but the .22 shotgun he'd purchased to teach the boys to shoot rabbits would do in a pinch. His house was on the highest hill in Sydney. It was painted white. Even on the darkest, cloudiest night, it could be a beacon to enemy planes and ships. He damn well wasn't going to leave his home and family undefended.

He should probably find his old uniform in the event Bobby insisted on him wearing it, but he certainly wasn't going to ask Sophie where it was.

—

Sydney
15 February 1942

Dear Sam,
I am going to assume you are well, even though you did not reply to my last two letters. You will never believe this. Your father was wearing his AIF uniform when I had dinner with your parents last night.

His superior ordered him to wear his army uniform and go undercover at Victoria Barracks to figure out how sly grog was getting in. I am no stranger to Australian uniforms, since my father wears his every day for his work at the memorial, but Sophie was not happy about it. She said if he gets injured like the last time he went undercover she will never speak to him again. I think she was also afraid the army would decide he was more useful with them than in the police force.

Your father and Sergeant Thompson are still working to solve the mystery, though, until the crims, as they called them, are in prison.

I hope you are still flying safely,
Marianne

THIRTY-THREE

VICTORY GARDENS

FEBRUARY 1942

From her perch on the balcony, Sophie watched Thomas pacing the width of the huge side yards on the northern and southern sides of the house.

Prime Minister Curtin had urged everyone in Australia to grow their own vegetables as a contribution to the war effort. Citizens had to do their part to provide food for themselves because the farms were sending all their food crops off to feed the army.

Thomas said he had never planted a garden on the scale she wanted. He would need help taking up the grass and getting the beds prepared, but he reckoned he could fit in enough vegetable beds to keep the Parkers plus Moira and him well-fed, plus have more than enough to share with a dozen families.

She called down to him. "Good morning, Thomas!"

Thomas looked up to her. His cap shaded his eyes but she knew from the tilt of his head that he was paying attention.

"Morning, missus."

"Can you meet me in the kitchen? I think I've found a way to get this done."

She hurried downstairs as Thomas wiped his feet carefully on the mat outside the kitchen door. Moira would have his hide if he tracked in dirt all over her freshly mopped floor.

Sophie entered the kitchen at the same time he did. "Come sit down, Thomas, and let's take a look at the plots now that you've had a chance to think about it all."

He hesitated at the threshold, his big frame filling the doorway. He didn't usually come in when the lady of the house was there, although she had always given him reason to believe he was welcome.

Sophie had already taken three mugs from a cupboard while Moira filled the teapot with hot water. "Come on in," Sophie said. "And have a seat. We have a lot to talk about."

Thomas settled at the big wooden kitchen table. Moira used it for everything—kneading dough, rolling out pie crusts, chopping vegetables—and it had been scrubbed clean so often that the wood was silky-smooth.

They'd stopped taking sugar in their tea, preferring to use their limited supply for the occasional batch of biscuits or a cake on an important occasion like birthdays. Flour was equally scarce, so the cakes were small but they were a much-appreciated treat that the whole household shared. Joe hadn't drawn a strong line between the Kellys and himself, and Sophie had continued the tradition.

She was so excited she thought she might bubble over. "I have wonderful news. I've spoken with my Aunt Flora. She has lots of room for more vegetable gardens and wants to find a place to donate what she grows. Alf and Vern, her gardeners, can help with ours."

"Beggin' your pardon, missus, but how is it they aren't serving?"

"Well, they aren't quite as able-bodied as they once were," Sophie began. "Alf lost a leg in the last war, and Vern lost an eye. But they're both able to work hard."

"And then there's me. I don't see so well myself anymore."

"That's because you refuse to wear those eyeglasses the doctor prescribed for you," Moira interjected.

Sophie waited while the couple went through their little routine. It never changed and it was always amusing. "Now Moira, you know

I don't like havin' them things on my face all the time." As he spoke, he carefully pulled his eyeglasses from his shirt pocket, made a show of wiping them thoroughly, and hooked them over his ears. The poor man was so farsighted that his eyes were magnified to twice their size. Moira fiddled with his glasses until she was satisfied they were straight.

"Right," Sophie said after Moira poured tea for the three of them. "Thomas, I'd like to drive over to my Aunt Flora's home so you can take a look at her grounds. I suspect you, Alf, and Vern will need another couple of bodies to help do the initial work. But we'll all know more after you've talked."

"I can probably get a couple of lads from St. Mary's," Thomas offered.

"Joe suggested some of the minor miscreants he's come across lately," Sophie said. "There are several boys who aren't in school any longer but they aren't old enough for the army or militia. They have too much time on their hands and are a little too good at getting into mischief."

Thomas looked down at the table. "Do you really want that sort around your place? And your aunt's place?"

"Well, we won't know unless we give them a chance, will we? Joe thinks they're good boys underneath it all. They're just hungry and bored. There's not enough at home to keep them fed and not enough jobs for thirteen-year-olds to keep them employed. We couldn't pay them very much, but once the gardens are growing, they'd go home every day with food for their families."

Moira Kelly had been listening to her husband and her mistress while another thought began to take shape in her mind. "Mrs. P, we have enough room here for a few more chickens."

"That's a brilliant idea!" Sophie thought for a moment. "I don't think Aunt Flora keeps chickens any more. But she has space for them. The coops probably need to be repaired or rebuilt." Another thought occurred to her and her eyes brightened again. "We don't have room for goats, but she does. Three or four goats could mean milk and cheese!"

Thomas bit back a smile. "If she's going to have a little farm, what about keeping pigs too? A bit of bacon and ham now and then would be a treat."

Sydney
27 February 1942

Dear Sam,
Sophie and Thomas are turning the huge lawns on either side of the house into vegetable gardens. Mrs. Kelly told me you, Jean-Luc, and your friends used to play cricket and football on one side and tennis on the other. I suppose you will have to find somewhere else to play.

Marianne

THIRTY-FOUR

DO UNTO OTHERS

MARCH 1942

Despite having been raised in her mother's Anglican faith, Sophie's need to belong to any church had faltered sometime between arriving at the American Hospital in Paris in 1915 and leaving it in January 1919. So when she presented the idea of distributing food to the city's needy to Monsignor Sullivan at St. Mary's Cathedral, the seat of the archbishop in New South Wales, she was nearly rebuffed.

"This is an interesting idea, Mrs....?" Moira Kelly had told her Monsignor Sullivan was a conservative man, with conservative views. She also said it might embarrass him that none of the wealthy ladies in his congregation had come up with such an audacious idea—growing food on their own grounds specifically to feed the lower classes—especially coming from a woman who wasn't even Catholic!

Young Father O'Donnell rallied to her side. "Monsignor, Mrs. Parker and her husband are well known to several of our parishioners. Their housekeeper and caretaker, Moira and Thomas Kelly, are members of our parish. The Parkers have been integral to keeping the Johnson and Flanagan brothers out of trouble, giving them work to do instead of hanging around and causing trouble. Their mothers are most grateful that the boys have been able to help feed their families while their dads are off at war."

The old priest frowned and remained unconvinced.

"Monsignor," Sophie said. "It's because the Kellys are connected with this church that I thought to come to you first. But I understand your discomfort with dealing with someone who isn't a member of your congregation. My aunt and mother, who are members at St. Andrew's, suggested splitting the food between the two churches."

That's when Father O'Donnell worked his magic. "Thank you for considering St. Mary's, Mrs. Parker. I'm sure St Andrew's congregants will be happy to be the sole beneficiaries of such largess."

"Erm, I see," Monsignor Sullivan sputtered. "Let's not be too hasty. Perhaps we can come to an arrangement that will benefit the hungry people of Sydney. Mrs. Parker, you say you grow vegetables... Any chokoes in your garden?"

Sophie encountered similar resistance at St. Andrew's Anglican Church. The young vicar had been in favor of the idea and the old one opposed to it even when she hinted that St. Mary's would be happy to take the entire load.

It seemed the need to perpetuate the Protestant-Catholic divide was stronger than the need to feed Sydney's hungry.

She shared her frustrations with Joe later that night. She sat at her dressing table, running a brush through her hair. "It makes me crazy," she said. "They're so concerned about what their conservative members will say about working together with *that other* church that they're completely missing the point that there are people in this city who don't have enough to eat and children are going to bed hungry!'

She huffed and tossed her hairbrush on the table. Little bottles of perfume rattled. A cloud of face powder puffed up and drifted down.

Joe marked his spot in his book and put it aside on his bedside table. While Sophie was on the warpath he wasn't going to get anywhere in the chapter. On the other hand, she didn't worry as much about Sam and Jean-Luc when she was going full tilt on a project. This particular project, digging up their lawns and her Aunt Flora's to plant massive kitchen gardens and distribute the food among Sydney's hungriest citizens, had been taking up most of her time and energy for the past several weeks.

She was also particularly fetching when she fumed about an injustice, all dark eyes flashing and curls tumbling. Her expressions changed so quickly he could only watch in fond amazement. She reminded him of their first meeting in Paris back in 1916 when she told him about her brother Ben leaving university and volunteering to drive ambulances for the French. She'd been adamant that the United States should join the allies in the fight against the Germans, angry and disgusted that President Wilson was dragging his feet.

She stopped talking for a moment and sat, staring in his general direction but not at him. She wasn't expecting him to solve the problem, but they often bounced ideas off each other and even more often shared their frustrations with their respective jobs. He often marveled that the charitable work Sophie took on voluntarily rivaled his own professional workload, and her days and evenings were usually as busy as his.

Today, however, had been a mercifully quiet day. He'd arrived home in time for dinner and without a briefcase full of paperwork to deal with afterwards.

He wasn't exhausted, Sophie was extraordinarily alluring, and it wasn't even ten o'clock yet.

He wondered how he could get a word in edgewise, and suggest that perhaps they could take advantage of their available time to indulge in an activity that had nothing to do with vegetables or crime scenes or anything remotely related to world affairs.

Sophie pulled back the covers on her side of the bed and tucked herself in. She lay on her back, staring at the ceiling for a few moments. Then she turned on her side and faced him.

"What do you think, darling? Do you know any dark secrets that I can use to convince them to work together?"

Joe raised a brow at her. The corners of his mouth twitched. "Are you suggesting that I aid and abet you in a blackmailing scheme?"

Sophie grinned at him. "You know that's the real reason I married you, don't you? So, you could help me plan the perfect crime!"

By now she had draped one leg over his so he slipped his arm under her shoulders and pulled her close. "I'm sure you'll think of some idea to get the two churches to work together," he said and nuzzled his favorite spots along her neck.

"I'm sure you're right," Sophie agreed, humming when his lips reached her favorite spot for them. "At the moment, though, I have a different sort of idea entirely."

"Do you now?" Joe had already pushed priests, vicars, and vegetables to the furthest corner of his mind and was instead concentrating on the armful of warm woman filling his senses. "That's a remarkable coincidence. I think I have the same idea you have."

The next morning, Joe carefully detached his sleeping wife's arm from his waist, and headed to the bathroom to get ready for his day.

She roused and blinked at him when he came back into the bedroom to dress. "I know what I'm going to do," she said as he fastened his cufflinks.

"Oh? Did sleeping on it help?"

Sophie shifted under the covers and stretched luxuriantly. "A lovely, restful sleep always helps. I'm going to remind them again that the other church is more than willing to take on the task themselves. They're so competitive that they won't want the other to get all the glory. And voilà, the Catholics and the Protestants get to feed hungry people. Everybody wins."

Joe slid the knot of his tie up to his top button and smoothed his collar down. "Brilliant," he said. "I can see it now. You'll charm them into submission."

"I shouldn't have to," Sophie said. "They should be remembering the basic tenets of their faith. Do unto others. That which you do to the least of my brothers. Honestly, do you think they even try to practice what they preach?"

"I think," Joe said, leaning down to kiss her good bye, "that you'll do a very good job of reminding them."

Thirty-Five

A Body in the Church

March 1942

Sophie looked on with undisguised pleasure at the horse and cart parked in the street in front of her house. Angel was tethered to a fence post with a long enough lead that she could reach a bucket of water on the pavement if she was thirsty. Her long ears twitched at the flies buzzing around her. She also had a strategically placed bag on her hindquarters to keep the street clear of the inevitable messes.

Angel nibbled on a tasty patch of grass bordering the street, eliminating the need for Thomas to keep it trimmed. She didn't require any petrol, either, which was an added bonus, and especially important since petrol rationing was in strict operation.

Thomas and two of the boys Joe had recruited to help the old man tend the gardens at the Parker house and at Aunt Flora's house loaded the last two boxes of eggs beside crates of runner beans, carrots, and potatoes from Flora's gardens. There were also a few bunches of flowers to brighten the hall at St. Mary's Cathedral where the food was organized and distributed to those who needed it most.

The cart, a sturdy contraption, was a stroke of good luck. Thomas knew someone who knew someone who had a cart they couldn't keep and was willing to trade it for a weekly delivery of fresh veg and a few eggs. Sophie often thought that between Thomas, who had spent decades working Sydney's ferries before he retired, and Joe, who had years of policing Sydney's streets, the two men knew just about everyone in the city who was worth knowing. When she wasn't pulling the cart, gently driven by Thomas, Angel spent her days sharing the back fields at Aunt Flora's with four nanny goats and a billy goat.

"Ready Mrs. P?" Thomas called.

Sophie checked the pin holding her hat on her head and then pulled on her gloves. "Ready, Thomas," she said and climbed up on to the seat beside him. The two lads sat on a board at the back. They would help Thomas unload once they arrived at the church. Sophie, alongside Father O'Donnell, would supervise the distribution of the food.

When she and Thomas arrived at St. Mary's, Sophie took a few moments to wander into the cathedral. The huge space was quiet, its thick sandstone walls muffling the noise of Sydney's busy streets. Mid-morning sun slanted in through the stained-glass windows, painting the stone floor and wooden pews in swathes of jewel-toned color. She loved Gothic architecture—visiting the great cathedrals in Paris and London had been some of the joys of her life until her brother Ben's death. Then, not even the ancient splendor of Notre Dame brought her any peace. She'd found what little comfort she could visiting Ben's grave at the American Cemetery at Suresnes and then, after she met Joe, in corresponding with him during the last two years of the war.

In Sydney, St. Mary's and St. Andrew's offered Gothic grandeur, although the structures were barely sixty years old. Sophie preferred St. Mary's because of a sculpture that took her breath away every time she saw it.

She chose a pew beside the memorial to Australian soldiers from the Great War. In life-sized bronze, a young soldier wore a typical uniform: tunic, trousers, puttees, well-worn boots. The slab he lay upon was only a foot high, as if he had fallen in a sea of mud on the cathedral floor. The young man, probably barely out of his teens, still had a softness about his jaw that only time, had he lived, would have thinned out. He was beautiful and heartbreaking, the deep golden bronze burnished and warm.

If she prayed to anyone it was to the young soldier. Sophie closed her eyes for a moment, asking, pleading, begging for her sons to stay safe and alive. Sam had the sort of personality that would either allow him to get past whatever bad memories he brought home or be broken by them. Jean-Luc, the more cerebral of the two, would probably be so angered by his experience that he would rail against the stupidity and brutality of war until he was an old man. Either way, they would come home changed. The only thought that gave her any comfort was that both she and Joe had been through war and would understand what they'd been through in ways that their own parents hadn't.

As she prayed, Sophie became aware she wasn't alone. She hadn't seen anyone when she came in, or heard anyone come in after her, but someone was breathing close by. Then she heard a soft moan, and a trick of light made it seem like the bronze soldier had moved.

She swallowed hard and took a deep breath. Joe had taught her some self-defense moves years ago, and she prepared to use them if necessary.

"Hello? Is someone there?"

Then she heard another moan and she stood, fists clenched and heart pounding, doing a quick look around to see what she could.

A young boy was huddled on the floor next to the memorial. She rushed to his side, heedless of possible danger.

He couldn't have been more than eight or nine years old. Knobby wrists showed below cuffs whose sleeves were far too short. Jagged rips ringed with smears of blood marred his shabby shirt and ragged trousers.

Her years of nursing experience came flooding back as she knelt and examined the boy. He was too thin and far too hot. Fever, she decided, and automatically pressed her fingers to his wrist to feel his pulse. Fairly strong but fast.

She smoothed the boy's tangled hair away from his forehead. "What's your name?"

The boy's pale lids fluttered, but didn't open.

"My name is Mrs. Parker. I'm going to get help. I'll be right back."

Running to the side door closest to the parish hall where the day's food was being distributed, she flung the door open. "Thomas! Father O'Donnell! Come quickly! I need your help!"

She returned to the boy and knelt beside him, confident the two men would be right behind her. They skidded to a stop next to the granite base of the memorial.

She looked up to Father O'Donnell. "Do you know this boy? Have you ever seen him before?"

Father O'Donnell peered at the youngster. He shook his head. "I'm fairly new to this parish. Sorry."

Thomas said, "He could be one of the O'Brien boys. Sad story. Father enlisted last year and hasn't been heard from since. Last time I saw her, his mother was expecting. There were two other kiddies, little ones. They haven't been to Mass in a long time."

"If something has happened to the mother, the children will be taken to a children's home," Father O'Donnell replied.

"Those places are little more than warehouses for surplus children!" Sophie cried.

Father O'Donnell shrugged. "I'm sorry Mrs. Parker. The orphanage is already full to the brim."

Sophie let out a disgusted huff. "Let's get him into a bed and have a doctor look at him. Is there a spare bed in the rectory?"

"Yes, yes," the priest said. "I'm sure we can find one."

"Thomas? Would you..." Sophie began, but Thomas already had his arms under the boy's shoulders and knees.

"Lead the way, Father," the older man said, rising with the boy in his arms.

"He's malnourished and those cuts are badly infected," the doctor pronounced after he had examined the boy. He put his stethoscope back in his medical bag.

Sophie looked up from the basin of water where she was wringing water out of a cloth. She had already cleaned the boy's face, and stepped back to the bed to wipe down the boy's hands and arms.

"Luckily I don't see any signs of head lice," she said. "Does he need to be in hospital?"

"I don't think so," the doctor replied. "A week or two's worth of rest and regular meals should do the trick, I reckon. The cuts on his legs and arms need to be kept clean and dry so they will heal."

"That's what I thought, too," Sophie said. "I was a nurse during the last war," she explained when the doctor's brows rose.

"Well, Father, it looks like you'll have a guest for a few days," she said. "I know it's hot today, but does your housekeeper have any soup in the kitchen?" She gave the boy another appraising look. "He'll need milk, too, and eggs, to get his strength back."

Monsignor Sullivan had come in during the examination. "I don't know how we'll manage all that on our rations," he said.

"You have a parish hall full of food twice a week," Sophie countered. "We'll just have to appropriate some of it for our patient. In fact, I'll go do that right now."

"But..." the older priest began.

Sophie smiled to herself as she turned and left the room. Thomas' voice tended to carry and she heard him speak to the priest.

"Monsignor, I've found it's best not to argue with the missus when she gets hold of a thought," Thomas said. "After all, growing all those vegetables and raising chickens was her idea."

THIRTY-SIX

ONE BOY

MARCH 1942

At breakfast the next morning, Joe drizzled a bit on honey from Flora's hives on his toast. Mrs. Kelly was cutting the bread thinner and thinner these days, and they were making the butter stretch further and further too. At least they had plenty of eggs, and Mrs. Kelly made sure he had as full a breakfast as possible before he headed to work.

This morning's offering included scrambled eggs and a fried tomato, which was delicious. Sophie's giant gardens were keeping them well-fed in spite of the food rationing in effect.

Their coffee supply was carefully meted out so they could manage a cup for him and one for Sophie in the morning. The state of New South Wales provided all the tea he could drink at the office and at the various police stations.

Sophie floated into the dining room in a cloud of dressing gown and tumbled curls. She sank into a chair and stifled a yawn behind her hand.

"You're up early," Joe observed. "I didn't expect to see you again until this evening."

Sophie yawned again, waiting patiently for Mrs. Kelly to pour her cup of coffee before she spoke. She took her first sip, and then a second.

The second sip did the trick. Sophie eyes fluttered to fully open. "I couldn't get to sleep last night."

"I know I wasn't snoring," Joe said, "because I don't remember you pushing me to roll onto my side."

Sophie shook her head. "No, darling, it wasn't you. I kept thinking about that boy I found in the church yesterday. Thomas thought he recognized him, but he wasn't certain. We still don't know what his name is or where he lives. I'm going to check on him today. Perhaps he'll be in better shape to speak."

Joe paused in between forkfuls of scrambled egg and gazed at her. "Sophie, it may be that he doesn't have a home any more. From what you told me last night..."

"I know. If there's one boy out there hungry and living on the streets then there are probably more. That's what worries me."

Joe refrained from saying that there had always been hungry, homeless kids living rough in Sydney. He'd run across enough of them to know this was true. Wartime meant circumstances were even worse for kids like that and they often turned from petty thieving to feed themselves and their families to more nefarious crimes. The criminal elements were always looking for youngsters to run errands and worse. The added benefit was they couldn't be tried as adults if they were caught.

"Is there something about this particular boy that's bothering you?"

Sophie looked off into space for a few moments. "I don't know. Perhaps it was the circumstances of how I found him, lying next to the bronze soldier. I love that sculpture, Joe. The young man is so perfectly depicted. He looks so peaceful in spite of the fact that he's dead because of a bloody awful war." She blinked rapidly and shook her head. "All I know is that I found that boy and I have to make sure he's all right."

Joe reached across the table and folded her hand in his. "If you're able to get his name, let me know. I'll have a constable find his family and let them know where he is."

"But what if Father O'Donnell was right? What if he ran away from a children's home and..."

She stopped speaking and looked off at nothing again. Her eyes narrowed. Joe could almost see the gears turning in her head. If anyone could convince the boy to speak, it was Sophie.

He finished his coffee and rose from the table. "I need to get to the office."

Sophie followed him to the entry hall, like she did every morning when she was up, and watched him gather his hat and briefcase.

"Be safe, darling," she said, and straightened his already straight tie.

Joe kissed her cheek. "I will. Let me know if there's anything I can do to help."

Before she went into her bedroom to get dressed to go check on the boy at St. Mary's, Sophie marched into the room where Sam and Jean-Luc had stored their boxes and possessions while they were away. The boy needed a pair of trousers and a shirt that weren't two sizes too small like the clothes he'd been wearing when she found him yesterday.

Sam was much too tall to have left anything that might fit the boy. Jean-Luc was shorter, and thinner, than Sam. Hopefully she could find something in his boxes that would do.

Sophie was glad she had decided to do this task first; by the time she'd shifted boxes to get to the one labeled 'Clothes' she was sweating. How could one 25-year-old have acquired this much stuff? To be fair, most of Jean-Luc's boxes were full of books, school papers, and the jars of specimens he loved to collect. When she introduced Jean-Luc to Joe, Joe had told him that a Frenchman had been one of the first Europeans to land in Australia back in the late 1700's.

Jacques-Julien Houtou de Labillardière had been on a voyage of discovery and exploration, much like Charles Darwin's expedition several decades later. Like all explorers of his age, Labillardière had collected specimens of flora and fauna to take back to France.

Jean-Luc hadn't remembered his meetings with Joe in Paris, but when they were reacquainted in Sydney, he liked the quiet man who treated him almost like an adult, not like a mere schoolboy. Joe had loaned him one of his own books on natural history and Jean-Luc had poured over the illustrations. Everything in Australia was so different from what he was used to. Ficus trees with labyrinthine above-ground roots and trunks so huge that he couldn't span their diameter even with Sophie's help. Banksias, waratahs, and proteas whose flowers looked like no flowers he'd ever seen before. For several years he was certain botany would be his profession until he grew older and learned to appreciate wine. He'd wanted to learn how to grow grapes and turn them into wine. He'd never looked back after that moment.

It was no wonder, Sophie thought, moving yet another box full of clinking jars, that Jean-Luc saved all of this. It was the work of his life so far. Every jar represented a step towards doing what he loved.

At least she was only sniffling and not sobbing as she reminisced, although being used to Jean-Luc and Sam off at war was rather disconcerting.

She finally reached the box of clothes he'd traveled to Australia with all those years ago and made short work of sifting through and finding a couple of cotton shirts, a pair of sturdy canvas trousers, a belt, and a woolen jumper that was a little the worse for wear but still serviceable. Perhaps Mrs. Kelly could fix the pulls in the yarn while Sophie bathed and dressed. She gathered up the clothes and headed downstairs to ask Mrs. Kelly for her help.

After Mrs. Kelly fixed the jumper, tightened a couple of buttons on the shirts, and patched a tiny hole on the trousers, Sophie packed a bag containing the clothes and set off for the church. An idea was taking shape in her mind. She couldn't save all the homeless children in Sydney, but she might be able to save this one.

Two hours later, armed with the information she needed, Sophie walked from the church to Joe's office since the forensics department was housed in the central police headquarters just a few blocks down College Street.

The ancient and venerable Miss Pringle peered up through her round spectacles.

"Good morning," Sophie said. "I don't know if you remember me. I'm–"

"Of course, I remember you dear," Miss Pringle said, the polished lenses and steel frames of her eyeglasses flashing as nodded. "You're Mrs. Parker. I never forget a face. I've been working for the police for years. I make it my business to remember everyone I meet."

"Oh! Good. Is my husband available? I just need a few minutes."

"I'm afraid he isn't. He's gone over to a crime scene. Someone reported their kitchen window was broken while they were away and most of their food was stolen." Miss Pringle's thin cheeks hollowed as she pursed her lips. "It's small change for a Detective Inspector. But I suppose with everything being rationed he can't let this go unpunished."

"Oh!" Sophie was beginning to feel like a scratched gramophone record, the needle bumping the scratch and never getting past it.

"Is there a message you'd like to leave? I'm afraid I don't know when he'll be back."

Sophie would have preferred to tell Joe her news herself, but he'd offered his help and she didn't want to wait. Perhaps, if she was lucky, Joe would be back in the office soon and could get the ball rolling on the information she had about the boy.

"Yes, please, Miss Pringle. Would you tell him that the boy's name is Teddy O'Brien. He's nine years old. He lives with his mother and two little sisters at this address." Sophie handed over a slip of paper with an address in The Rocks, a very poor, old area of Sydney. She knew the neighborhood had become unsafe in the last few years.

Being close to the waterfront it had always been a rather dubious location, but after the economic downturn in the 1930's it had become quite seedy. Sophie was tempted to go over there herself and knock on every door if necessary, but she had promised Joe long ago that she wouldn't take on a task that the authorities should handle.

Miss Pringle had written down everything in a perfect, spidery, hand. Joe still needed a secretary who knew shorthand and could type, quickly, but he wasn't willing to give up Miss Pringle. She proved her worth immediately yet again. "Hmmm. It's a terrace, dark brick, with broken shutters. There must be twenty people living in it. Not unusual for the area. I'll pass your message on, Mrs. Parker."

Sophie's next stop was her Aunt Flora's home. She walked to Circular Quay and caught the ferry to Vaucluse. That plus a half mile walk would get her to Flora's in time to meet Thomas. Not only were the Sydney ferries a great way to get around the city, they were a lifesaver in times of strict petrol rationing.

She met Thomas and Flora's two gardeners coming around the side of the stately house that her aunt and uncle built in an elegant, Georgian style. There wasn't a whiff of the twentieth century on this estate, no Art Nouveau curlicues or Art Deco curves. She could have been in the English countryside, peering up at the local baron's country home. Whomever had done the actual construction understood the genre perfectly: multi-paned windows stacked one above the other, classical columns flanking the front entrance, a fanlight above the door that let natural light softly illuminate the marble-floored entry hall.

Around the back, great lawns had once boasted a tennis court and a croquet green, and then given way to a width of shrubbery that shielded the views from the house of a working estate: kitchen and cutting gardens, a sizeable chicken yard, complete with crowing roosters, stables that had once housed a couple of thoroughbreds and ponies for the children of the house.

The thoroughbreds had been taken in the first war, as had most of the horses in Australia, New Zealand, and England. The Australia government had refused to allow war horses back in the country afterward, citing disease as its reason, but Sophie knew so many horses had been killed in France that no one in Australia would have received nearly as many as they'd given up. Her aunt and uncle had been allowed to keep their old mare and an even older stallion at their farm in the country to pull carts and plow the fields. Somehow, the two old beasts had found enough energy in their waning years to produce a perfect little white foal. She had been named Angel. Now she spent her twilight years grazing the back fields when she wasn't pulling the cart to Saint Mary's.

Like Angel, Thomas and the two gardeners, Vern and Alf, were also in their twilight years. All three men had done their bit for King and country in Gallipoli, had been wounded or sick enough to be repatriated instead of sent to France. The two gardeners, best mates before the war and best mates after it, had presented themselves to Sophie's uncle Randolph and asked for work in exchange for a place to sleep every night and a meal to fill their bellies every day. They'd been with the family ever since, and Flora trusted them to keep the place in tip-top shape.

"Hello Thomas!" Sophie called. "And hello Vern and Alf!"

All three men tipped their caps to her. "G'day, missus," Vern and Alf replied in unison.

"Thomas, I've come to tell you I found out the boy's name is Teddy O'Brien."

"Ah, so he is one of the O'Brien boys," Thomas said.

"There are more?" Sophie thought back to what the boy had told her. "He only said he had two younger sisters and another baby on the way."

"There's an older brother," Thomas said. "He ran off...maybe two or three years ago. Dunno where he went. The family stopped comin' to Mass regular after that."

"Hmm. Well," Sophie continued, "I have an address and I took it to Joe's office. He said he'd help if he could."

Vern and Alf had been looking on and listening to the conversation with interest. Thomas had informed her that coppers weren't their favorite people since they'd both had plenty of run-ins with them in their youth, but they thought Inspector Parker wasn't a bad sort.

Alf spoke up. "Will you be wanting to inspect the fields after lunch, missus?"

"Yes," Sophie replied. "I'm wondering if there's any way we can plant another bed of potatoes. There was a line of children at St. Mary's this morning when I went to check on Teddy. Since today wasn't a distribution day, I have to believe they were hoping we'd show up anyhow."

Vern shook his head slowly. "I don't know that we can squeeze in anything more, missus. Not and leave room for Angel and the goats to graze."

"Darn it," Sophie said, sighing. "We'll think of something, gentlemen. We just have to put our minds to it."

THIRTY-SEVEN

TWO LITTLE GIRLS

MARCH 1942

Sophie rarely woke fully when Joe slipped into bed beside her after a late night. Tonight, though, she startled awake to Joe's weight on her side of the bed and his hand stroking her arm.

"Wake up love," he said. "I need you to come downstairs."

"Umph. What time is it?"

"It's just gone two." He stood and she could see he was still dressed in the same suit he'd donned hours ago.

He was safe and her initial panic eased a little. "What happened?"

Her husband hesitated, as if he wasn't sure how to tell her. Panic rose again. "It isn't one of the boys, is it? Have you heard something?"

"No, no, it's nothing like that. Mrs. Kelly and I need your help."

Mystified, Sophie rose, pulling on her robe and following Joe out of their bedroom.

The entry hall was dark, with the exception of the little lamp she left on when he was out late. He led her through the dining room and into the big kitchen at the back of the house.

Sophie squeezed her eyes in an effort to get used to the bright light. Mrs. Kelly had her back to the door, tending to something on the stove.

Nothing seemed amiss except the ungodly hour. Then Sophie realized there were two small girls sitting at her kitchen table.

Two very dirty faces turned, gazing solemnly at her until Mrs. Kelly cooed, "There we are lovies, some nice warm milk to have with your bread and jam."

As Sophie watched, Mrs. Kelly placed two mugs on the table and cut two slices from a loaf of bread. She spread each piece with a generous amount of jam and pushed plates in front of the little girls. They stared at the food until she said, "It's all right. That nice lady over there is Mrs. Parker and this is her house. The nice man who brought you here is her husband. I think she'll agree you need to get some food in your tummies."

Still dumbfounded at the events unfolding in her kitchen at two in the morning, Sophie nodded. "Yes. Please. Eat."

The little girls must have been starving. They wolfed the first bite, and then another and another, pausing only to take a drink of milk.

Joe tugged gently on Sophie's sleeve and motioned her back to the dining room.

Sophie kept her voice low. "Who are those children?"

Joe blew out a breath. "They're Teddy's younger sisters. We found them at the address you managed to get out of him."

"They look like they haven't eaten in days! Where is their mother?"

Joe pulled out a chair, and sat down wearily. "She's dead."

"Please don't tell me those little girls were there with their dead mother?"

"It gets worse. There was another child. Just a babe in arms, only a few hours old. The mother was wearing a crucifix, so we got the chaplain at the hospital to baptize the baby. The doctor said there was nothing they could do. He'd been born at least a month early..." Joe shoulders slumped. "It looked like the mother hemorrhaged after giving birth, but we won't know for certain until after we get the autopsy results."

Sophie sank into a chair. "No."

Joe nodded. "The place was practically empty. No food, no furniture, only a mattress on the floor and a couple of wooden crates to sit on."

"Oh God, Joe."

"We had to break the door down to get in. Welfare didn't answer the phone so I couldn't leave them there. Thompson offered to take them home, but…"

"But Mary's pregnant with their fourth and they're already cramped in your old cottage."

"Right. So, I brought them here. Honestly, it's so late I didn't have any other ideas."

"It's fine," Sophie assured him. "You did the right thing. They're safe here. We can get them cleaned up and fed and keep them as long as they need to stay." She got up to go back to the kitchen but stopped before she opened the door. "Joe? What about Teddy? Does he know about his mother and sisters?"

Joe shook his head. "No. I went to the church before we found them. He was so worried about his little sisters and his mother and the baby that he confessed. He broke a window at a house and stole food for them. That's how he got the cuts on his arms and legs. He thought if he hid in the church he couldn't be sent to jail for stealing." Joe leaned back in his chair. "I assured him he wouldn't go to jail. He'll have to atone for what he's done, but that can wait until we get all of this sorted out."

"What business does a nine-year-old have knowing about sanctuary?" Sophie rolled her shoulders and came to a decision. "I'll help Mrs. Kelly. You go upstairs and get to bed. You look done in, darling."

"I am done in," Joe replied. Sophie gave him a tight, quick hug before he left the dining room and wearily trudged up the stairs.

An hour later Sophie got into bed as quietly as she could, hoping she wouldn't wake Joe.

She thought she'd been successful, but as soon as she pulled the covers up and settled in Joe turned to face her.

"Everything okay?" he murmured.

"Yes. Mrs. Kelly and I gave them a quick wash in the downstairs lavatory. She's brilliant, Joe. She told Thomas to go through the rag box and find two of his old undershirts. We put them on the girls for nightgowns. We tucked them in Jean-Luc's bedroom." The clean, soft cotton shirts had dwarfed the girls, but neither Mrs. Kelly nor Sophie possessed anything small enough or better suited. But before that, Sophie had to bite the inside of her cheek to keep from crying at how thin and tiny the little girls were. Despite being so hungry, they said thank you when they finished their bread and milk. What a heartbreaking contrast. Good manners and hunger often didn't go hand-in-hand.

"Joe, what was the mother's name?"

"Catherine O'Brien, according to the landlady. The husband's name is Patrick. Did the girls ever tell you what their names are? Or how old they are?"

"Katie is five and Cora is three." Katie was old enough to know something dreadful had happened, that their lives had been completely upended. She had given their names and ages and then slipped into silence while Cora simply took in everything, wide-eyed. "I'll go by the church in the morning and tell Teddy they're safe."

"Good," Joe mumbled. "Good."

Sophie leaned forward to kiss his cheek but Joe was already asleep.

She had a harder time falling asleep. Her brain wouldn't stop imagining the girls in the dire straits before Joe and Fred Thompson found them. She got out of bed and peeped in their bedroom. Katie was spooned around Cora, holding her little sister close. The night was so quiet Sophie could hear their slow, quiet breaths of deep sleep. She tiptoed back to her own bedroom, leaving the door ajar so she could hear if they stirred or they could find her if they woke during the night.

THIRTY-EIGHT

TEARS AND A BUBBLE BATH

MARCH 1942

Three hours later, Joe woke, rubbed his eyes and scrubbed his hands over his face, and contemplated whether he could just go back to sleep for the next twenty-four hours. Then he remembered that Sophie and he had two tiny guests in their home whose futures needed to be sorted out. Coroner first, and then he'd stop by Welfare on this way to his office. He was much more likely to be seen and heard if he showed up in person instead of telephoning. Besides, the recently appointed head of the department was an old friend. If necessary, Joe could appeal to him to get the wheels moving faster to find a place for the girls and Teddy.

He got out of bed and headed to the bathroom. Emerging washed, shaved, and feeling almost human again, he pulled underwear and socks from his dresser drawer.

The bedcovers rustled. He turned and saw Sophie stretching and blinking at him.

"What time is it?"

"Almost half-six," he replied. "Go back to sleep for a while."

"Humph."

Joe smiled. Early mornings were not Sophie's forte. She was often still asleep when he left for the day, only briefly rousing long enough to kiss him good-bye before she snuggled back under the covers.

"I'm getting up too." She threw off the covers. "I can't leave Mrs. Kelly to get your breakfast and deal with Katie and Cora. Would you mind telling her I'll be down in just a few minutes?"

Joe had already finished dressing and was opening their bedroom door. "I think you can tell her yourself," he said. "Take a look."

Sophie grabbed her robe from the foot of the bed and pulled it on as she joined him in the doorway.

"I'll go down," Joe said, "and leave you ladies to dress in privacy."

Moira was in Jean-Luc's bedroom, pulling open the curtains and calling softly to the little girls still snuggled together in the big bed.

"Good morning," she said when Sophie entered. "I've brought up the clothes they were wearing when they arrived. I gave them a launder before I went to bed. I didn't have a chance to iron them but they're nice and clean and dry."

"Oh, Mrs. Kelly, you're a jewel," Sophie said. "Thank you."

Moira shook off the compliment. "Well, we couldn't have them putting on dirty pinafores, could we?"

"No, we couldn't," Sophie replied. "I'll have to get them some more clothes today." She remembered the ragged little boots the girls had been wearing. "Some new shoes, too, I think."

By this time, Katie was sitting up in bed, rubbing her eyes.

Sophie said, "Good morning, Katie. I'm Mrs. Parker and this nice lady is Mrs. Kelly. Do you remember us?"

Katie nodded but didn't say anything.

"Are you hungry? Would you like some breakfast?"

Katie nodded again, but still remained silent.

"May I help you and Cora get dressed while Mrs. Kelly makes us all some eggs and toast?"

Cora had been paying attention after all. "I want eggs!" she cried.

"Good! Let's get you dressed and we'll all go downstairs." Sophie shared a conspiratorial smile with her housekeeper. "I'll take over here, Mrs. Kelly."

Fifteen minutes later, Sophie led Katie and Cora downstairs. Joe sat at the dining table, eating his breakfast and reading the newspaper at the same time.

He rose when he saw the three of them. "Good morning, ladies," he said. His tone was friendly and quiet, the product of years of dealing with all sorts of citizens over his long career. He was unfailingly polite to everyone except the most obnoxious criminals.

Sophie could have kissed him for being so sweet to the little girls. He'd rescued them from a dire situation, brought them home with him, and was now treating them with grave respect.

Katie looked at him with her solemn eyes. Cora smiled at him around the fingers stuck in her mouth.

"Come along, girls," Sophie said. "Let's see what Mrs. Kelly has made you for breakfast." She led the little ones into the kitchen and sat them at the big wooden table.

Mrs. Kelly plated scrambled eggs and toast for the girls, and then prepared a plate for Sophie and poured a cup of coffee for her. "If you don't mind taking this to the dining room yourself, the inspector wanted to speak with you. I'll help the littlies."

"Of course, I don't mind," Sophie answered. "Katie, Cora? Would you excuse me for a few moments?"

She sat down with Joe. "What's the plan?"

He had finished his eggs and toast and took the last sip of coffee. "First off, the coroner's office. I'm hoping I can get him to schedule the autopsy on the mother tomorrow. It should be fairly straightforward. Then he can release the bodies for burial."

"Joe, what about Teddy? Should we let him see his mother? I think Katie and Cora are too young for that, but he's old enough to do the identification, isn't he?"

Joe's head rocked back and forth a couple of times. "It would be better if we had an adult to do it," he said. "Then Teddy could see her afterwards at the funeral. Under normal circumstances, where do you think she would be buried?"

"If she is...was...a member of St. Mary's, it should be the Catholic cemetery," Sophie said. "I'll speak with Monsignor Sullivan and Father O'Donnell about that. They must have some sort of fund or something to deal with situations like this.

"One would think so," Joe said. "After I speak with the coroner I'll go over to Welfare. I have a feeling they're going to tell me they won't be able to keep the kids together. In fact, they may not be able to take all of them or Teddy."

Sophie's shoulders sagged. "We have to think of something. I hate the idea that they could be separated."

Joe checked his watch. "Thompson is picking me up in a few minutes. Did you want to ride into town with us? We can drop you at the church."

"As tempting an offer as that is, I'll forgo a lift with Sydney's finest," Sophie said. "I think I should help Mrs. Kelly look after the girls for a while this morning. I want them to feel as comfortable and safe as possible. Poor lambs, they've had a horrible time of it. I'll go by the church to speak with Teddy after lunch."

"Right." Joe rose from the table. "I'll see you this evening, then, love. Leave a message with Miss Pringle if the girls tell you anything you think I should know before then."

After Joe left, Sophie lingered to finish her coffee and read the latest news. Moira Kelly came in to clear the breakfast plates and cups from the dining room.

"The girls are having a second piece of toast," she said. "I'm not sure when they last had a decent meal. They'll need a bath and a good scrub, too, more than we were able to do last night. I'll have to do that after I go to market."

Sophie stifled a yawn. "I can bathe them while you do the shopping."

"Are you sure? Didn't you have a luncheon scheduled today?"

Sophie nodded. "With the Red Cross. I'll call them and beg off. The girls will need both of us close today. They've had a huge upset to their lives. I don't want them to feel like I've abandoned them."

"I'm happy to do it," Moira said, her hands full of crockery.

"We'll need to divvy up the work," Sophie said. "But for today, if you can watch the girls after I bathe them, I'll go over to Myers and pick up some clothes, underthings, and shoes. Then we can figure out the next steps."

—

"Katie, Cora, I have a wonderful idea," Sophie said as she trailed Mrs. Kelly into the kitchen. "Would you like to take a bubble bath?"

Cora's eyes widened. Katie shook her head. "I want mumma. I want Teddy."

Sophie and Moira shared a look. The only real experience Sophie had with small children was helping to look after Jean-Luc when she shared a flat in Paris with his mother, her best friend Natalie. Her best hope was distraction until she discovered how much Katie knew about her mother's death. Distraction had worked when injured soldiers asked hard questions she couldn't answer. The same tactics should work with the little girls, especially Katie. The poor child was probably traumatized in ways that would manifest themselves as time went on.

"I know you do, sweetheart," she said, her voice catching as she spoke. "And we can talk about that in a little while, but I'll need your help to wash Cora's hair first. Can you do that?"

Sophie held her breath, hoping her request would delay the inevitable questions for a little while. The ploy didn't work. Katie's lower lip quivered and she shook her head, causing fat tears to spill down her cheeks. Cora's method of coping seemed to be using her thumb and forefinger to comfort herself, but she didn't look distressed so Sophie banked on Katie not wanting to let Cora out of her sight. She held her hands out to Cora, who promptly put her arms up to be lifted from the chair.

Sophie cuddled Cora for a moment, sensing Katie was watching and judging her sister's reactions. When Cora giggled as Sophie dabbed her cheeks with a napkin, Katie's rigid stance softened a bit.

"What do you think, Cora? Shall we ask Katie to join us upstairs?" As Sophie spoke, she shifted Cora's weight to one arm and beckoned to Katie with the other.

Moira, who had been rinsing dishes to allow the girls to concentrate on Sophie, bustled back into view and addressed Katie. "Doesn't a bubble bath sound grand? And afterwards you can help me gather eggs and feed the chooks. Would you like that?"

Sophie's voice caught in her throat several times again after she started the tub filling and began undressing the girls. Their little bodies were so thin that their ribs were clearly visible. As she soaped and rinsed Cora first and then Katie, she was pulled back to wartime hospital memories of how fragile human bodies were. The girls were so small and defenseless that a primal urge rose in her to protect them from the evils of the world.

Cora playing with the bubbles distracted her from tears more than once and Sophie was relieved neither girl bore any signs of rough handling, only typical light bruises and scrapes on their knees, shins, and elbows. Their mother may have been dirt poor but her daughters seemed to have been cared for. Their mental healing would revolve around the trauma of losing their mother and her baby, but not, luckily, around physical abuse.

Drying the girls after she lifted them from the tub, Sophie became aware that she'd unconsciously been pondering their less than rosy future. Welfare would surely place them in foster care, but how could she be assured they would be placed somewhere safe? Or even kept together? Cora was young enough to appeal to a couple who wanted a child, but Katie was old enough to be trained up as merely a body to do mind-numbing chores. The possibility that she might never go to school loomed large, and Sophie resolved to do whatever she could to assure Welfare placed them together in the best home possible.

But first, she needed to get the girls dressed and delivered back downstairs to Mrs. Kelly's capable hands so she could shop for some decent clothes to replace their ragged ones.

THIRTY-NINE

ON THE ROCKS

MARCH 1942

Joe finally arrived in his office three hours later than usual. He'd been to the coroner's office and Welfare, and now faced a stack of paperwork on his desk that he'd been too busy to deal with for the last couple of days. Being one of the police officers who'd been selected to stay in Sydney was a blessing and a curse. He had a lovely home to go home to every night, his wife was a treasure, and he was doing a job he loved.

Jobs, he corrected himself. He was doing two jobs. His official job as head of the forensics department was completely different than active policing. He'd worried about making the transition his first day on the job. Making the change had seemed like a great way to remain on the force after he'd been shot last year. He'd be able to continue to solve puzzles, which was how he viewed solving crimes, without the constant threat of possible injury. Which, after thirty years of policing, had taken a toll.

The sense of being able to relax a little bit hadn't lasted long. War, once again, had changed everything. He felt a little guilty for being relieved he didn't have to fight again. Then he caught sight of the photographs of Sam and Jean-Luc in their uniforms and remembered the ongoing drama caused by Sam not replying to letters Marianne had written to him. Joe was only involved peripherally—he knew about it because he'd overheard Sophie and Marianne having a worried conversation which had set Sophie on edge because they hadn't heard from Sam either. How long could it possibly take to pen two or three sentences home? But when he allowed himself to think about it further, he remembered not responding to one of Sophie's letters and how worried she had been. At the time, he'd been too shaken by his actions after the battle at Villers-Bretonneux to answer her, believing Sophie would never want to have anything to do with him if she knew what he'd done. What if Sam was in a similar situation?

Sighing, Joe sifted through the files on his desk. Miss Pringle had placed them in the order she thought had the highest priority.

He had discovered she was usually right, but today he was looking for something a little easier to start with. His office was currently working on providing forensic support for three cases that were coming to trial, but with the newer, more efficient equipment he'd managed to extract from the Commissioner in exchange for staying in Sydney instead of going back into the army, Joe could rely on his technicians to handle processing the evidence for those cases.

In addition, there was the ongoing sly grog investigation, a murder-suicide at the fish markets in Glebe, and Teddy's case. The murder-suicide was being handled by the coppers at the station closest to it. The senior sergeant had phoned in the results of the previous day's canvassing of the area. Joe took a quick look at the report, decided the local boys were progressing as they should be, and put that file aside. He'd already done everything he could in Teddy's case. The deep gashes in the boy's legs and arms were healing and the infection and fever were under control. The boy was still ensconced at the rectory at St. Mary's and would be there for another day or two.

That left the sly grog case. He'd managed to place a constable in the guise of a cook inside the barracks, but so far, the young man had had nothing to report. They were getting nowhere fast. Joe blew out a frustrated huff of breath. The last thing he wanted was to don his army uniform as the assistant commissioner had suggested, but he needed results.

He grabbed his hat and left his office. "I'm heading down to Harry's," he told Miss Pringle.

Miss Pringle had a wicked sense of humor. "Taking a long lunch, sir?"

"Something like that," Joe chuckled. Harry's Pies on Wheels was famous for serving hot pies quickly and cheaply. Downing one would take a maximum of ten minutes, fifteen if he stopped to watch the gulls flying around the waterfront. "I just need to be out amongst people, put an ear out for anything unusual that might be going on."

"I hear there are some new girls working that area," Miss Pringle countered. "Perhaps you could have a look? Make sure they haven't been roughed up?"

Honestly, Joe thought, the woman really might be worth her weight in gold. He had no idea how she came into the information she offered on a regular basis, but she'd been right enough times since he came on this job that he'd learned to listen when she dropped tidbits like this one.

"I'll keep my eyes open as well as my ears," he promised, tipping his hat to her and striding out of the department. "I'll be back in a couple of hours."

Joe had been an active police officer for too long to avoid recognition by the thugs and miscreants who made Woolloomooloo their base of operations. Another reason why going undercover at the barracks wouldn't work, he thought. They'd all either hidden themselves away when they saw him coming or, more likely, they were busy preparing for whatever business they would be conducting come nightfall.

After an hour of wandering the streets, he decided to head over to The Rocks and take another look at the flat where Teddy's family had lived. Perhaps they'd missed something, although he doubted it. The one room had been practically barren when he and Thompson found the girls and the mother and baby.

The landlady glared at him when he inspected the tape across the door that marked it as a police scene. Someone had already repaired the door jamb and replaced the lock.

"How'm I s'posed to keep respectable tenants with p'lice breakin' down doors and comin' in whenever they feel like it?" she groused.

Joe resisted the urge to roll his eyes. Good manners would get him further than sarcasm.

"Mrs. Albert, I apologize for the damage. Unfortunately, it was unavoidable since we didn't have the key and didn't know where to find you at the time."

"I was asleep in my bed, like the respectable woman I am," she declared. "It's not my fault I sleep like a log. Ya shoulda knocked harder. I woulda woke and let you in."

A soused log, more like. Joe remembered the woman stank of cheap gin when she'd appeared after Thompson had applied his powerful body to the door. The lock had been so flimsy it barely held.

"I'd like to take another look, Mrs. Albert. If you don't mind, of course" he said, sticking with politeness.

"Nah, go ahead. But be quick about it. And can you take that police tape off? I've got another tenant lined up to take the room and I don't want you scarin' him away."

"I will if I can," Joe said. He eyed the new lock and badly repaired door jamb. "If you would be so kind?"

Grumbling under her breath, Mrs. Albert produced a huge ring of keys from her skirt pocket and unlocked the door. "Lemme know when you're finished," she said. "Don't want nobody comin' in who's not s'posed to."

There was absolutely nothing in the flat, not even the blood-stained mattress in the corner or the two crates. Nothing in the tiny cupboard that had served as a makeshift kitchenette. It didn't make sense. Surely Catherine O'Brien would have had a bucket to fetch water or a hairbrush or something.

The landlady must have disobeyed the police tape and removed everything. Joe couldn't think of any other explanation.

First things first, Joe thought as he closed the door of the shabby room and climbed the stairs to where Mrs. Albert watched him from her open door. The whole place gave off a smell of stale sweat and musty wool, underpinned by traces of bodily excretions. Those scents mingled with the stink of over-boiled cabbage.

This is what despair smells like, he thought, wrinkling his nose and blinking away the dust. His eyes widened in spite of it when he caught sight of the sheer amount of stuff crammed into the front room. It looked like a miniature warehouse: a stack of ratty mattresses in one corner topped with a stack of equally ratty looking blankets.

Another corner housed chairs and tables, also stacked, but in a precise manner so as many as possible could fit in the allotted space. A maze of wooden legs grazed the ceiling.

The third corner held piles of clothes: men's jackets, trousers, and shirts, women's dresses, the patterned cottons contrasting with the browns and greys of the men's clothing. There was a smaller pile of children's clothes, too, and crates of shoes and boots.

He cleared his throat. Mrs. Albert scowled at him. "Whatcha lookin' at?" she groused. "You finished downstairs?"

Joe had an overwhelming suspicion that the possessions of the O'Brien family would be found in this room. He had several courses of action: he could walk away, having neither the time nor the wherewithal to go through the mountains of things in this room by himself. He could drag Mrs. Albert down to the station and try to get an explanation out of her. He doubted she would go quietly;

she'd kick and scream all the way down the stairs and into the police car, alerting any and all who might be her accomplices in her larceny.

He chose another option. "Mrs. Albert, have there been any thefts in this building?"

She squinted at him. "I heard nothin' about thefts."

Of course, you haven't, you old harridan, you've been committing them. Joe wasn't a fisherman. He'd never caught a fish in his life. But he understood the concept of using the right bait and the patience required to land a wily fish. Somehow, the O'Brien's room had been emptied. Teddy could probably identify his family's belongings in this mass of stuff. Teddy wasn't quite up to the task yet, though. His body was healing nicely but he'd need some time to get over the shock of his mother and baby brother being dead.

Joe made a show of mentally cataloguing the contents of the crowded room. "Hmmm."

Mrs. Albert's face twitched. "I need to rent that room out. I can't be refusin' good money when it comes to me."

"I understand," he said, casually slipping his hand in the right pocket of his trousers and jingling the coins there. "We're just trying to figure out what happened to that poor woman and I don't have enough men to do all the legwork."

The expected greed glinted in her squinty eyes. "I might be able to help."

Joe pulled out his loose coins. He was certain that once he held his palm open that she'd take every penny he had.

Mrs. Albert was even better than he expected. From a distance of four feet, she counted the coins. "That'll do for a start," she cackled.

Joe crossed the room and hesitated before he tilted a few coins into her waiting hand. "Any idea what happened to all the furniture in that flat?"

"She was skint. Her old man was outta work and the dole wasn't enough. Reg'lar pay is the only reason he enlisted. I gave her a fair price. She still owed me rent. I just tried to cover my losses."

Fair price, my arse, Joe thought. He fiddled with the remaining coins he held. "And what about personal possessions? Children's toys? Clothes? Letters?"

Mrs. Albert eyed his hand. She blew out a cabbage and gin-scented breath. By way of answering, she shoved the pennies she'd already acquired into one pocket and picked some ragged pieces from the piles of clothes. "No letters, no toys. What would letters be worth anyway?"

Sophie and Mrs. Kelly probably wouldn't want the clothes, but he wasn't going to let this old crone gain anything else from the family. He plucked the rags from her claws and let a couple more pennies fall into her palm.

"Anything else?"

"There's only a photo," she protested. "I only took it for the frame. I was gonna give the picture back to her."

Then she glared at him and rummaged through a box containing knickknacks and handed Joe a carved frame holding a wedding photograph, taken before the effects of children, economic depression, and war had overtaken the family. Catherine must have been truly desperate to give this up.

Joe waved an impatient hand that encompassed the room's packed, shabby contents. "I'm willing to overlook all this in exchange for you identifying Mrs. O'Brien's body. You wouldn't want a nine-year-old boy to have to identify his dead mother, would you?"

Her shoulders slumped. She shook her head.

"Thank you, Mrs. Albert." He gave her his remaining pennies. "I'll see you at the Central Station morgue tomorrow morning at eight. Until then."

With that, Joe pulled his hat down more firmly, gave her a long look tinged with warning, and made his way down the narrow stairs to the street.

"Nice doin' business with ya," she called in effort to regain her battered dignity.

FORTY

ALL NEWS IS BAD NEWS

MARCH 1942

As March began, Joe became increasingly frustrated with the search for the dead woman's husband. He first contacted the army's paymaster office for information on her husband's current whereabouts, but hadn't received any responses from them yet. He checked with the militia and the jails too, neither of which turned up anything.

The month was made even more miserable by Katie's sorrow when she finally understood she would never see her mother again. Mrs. Kelly had been trying to comfort Katie by telling her that her mother was with God in Heaven, but the five-year-old had only limited understanding of the concept of death, much less everlasting life. The poor child cried herself to sleep most nights, even with Sophie cuddling her close and whispering comfort. Three-year-old Cora had had an easier time of it, although Katie's tears often set her off crying too.

In spite of all the bad news and tears, there were two bright spots in the month: the knowledge that Jean-Luc was en route to Australia from Egypt and Teddy's recovery from his infected cuts. Sophie and Thomas Kelly collected Teddy from St. Mary's rectory and brought him home to be reunited with his little sisters.

However, it had become clear that they had no good answers for the children. The army finally identified several men named Patrick O'Brien who could be the children's father. After Joe urged them to delve deeper, they found only one man who had a Catherine listed as his wife and three children. As they did for all servicemen, the army had deposited the bulk of Patrick's pay locally for his family's use, but Catherine must have been physically unable to get to the post office and withdraw the funds. Joe had questioned Teddy about his family's circumstances, but getting information out of a young boy required gentler tactics than questioning a criminal suspect. According to Teddy, his father had been out of work before he enlisted but the boy couldn't remember for how long. With even a minor wait between Patrick's final dole payment and his first army pay, Joe figured the family had been living hand to mouth for some time. Catherine must have been desperate to pawn everything they owned to the unscrupulous Mrs. Albert. If nothing else, it helped to explain why Teddy had taken matters into his own hands and broken into someone's home to steal food.

"I woulda done it again," Teddy declared. "Didn't count on getting cut up and sick because of it."

When word finally came from the army regarding Patrick's whereabouts, the news wasn't good. His battalion had embarked for Egypt and, after training there for several weeks, had then been sent to fight the Germans in Crete. The man was listed as wounded and taken as a prisoner of war. There was no telling how long he would be a prisoner, or even if he would survive prison camp.

That evening, he and Sophie settled in the drawing room after dinner to outline the few options available for the children.

"Welfare has found two spots at a state home for girls, but the boy's homes in our part of the state are overflowing," he said.

"What do they suggest we do with him?" Sophie's voice always rose at least half an octave when she was upset. It rose even higher than usual. "Set him loose on the streets?"

Undeterred, he continued. "They're checking further afield. There's a family in Bathurst that might take him on to help in the fields."

"Bathurst? That's three or four hours away by train, if they're even running the regular passenger routes any more. Would they send him to school if he's working as a field hand? And he would hardly ever get to see Katie and Cora."

He threw up his hands. "I know. But that's all Welfare has available."

Sophie set her coffee cup in its saucer so hard that the china clunked and the spoon rattled. "Those are not acceptable solutions!" She folded her arms across her chest and fumed for a moment, gazing into the distance at nothing in particular.

"I agree they aren't ideal, but—"

"What if they were our children? We wouldn't want them separated and farmed out to places where they'll hardly be cared for, much less cared about."

"No, we wouldn't."

Sophie jumped up and paced the room, eventually stopping in front of the family photographs atop the mantelpiece, her expression morphing from angry to frustrated to thoughtful. "Joe."

"Yes, love?"

"I know how to solve this. The children should stay with us."

She turned so she was facing him. "They're already here. The girls are used to us and the Kellys by now. It won't take long for Teddy to settle in. We have plenty of room. We have the financial resources to look after them. We can send them to school, feed them properly, clothe them."

"What about their father? We need to inform him his wife has died but his children are safe and being cared for. He may be able to tell us if there are other relatives who can take them."

"Well of course those are possibilities. But they aren't options at this particular moment, are they? The answer is simple. They stay here. We take care of them until something changes."

Joe gazed steadily back at his wife. "All right. Let's go through that scenario. Neither of us has raised three young children."

"I helped Natalie with Jean-Luc when he was little."

"And I had my mother's help with Sam in Melbourne and Mrs. Kelly's help here in Sydney. My point is we each had one child, not three. You're already running full tilt with the vegetable gardens and all the other aid and comfort projects you've committed to, aren't you?"

"The vegetable gardens don't require much of my attention any more. Thomas manages them almost on his own."

"All right. What about Mrs. Kelly? She would have the added burden of laundry and feeding the children. Making their school lunches, ironing their school uniforms. Someone has to get Katie and Teddy to and from school every day and look after Cora all day."

Sophie shot him a half-hearted glare. "I know how to iron and make sandwiches, Joe. And I'm perfectly capable of doing a daily school run. The burden wouldn't fall entirely on Mrs. Kelly's shoulders."

"But she isn't as young as she was when Sam was in primary school. I leave the house at seven every morning and I'm hardly ever home before seven or eight o'clock at night. There are many nights it's later than that. It isn't fair, but you would bear the brunt of most of it."

"I don't mind. Those children need care and a stable environment. We can provide that."

"We can," Joe said. "But we should ask Mrs. Kelly before we make the decision. Is she still here or has she gone home already?"

Even though the Kellys lived in the cottage at the rear of their property, the Parkers made a habit of not disturbing them once Moira finished cleaning the kitchen after dinner.

"Let's go check," Sophie said.

Moira listened carefully while her employers laid out the idea of keeping the children for the duration. Joe, as usual, was methodical and Sophie, as usual, was passionate. But they didn't need to persuade her. She and Thomas hadn't been blessed with children of their own. Helping to raise Sam had been one of the great joys of her life, and until he or Jean-Luc settled down and started families there wouldn't be any surrogate grandchildren to cuddle and spoil. The O'Brien children needed a home. They already had a place in her heart.

"It's best for everyone if they stay here, isn't it? We've already settled into a routine. If you can get Teddy and Katie to and from school, we can take turns looking after Cora during the day."

After they bid her good night and turned to leave the kitchen, Moira saw Sophie wrap her arm around Joe's waist and Joe press a kiss to his wife's temple. She was fairly certain the children already had a place in the Parker's hearts too.

The next day, Joe sat down to write the kind of letter he'd written too many of during the last war. He hoped he would never have to write another one like it.

Sydney
22 February 1942

Dear Pte O'Brien,
It is my sad duty to inform you that your wife, Cather-
ine O'Brien, died after giving birth last month. Your
son survived long enough to be baptized. I took the liber-
ty of asking the priest to baptize him using your name.

> *Mother and child are buried together at the Catholic
> cemetery.*

Joe paused, wondering how much detail he should include, and finally deciding to give a pared down version of the facts. There would be time enough when Patrick came home to tell him his daughters had been present for their mother's death.

> *The Sydney police were alerted to your wife's demise
> because your son Teddy injured himself breaking a
> window and stealing food for his mother and sisters.
> My wife found him hiding in St. Mary's cathedral. He
> supplied his home address, which is how we found your
> wife's body and your surviving children.*

> *The department has exhausted all avenues of state care
> for your children. Since there was nothing acceptable,
> my wife and I are caring for them in our home. They
> are healthy and well. Teddy and Katie are in school
> at St. Mary's parish school. Cora spends her days with
> my wife and our housekeeper. Our housekeeper and her
> husband are Catholic and the children attend Mass
> with them weekly.*

He paused again, comparing the life the children were now living compared to the rotten flat they'd been living in. Still, nothing would ever make up for the loss of their mother. He knew too well how much extra care Sam had needed after Annie's death. Thank God for his mother and Mrs. Kelly then and Sophie and Mrs. Kelly now.

> *My wife and I are fully prepared to look after the
> children until you are safely back home in Australia.*

*Please accept my sincere condolences, and let me know
if there is anything you need to alleviate the suffering
you must be feeling from your loss, as well as the deprivations prisoners must be experiencing.*

He handed the letter to Miss Pringle when he finished.

"Would you type this on department letterhead with my full
name and titles and figure out where to send letters to prisoners?"

She read through it quickly. "You covered everything very nicely
indeed."

Joe scrubbed a hand through his hair. "I wrote too many letters
to relatives during the last war. I need a break. I'm going to get some
lunch. Can I bring you anything?"

"No thank you." Miss Pringle lifted a neatly wrapped sandwich
from the voluminous bag she carried every day. "I'll have this letter
ready when you return."

He left the office to the slow clatter of her hunt and peck typing.

When he returned, he signed the letter and Miss Pringle gave him
a nod of approval after she blotted the ink. "Am I correct in guessing
that you and Mrs. Parker bought a headstone for mother and babe?"

"Sophie didn't want Teddy and Katie to see their mother and
baby buried in an unmarked grave. And now we have to tell them
their father has been wounded and is in a German prison camp. I'm
not looking forward to that."

—

*Sydney
23 February 1942*

*Dear Sam,
Your parents have taken in three children! Teddy,
Katie, and Cora. Their mother died and their father*

*was fighting in Crete and has been taken prisoner.
Cora is three, Katie is five, and Teddy is nine. Katie is
very quiet, Cora loves to play with Howard, and Teddy
reminds me of my brother because he is always getting
into things he should not.*

*Please let us know if you are safe and well. Your parents
are worried about you,
Marianne
P.S. Sophie and I have not read your name in the casualties lists, so presumably you are still alive.*

*Somewhere in the ACT
28 February 1942*

*Dear Marianne,
Apologies for the delays in responding to your letters.
All is well but very busy here. New cadets to train,
new manoeuvres to learn, etc., etc. No need to check the
casualties lists! I'll do better.*

*Poor kids. Sophie adopted Jean-Luc and Dad has a soft
spot for lost kiddies, so I can't say I'm surprised they've
acquired three new ones. How is everyone coping with
the houseful?*

*Sew straight,
Sam*

FORTY-ONE

THE GOOD, THE BAD, AND THE HOPEFUL

MARCH 1942

In early March, Joe tossed the newspaper onto the dining table. "Bloody—"

"Language, darling. The children are within earshot." Sophie picked up the paper and scanned the front-page headlines. 'Japanese occupy Lae and Salamana.' 'Battle of Sunda Straits, HMAS *Perth* and USS *Houston* sunk, no word on survivors.' "What is it this time?"

"The government is going to shut down the nightclubs. Which is asinine, because drinking won't stop. It will just continue at all the sly grog places that will pop up."

"Which will make it harder for the police to keep up with."

"Exactly." Thoroughly annoyed, Joe downed the last of his coffee and rose from the table. "I need to take the kids to school and get to the office. This day can't end soon enough."

—

Somewhere in the ACT
10 March 1942

Dear Dad and Sophie,
*Sorry to have been incommunicado. Marianne has
scolded me thoroughly. I'm safe and well, just incredibly busy with new cadets as I'm sure you are with the
new additions to the household. Have you had any news
from Jean-Luc?*

Love to all,
Sam

Sydney
20 March 1942

Dear Sam,
*Jean-Luc's battalion arrived in Adelaide a few days
ago and he will have some leave before they're sent
to wherever they're going next. He says the officers are
housed in private homes and the troops are billeted
in tents at the cricket grounds. Apparently, the local
Cheer Up Society is providing refreshments and feminine company. Needless to say, we're waiting with bat-
ed breath to hear if and when he can get home for a
visit. We would be thrilled to see you too, as always.*

Much love,
Sophie

FORTY-TWO

GOOD FRIDAY

3 APRIL 1942

At the ripe old age of nine and a half years, Teddy O'Brien believed he had far more important things to do—like staying on the lookout for the enemy—than going to school.

But no matter how much he protested, every morning Joe dropped him and Katie off at St. Mary's school. Every afternoon Sophie picked them up and asked what they had learned that day.

Thomas had caught Teddy slacking off more than once, usually up a tree or on top of the chicken coop, while the homework he was supposed to be doing languished on the dining room table.

"Teddy's not much for the books," Thomas had reported to the Parkers. "He's convinced he'll spot enemy planes and ships. And if he's not doing that, he's dragging that little wagon up and down the street collecting bits of paper and metal. He wants to win some competition at school."

Joe knew something about raising a boy who was high-spirited. Sam had required a lot of attention and activity to get him to hunker down and hit the books. Jean-Luc had been easier. He required far less physical activity and was more studious. Joe was willing to put in whatever effort was required. It was just that Teddy was cut from different cloth than the two boys he'd already raised.

He motioned for Thomas to follow and they went to ask Sophie if she had any ideas.

Sophie looked weary. She'd spent most of the week with her nose buried in ledgers and in meetings with their accountant. The sheep stations she'd invested in before they married were extremely profitable, providing wool to His Majesty's armies for uniforms. And they would continue to be, as long as there was a war on. What she wanted now was to figure out how to keep the stations running during times of drought since wool was a huge part of the Australian economy. She often wished her father, who had been a civil engineer, was still alive to advise her about drilling bores and diverting creeks.

"I don't know what to tell you," she said when Joe and Thomas rapped on the door to her study and posed the problem. "We need to figure out how to keep him on track. He gets distracted so easily."

"Agreed," Joe said.

"Let's revisit the subject after we get through the holiday festivities," Sophie suggested. "The kids are so excited that I think we'll be working a miracle just to keep them contained for the next two days."

Thomas nodded. He ended up spending the most time with Teddy, and Joe and Sophie always included him in discussions about the O'Brien children. "I'll say good night, then, missus. Inspector." He ducked his head and took his leave.

"I brought home a briefcase full of files," Joe said. "I didn't want to be driving home at midnight yet again. Are you going up anytime soon?"

Sophie shook her head. "I have another hour or two before I'm finished with the accounts."

FORTY-THREE

TWO INTRUDERS

4 APRIL 1942

Teddy also thought he was far too grown-up to believe in the Easter Bunny that Miss Sophie and Mrs. Kelly kept talking about. He pretended to believe, but only because Katie and Cora believed and because the adults had asked him not to spoil it for his sisters. If he had had even the tiniest hope that a magical Easter Bunny who granted wishes was real, it had vanished after listening in on the conversation between Thomas and the Parkers last night.

Teddy had learned that he could position himself just out of sight at the very top of the stairs and hear almost every word spoken in the dining and drawing rooms. He'd convinced himself he had to listen in because, as nice as it was living in this big house with the Parkers and the Kellys looking after him and Katie and Cora, they weren't family. The adults could decide at any moment that the children needed to be sent to the home for orphans. He could be sent somewhere where he had to work on a farm or a cattle station, or a coal mine, even. Teddy didn't like being in small, dark, deep places. And he certainly didn't want his little sisters to be sent someplace where they'd be put to work in the fields.

So, on Easter Eve, he'd gone upstairs to the bedroom everyone had begun to call his, changed into his pajamas, and stared out the window instead of getting into bed. If the Parkers didn't have to worry about him then they would be happier about keeping Katie and Cora. They were too little to be sent away. He was a burden, never doing what they wanted him to do, but the little girls were young enough to learn exactly what adults expected of them.

He'd wait until after Easter to enact his plan to run away. Katie and Cora were so excited about the Easter Bunny and hunting for eggs that he couldn't bear the thought of spoiling their enjoyment. He'd pack his clothes into a bundle tomorrow night, wait until everyone was asleep, tired from the day's festivities, and he'd be on his way. He'd saved a few pennies, found a few more, and he knew where Mrs. Kelly kept the housekeeping money. She would be angry when she discovered that he'd taken a pound, but Teddy hoped everyone would understand it was for the best that he was gone.

Satisfied he had a plan, Teddy climbed into bed and fell asleep.

—

Teddy's eyes flew open. Someone was downstairs. For a moment he believed there might really be an Easter Bunny after all.

He froze in his bed, wondering why the Parkers weren't racing downstairs to catch the intruder. Then he remembered how tired they'd sounded earlier, and how much work they said they still had to do before they went to bed. But why wasn't Howard barking? Dogs were supposed to guard for things like this weren't they?

If the adults weren't going to protect the household, he was going to have to do it himself. He slipped out of bed and down the hallway to his listening position at the top of the stairs. Something was rustling in the drawing room.

Teddy's heart was pounding so hard he could barely swallow. A long shadow appeared in the entry hall. The shadow swung something from its shoulder and a bag clunked on the tiled floor. Then, just when he thought he couldn't be more frightened, Teddy saw a second shadow and two figures moved across the entry hall and into the dining room. The barest hint of light came on downstairs. The intruders were in the kitchen.

He scrambled back to his bedroom, panting and shaking. Maybe the Parkers would keep him here if he could prove he could protect their home. He lifted the cricket bat that had belonged to one of the Parker's sons and crept down the stairs.

He could hear two men talking and laughing in the kitchen. Teddy crossed himself for courage, took a huge breath, and pushed the kitchen door open. He lifted the bat, ready to swing if the men tried to attack him.

He meant to shout "Who are you? What are you doing here?" at the top of his lungs. That would awaken Joe and Sophie who would come racing down the stairs and take over. Then they would realize that he had an important role in the household, and they might not send him away after all.

What happened was not at all like Teddy imagined.

Nothing came out when he opened his mouth to shout. Instead of two burglars in black caps and dark clothes, Teddy stared at two young men in uniform. One was tall and fair in an RAAF uniform. The other was shorter and dark in an AIF uniform.

The men stood at the kitchen table with the platter of roast mutton and a bowl of potato salad left over from dinner. The taller one had two bottles of beer in one hand and the bottle opener in the other. The shorter one had a carving knife and was cutting thick slices of meat. Howard had been shushed with a bone, which he gnawed on under the table.

The tall one carefully placed the bottles and the opener on the table and raised his hands in a gesture of surrender. The shorter one put the knife down and put his hands up too.

Good. They would not fight him. Teddy's courage returned along with his voice.

"Who are you? What are you doing here? Why're you eating our food?"

The tall one choked back what sounded like a laugh. Teddy glowered at him and clenched the cricket bat tighter. "I said..."

The shorter one gave the tall one a look and spoke. "Please put the bat down. I'm Jean-Luc and this bloke is Sam. We live here. Well, our parents live here."

"Where've you been?" Teddy did his best to sound grown up and stern. "I've never seen you here before. Why were you sneaking around?"

The one who said his name was Jean-Luc spoke again. "We were going to surprise our folks earlier, but..." Jean-Luc shrugged and cocked his head at Teddy.

"Don't believe you," Teddy said.

"Crikey," the one called Sam said. "You must be Teddy. I've heard about you. There are photos of us all over this house. Haven't you seen the ones on the mantelpiece?"

"I'm not tall enough to see up there."

"Listen, nipper," Sam said, "we're telling the truth. Go upstairs and wake my father and tell him we're here."

Teddy shook his head. "You'll run away."

Sam rubbed his eyes and Teddy thought he looked just like Joe when he rubbed his eyes after he'd been reading too long. "All right. Here's more proof. That cricket bat you're holding has the initials SLP carved in the handle, doesn't it? SLP is for Samuel Lawrence Parker. That's me. Joe Parker is my father. Sophie is his wife and my stepmother."

Teddy turned to Jean-Luc. "Now you say something."

Jean-Luc thought for a moment. "Sophie adopted me when I was twelve. Mrs. Kelly is their cook and housekeeper. Her husband Thomas takes care of the gardens and fixes things that need fixing."

All of this sounded believable from what Teddy knew about the family. The cricket bat did have SLP carved in the handle. Jean-Luc knew about Thomas fixing things.

But he couldn't take any chances.

"Come with me," he commanded the two young men, trying to sound as grown-up as possible. "Keep your hands up and don't try anything funny."

Teddy marched them to the foot of the stairs and prodded Sam in the back with the cricket bat. "If they're really your parents, tell them to come downstairs."

FORTY-FOUR

EASTER SUNDAY

5 APRIL 1942, MORNING

Despite the entire household being awakened by Sam and Jean-Luc shouting from the bottom of the staircase in the middle of the night, Easter Sunday morning was an unqualified success.

The greatest gift of all, according to Joe and Sophie, was Sam and Jean-Luc's presence. Neither of them could quite believe their boys had made it through two years of war in one piece. Sam hadn't crashed his plane or been killed in a training accident. Jean-Luc hadn't been injured, or worse, in Lebanon and Syria. Joe clapped both young men on the shoulder multiple times. Sophie hugged them every chance she could.

The greatest gifts of all, according to five-year-old Katie and three-year-old Cora, were those that the Easter Bunny left for them. Katie had asked for her own set of garden tools so she could help Thomas in the flower beds. Cora had asked for a real pony, which she did not get. Instead, she received a toy horse and a promise that she could sit on Angel's back, with an adult's help. But there would be no galloping.

The greatest gift of all, according to Teddy, despite how pleased he was to receive a pair of his own binoculars, was Joe taking him aside before they all went to bed and asking what he thought he was doing by attempting to investigate intruders in the house all by himself. Teddy finally managed to mumble out the truth, that he wanted to prove his worth to the household so he wouldn't be sent away.

Joe stared at him incredulously. "Why on earth did you think we were going to send you away?"

Teddy focused on his toes as if they were the most interesting thing in the world.

"Teddy?" Joe's voice was quiet, not angry, and Teddy decided to risk telling the truth.

"I heard you and Miss Sophie talking. She said you were going to send me to boarding school because I'm not good at the church school." Teddy stole a glance at Joe.

"You were listening to our conversation?"

Teddy nodded. No matter how hard he tried, he couldn't stop his eyes filling with tears. "Please don't make me go to boarding school. I want to stay here with you and Katie and Cora and Miss Sophie. I'll try harder at school. I promise I will. Please."

Joe scrubbed a hand over his chin, trying to figure out when Teddy would have heard such a thing. It must've been that conversation Sophie and he had a couple of nights ago. They'd been sitting in the dining room, finishing a late supper. Sophie rose from the table, and he followed her into the kitchen. Before she opened the kitchen door, Sophie said "Boarding school..." When the door closed behind them, she finished her thought, "...would be a terrible choice for Teddy. He'd be miserable."

Joe shook his head. "No, you've got the wrong end of the stick. Miss Sophie does not want to send you away to boarding school." Teddy's eyes had brightened and he sniffed. Poor lad. "And I don't want you to go either. We'll work something out with school. But right now, it's time we were all in our beds."

Sophie had come into the hall after getting Katie and Cora back to sleep. "I'm putting the boys in Teddy's room. Teddy, do you mind giving up the bed for one night? I made up the cot in Katie and Cora's room for you. We'll get all the beds sorted out properly tomor—"

She stopped short at the sight of Teddy flinging his arms around Joe's waist and giving him a swift, tight hug. Then Teddy hugged her too before he disappeared into the bedroom where his sisters were already asleep.

—

Sophie swept her gaze around the dining room table, still cluttered with breakfast dishes, and smiled contentedly. The adults were lingering over second cups of coffee and tea. The little girls and Teddy were sprawled in the drawing room reading and playing. Easter lunch with Sophie's mother and Aunt Flora was still hours away and the family had a few minutes to chat before getting dressed and going to Mass.

"How long have we got you for? Where are the air force and the army sending you now? And why the moustache?"

She nearly burst out laughing as Jean-Luc stroked the moustache he'd grown while in Lebanon. "Let me just say it was useful as a means of blending in when I wore local garb and listened to conversations in French the Australians were not privy to."

With his dark curls and suntanned skin, he could very easily have passed for a local. "You were a spy?"

The young man shrugged a very Gallic shrug. "Just...a listener. As for what's next, I have to report to Ingleburn next Monday. After that, I suspect we will move to Queensland at the end of the month."

"Oh God." Sophie pitched her voice very low so the children in the drawing room wouldn't be able to overhear. "You'll be defending the coast."

"Perhaps. I can't say more than that because I don't know."

"Please tell me you aren't going there too," Sophie said to Sam.

"No worries, Sophie." Sam winked at her. "I'm too smart for that. My squadron is moving to Canberra." Sam leaned back in his chair, ran a hand through his untidy fair hair, and blew out a breath. "I have to get back by noon tomorrow. Since the Japanese bombed Pearl Harbor and America declared war, the betting lines are that Japan will turn its sights on Australia. Almost all Australian pilots are being sent back home from Europe and Africa, but we're still short of 'em. We'll need all the pilots we can get as fast as we can train them."

When the doorbell rang, it was Teddy who jumped up and ran to the entrance of the dining room.

"I'll get it," he said. Sophie looked at Joe, who returned her look with one of pure innocence.

He lifted his hands, palms out. "I've no idea who it is, love. I'm not expecting anyone."

She gave him a look that said she wasn't quite certain she believed him. He'd promised he had the day off, but just because it was Easter didn't mean Sydney's criminals knew about his promise.

She heard, "*Bon jour*, Teddy!" coming from the entrance hall, and her fears evaporated. Marianne was due to arrive a little later than this, but she was practically family by this point, so Sophie didn't think Joe would be horribly embarrassed to greet her while clad in his pajamas and dressing gown.

"Let Teddy have a moment," Sophie whispered to the men in her dining room. The boy had a terrific crush on Marianne, and Sophie knew he was a little envious of all the attention she gave his sisters.

"Marianne, Marianne!" Katie and Cora tumbled into the entry hall at full steam. The little girls adored the young French woman who told them tales of crossing the big, wide oceans and coming to live in Australia.

"*Joyeuses Pâques, les enfants!* Happy Easter children!" she greeted them in her charming way, mixing English and French. "*Tu vas bien?* You are well? *Où est Madame Sophie et Monsieur Joe?*"

"They're in the dining room," Teddy said.

"Good," Marianne said. "Because I have some little gifts for you. You can open them while I say hello to the adults."

The men took that as their cue to rise from the table, but Sam leapt up first. "Give me a minute."

He met Marianne as she turned away from the children.

Sophie couldn't see Sam's face, only Marianne's. Sam's head tilted sideways, a movement that was remarkably like something Joe would do. But Sam said nothing.

Marianne stared at Sam, and then blinked, and then flung her arms around Sam's neck.

In a matter of less than a second, Sam reached around Marianne's waist. From what Sophie could tell, he enthusiastically returned Marianne's hug and offered her one of his own.

Sophie's head swiveled to Joe. "Did you know about this?" she mouthed.

Joe was watching the tableau in the entry hall open-mouthed. Clearly, he hadn't known. She turned to Jean-Luc, who was biting his bottom lip and trying not to grin.

"You knew?" Sophie mouthed to Jean-Luc.

Jean-Luc waggled his head. "They've always been crazy about each other," he whispered. "They just don't know it yet."

"Always?"

Jean-Luc nodded. "Yes. Always. You really didn't know?"

"How would we know?" Sophie silently demanded, and yet, as the two young people continued their embrace, chaste though it was, the attraction between them was palpable.

Then, to the continued amazement of the assembled adults and children, Marianne pulled back from Sam's arms, set her shoulders, and frowned at him.

"How could you not tell me you were coming home? You don't send me a letter to say you would be here. *Pourquoi pas?*"

Sam shoved his hands in his pockets and his fair head hung down. Sophie knew that stance from his early teenaged years. Sam had always had the good grace, and good sense, to admit when he was wrong.

"Sorry," Sam mumbled. "I just wanted to surprise you, that's all. I was picked to help pilot a plane from Adelaide to our new digs. I got a hold of Luc and we wrangled him onto the same flight. Then we hitched a ride up to Sydney. We didn't know when we would arrive." He stood straighter, meeting her eye, and removing his hands from his pockets. "Does this mean you're not happy to see me?"

"Happy? We talk about this later," Marianne said. Her command of English tended to slip a little when she was upset or excited. "Now I am going to greet your parents and your brother with much better manners than yours!"

Her voice was stern, but she slipped her hands into Sam's and pressed three gentle kisses to his cheeks, the French greeting that is reserved for only the very dearest of family and friends.

Then she cleared her throat and faced their onlookers. "Happy Easter, everyone! Good morning!"

Sophie rose and rushed over to the young woman. Marianne was blushing furiously, a lovely pink flush spreading over her cheeks. Sophie kissed her cheeks three times, partly because she adored Marianne and partly to reassure her that a romantic relationship with Sam met with her approval. She would tell Marianne later, in private, that if she didn't pursue a relationship that was all right with her too.

Joe had risen from the table also, clearing his throat self-consciously. "Sorry for our, erm, less than formal attire," he said, tightening the sash of his dressing gown. He normally didn't kiss anyone's cheek except Sophie's but he knew exactly what was needed, because he kissed Marianne three times too.

Jean-Luc was the last to greet her. He was grinning like a lunatic when they exchanged kisses. "You are just as bad," she accused, swatting him on the arm. "You don't write either."

"To be fair, I was on a troop ship for six weeks and marooned in Adelaide for another three," Jean-Luc replied.

Marianne glowered at him for a moment. Then she turned to Sam, who had his hands back in his pockets and was nonchalantly lifting himself up and down on the balls of his feet. "If you don't write to me, how am I supposed to tell you when I meet someone better to write to?"

Sam gaped like a fish. Jean-Luc burst out laughing. "You deserved that mate," he told Sam. "And you, *mademoiselle*, you should know that this idiot talked of nothing but you and your parachutes, without stopping, from the time I got on his plane in Adelaide. I think you should forgive him a little."

"All right. I forgive you a little," Marianne said to Sam. "But we must talk about this."

Since the morning's schedule was a little rushed with the addition of Sam and Marianne's drama, Marianne helped Katie and Cora into their new dresses while Sophie and Joe dressed. He finished first, and went across the hall to see if Teddy needed help with his tie. Sophie had insisted they were all going to attend the 11 o'clock Mass at St. Mary's. Normally Moira and Thomas took the children to Mass with them on Sunday mornings, but Sophie thought it was important that Monsignor Sullivan and Father O'Donnell see for themselves that she and Joe, who were not Catholic, were committed to raising the O'Brien children in their parent's faith for as long as the children were in their care.

It seemed Teddy didn't need his help this morning. The youngster had Sam and Jean-Luc standing behind him at the mirror over the dresser. The young men had found a box for Teddy to stand on and they were teaching him by example.

Teddy had his lower lip tucked into his teeth as he concentrated on doing the same thing Sam and Jean-Luc were doing. "That's right, around twice and then the rabbit goes down..." Sam said, repeating the same mnemonic Joe had used to teach him and that he had learned from his father.

Joe wondered who had taught Jean-Luc. He'd never thought about it before. Jean-Luc's father had been killed in the Great War when Jean-Luc was only a toddler. Perhaps it had been Natalie, his mother.

Jean-Luc helped Teddy into his jacket, another item of new clothing Sophie had insisted on. She worried that when the children's father came home he might be resentful that his offspring had lived as well as they were living now. Joe just hoped the man would come home intact and undamaged.

Then he looked at his own sons, Sam in RAAF blue and Jean-Luc in AIF khaki, and prayed they would come home safely too.

—

Sophie glanced down the pew as Monsignor Sullivan gave the final blessing.

Jean-Luc and Sam sat on either side of her, with Marianne beside Sam. Were Marianne's fingers close enough to entwine with Sam's? Perhaps it was only wishful thinking. Regardless, she was overjoyed both boys were home, and she took Sam's hand and Jean-Luc's hand and squeezed.

Katie, wedged between Moira and Thomas, had been attentive during the high Easter Mass. She would make her first Communion after her sixth birthday, and she took Mass very seriously. She and Moira had exchanged a few whispers during the service.

Teddy fidgeted next to Jean-Luc with Joe on his other side and Cora beyond that. Only half of their group was Catholic but Sophie didn't think God would care too much, if He even had time to check off who was and wasn't Catholic in the crowded cathedral. Besides, enough people knew the circumstances surrounding the children's situation, as well as her work to bring food to the church's hungry, that the Protestant-Catholic divide had been bridged, at least a little. Plus, it was interesting to upend expectations by taking up an entire pew with their gaggle of mixed faith family.

At some point during the sermon, Cora started yawning, crawled onto Joe's lap, and dozed off. Monsignor Sullivan blessed the congregation, who rose and sang the final hymn while he and half a dozen altar boys and several priests processed out of the cathedral. Cora slept through Joe lifting her and maneuvering out of the pew. Sophie glanced at the little girl's head lolling on her husband's shoulder, and she smiled at Joe when he met her fond gaze.

FORTY-FIVE

SACRIFICE

5 APRIL 1942, AFTERNOON

As she and Sam exited the church, Marianne steered them to the edge of the broad plaza in front of the cathedral and motioned to Hyde Park across the street.

"Could we take a stroll before we return to your parent's house?"

A lull in traffic gave them enough time to dash across College Street. Sam grabbed her hand as they ran, but let go once they crossed.

They sidestepped a throng of American sailors and Australian girls having their pictures taken by a stand-up photographer and headed for the meager shade of young Moreton Bay fig trees lining the broad paths through the park.

While they walked, Marianne wondered how to broach the subject that had been bothering her for weeks, but Sam spoke first.

"Sorry I haven't written," he said. "There hasn't been much to say."

"What about the crash back in January? That's news, Sam! You could have died or been burned alive. Or..."

Sam seemed to have no reason he could, or would, articulate beyond "Neither of those things happened, so there's no need to worry about them." He kept walking, his gaze caught by the Anzac Memorial dedicated to those who had lost their lives in the Great War at the far end of the park. "Have you ever been in there?"

"I came with Sophie a few weeks after we arrived in Sydney from France," Marianne said. "Why do you ask?"

"My father and Sophie brought me and Jean-Luc to the dedication. We all stood in the Hall of Silence and stared up at the statue. You know the one?"

Yes, she knew the statue Sam mentioned. It was called Sacrifice. Cast in bronze and fifteen feet tall, three women, one holding a baby, held a shield above their heads upon which their dead husband, son, brother lay. Sophie's eyes had filled with tears which didn't abate as they gazed at it from below or when they mounted the stairs to view it from above.

Marianne had seen her mother Hélène tear up when they visited the Canadian national memorial at Vimy with its towering, grief-stricken Mother of Canada statue. But as heartbreaking as that memorial had been, to Marianne it paled beside the lean, nude man held aloft on his shield with his lifeless arms supported by his sword. The plaque describing the statue had mentioned Spartan women carrying their dead men, but it reminded Marianne more of a crucified Christ.

The thought of being one of those women terrified her.

"Someone I trained and was responsible for died. It's bad enough that it happened and I couldn't do anything except watch it happen." Sam wrenched off his forage cap and twisted it in his hands as if he was witnessing anguished screams and twisted metal all over again and couldn't turn away. "Did I fail him somehow? What could I have done better? He had a wife and a baby. That statue was all I could think about when I wrote to her. I couldn't write about it again."

Marianne studied Sam's face as he stared at the memorial. Dark smudges under his eyes and a new crease between his brows took her aback. This wasn't the seemingly carefree young man he'd been when they first met eighteen months ago. The man in front of her was careworn and subdued. "Could you write about anything but flying? Like what color the sky is when you wake up in the morning. Or what you're reading. Anything. Please. I can't get letters from my parents or my brother. I have no idea how they're coping. I have no idea if Chris is still alive. I can't help them, but perhaps I could help you."

Sam fitted his cap back over his fair hair, automatically placing it the regulation angle, and cocked his head toward College Street. "I'll try to do better. C'mon. Let's get back to my parents' house, have lunch with the family, and head to Bondi afterwards. I need some surf after being stuck inland for months."

"You're not going to see Isobel while you are home?"

"Isobel?" Sam seemed to not recognize the name for a moment. "We haven't spoken in over a year."

Marianne was only a fair swimmer, not as good as Jean-Luc, who had agreed to join their trek to the beach, and not nearly as strong as Sam who had grown up swimming at all the beaches around Sydney. When she tired of fighting the waves, she trudged out of the water, made her way to the gate through the maze of concrete pilings and wire designed to keep Japanese from coming ashore, and sat on the blanket they'd spread on the sand. Jean-Luc followed not long after.

Sam's fair head bobbed in the waves for another ten or fifteen minutes before he emerged from the sea. The eyes of every woman on the beach followed him—sleek, tanned, fit—striding from the shallows across the sand.

A group of merrymakers hailed Sam. The men shook Sam's hand when he walked over to greet them. The young women bounced up and hugged him.

"*Comment il reste ami avec toutes ses anciennes petites amies est un mystère*," Jean-Luc said.

It had been a long time since anyone had spoken to her in French, but Marianne automatically made the switch from English. She peered more closely at the group over the top of her sunglasses. "All three of them were his girlfriends? Whatever happened to Isobel? She seemed completely smitten with Sam last year."

"He hasn't mentioned anyone named Isobel. None of those three were serious, though. He isn't interested in women who only want to find a husband." Jean-Luc shook his head. "The women who intrigue him are much more independent than that. He is very particular."

His gaze still on Sam, now lounging on the sand with his friends, Jean-Luc said, "He is a good man, and I love him like a true brother. I hope he can find who he truly wants."

Marianne struggled to reconcile what he'd just revealed about Sam with her own deductions about Sam's character. He was protective of his father and Sophie. His usual outward appearance was friendly and carefree, but after their conversation about his father being afraid he'd have a flying accident, and his obvious anguish when he'd spoken of the letter he had written to the dead cadet's wife, that could be a façade masking some deeper fears and insecurities. Sam was obviously haunted by the incident. What else had he revealed by fixating on the Sacrifice statue at the Anzac memorial in Hyde Park?

Those questions warranted further thought when she had time to puzzle through them, so she turned her attention back to Jean-Luc. "*Et toi*? Do you live up to the reputation of the romantic Frenchman? How is your girlfriend Violet?"

Jean-Luc huffed a rueful breath. "I'm afraid not. Violet is engaged to a widowed sultana farmer who she met while she was working on his farm with the Women's Land Army."

"*Désolé.*"

"No need to be sorry. We were not serious. She wants to stay in Australia forever and I want to see the rest of the world. I'm happy for her. And you? Was there some gallant French farmer you left behind when you traveled here?"

Marianne shuddered. "No farmers, please! I cannot abide rural life. That's one of the reasons I took a job with a dressmaker in

Amiens the day after I left school. It was lucky that I have a talent for fine needlework and an eye for what works on different figures. I want to have my own shop."

She grasped a handful of sand and let it trickle though her fingers. "That was before. Now I am still here and I have no idea when I can go home. My plans have been taken away by this war."

Jean-Luc seemed sympathetic, but she didn't want to dwell on what she couldn't do, so she asked, "What will you do when the war is over? Go back to the winery?"

"I want to keep making wine," he said. "But I don't know where yet. I would like to go back to Lebanon." He stared out to sea for a few moments. "Such a beautiful country. You cannot imagine. Centuries-old vineyards and orchards. Roman and Phoenician ruins that go back thousands of years. And Beirut is such a crossroads of people and cultures. If you close your eyes, you can practically feel the history of the place seeping into your bones."

"For someone who claims not to be, that was quite a romantic declaration! But you would leave Australia? I had the impression you adopted this place as yours."

"I have. Had. I don't know how to explain it. I traveled a bit before I settled on making wine instead of botany. French Polynesia, Noumea, Indochine. Then the west coast of America after I chose wine. I've only been to Lebanon for war, but it felt like home to me."

She understood. It was the same feeling she'd had standing on the Parker's balcony and drinking in the immense vistas of land, sea, and sky, as if she had always been meant to be in Australia and not the battle-scarred Somme valley of her birth. "Does Sam know how you feel? Or Joe and Sophie?"

Jean-Luc turned to her. "*Non*. I haven't said a word to anyone except you. Please don't tell them. I'm not certain I can go back there, and with the war...none of us know what will happen."

Her eyes on Sam, who was making his way back to them from the knot of friends he had been chatting with, Marianne nodded. "I will keep your secret."

"And I will keep yours," Jean-Luc said.

"What do you mean? I don't have any secrets."

Sam was still several steps away when Jean-Luc said, "Ah, but I think you do. I think you are wondering what it would be like to remain here because of our mutual friend."

Her jaw dropped. She turned to Jean-Luc and managed to pull it up enough to sputter, "*Je ne... Je ne suis pas—*"

Sam crouched on the blanket between her and Jean-Luc. "You aren't what? Enjoying your sunbake? Did the wire catch your skin? The beach patrol has a first aid—"

Oh, mon Dieu. How had Sam reached them without her noticing? And how much had he understood what he'd overheard? "*Ri... rien,*" she stuttered. It wasn't helping that his glance was flicking over her body, even if he did seem to be looking for telltale scratches rather than appraising her figure. Her bathing costume was modest, but it couldn't hide the generous bosom she had inherited from her mother and the long legs she'd inherited from her father.

Scrambling to distract him, she jammed the wide-brimmed sun hat Sophie had lent her over her windblown hair. "Nothing. We were just—"

Mercifully, Jean-Luc jumped in. "We were just talking about what it's like to live in another country." He lifted his chin toward the group across the beach. "How are the ladies?"

"The same as ever," Sam said. "Only now they've all paired off and are flashing their engagement rings." He shifted and lay on his back, closing his eyes, like a large cat drowsing in a sunny patch. "Back to the more interesting subject. I like visiting, but I never thought about actually living in another country. I suppose it would depend on where. And who I was with."

Jean-Luc eyed his brother, a thoughtful expression crossing his features. "I think I'll take one last dip before we leave," he said, and pushed up from the blanket.

Left alone with Sam, Marianne watched the surf for a few moments before she dared to glance at her companion. He seemed to be asleep, limbs loose, lashes resting on his cheeks. Waves had pushed them together in the water, but she had never lain so close to a man, and certainly not one clad in only swimming trunks. His closeness set her skin humming. Several grains of sand caught in golden stubble on his jaw called to her to brush them away, to touch him, if only for a second.

She reached, but her wrist was trapped, vise-like. Sam loomed over her. Alert. Wary. Muscles coiled, ready to pounce.

"I didn't mean to startle you," she gasped.

He released her wrist. "Reflexes," he huffed as he fell back to the blanket. "They trained us to be vigilant, even when we're sleeping. Good to know it worked."

"You have some..." She gestured to her own jaw.

When Sam made no move to brush the sand away, she reached again, willing the tremor in her hand to still so her fingers on his skin would be as light as a feather.

Sam's eyelids fluttered at her touch. "I'm sorry."

"Whatever for?"

"For my behavior earlier. For not replying to your letters. I've been unforgivably selfish. I can only imagine what you're going through, not knowing what's happening with your family."

He finally looked at her, the intensity of his gaze lighting a spark between them that steadied and glowed until a shadow and a cleared throat signaled Jean-Luc's return from the surf.

Sam rose from the blanket, smoothed his tousled hair and brushed sand off his arms, his features transforming to the sunny, friendly grin she hadn't seen since before he'd gone off to war. "Am I presentable?"

She couldn't help but grin back, shaking her head at his cheekiness, but grateful for the glimpse of him unburdened, before wartime responsibilities weighed him down.

Afterwards, they repeated the bumpy tram trip in reverse, sunburnt and sandy. When the tram came to a stop, the jolt pressed Sam's body to hers and in a moment of clarity she was certain, even if nothing ever happened between them, that she would always need to know he was alive and not borne on a shield by the women who loved him.

Forty-Six

Chez Marianne

5 April 1942, Evening

Back at the Parker home, Marianne gathered up her belongings while Sam said his good byes to his parents and Jean-Luc.

Sophie reluctantly released him from a hug. "Are you sure you can't spend the night? Head to Canberra at first light?"

Sam shook his head. "If I leave now, I can be back to base in time for a good night's sleep. Be raring to go in the morning. Besides, I'm going to take Marianne home on my way out of town." He lifted his chin in the direction of the three children who needed baths and stories before bed. "That way dad doesn't have to leave you alone with the young ruffians."

Marianne held on tightly for the entire ride to her flat on the back of Sam's motorbike, curving her body to his, wondering if this might be the last time she could. Sam navigated Sydney's streets, lit only by wan moonlight, more slowly than he had when they went to Mascot.

He helped her dismount and walked up the steps with her. "Would you like to come in? I could make you a cup of tea before you're on your way."

"Won't your flat mate mind?"

"Patricia wouldn't mind in the least. She would be thrilled to finally meet you, but she isn't here. She's at her parents' home until tomorrow."

"Righto," he said, stifling a mighty yawn. "Might help me stay awake on the road."

He was so close when she unlocked the door that she felt his breath on her neck. Flustered, she fumbled for the light switch. Her keys dropped beside the little bowl rather than in it.

"So, this is *chez* Marianne." Sam stood in the middle of the living room, turning to take it all in—the armchairs she had covered so they finally matched, an album full of newspaper clippings on the coffee table, maps of Europe and Australia on the walls, framed photographs of her family on the mantle.

"You favor your dad," Sam remarked, comparing a photo to her. "Is Marianne a French name?"

"In a way, yes. My parents named me after the symbol of the republic of France."

Sam moved to the maps, studded with pins where her brother might be in France and where he and Jean-Luc had been.

"I'm a good pilot," he said, pacing the room. "I do my best to teach the new cadets to be good pilots too. But sometimes things happen that are beyond our control. When that happens, we're all completely cut up about it, but we can't dwell on it. If we do, we'll never go up again. We have to keep going up. Too many people depend on us. Do you really need to hear about it from me?"

Marianne placed a hand on his forearm to still him, to calm the nervous energy humming beneath layers of dark blue wool and pale blue cotton. "I care how it affects you. I might not be flying or fighting, but people I care about are. People I love are. My brother Chris. His friend Nick. Jean-Luc. You. And more than anything I want all of you to come through it alive. I need to know you're still alive."

She broke off with a sob. So many members of her family had been killed during the last war that she could count her closest relatives on one hand. The Parkers had become her second family. Was it any wonder she had come to include Sam and Jean-Luc in her list of loved ones? Jean-Luc like another brother and Sam like no one she had ever imagined before.

"People you love?" Sam's eyes searched hers, but his thoughts were unreadable aside from a miniscule tightening of his features. He pulled a handkerchief from his pocket and handed it to her. Feeling wretched and embarrassed by her slip about love, she could only crumple it up after she dried her tears and wiped her nose.

"Keep it," he said. "I have another one."

She managed a hint of a smile. "You sound just like your father."

"I learnt it from him." His expression softened as he smoothed an errant strand from her cheek and tucked it behind her ear. She leaned into his touch, longing for more. "Always carry two, in case a beautiful woman needs one."

"But I'm not—" She was nothing like the stunning women who had bubbled around him at the beach.

"Yes, yes you are," Sam said, his eyes dropping from hers to her lips and back again, as if he was wondering whether his kiss would be welcome.

She was tall, but he was taller, so she stood on her toes and slipped her arms around his neck, pressing her lips to his so he would never have any doubts that his kisses would always be welcome.

Sam's hands spanned her waist, pulling her even nearer as they deepened their kiss, which led to another, and another, and another. The more their hands roamed, the more eagerly she responded. She had never made love before, but now, with her soft curves molding to his firm angles, their bodies so warm and close that she couldn't tell where she stopped and he began, she wanted to, more than anything.

But Sam took a step back, breaking contact. His arms fell to his sides. "Sorry," he mumbled through a heaving breath. "I shouldn't have done that."

"Yes, you should have." Need, desire, longing still thrummed in the space between them. "I want you to."

"I can't."

"Is there someone else?"

He shook his head. "No. There's no one else. But I can't risk... As much as I would like to, I can't be involved with anyone right now. I've seen how badly people are affected when... I won't be responsible for you wondering and worrying about me any more than you already do."

Didn't he understand she was perfectly capable of making decisions for herself? Or that they might never have another chance? "I am responsible for myself, Sam. I will wonder and worry about whomever I choose."

"Don't. Please. You have enough worry about your family as it is. Thanks for the offer of tea, but I should get on the road."

He opened the door and stepped out, but didn't look back before he drove away, no matter how fervently she willed him to. She stood in the doorway until the motorbike's rumble faded in the night.

—

Sam's mind was still reeling halfway to Canberra.

He forced himself to concentrate on the road when he left Marianne's flat. Sydney's streets were dark and the route to Canberra wasn't one he had traveled often.

The old girlfriends at the beach were all conventionally pretty, but nothing like Marianne with eyes the color of jade and hair that gleamed gold and copper in the sunlight. He had watched her pupils grow wide and dark and her lips part in that long moment before Jean-Luc came back to them.

None of them had ever looked at him like that.

He couldn't imagine asking any of them to look after his loved ones, or that they would write letters that were funny and teasing, full of family news, scolding when he neglected to let everyone know he was still safe.

The enormity of her worries had stared him in the face when he saw the pin-studded maps on her wall. He'd wanted to tell her everything would be fine, that everyone would come home safely, that she had nothing to worry about, but they both knew that wasn't true.

And then she kissed him like he'd never been kissed before, as if she was offering her heart and soul as well as her body. It had taken every ounce of his willpower to pull away when all he wanted was to make love with her until their shadows and terrors faded into oblivion

He longed to turn around, speed back to her, and give her all of himself, but he couldn't. Not when his future and the future of everyone she loved was so uncertain. Not now. Not yet.

FORTY-SEVEN

TOO CLOSE TO HOME

MAY 1942

S ophie was becoming quite proud of her proficiency at decoding letters from Sam and Jean-Luc.

Somewhere in QLD
1 May 1942

Dear Sophie and Joe,
We finally arrived in Queensland a couple of days ago,
and 7 Division was assigned to I Corps, First Army.
Because of the air raids that happened at Pearl Harbor
and Darwin, we've been involved in defensive duties
and training. I don't need to explain why, but I have
to admit we're a combination of worried that the worst
could happen and adamant that the worst could never
happen.

In any event, I've been told to be grateful we're here in
late autumn because apparently northern Queensland
is unbearably hot and humid in the summer. Sophie,

would you please send supplies? Edible and otherwise? The usual, please. Socks, foot powder, Vaseline, some of Mrs. Kelly's biscuits? I'll write again when I have more news.

Yours affectionately,
Jean-Luc

In light of the newspaper article she had just finished reading about the naval battle in the Coral Sea, she deduced Jean-Luc's division could be on the front lines and bear the brunt of Japanese displeasure at their losses in the Coral Sea if they turned their sights to New Guinea and Australia. While Prime Minister Curtin had announced Allied success in the week-long battle, he also said "Nobody at this moment can tell what the result of this engagement will be. If it should go advantageously, we shall have great cause for gratitude, and our position will be clearer. This battle will not decide the war, but it will determine the tactics which will be pursued by ourselves and the enemy."

Somewhere in Sydney
10 May 1942

Dear Jean-Luc,
We've all received so many letters beginning with "Somewhere in" that I decided to make a little joke of it and do the same. After all, if we can't find a tiny bit of levity here and there, we shall go mad.

I'm sure by now you've heard that the war came to Sydney in the form of three Japanese midget submarines. One of them shelled Bondi Beach, but the boom net caught it and the crew apparently killed themselves rather than be captured. I can't imagine ever thinking death is preferable to living.

The second submarine fired two torpedoes at an American ship in the harbor. The torpedoes missed the ship, but one of them hit and sank a ferry that was being used as a depot of some sort. Twenty-one sailors were killed. The other torpedo exploded on the eastern shore of Garden Island, but there were no Australian casualties. The third midget sub disappeared out to sea and no one knows where it got to.

Naturally people here are very shaken, and many locals are leaving the city for points further inland now that the war has finally come home to us. My mother and Aunt Flora have left Sydney for Flora's place in the Blue Mountains, but Joe and I are resolved to stay, as are the Kellys and Marianne. We keep the blackout curtains firmly in place at night and Thomas and the boys who tend the vegetable gardens reinforced the sides of our air raid trench. Since our house is at the highest point in the neighborhood, there's always someone on our balcony watching for planes. We try to limit conversations about the war when the children are within earshot, but Teddy insists on bringing it up every time he sees a ship on the horizon or a plane in the sky. He has taken to recording every sighting in a little notebook that he carries with him constantly.

Speaking of the children, we had hopes Welfare found a good home where all three could be placed together. Let me just say that Welfare's definition of "good" is nowhere near mine. I realized they're stretched to the limit, but I suspect some of their "homes" are no more than fronts for child labor gangs or worse. So, the kids are still with us and we're muddling along as well as we can.

I've sent the supplies you requested, and added a few little extras. I won't tell you what, though. I'll let them be a pleasant surprise.

Sam has called home several times, and said to tell you to "watch out for the killer mozzies." Please take care of yourself and write again when you can.

Everyone here sends their love to you, me most of all.
Sophie

FORTY-EIGHT

STARTING OVER

MAY 1942

I t was time, Marianne decided, to try and smooth things over with Sam. As much as she had wanted to kiss him forever on Easter, keeping her promise to look out for his parents was more important. Not that she would ever be able to forget their kisses. They were kisses to judge the next ones from a man of her choosing, but she wouldn't allow herself to pine for Sam.

Sydney
25 May 1942

Dear Sam,
I apologize for being so forward when we parted last month. Can we start over?

I am sure you have heard about the incidents here with the midget submarines earlier this month. Sophie and Mrs. Kelley were very anxious afterwards. I think your father and Thomas might have been too, but they did a better job of hiding it. It is always surprising to me how life simply goes on after a disaster. Even though there was death and destruction in Sydney Harbour, the sun still rises and sets. The birds are still singing. A few people have broken hearts because they have lost loved ones, but the rest of us go on as usual. Is that your experience too?

Fly safely,
Marianne

Somewhere back in NSW
31 May 1942

Dear Marianne,
Not too forward, just very bad timing. I apologize too. I hope you'll keep writing to me. Your letters are always a bright spot in my day. I suppose my experience is mostly the same as what you've described. There are so many new cadets that I can barely remember their names after they're assigned elsewhere. They aren't here long enough to get to know most of them, only the few that I feel an immediate affinity for. I'm sorry to admit that, and I hope you don't think less of me because of it. I'm relieved everyone at home is still safe.

Sew straight,
Sam

Hours later, when she was drifting off to sleep, Sam's words rose in her mind. He had actually written something insightful about how he was feeling. Finally! And then there was his opening: *Not too forward, just very bad timing*, plus his words at Easter, *as much as I would like to*. What, exactly, had he meant?

Forty-Nine

An American Friend Arrives in Sydney

June 1942

When US War Department writer Edmund Stone arrived in Melbourne from the United States in late April 1942, the first waves of American servicemen had already landed in Australia and caused a sensation. When he suggested to his superiors that something needed to be done to keep the thousands of Americans who were passing through Australia in line and to keep the locals from resenting their presence, they bumped his WWI-era rank of lieutenant up to captain and gave him three months to come up with something to handle the situation.

He quickly set out to interview as many people as he could to find out how the locals were reacting to the invasion. Young Australian women told him the Americans were fascinating and generous, with manners far superior to their Australian counterparts.

Young men in the Australian forces told him they weren't nearly as pleased with the influx of American GIs, who were well-fed, well-paid, and cocky as hell. The GIs hadn't spent the past two years getting shot at in Crete, Lebanon, and North Africa, only to be sent home with a few week's leave before they retrained to fight in New Guinea's jungles.

On the other hand, America had been severely bombed by the Japanese at Pearl Harbor, just like Darwin had been attacked, and Australians felt a lot of sympathy for Americans in general. Specific Americans were another story entirely. And the American access to booze, when Australian bars closed at six pm sharp, rankled deeply.

Edmund did his best, in whatever time he had the attention of the Australians he was speaking with, to inform them that most of the Americans had never been more than 50 miles from their homes until they were sent to army or navy training camps and had little or no idea that Australia existed, much less was a thriving and modern country. All they could see were the differences and were too unsophisticated to know that the American way was not the only way of doing things.

Taking that tack seemed to lessen the irritation of the locals, at least a little bit.

He also learned that the rivalry that existed between the young men of both nations could often be channeled onto sporting fields—football, basketball, swimming. At other times, though, rivalries played out in dark alleys, where fists ruled and the game was every man for himself.

He wasn't sure what he needed to do to handle the situation, and hoped Joe and Sophie Parker could help. He had met them in Chamonix in 1939 when his friend Will Ryan had befriended them in Villers-Bretonneux and invited them to Chamonix. He'd been impressed by the quiet, wry Australian and his bubbly American wife. After spending a week in Melbourne and assessing the situation there, Edmund had some ideas, but he wanted someone who knew both cultures to bounce ideas around with. His letter to the Parkers resulted in an invitation to stay with them in Sydney for a few days. He'd booked a berth on the overnight train and cabled Sophie and Joe with his arrival time. He would see them in a few days.

Buffeted by the crush of khaki-clad men swarming the platform at Sydney's Central Train Station, Sophie felt as if she was transported back to the Gare du Nord in Paris when troop trains packed with soldiers of many nationalities arrived from the Western Front on leave. While these men were distinctly Aussies with their slouch hats and friendly insults shouted to each other, the comingled smells of wool and male sweat, cigarettes and ground-in dirt, plus hot steel and soot, were the same regardless of decade or locale.

Too short to see over the mass of humanity pressing from all sides, she found a bench, stood on it, and scanned the crowd from her perch. She soon caught sight of Edmund Stone: he had waited until the initial throng had exited the cars and was surveying the crowd from the top step.

"Edmund!" she called, waving wildly to catch his attention. He waved back and pushed his way through to her.

"Sophie! You look lovely, as always." Edmund placed his duffle bag and portable typewriter on the floor and returned her hug.

"And you look very dashing," Sophie replied. "Your officer's uniform is a far cry from the hiking shorts and boots you were wearing when we said our goodbyes in Chamonix."

Edmund wiggled the knot of his tie and slipped a finger under his shirt collar. "This uniform isn't nearly as comfortable as my hiking gear."

"We've seen a lot of American servicemen here in Sydney, but not many officers," Sophie said. "You should see the streets in the evening. American soldiers and sailors as far as the eye can see."

"It's the same in Melbourne," Edmund said. "The Cricket Ground is the epicenter for American servicemen. The field is a parade ground and the stands are crammed with cots. Heck, there are so many GIs there that many are billeted in private homes too."

Knowing Edmund wouldn't feel free to talk about anything of importance while they were in public, Sophie led him to the station's exit. "Let's get you home and settled in. Marianne will join us, Joe promised to leave the office early today, and Mrs. Kelly is preparing a feast for your arrival."

"A feast? I'm always up for one of those, especially since we've all been on short rations. Lead the way," Edmund said.

"My car is just there." Sophie pointed across the tram tracks that ran alongside the station. They waited for a tram to pass and loaded Edmund's bag and typewriter in the car's trunk.

"I thought I'd take the scenic route home so you can get a little bit of an idea of the city. Then tomorrow I'll take you for a ferry ride or two and we can walk through the Botanic Gardens and we'll visit the areas where the Americans are headquartered."

"Sounds like a great plan."

"Oh, and I have to warn you. We're doing the school run on the way home. We've taken in three children until their father comes home."

"Like what they're doing in England, evacuating kids from London and sending them to the country?"

"Not quite. They lost their mother a few months ago and their father was taken prisoner in Crete. He's probably somewhere in Germany or Poland by now."

"I sense there's a heck of a story there."

"Indeed, there is. I'll fill you in while you're here."

She parked alongside the school at St. Mary's and waved for Sister Anna Joseph to release Teddy and Katie from the line of children waiting for pickup.

Teddy, whose eyes widened to the size of saucers when he saw an American officer sitting in the passenger seat of Sophie's car, kept up a volley of questions at Edmund, who answered patiently until they arrived home.

Edmund's first reaction when Sophie pulled up the drive to the Parker's house on the hill was, "God, what a view!" He swiveled to take in the Pacific to the east and Sydney Harbour to the west. Australian and American warships lined the horizon.

Katie, always subdued compared to her siblings, shyly pointed out the extensive vegetable gardens surrounding the house.

"You weren't kidding about growing loads of vegetables," Edmund said. "Folks in the States are starting to do the same thing. They're called Victory Gardens."

Then Cora, who tumbled out of the house with Howard at her heels and Moira in close pursuit, tugged Edmund to the chicken coop and removed her fingers from her mouth long enough to capture the most patient hen and present her to Edmund for petting.

"Welcome to our three-ring circus," Sophie said as Edmund gingerly stroked the hen's feathers.

After Joe arrived home, bringing Marianne with him, Edmund proposed the first toast after Joe passed around coupes of sparkling Australian wine to him, Sophie, and Marianne. "Here's to friends from all over the world," he said.

"I met your Sam in Melbourne," he added after everyone had their first sip of bubbles.

"How did you...?" Sophie looked to Joe and then to Marianne. "He can't really tell us his movements very often. He's in Melbourne?"

"I don't know for how long or why," Edmund said. "But he was there last week. When we parted, he asked me to give you a kiss on the cheek, Sophie, and a clap on the back for you, Joe."

Edmund set his glass down, and gently took Marianne's hand in his. "There was one more message from Sam. I'm to tell you he hasn't found anyone better to write to and he hopes you haven't either."

Marianne met Edmund's gaze. "Sam and I are only good friends."

He appraised Marianne fondly and Sophie wondered what Edmund was reading in the young woman's demeanor that she wasn't. "All right. I have to tell you, though. I thought your Sam was a great guy. Funnily enough," Edmund continued, "the words crook and mate were the reason I met Sam."

"Do tell," Sophie said, topping up their coupes with the last of the bubbles before she settled next to Joe on the sofa.

"I was coming out of the Houptoun Tea Rooms in the Arcade..." Edmund began.

"They used to have lovely cakes," Sophie enthused. "I wonder how they're managing with the rationing."

"Fairly well," he continued. "I and another officer went there for high tea."

"Good place for it," Joe agreed.

"Anyhow, when we left there was a minor scuffle going on at the entrance to the Arcade. A couple of American boys were involved, so naturally we high-tailed it down there to see what was going on. Turns out the two Americans...midshipmen, they turned out to be...had been bothering a couple of Australian girls. The girls were trying to pass and the two sailors wouldn't let them." Sophie stiffened and she saw Marianne had too. "Not that kind of bothering, ladies. I'm fairly certain the sailors were indeed just being overly friendly and didn't like being ignored by two pretty girls."

"I suppose no man likes being ignored by a pretty girl," Joe said wryly.

"Just before my friend and I got to the entrance, a youngish man in an RAAF uniform stops, asks the girls if they're all right, and tells the sailors to leave the girls alone, that they're crook. One of the sailors said something, and the airman said 'Listen mate, don't you know when your attentions are unwanted?' That's when the sailor says 'I'm not a crook and I'm not your mate, buddy' and takes a swing at the Australian."

Edmund paused and sipped his drink.

—

Joe tensed, wondering if Edmund was going to say Sam had responded so enthusiastically that he injured the American. Sam was so much like Joe's younger brother Robbie that he often expected Sam to act the same way Robbie would in certain situations. When they were kids, Robbie had never backed down from a fight or a dare. Joe, being the older brother and therefore tasked with looking after his younger brother, had often been on the receiving end of their father's ire when they came home with bloodied noses or torn clothing because Robbie simply wouldn't back down or walk away, no matter what Joe said.

Consequently, Joe had spent a lot of time with Sam during the boy's childhood and especially during his teenage years, teaching him how to control his reactions to the usual situations boys found themselves in. Joe usually thought he'd done a pretty fair job of it. Sophie sometimes said he didn't give himself or Sam enough credit, but Joe still had occasional doubts that he'd taught Sam everything he needed to know or that Sam had learned the lessons.

The situation Edmund was describing was a perfect example of his worries about how Sam had responded. Joe's fingers tightened on the crystal coupe he held and waited to hear the rest of the story.

"So, the Australian—by now we were close enough to step in if we needed—ducks the punch, grabs the sailor's forearm, and twists it behind his back—not hard enough to hurt the guy, but quickly enough to grab his other hand and pull it behind the guy's back."

"That's a police move," Sophie said.

"That's what I thought, too," Edmund replied. "The other sailor was so surprised his buddy has been contained that it takes him a couple of seconds to get his fists up. The Australian shifts so the sailor he's holding will be the one who gets punched when the other sailor swings, and very calmly tells the young ladies they should be on their way."

Sophie shifted beside him. "Did you teach Sam to do that?"

Joe shrugged. "I taught Jean-Luc too. I figured they might need to know how to react if they needed to."

Sophie raised her brows at him. "Hmmm. It's probably good you did." She turned to Edmund. "When did you discover the Australian was Sam?"

"Some high-ranking RAAF officer came out of the tobacco shop and saw what was happening. By then...you have to understand, this all happened very quickly...my friend and I were right there. We were just about to take the sailors to task and whistle for the MPs when this officer says 'Parker. What's the problem here?' He looks around, sees there are two American officers, and orders his man to stand down at the same time we're ordering the sailors to settle down."

Right, Joe thought, this is where I hear about Sam being disciplined in front of officers for defending Australian girls from the advances of American servicemen.

Edmund must have seen his discomfort because he raised his glass to him. "My friend and I introduced ourselves to the officer right away and told him that his man had acted entirely properly and had possibly avoided a nasty situation. The sailor who'd taken the swing complained that this Aussie had called him a crook and that he had the right to defend himself when someone insulted him."

Edmund chuckled. "That's when I understood what had happened. It was a simple matter of the same language separating two nationalities. I told the sailors that crook is the Australian equivalent of not feeling well and there was no reason to be insulted by it. Then I told the airman that crook is the American equivalent of someone who breaks the law. Anyhow, there are handshakes between the airman and the sailors and salutes all around for the officers.

"My friend and I ordered the sailors to apologize to the two young ladies, who hadn't left. They'd only moved to the other side of the arcade and had witnessed the whole thing. The sailors begged their pardon, and we took them aside and gave them a piece of our minds about bothering women in general and Australian women in particular, took their names, and sent them on their way. The whole time, I'm thinking there was something about the way the airman held himself that struck me as familiar. Then I remembered the RAAF officer calling him Parker so I asked him his name. When he said 'Flight Lieutenant Sam Parker' I asked him if Joe Parker was his father.

"When he said yes, I explained how I knew his father, the RAAF officer and my friend looked impressed, and Sam suggested we all go for a beer to show anyone who's watching that Australians and Americans can get along."

Joe leaned toward Edmund. "You're telling me that my son came to the aid of two young women, was prepared to defend himself against two attackers, and then invited his superior officer and two fairly high-ranking American officers to have a beer with him?"

Edmund nodded, smiling. "That's exactly what I'm telling you. You raised a fine young man, Joe. You should be proud of him."

Joe downed the last of his drink, blinking as the bubbles hit the back of his throat. Robbie would have hit first and asked questions later. Sam had done something else entirely. There had been so many times he wasn't sure he'd done a good enough job raising Sam, but it seemed like he might have, after all. "I am," he said. "I am."

FIFTY

INSTRUCTIONS FOR AMERICAN SERVICEMEN STATIONED IN AUSTRALIA

JUNE 1942

The next day, Sophie read through Edmund's handwritten notes for 'Instructions for American Servicemen Stationed in Australia' while he perused the morning papers.

"This is really very good," she said, looking up from the pages. "I have a couple of ideas and a suggestion or two, but why don't you wait until after Joe has read it and then the two of us can tell you what we think. He promised he'd be home early."

"Sure," Edmund replied. "I'll type it up so he has a clean copy to read." He'd written the first draft on the ten-hour train ride from Melbourne to Sydney, often pausing mid-sentence to take in the Australian countryside swishing by outside his window and referring to the maps of the world and Australia that he'd brought with him. This country was almost as big as the United States and seemed to be as diverse in terms of landscape, regional industries, and immigrants.

"You're a particularly interesting subject," he told her. "Half American, half English, married to an Australian. I'm not sure I could find a better combination to help me with this project."

—

That evening, after Sophie, Joe, and Edmund finished dinner and had retired to the drawing room with their coffee and slices of Mrs. Kelly's lemon cake, Edmund asked Joe for his opinions on the draft of instructions.

"Sophie has read through it a couple of times, but I thought it best to hear what you had to say first, since, of course, you're the home-grown Australian in the crowd."

Joe nodded. He had enjoyed meeting Edmund in Chamonix when he and Sophie were there in July 1939, and he had been very impressed with Edmund's insights into the state of Europe at the time and the prospects of the impending war they were in now. Joe's opinions of Americans in general were fairly high, since his battalion fought with Edmund's unit at Saint Quentin Canal in late 1918. The American troops had been green and not as well prepared as they should have been, but with the help of the Australians, they had contributed to the further destruction of Germany's Hindenburg Line.

"I think there are a lot of similarities between Australia and America," Joe began. "Even though the United States is independent of Britain, both countries were originally populated by English-speaking immigrants. Yes, Australia was originally a penal colony, but that's probably not as germane as the fact that people immigrated to both countries to make a better life for themselves."

"And pushed the original inhabitants of both continents to the brink," Sophie said, frowning.

Edmund nodded. "Agreed, although this publication isn't the place to go into those points. It has to be short enough and punchy enough that GIs will absorb what they need to know at this moment. Most pages will have illustrations, too."

"What about money? I'd add that and definitely include pictures."

"Good point, Sophie. Most of these boys simply can't fathom that the dollar isn't the only currency in the world. You tell them pounds and they think you're talking about weight. They usually pull out a fistful of money and tell the person to take whatever is owed."

"You've said that the two countries are about the same size," Joe continued. "You've compared basic industries in both countries. What else could you include?"

"I've been working on a section about animals that are only found in Australia," Edmund said. "The kids I've talked to couldn't believe their eyes when they saw kangaroos and koala bears. They really couldn't believe how fast kangaroos can move and how hard they kick."

"Good. Be sure to say something about the spiders and snakes here," Joe said. "We have some of the world's most deadly. Oh, and koalas aren't bears."

Sophie had been listening patiently while Joe offered his opinions. She had thought of many of the same things but there was something neither man had mentioned yet. "Edmund, what about sports? Australians are crazy about sports. There are three kinds of football here, plus cricket, basketball, wresting, boxing, tennis, sailing, rowing, and horse and dog racing. I think that's an area where both countries are very much alike. Although I don't think the state of Kentucky has a public holiday the day the Kentucky Derby is run like the state of Victoria has for the Melbourne Cup."

"Good, good," Edmund said, nodding and making notes at the same time. "None of these boys know anything about Aussie Rules Football or cricket. I bet they'll love both games if they can figure out the rules."

"And don't forget winter sports,' she said. "We have the Australian Alps that straddle the border between New South Wales and Victoria. Skiing, climbing, you name it."

"I like the tone you used in your draft," Joe said. "It's like you're speaking to each man as someone who believes they can process what you're saying and understand it. Does that make sense? You don't ever talk down to them."

"Good point, darling," Sophie said. "What if you…" she paused for a moment, thinking something through. "What if you present all this information in a sort of compare and contrast format? That way you can emphasize the things that are great about each country. You could make the point that just as Americans are proud of say the ancient redwood forests in the Northwest, Australians are proud of the Great Barrier Reef. Size, unique animals, sport—the two countries have lots of things in common.

"And then there's the language and the beer," Edmund said. "I'm definitely going to include a glossary of slang and common phrases. I have some great ones that Will taught me over the years. Like arvo for afternoon and fair oil for what's the real story."

"Don't forget pronunciation, Edmund," Sophie added. "I'm still surprised when I hear the word t-r-a-i-n pronounced trine instead of trane."

"And I'm still surprised to hear you pronounce every R in words," Joe added.

She brushed Joe's shoulder fondly and smiled at Edmund. "I'm going to go say goodnight to Katie and Cora and check Teddy's homework. I'll be back down in a little while."

She went upstairs to the sounds of Joe reciting words Edmund needed to define.

"Cobber, drongo, digger…, but you already know that one.

"I knew cobber, too."

"Sheila, cliner, sninny…

"Is cliner with a c or a k?"

"C. Shivoo, imshi, chivvy…

"Shikkered, plonk, shout…

"Wowser, fair cow, and last but not least," Joe said, "hard yakka."

"This is great!" Edmund said, scribbling furiously. "Exactly what I had in mind. Once the army approves the content, they'll get it printed and distributed."

"But will it help?"

"God, I hope so. Only time will tell, won't it?"

FIFTY-ONE

NEW WORDS

Sydney
1 June 1942

Dear Sam,
Your father and Sophie are doing well. Edmund Stone,
my honorary uncle who you met when you rescued those
two girls from the sailors, was here in Sydney to enlist
their help in creating a little handbook for American
servicemen to understand the country where they are
stationed.

It was wonderful to see him. He and my father became
friends during the last war, and they have remained
friends ever since. He had news from my parents who
have settled in London for the duration. They had a
letter from my brother, who is well, but I worry how safe
he is. Edmund asked me to accompany him to a dinner
dance for American officers while he was here. It was at
the Australia Hotel, and I wore a new-to-me dress that

I sewed from one of Sophie's old evening gowns, so that was a nice change of pace.

Edmund spent a few days at your parents' house coming up with the general outline for his handbook and your father supplied him with some of the more obscure Australian phrases and swear words they might encounter. Despite having an Australian father, I learnt some new ones!

Fly safely,
Marianne
P.S. Of course I will continue writing to you. Your letters are a bright spot in my day too.

Somewhere in NSW
7 June 1942

Dear Marianne,
Which words? Good to know you heard from your family. I enjoyed meeting Edmund in Melbourne.

Sew straight,
Sam
P.S. The Australia Hotel? That's classy. Edmund didn't introduce you to any Yank officers who want to whisk you away from Aussie pilots, did he?

Sydney
18 June 1942

Dear Sam,
The words were mostly related to beer. It is not my

*beverage of choice, and even less so since this country has
ridiculous rules about women allowed to sit only in the
ladies' lounges.*

Fly safely,
Marianne
*P.S. There were no Yanks who wanted to whisk me
away from Aussie pilots. As you can see in the photo, I
am on Edmund's arm, no one else's.*

Marianne included the newspaper photo taken at the dinner with
Edmund. Normally she wouldn't have made a poppy red dress for
herself, but the silk from Sophie's gown slipped deliciously over her
skin. The skirt and sleeves fluttered when she moved. The strand of
tiny pearls her parents had given her for her twenty-first birthday
nestled above a keyhole neckline fastened with thin red ribbons. She
had barely recognized herself in the mirror after Patricia pinned her
hair back on one side with a small white orchid and dotted her lips
with her precious red Coty lipstick.

Somewhere in NSW
22 June 1942

Dear Marianne,
*I think ladies should be able to sit wherever they like,
although even I don't like being in a bar during the six
o'clock swill.*

Sew straight,
Sam
*P.S. You look a picture in the newspaper photo you sent.
What was wrong with those Yanks? You're eminently
whiskable.*

Sydney
23 June 1942

Dear Sam,
The swill is disgusting! Who thought of such a dreadful thing? The government changed the hours for hotel bars so late shift workers can drink after work. Now there are two times when men come staggering out of the bars only to see the Americans parading around with enough money to buy liquor whenever and wherever they want to. I am tired of dodging drunks and avoiding fights on my way home from work at night.

Luckily my papa taught me a few useful moves to defend myself.

Keep flying safely,
Marianne
P.S. Thank you for making me laugh! All I could think of after reading your postscripts was whisks for cooking, even though I have never used one. Have you?
P.P.S. Is whiskable really a word? Should I find an English dictionary?

Somewhere in NSW
28 June 1942

Dear Marianne,
The temperance unions were responsible for bars closing at 6 pm sharp. Now everyone has to drink as much as they can, swilling it down like pigs, before closing time. If you ask Dad, he'll tell you those laws are responsible

for most of the sly grog trade.

I think I can guess what useful moves your father taught you, and I have only one thing to say: Ouch! But I'm still worried about you getting home safely.

Please be careful because we need you sewing straight.
Sam

P.S. The first time I asked Mrs. Kelly to make a pavlova, she handed me a whisk and her copper bowl and taught me how to whip egg whites. So, yes, I have used a whisk. In fact, I learnt to be pretty handy in the kitchen. The next time I'm home I'll prove it to you. P.P.S. If whiskable isn't a real word it should be. And if the dress you're wearing in the photo is an example of your talents, I'd say you're well on your way to that dressmaking shop you want.

FIFTY-TWO

SUFFER THE LITTLE CHILDREN

JULY 1942

In addition to the long-term strain of not knowing whether her sons or her home, city, and country were safe, the addition of the O'Brien children to the household wreaked havoc with Sophie's daily routine. Early mornings, which were previously spent sleeping or snuggling with Joe before he had to get ready for work, were now spent getting the children up and dressed while Moira made their breakfast and school lunches.

Now, after Joe and the two older children left the house, Sophie began her ritual of pouring over the newspapers, memorizing maps, and listening to the news on the wireless while she ate her breakfast. She had absolutely no control over the war, but she clung to anything that gave her the illusion of feeling less helpless.

The remainder of the mornings she and Moira spent sharing household chores and looking after Cora, who still insisted on sucking her fingers as a means of self-comfort despite their best efforts to get her to stop. Marianne had sewn a little cloth rabbit for her in the hopes of a distraction, but the rabbit's ears were usually sodden by bedtime. Sophie was loathe to let the thing in bed, but Cora was adamant about keeping it with her. Marianne had solved that problem by sewing two more rabbits, so that one was in Cora's hands, one was being washed, and one was ready to replace. But otherwise, she was a happy child, far less traumatized by her mother's death than Katie and far less likely to get into mischief than Teddy.

At the moment, Cora and Howard were playing a noisy game of fetch in the fenced off area between the main house and the Kelly's cottage. Cora hadn't yet mastered throwing a ball as far as Howard would like, or even much more than a few feet, but he fetched the ball from wherever it landed and brought it back to her, dropping it at her feet and yipping impatiently for the next throw. Thomas was working in the vegetable gardens, Teddy and Katie were at school, and Joe was at work. For Sophie and Moira, it was laundry day.

"Thank heavens Cora has finally stopped wetting the bed," Sophie said as she and Moira worked together to hang clean clothes on the line. They straightened seams and smoothed out wrinkles to minimize the amount of ironing they'd need. A stiff breeze and bright sun meant the first clothes they'd hung were half dry by the time they finished hanging the basketful. If she could, she would have hired a young woman to help with the extra laundry and cleaning generated by the three additions to the household. But the government had decreed household help was not war-related employment, and anyone she might have hired was working in a munitions factory or some other vital industry. If Moira and Thomas weren't in their sixties, they would have been requisitioned for war work too.

"Aye, that's a relief. And thank heavens for the machine," Moira replied. "Otherwise, washing sheets and bedclothes every day would have taken a lot more time. But who would have guessed a lady like you would be so good at doing laundry?"

"I learnt an awful lot about how to do it during the last war. The newest nurses had to prove they were willing to do the worst jobs before we were allowed anywhere near the patients."

She tried, and failed, to stifle a huge yawn as she moved to help Moira fold the dry sheets.

"Judging from the size of that yawn, Katie isn't sleeping much better than when she and Cora first arrived," Moira said.

"No, not as well as I'd hoped she would by now," Sophie admitted. "She still has bad dreams several times a week. I'll hear her moaning in her sleep and run in to comfort her before she wakes Joe and Cora." Katie's heartbreaking whimpers and nightmares reminded Sophie far more of her nursing days than laundry did. After spending four war years nursing injured troops at the American Hospital in Paris and then ten years nursing her first husband's patients after the war, she knew that when one man began a noisy nightmare, it wasn't long before half the ward could awaken. Then it was always a race to quiet the patient before that happened. Now it was a race to quiet Katie before she woke Cora, who slept in the same bed, and Joe, who woke at the slightest sound. Luckily Teddy slept like a hibernating bear.

"I'm always on edge waiting for her to wake...then trying to get her back to sleep... And after that, waiting to make sure she's really asleep."

"I figured you weren't getting enough rest," Moira said. "I hope I'm not overstepping, but you've been looking tired ever since the girls arrived. Would you like me to set up a cot in their room? I could stay with them one or two nights a week. That would take some of the burden off of you."

"That's a very kind offer, but I don't know whether it would help or not," Sophie said. "It's the only time Katie willingly accepts my help. But I admit the interrupted sleep is taking a toll." Who was she kidding? She's so exhausted she's swaying on her feet. If she's lucky she gets four or five hours of sleep a night. What was she thinking, saying they should take in three children? She and Joe should have pushed Welfare to keep looking for a placement.

"I've heard new mothers should nap when the baby naps," Moira continued. "Perhaps you should rest while Katie and Teddy are at school."

"That's one of the few times I can get anything else done. Besides, I always wake up from naps feeling groggy and annoyed that I've lost time when I could have been doing something useful."

The annoyance that had been simmering boiled to life. She was spending too much time and energy on mindless, mundane tasks like laundry instead of the things she was good at like organizing fundraisers, convincing wealthy Sydneysiders to donate large sums, and cajoling city officials to allow the use of their facilities at little or no cost. Why hadn't Joe nixed her insistence they take the children in? It was easy for him. He wasn't here all day, every day. He hadn't given up his professional life.

She snatched the last of the children's clothes from the basket and slapped them on the line, savagely pushing down clothes pegs.

And worse, she didn't have the time to tend her secret cache of worries about Sam and Jean-Luc. It's as if she's grieving them in advance so that if something does happen, she'll be prepared for devastation. Then there was her fear that the Allies might lose the war and revulsion towards being subjugated by conquering forces who believed their emperor was divine or that Aryans were the only race that deserved to live. How on earth could she live like that? And what would they do to the people she loved? She knew without a doubt she would do her best to kill anyone who touched a hair on their heads. She would probably be killed in the process, but it would be worth it if she could keep them safe. Doubly so if she managed to take some of the enemy with her.

She kept most of her thoughts to herself, not even sharing them with Joe. Anyhow, what would talking about it accomplish, except to increase their wondering and worrying?

She'd thrown out hints about her fears, though. We'll join the resistance, just like the French, she'd said when a dinner discussion had taken a dark turn. She'd shut up when Marianne's face turned pale. The poor girl had enough to worry about with her homeland occupied, her brother in the French army, and her parents decamped in England where invasion was still a possibility.

The pendulum swung to an overwhelming guilt that she offered a life to the children that she couldn't sustain because she was so engulfed in her worries, and shame that she couldn't seem to be what they needed. This morning she had snapped at Teddy for not tying his shoes and had been impatient with Katie when she couldn't manage a button on her uniform skirt.

Then her deepest sorrow, the one she tried never, ever to think about, the miscarriage she'd had when she was married to Michael, erupted to the surface. Their marriage was already deteriorating at that point, and she'd been relieved to not bring a child into it, but the guilt of feeling relieved had never gone away. Would she have been as rotten a mother to her own child as she was being to another woman's? She had managed to help care for Jean-Luc when he was Cora's age. There was a war on then, too. Why were these three so hard now?

Just as suddenly she couldn't bear the idea of not taking care of the children. Their clothes were so small, their bodies and hearts so fragile. Cora raising her arms to be held and cuddled, even as a saliva-soaked rabbit ear seeped through her dress. Teddy, racing indoors, hands and knees grubby, to inhale a snack or show off some treasure he had uncovered, before racing back outside. Those two were thriving despite her. Still grieving her mother, Katie was often lost in the shuffle between her more outgoing siblings. She seemed to prefer it there, rebuffing everyone's efforts to bring her out of her shell. None of this was their fault. They needed love and care, like all God's creatures. What was it Moira had said when they first contemplated taking in the children? Suffer the little children...

Feeling thoroughly wretched, she rolled her neck and shoulders and examined new rips in the knees of Teddy's trousers. "I'll do the mending later this week," she said when Moira pointed out a loose hem in Katie's skirt. "Otherwise, these children are going to look like ragamuffins."

But before she could tackle the pile of mending, there were phone calls to make, accounts to balance, bills to pay while Cora napped after lunch. Then there was the afternoon school run when she took the ferry or the tram to collect Teddy and Katie from St. Mary's. Driving would take half the time, but petrol rationing made her hoard the petrol she did have in case of rain or emergencies, and she didn't trust Teddy on his own. Knowing him, he'd dawdle and explore and drag Katie along for the adventure. They'd be late getting home, late to do their homework, late for supper, late for baths and bed.

Breathe, she reminded herself. Slowly. In. Out. In. Out.

FIFTY-THREE

CONFESSION

JULY 1942

Sydney
3 July 1942

Dear Sam,
My apologies for not writing sooner, but work has been
so busy that I can hardly keep my eyes open when I
arrive home at night. You must be training many new
pilots because orders for parachutes are flooding in. We
are also sending them to England. Working six days a
week might not be enough to keep up with demand.

I think you might have been right to worry about your
parents withdrawing from each other. Sophie looked so
tired when I had dinner with her and your father last
night. He kept asking her if she was all right, but all
she said was I'm fine every time he asked. He did not
look like he believed her and she did not sound like she
was. Perhaps I imagined it, but it seemed like they were

on the verge of an argument. I did not stay long after dinner. I felt like I was intruding.

My parents have their own code phrases for those times when they are upset. Is 'I'm fine' code for your parents?

Fly safely,
Marianne

Somewhere in the SWPA
27 July 1942

Dear Marianne,
I think you're right. When dad was recovering from those gunshot wounds three years ago, he used to say I'm fine every time Sophie asked how he was and it seemed to set her on edge. He wasn't fine, and she knew it, but she kept such a close eye on him that he might have felt like she was suffocating him. It sounds like the reverse is true now. Thanks for letting me know.

Sew straight,
Sam
P.S. Please take care of yourself so we don't have to have a code.

Joe came home from work after dark, checked the perimeter of the house for any light escaping their blackout curtains, and let himself in quickly to minimize the crack of light from the door opening.

The downstairs was dark except for a lamp glowing in the drawing room. With a quick glance around the shadowy room, he took in a pile of clothes and an open sewing box on the coffee table. Sophie sat in a pool of light, sucking her finger while tears streamed down her cheeks.

He dropped his briefcase and rushed over to her. "What's happened? Have we had a telegram? Did something happen to one of the boys?"

"No, it's nothing like that. I'm fine." Joe raised a brow. She'd been hiding her worries for weeks and he knew it. They'd made a promise they would share their troubles and she wasn't keeping her end of the bargain. He knew that too.

Halfheartedly, she showed him the pair of Teddy's trousers on her lap. "I knew better than to try to mend something dark without proper light, but I did it anyway. Not only am I making a mess of the job, but I also stabbed the living daylights out of my finger."

"Does that explain the tears?"

"Yes and no. I've had a rotten day, darling, and I've been feeling a little sorry for myself."

"Give all that to me." He took the trousers, needle, and thread from her, placed them on the table, and joined her on the sofa, putting his arm around her shoulders. She leaned into him and rested her cheek on his chest, the thud of his heart slowing after the surprise of finding her crying alone in the dark. "Now. Tell me why your day was rotten," he said.

"I don't think I can. I had some really awful thoughts today. I'm afraid you'll think less of me if I tell you."

"Love, there's nothing you can say that would do that."

A shuddering intake of breath. "I had a moment, just a tiny moment, when I thought we shouldn't have taken in the children."

"Ah." He let her admission hang in the space between them, knowing that if he kept quiet, she would feel compelled to fill the silence.

"Actually, it was more than just one tiny moment. It was several. Many." Another long pause. "I'm not proud of them. I just need to work through it. I'll be all right once I do. Until then..."

Another shudder brought a fresh onslaught of tears. Joe reached for his handkerchief and handed it to her.

"Th-thank you." She pressed it to her nose and pulled away from him abruptly. "Damn it, I cannot cry all over your suit jacket."

"Of course, you can."

"No, I can't. Because then we'd have to deal with one more piece of laundry and there's too much of it already that we can barely keep up with and... and... there just isn't time for all the bloody laundry!"

He scrambled to understand why his usually cheerful, competent wife was losing her composure over something as mundane as laundry. In the absence of all the facts, he did the one thing he could do, gently dislodging his arm and rising to remove his jacket. "Better?"

"Waistcoat too. And your tie. In fact, take off your shirt as well. It'll save having to wash that too."

Rather than strip down to his underwear in the drawing room, Joe glanced at his watch. "Are the kids in bed?"

"I finally got them all to sleep about nine." Sophie used his handkerchief to blow her nose, crumpling in in her fist afterwards. "Damn it!" she cried, as another round of tears fell.

He held out his hand. "Come on. Let's go upstairs."

"I haven't finished mending—"

"Will it keep until the morning?'

"Yes, but—"

"Then come with me."

When they reached the door to their bedroom, Joe pressed his hand to her back and guided her over the threshold before slipping into their en-suite bathroom and turning on the tub faucets.

He came back to the bedroom while pulling off his tie and un-buttoning his shirt. "You too. Undress."

She sank to the edge of the bed shaking her head. "I'm really not in the mood."

"All we're going to do is take a bath. You've clearly had a long, hard day and I have too. Warm bath, pajamas, bed. During that time, you can tell me as much or as little as you want to about what's bothering you."

Sophie released a huge sigh after they settled into the tub, her back resting against his chest. "God, I've missed this. I miss us. We're so busy that I hardly see you anymore."

She lay quietly for a few minutes, considering what to say. It would be easier to confess when she's not facing Joe, so she began with her thoughts while she and Mrs. Kelly hung the wet clothes and folded the dry ones. Not the entire story of course. She left out the bits about her secret store of worries. And resenting him for not stopping her. What good would it do to tell him all that?

Joe started to massage her shoulders. They were tight and hard. "Sit up so I can do a proper job of this." When she did, he continued. "What else?"

"I may have cursed the entire Catholic church for not allowing birth control before I realized I was judging people I have no right to judge. Catherine took care of her children as well as she could. They were loved. Katie wouldn't miss her as much as she does if she hadn't. Cora wouldn't be as sweet, and Teddy wouldn't have risked everything to try to provide for his mother and sisters."

He continued massaging, moving from her shoulders to the muscles lining her spine.

"God, Joe. I'm so ashamed. The children don't deserve the lot life has handed them. I have everything compared to them and all I could do was feel selfish and sorry for myself."

"You are the least selfish person I've ever met. I suspect you're exhausted and it has all caught up with you. What needs to happen to solve this problem? What can I do to help?"

"Honestly, I don't know. I'm so tired I can't think straight anymore. I need sleep. I need Katie to sleep through the night. Mrs.

Kelly offered to camp out in the girls' room a couple of nights a week but she already has her hands full with all the extra work that came with taking in the children. I'm so busy I can hardly keep up with our accounts, much less the accounts for all the organizations I work with. But if I stop doing them, I won't be doing my bit. I want to accomplish everything I can." As if doing everything she can will somehow affect events of the war, even the outcome.

She'd long wondered if Joe thought she'd been involved in far too many projects even before the children arrived, but if he did, he refrained from voicing that opinion outright. "Is it possible that providing a safe, loving home for a soldier's three motherless children is also a worthy accomplishment?"

Sophie reached for Joe's hands and leaned back again. Perhaps he was right, but she was too tired to think. He shifted so she could guide his hands wherever she wanted them, but instead of her usual movements, her head lolled and her fingers went slack. The next thing she knew, Joe was gently pushing her back to a sitting position. "Time to dry off and get in bed," he said.

FIFTY-FOUR

SMALL VICTORIES

JULY 1942

After Joe and the two older children left for work and school the next morning, Sophie heard dishes rattling in the sink and Moira Kelly admonishing Cora to play quietly in the kitchen for a moment.

"Mrs. Parker, may I have a word?"

Startled, Sophie looked up from the newspaper. Mrs. Kelly stood in the doorway between the kitchen and dining room with her hands on her hips. Usually, she called her Mrs. P. Sophie had no idea what she could have done to upset her.

"I thought we agreed that you and the inspector would leave your dishes in the sink when he comes home after a late night and I would wash them with the breakfast dishes."

Mystified, Sophie nodded. "We did."

"Then why were there clean dishes on the drainboard this morning? What's more, I found the tables set for breakfast when I came in." The older woman's stance softened. "Trying to save me a bit of time and work is a kind gesture, but you're barely getting enough sleep as it is. If you won't let me help with Katie's sleeping–"

Sophie had a jumbled recollection of Joe kissing her temple and saying he was going downstairs to get a bite to eat, but aside from that, she was clueless. "Mrs. Kelly, I didn't do them. It must have been Joe."

Moira didn't look convinced, and returned to the kitchen, shaking her head and sighing heavily.

It wasn't until after Sophie finished her share of the day's housework—today was cleaning the two upstairs bathrooms, where the two males in her household had neglected to put the toilet seats down yet again—ate lunch, and put Cora down for a nap that she recalled her earlier conversation with Moira. Sophie hadn't shared Joe's late meal, much less set the tables for breakfast. Come to think of it, she hadn't been awakened by Katie either.

Chalking it all up to Joe's habit of raiding the larder when he missed dinner due to working late and sheer luck that Katie had slept through the night, Sophie went upstairs to freshen up and change clothes for the afternoon school run. She caught sight of her forty-five-year-old body in the cheval mirror and gave herself a critical once-over. Several silver strands mingled with her deep brown tresses. Dark smudges seemed to have taken up permanent residence under her eyes. On the other hand, months of lifting Cora and laundry baskets had delayed the dreaded onset of jiggly upper arms. Far less butter, cream, and sugar in their daily meals had melted the slight layer of fat around her midsection that had stealthily appeared when she turned forty. And all the school run walking meant her thighs and derrière were almost as firm and trim as they'd been when she was in her twenties.

Well then. Maybe some clouds did have silver linings.

Deciding she would celebrate even the smallest of victories, Sophie dressed and donned her favorite blue woolen coat and set off to collect her youngsters.

As usual, Teddy ran ahead during the walk from the ferry back to the house. As usual, she kept an eye on him while she tried to engage Katie in conversation.

Today Katie actually spoke first. "When will my daddy come home?"

Oh no. The question she dreaded most. "We're doing everything we can to find out. You and Teddy must miss him very much."

"Daddy said Teddy is stupid because he gets bad marks in school."

Sophie's heart cracked a little for the poor boy. Teddy might not be a very good student, but he was far from stupid or lazy. He just needed help to keep him focused. She almost didn't want to know anything else. "Oh. Well, perhaps—"

"Mr. Parker let me have a midnight snack," Katie announced.

That was an unexpected change of subject. "Did he?"

Katie nodded. "I was having a bad dream and he came in and took me downstairs."

That explained not being awakened.

"He let me have two biscuits with my glass of milk."

That explained one set of dishes.

"After Mr. Parker ate his supper, he washed our dishes. Then I helped him set the tables for breakfast to surprise Mrs. Kelly. Mr. Parker says he can't surprise her very often because she knows almost everything."

That explained the other set of dishes. And the tables being set for breakfast.

That man. What a sweetheart. Maybe she wouldn't fuss at him for leaving the toilet seat up after all. She would gently remind him. She would fuss at Teddy, though. Fishing Cora out of the toilet bowl when she didn't notice the seat was up just added to the laundry burden.

"Yes, she does."

"If you want, you can have a midnight snack with us next time. But don't tell Teddy. If he knows he'll try to eat all the biscuits."

Sophie tried valiantly to keep her reactions and voice as matter-of-fact as possible. "I won't breathe a word of it to him. Cross my heart." Impulsively, she stretched her hand out.

Katie held it the rest of the way home.

Small victories indeed.

—

Sydney
31 July 1942

Dear Sam,
Everything seems to be better with your parents. I do not know what happened to bring that about, but Sophie seems more rested and relaxed and your father seems less concerned about her.

They are still worried about you and Jean-Luc, though. I know sometimes you are simply too busy, but could you write home a little more often, even if it is just one line to say you are safe and well? That might help. But I am glad you telephoned during dinner when I was there. Hearing your voice raised their spirits immeasurably. Mine also.

Fly safely,
Marianne
P.S. You must take care of yourself too.

FIFTY-FIVE

THE PACIFIC WAR HEATS UP

AUGUST 1942

"**S**ophie!" Joe called from the front hallway. The post had just arrived, and instead of sorting it into neat piles like he usually did, he snatched up the envelope bearing Jean-Luc's neat cursive. "We have a letter from Jean-Luc."

Sophie appeared as if out of thin air. Not for the first time, Joe wondered if she could hear the sound of an envelope opening from every room in the house.

"What does he say?" she demanded, slipping her arm around his and squeezing in as close to him as she could.

"He can't say much, it appears," Joe said. "I think he's trying to beat the censors. We'll have to guess based on what we've read in the papers and heard on the wireless."

Somewhere in QLD
3 August 1942

Dear Sophie and Joe,
We've finally received our next orders. We're being dis-

*patched to the boat town on the south side of the big
island just north of here.*

"Big island?" Sophie mulled that for a moment. "He must mean
New Guinea."

Joe nodded. "Boat town must mean Port Moresby. They're going
to reinforce the Militia units on the Track."

"Oh God," Sophie breathed. "Please not Kokoda."

The news from New Guinea, Australia's protectorate, had been
especially grim. The Kokoda Track was a barely-there path from
the south side of the island through the Owen Stanley mountain
range to the north side of the island. The Kokoda Track campaign
had become a vicious, seesaw battle between the Japanese and the
Australian militia troops who had been conscripted to defend Australia and sent to fight in New Guinea. Two posthumous Victoria
Crosses had already been awarded and the casualty lists of killed and
wounded had been horrendously long. Now the AIF was heading
to New Guinea to reinforce the militia.

Sophie's grip on his arm had tightened considerably. In an effort to redirect her emotions, Joe quickly read the remainder of
Jean-Luc's letter.

*Sophie, would you please send supplies again? We've
heard that parcels often get lost along the way, so perhaps send several small packages instead of one larger
one. Socks, as usual, and foot powder...*

Joe chuckled. "I'm glad to know he listened when I told him to
take care of his feet. At least he won't have to worry about frostbite
like I did."

Sophie gave him a withering look and he immediately regretted
trying to make even a small joke to alleviate the tension. "Trench
foot will still be an issue in the tropics," she said.

Deciding discretion was the better part of valor, Joe continued reading.

> *... plus soap and any kind of antiseptic you can find. We've been issued Atabrine tablets, but send quinine tablets if you can find them in Sydney. Underwear and bootlaces. Waterproof matches. Cigarettes. Sophie, I know you hate smoking, but they're useful for trades and barters. Woodbines are best but Capstans will do.*

"I'll send some toothpaste and spare toothbrushes, too," Sophie interjected.

"Always a good idea." Her grip on his arm had eased, so Joe resumed reading.

> *I will write again when I can. All my best to you both, plus Sam, the Kellys and Marianne.*
>
> *Yours affectionately,*
> *Jean-Luc*

Joe handed the letter to Sophie. The Japanese air raid on Townsville late last month had rattled them both. No matter how often she said she was fine, he knew she was terrified by the possible consequences of both boys being at war. Having a specific task to accomplish would go a long way towards staving off her panic. "For your list," he said.

Sophie nodded eagerly. "I can go shopping tomorrow and post the packages the next day."

He slipped an arm around her shoulders. "Excellent plan."

Somewhere in QLD
31 August 1942

Dear Dad and Sophie,
Seems I just missed Jean-Luc and his mob. We're now
where he was, and I have every reason to believe we'll be
sent to support them soon. Knowing him, he wrote with
a full list of supplies. Could you send the same to me?
Love to all at home,
Sam

Somewhere in QLD
31 August 1942

Dear Marianne,
Put another pin in your map. I think every squadron is
here or has been here, along with every type of aircraft
we have. The town's main claim to fame is growing
baked beans for the US forces. The Yanks call them
navy beans and it's all they eat if the local farmers can
be believed. It's a good thing there's a local CWA to
keep us supplied with biscuits and the occasional cake.
We were even invited to a dance they organized for the
Land Army girls who are working on the farms around
here. They were dancing with each other and the lo-
cal ruffians (think Teddy) when our mob of airmen
showed up.
Sew straight,
Sam

FIFTY-SIX

A FRENCH GIRL IN SYDNEY

SEPTEMBER 1942

Marianne unlocked the door to her flat, wearily rolling her head and shoulders in an effort to shake off the tension of sewing miles of fabric all day, every day, for weeks. Thank goodness they had finished the orders for additional parachutes in addition to the usual output. She wasn't sure she could have done it if she had been asked to work late again today.

Patricia's head appeared around the kitchen door jamb. "Oh good! You're not working back this evening. Kettle's on and soup's ready," she said. "I had a letter from Emma today. She actually rode in the same lift as MacArthur himself! Can you believe it!"

"That's—"

"She was too afraid to speak to him though. Imagine, my big sister, in the same space as the supreme commander. I'm so excited for her!"

Before Marianne had a chance to respond, Patricia bubbled on. "There's an article about an Australian girl who managed to escape from France and get home. She's like you only with nationalities reversed. I'll bring the tea and soup and we can read it while we eat."

"All right," Marianne said, reeling from her flat mate's exuber-
ance. "Meet you there in ten minutes. I'll put my things away and
wash up."

Settled in the armchair that had become hers because of its prox-
imity to the better lamp, Marianne rifled through the newspaper
until she found the article. She scanned the headline and first para-
graph while she ate her soup.

"This is good," she said between spoonfuls.

"It should be. I made it from the last of that stew you brought
from the Parker's. Their cook is better than I'll ever be."

"Are you ready? It's a long one."

"Fire away," Patricia said as she sat back with her soup bowl.

"A Sydney girl in France," Marianne began. "How the people
suffer. Propaganda against Britain by Alice Bolger."

"Wait a minute," Patricia said. "Who's saying something against
home?" Like many Australians, she referred to England as home,
even though her family had emigrated from England several gener-
ations ago.

"I don't know yet," Marianne said. "Just listen and we'll find out.

"The writer," she read, "who has just returned to Sydney after an
absence of some years, was resident in France on the outbreak of
war, and saw the capitulation of June, 1940, from the inside. She
witnessed a trickle of the great river of refugees reach the small town
of Eauze, in the southwest of France, near the Pyrenees, and endured
many privations in the subsequent months. Finally, she got away via
unoccupied France through Spain and Portugal, after a harassing
delay of four months at Perpignan, on the Franco-Spanish frontier."

"Stop right there," Patricia said. "Where *are* those places?"

Marianne rose and crossed the room to the map of Europe they'd
pinned on the wall next to the Australian map. She pointed out the
general vicinity mentioned in the article, southwestern France and
northwestern Portugal, then returned to her chair.

"My story begins with the great flight of refugees from the north
of France, which took place about three weeks before the Armistice.
To me this was one of France's greatest trials and sufferings. Unlike

Britain, France, apart from the north, had few bombardments, her sufferings lay in other directions such as her great lack of food and also this exodus of refugees."

"But why was there no food?"

"Probably because the Germans stole it all."

"Oh." Patricia, like many people, had no real idea what a conquering army was capable of. Marianne had been born just before the last war was over and raised in a town that had been shelled nearly into oblivion. Her earliest memories were of her father constantly patching up their house and their neighbors' houses with whatever materials he could scrounge from the ruins and her mother coaxing and cajoling vegetables to grow in the garden.

"No sadder sight than this great flight of a people could be imagined," Marianne continued, "and I only wish I could blot it from my memory. It was our duty to go out in lorries to meet the refugees, and the sight of these poor people trudging along the roads, exhausted, was terrible. Mothers bore their babies in their arms, some wounded and others just dragged themselves along carrying the few belongings that they had managed to bring with them."

"Oh, the poor things," Patricia said.

Marianne read ahead quickly. Alice wrote of two mothers who had each buried a child on the roadside when they were victims of Nazi machine-gunning. She felt sick to her stomach. "It gets worse," she said, scanning the two long columns of the article until she came across something that was less fraught than the mothers who had buried their children on the side of a road.

"I find that Australians greatly under-rate the severity of the food shortage in France. Towards Christmas of 1940 food was gradually becoming scarcer and scarcer, rationing was becoming more severe, all stocks were becoming exhausted. The climax came in the beginning of January, 1941, when German commissions went right through France and made a clean sweep of all the food. The following morning, on entering the shops, all that greeted us were empty shelves. Germany had agreed to supply France with certain foods in place of what had been taken, but the Germans did not keep their promise; they merely sent trainloads and trainloads of swede turnips."

"Ugh. I hate turnips. At least your friend Mrs. Parker keeps us well-supplied with *good* veg."

Mon Dieu, this young woman Alice had been so courageous.

Marianne recalled the last letter she'd received from her mother almost two years ago telling Marianne that she and her father had fled to England. She had started shaking as she read, terrified she might never see her parents again.

A wave of guilt swept over Marianne. Simply telling Sophie three years ago—three years!—how could so much time have passed?—that she wanted to go to Australia had magically transformed into reality. She was in comparatively peaceful Australia and not occupied, war-torn France by sheer good luck. She was suddenly very glad she had quit her department store job to sew parachutes to help the war effort.

Patricia's "You've gone awfully quiet," broke into her reverie. "Let's talk about something more cheerful. How about those Yanks TJ introduced to me and Lucy at the Red Cross dance last Sunday? They're still in town on leave. TJ said they'd all come by tomorrow."

TJ, an American sailor from Texas, was Patricia's new beau. "What? No. I'm not—"

"Why ever not? You deserve to have a bit of fun. It's not like you have to marry one of them."

Why did Patricia always bring marriage into it? In France, marriage inevitably meant babies and being tied down to one place and it seemed things were the same here in Australia, especially if the married women at the factory were anything to go by. After Elsie, another seamstress who sat at the sewing machine next to Marianne, complained that her husband would have a fit if his tea wasn't on the table when he got home from work, the factory foreman never held back the married women when overtime was required. If she ever got married, her husband was going to be willing and able to make his own damned tea. She wasn't going to succumb to a life of drudgery for the sake of a man who couldn't feed himself. "Patricia, I'm not interested…"

"Trust me," Patricia said. "The Yanks have better uniforms, their pay is better, and they have that thing called the PX where they can get all the cigarettes and chocolate and whatever else they want. Not like Australian shops. TJ says he'll bring us a surprise when they come. I hope it's nylons." She eyed a smudged line on the back of her calf. "I'm sick of drawing lines on the backs of my legs so it looks like I'm wearing stockings."

Patricia kept everything TJ brought her, but Marianne knew many girls often resold or bartered away the gifts of chocolate, flowers, and liquor American servicemen gave them. She didn't blame them. Prices were high because of shortages, wages were low, and luxuries were almost nonexistent. Sometimes selling gifts helped pay the rent and put food on the table.

"I don't have time. I have dresses to work on for three of the girls at work." With clothing rationing in place, and no new evening frocks available in the shops, word had spread among her work mates and their friends that she had a gift for quickly refashioning old dresses into something new. Her abilities were much appreciated by girls who wanted pretty dresses to wear when they went out in the evening.

"All right. Just remember what I've said about all work and no play." Patricia picked up the paper that Marianne had discarded and scanned the page.

"Listen to this. Establishment of the Australian parachute industry is one reason why the Government has had to freeze silk, and why women find it difficult to get silk stockings." Patricia lowered the paper. "If they'd explained it like *that* instead of just saying we can't have them because of the war, I wouldn't have grumbled so much. Of course, parachutes are more important than stockings.

"And listen to this one," Patricia continued. "Sydney Girls' Tribute To RAF Ace. Flight-Lieutenant James "Ginger" Lacey, 23-year-old RAF ace, wearing the first Australian-made parachute to reach Britain and a silk scarf that was sent with it. The scarf was made by the girls of the Sydney factory which made the parachute, and bears 85 signatures. Flight-Lieutenant Lacey has made nine parachute descents during battles and claims to have brought down 24 Nazi planes. He has won the Distinguished Flying Medal and Bar. Is that the one you told me about?"

"Mm-hmm."

"Just imagine. An RAF ace. I wonder if Australia will ever have one. It could even be your Sam."

Ignoring Patricia's comment about Sam, Marianne said, "I thought you were more interested in American sailors."

"Just the one American sailor." Patricia rose from her chair and collected the tray of crockery. "I'll do the washing up and then I'm going to have an early night of it. I want to get to the office early in the morning so I can leave early and have time to get dolled up for my lovely Yank friend. We're going dancing at the Trocadero."

"Go on. I'll finish hemming your dress tonight," Marianne said. "You will look beautiful for TJ tomorrow."

Patricia blew a kiss her way and danced out of the sitting room humming Glenn Miller's "Chattanooga Choo Choo."

Before she opened her sewing box, Marianne perused the rest of the paper. One woman's letter suggested that Australian women who were married with children wanted to help but couldn't because of the hours. Why couldn't employers arrange shifts that would allow them to work while their children were in school? Then, an article calling for more air cadets caught her eye. "There are now 1,870 cadets in this State, and more than 100 enrollments are being received each week," she read, "but further cadets are required for both air crew and ground staff."

No wonder they'd had the extra orders at work. As usual, when parachutes came to mind, so did Sam and her prayer: *Please fly safely. Please don't make us carry you on your shield.*

Somewhere in Sydney
4 September 1942

Dear Sam,
*My map has been pinned. What is a CWA and why
are they giving you biscuits and cakes? Does Mrs. Kelly
know about this?*

Please fly as safely as you can,
Marianne
*P.S. Who were the better dancers? The ruffians or the
airmen? I confess I'm not very good. The tallest girls
always got asked last at school dances.*

Somewhere in QLD
22 September 1942

Dear Marianne,
*No one's biscuits and cakes are better than Mrs. Kel-
ly's. CWA stands for Country Women's Association.
Imagine a dozen older ladies who do good works and
host gatherings to raise money and morale but out in
the country towns instead of the big cities.*

*I suspect we all had our toes stepped on at least once, but
everyone seemed to enjoy themselves. If nothing else, we
appreciated the respite from everyday life.*

Sew straight,
Sam
P.S. Those boys knew nothing. You're just the right

height. If you'd been there, I'd have danced with you until our toes were aching.

FIFTY-SEVEN

FLYING WITH THE STARS

OCTOBER 1942

Sydney
12 October 1942

Dear Sam,
Your parents still seem to be doing well. I think the ad-
dition of the three children to the household keeps Sophie
so busy that she has less time to worry about you and
Jean-Luc. Teddy is determined to win the competition
at school for collecting the most scrap paper and metal.
Cora is so fascinated with the hens that Thomas had
to fix the latch so she can't get in the pen by herself.
Katie is still sad about her mother's death. I don't think
she understands when Mrs. Kelly says her mother is in
heaven with the angels. I offered to teach her to sew, but
she said she would rather read her book about the stars.

Actually, it's your book. Sophie asked Thomas to build a
little shelf in the drawing room and fitted out a corner

with cushions for Katie to read in. Howard snuggles up to her when she reads. Your father says Rudy, the puppy you found when you were a little boy, did the same thing with you.

Fly safely,
Marianne

Somewhere in QLD
28 October 1942

Dear Marianne,
I was only a little younger than Katie when my mum died, so I know something about losing your mother as a child. She can have all my books if they will lessen her grief.

There's another thing that helped me – someone told me my mum was up in the sky with the stars. Dad used to spend hours in the back garden teaching me the constellations while I tried to guess which star she was hiding behind. I hadn't thought of that in ages. Maybe that's why I like flying at night so much.

Must fly, literally and figuratively. **Merci** *for all the home front news.*

Sew straight,
Sam

FIFTY-EIGHT

THANKSGIVING

NOVEMBER 1942

By November, Sophie realized with a start, the Parker household had settled into the reality of being at war with no end in sight of bad news interrupted by occasional bursts of good news.

In what the press labeled the Battle of Brisbane, two Australian soldiers bashed an American Military Police officer who had harassed an American GI. Americans and Australians began fighting with the despised MPs, one of whom shot and killed an Australian soldier. Thousands of people then joined in what became a riot that lasted two days. Businesses and public areas were closed for the duration.

Nine months after HMAS *Perth* and USS *Houston* disappeared without a trace in the Sunda Straits while on a joint mission, the Japanese finally admitted to torpedoing both ships and taking the few survivors prisoner. Hundreds of Australian and American sailors had been lost.

But there was good news from New Guinea, even though it was tempered by the knowledge that Jean-Luc was there and appalling numbers of casualties continued to be reported. In September, the Battle for Milne Bay marked the first time Japanese ground troops were defeated. Allied forces had interrupted and delayed Japanese supply lines to the point the Japanese were finally pushed out of the Owen Stanley Range in October. And within the last few days, Buna and Gona, on the northern coast, had been captured from the Japanese. It seemed Port Moresby might not be occupied after all. Perhaps Australia was safe from invasion. Perhaps Jean-Luc wouldn't be one of the casualties.

Then, a note from Sam arrived with a different sort of news.

> *Somewhere in QLD*
> *1 November 1942*
>
> *Dear Dad and Sophie, Mrs Kelly, Thomas, and Marianne,*
> *Quick note to say I'm still safe and well. Supplies received and many thanks for them. As I predicted, we're being sent north to look after Jean-Luc and his mates, plus help the Yanks.*
>
> *Love to all,*
> *Sam*
> *P.S. The chaps in my squadron loved Mrs. Kelly's fruitcake.*

By the time Sophie finished reading Sam's letter, the familiar seesaw of emotions began. Relief she'd dared to feel about Jean-Luc was immediately replaced with anxiety over Sam's news that he too would be in harm's way in New Guinea.

—

The third Thursday of November was an ordinary day on Australian calendars, but for Sophie and the American officers whom she had invited to dinner it was Thanksgiving Day.

She had originally suggested the idea to Edmund Stone, who loved it, and chose two friends to join the festivities. Since the US Navy had the best provisions and cooks, Neil, a navy pilot, brought a turkey, cornbread, and cranberry sauce, plus pumpkin and pecan pies. Edmund and Alan, an Army Air Force pilot, availed themselves of all the luxuries the PX had to offer and brought a bottle of Kentucky bourbon each for Joe and Thomas, perfume and stockings for Sophie, Marianne, and Moira, and Hershey's chocolate bars for the children.

Teddy was still enthralled by military regalia, and having the opportunity to examine and compare the uniforms, badges, ribbons, and caps of three branches of American forces firsthand was almost as thrilling as the prospect of Christmas next month. His excited reporting after Edmund's previous visit had earned him the envy of his classmates. He was practically bursting with anticipation at the opportunity to tell his news at school tomorrow.

Moira, whom Edmund had befriended on his first visit to the Parker home, invited him into her kitchen to check the progress of the turkey and cornbread dressing, and then shooed him back to the drawing room, where the adults were studying a map of the South West Pacific Area.

"We're fairly certain Jean-Luc's brigade is here," Joe said, indicating the area around Buna and Gona on the northern coast of New Guinea. "And Sam's squadron is at one of the airfields close by."

"US forces are there with them," Edmund said. "I've heard the fighting has been intense." He looked away from her when she caught his eye.

"Edmund? Please, if you know more tell us. Even if it's awful. The wondering and worrying are breaking my heart."

"I don't really *know* anything about the Australian troops," Edmund replied. "It's all second-hand."

"I'd like to hear it anyway," Sophie said. "We need to be prepared for what he might need when he finally comes home."

"All right. Allied forces managed to capture the Japanese beachheads."

By this point in the war, Sophie had virtually memorized the South West Pacific Area map. "Here and here," she said as she pointed to Buna and Gona on the northern coast and Milne Bay on the eastern tip of the island. "What about Kokoda? We think Jean-Luc's battalion was sent there."

"It's pretty chaotic out there. I spoke with only a few American GIs out of hundreds of troops." He paused, as if to gauge her reactions. She nodded for him to continue, so he pulled his notebook from a pocket and read through his notes. "The men I talked to heard tales of jungle so deep and thick that the enemy could be lurking within mere feet. Near constant rain and mud that resulted in ungodly trench foot and debilitating skin ailments. Then there's malaria and dysentery. Warm food and hot drinks were things of the past. Grumbles they had received less than adequate training and preparation for the terrain."

He tucked his notebook away. "I asked, but no one has seen a Frenchman wearing an Australian uniform."

Sophie was certain Edmund could have said more, that he knew more, but he wasn't sure she could bear to hear it. She finally said, "Thank you for telling us."

"It doesn't mean anything has happened to Jean-Luc, Sophie," Edmund said.

"Needless to say, it can be a little fraught around here with both sons in the thick of it there," Joe said.

A long silence followed, with Alan and Neil shifting uncomfortably, their eyes darting over the map. Sophie thought it must be one thing to be in the fight, but another thing entirely to see firsthand how the fight affected parents worried about their sons. Joe caught her eye, and she could see he was just as concerned as he was. What if Sam or Jean-Luc came back broken beyond repair? How could they bear it?

Neil spoke up to break the tension. "What kind of planes does your other son fly?"

"Sam flies Wirraways," Joe replied. "No 4 Squadron, flying close air support for the Australians. The Americans, too, I reckon. He flew for an aerial mapping company for several years before the war, so he had a lot of experience to start with. He spent a couple of years training air cadets before his squadron moved to New Guinea."

Alan let out a low whistle. "He's one of the Wirraway boys? That's what Admiral Halsey calls 'em. During the battle for Buna, Aussies flying Wirraways directed our artillery onto hidden Japanese gun positions." He paused, a look of awe crossing his features. "They have to fly so low the trees bump the plane's undercarriage. Pinpoint accuracy. Exposed to enemy fire the entire time but absolutely fearless. I've seen some damned, sorry ladies, fine flying in this war, and that was some of the best. I'd like to meet your son someday and shake his hand."

Hidden enemies. Flying at tree-top level. She recalled Sam's comment that he wasn't one of the brazen pilots the allies needed in Europe, that they needed his experience to train new pilots, but it seemed circumstances were forcing him to be brazen and brash after all.

Glancing at Marianne, all pale cheeks and wide eyes, Sophie knew the young woman was just as distressed as she was. Somehow, she had to calm Marianne's nerves as well as her own. She'd had plenty of practice doing exactly the same thing when tending wounded soldiers all those years ago. She should be able to do it know.

Sophie linked her arm with Marianne's and led the way to the dining room "Since Jean-Luc is infantry, I like to think he and Sam are somehow working together and taking care of each other. The news about Buna and Gona seems to bear that out, don't you think?"

Marianne leaned closer, which Sophie interpreted as agreement. She forced a lighter note into her voice. "And now I think we should sample our allied culinary efforts. It has been too many years since I had a proper Thanksgiving meal."

Dinner might taste like ashes in her mouth, but she had guests to entertain and a young woman to reassure. She could fall to pieces later.

When it came time for everyone to leave after dinner, pie, and sampling Joe's bottle of bourbon, Marianne motioned Edmund aside for a private moment.

She handed him a thick envelope. "Would you give Maman and Papa this letter when you see them in London next week?"

"Of course. Anything else?"

"Hug them both for me. Find out everything you can about Chris. I'm so worried about him. Could you take me with you? Just for a short visit?"

Edmund chuckled. "I would if I could. Now tell me, how are you coping with Sam based in New Guinea? I saw you fidgeting while we were discussing a certain RAAF squadron."

"Flying just above the tree tops? How can they be expected to do that?"

"How else can they show the bombers where to bomb? New Guinea is covered with so many trees that the Japanese are very well hidden from the air."

"But it can't possibly be safe. Parachutes are useless at that height."

"My dear, what you must understand is that pilots like Sam have trained for countless hours. They're very good at what they do. They know what their planes are capable of and they're confident in their abilities. You have to be just as confident in Sam."

Marianne's shoulders sagged as her indignation deflated. "I try to be. I'm just so worried about him and Jean-Luc. We will be devastated if anything happens to them."

"By the way, I'm happy to offer my approval on your mother and father's behalf. After all, I am your—"

"Honorary uncle. But Edmund, even if I did have feelings for Sam..."

"Mm hmm."

"...which I do not because I am too busy to have feelings for anyone..."

Edmund was appraising her with the same indulgent expression of disbelief she'd seen from him dozens of times when she and Chris were growing up and spinning a tale. It would be best if she stopped talking. "Sam does not have time for feelings either."

"Then he isn't nearly as smart as I thought he was. Dear girl, I've watched you grow up from a babe in your mother's arms to a smart, strong, beautiful young woman. You are what the GIs would call a real catch," Edmund replied. "There are plenty of other fish in the sea, you know. I'm sure I could round up some—"

"*Non, merci.* But I will let you know if ever I need help catching a fish," Marianne said, smiling in spite of her distress as she and Edmund kissed cheeks three times.

Sydney
26 November 1942

Dear Sam,
Edmund and two American pilots were here today for
Sophie's American Thanksgiving holiday dinner. The
Americans were full of praise for the Australians pilots
who guide them in and show them where the Japanese
are hidden by jungle.

I admit to being scared nearly senseless when they said
you have to fly so low the coconut trees brush the under-
side of your plane.

Please tell me you are being as careful as you can be,
Marianne

FIFTY-NINE

CHRISTMAS ON THE HOME FRONT

DECEMBER 1942

Sam's news back in November that his No 4 Squadron had been sent to New Guinea to support Jean-Luc's 7th Division, and the belief that both their sons were working together to protect each other and home, helped to counterbalance Sophie's worrisome thoughts about flying at treetop level and hidden enemies.

Their boys wouldn't be home for Christmas, but she plunged into helping to organize the nativity pageant at St. Mary's with a lighter heart.

———

Sophie swiped the back of her hand across her forehead. Despite having all of the windows open, and fans positioned at strategic spots to move air, the house was far too warm for comfort. Unless they got a southerly buster soon, with its cooling rain and wind, this Christmas was going to be a hot one.

Darn it. The pin slipped in her sweaty fingers because the boy standing on the coffee table was not as cooperative as he should have been. "Teddy, stop fidgeting before I poke you with a pin!"

After several rounds of soul-searching when she finally acknowledged her doubts about the wisdom of taking the children in, she had decided to ease away from all but one of the organizations she volunteered with, informing the boards that her energy and time were best spent providing aid and comfort to the three youngsters the war had unexpectedly placed in her path. She stayed on with the Red Cross, since she'd had a soft spot for it from her days in France during the Great War. Because she was already involved at St. Mary's via the weekly vegetable and egg donations, and she was there for pick up duties every weekday anyhow, she volunteered to help with the nativity pageant. Not wanting to step on any toes—she knew how territorial volunteer organizations could be, plus she wasn't a parishioner or even a Catholic—she accepted the tedious job of fitting, hemming, and mending costumes the church had in its vast stores. Teddy was going to be one of several shepherds and Katie one of the angels. Students from the upper years would be Mary, Joseph, the angel Gabriel, and the lead shepherd.

Sophie had briefly wondered if she could get Marianne to teach her how to use a sewing machine, but decided she could sew fast enough and well enough to do the hemming by hand. Katie was rummaging through the contents of the sewing box, but wasn't making a mess of things, so Sophie concentrated on the youngster who was proving to be a trial.

Teddy was impatient to get back outdoors. "I won't be able to see the ship once it passes Bennelong," he protested.

Sophie was nearly out of patience. "That's a shame. I'd be finished and you'd be outside by now if you'd stood still the first ten times I asked you to."

"But Miss Sophie!"

"No buts, Teddy. It will take me less than a minute to finish pinning this hem if you keep still. So you have a choice. Stand still now or keep fidgeting and it will take twice as long."

Chastened, Teddy grumbled something that Sophie didn't catch, but he stood still while he counted off seconds.

Determined to make good on her self-imposed deadline, Sophie pinned faster. As long as Teddy didn't trip over the robe, it didn't matter if it didn't hide his shoelaces. Besides, at the rate he was growing, the hem would reach his ankles by Christmas.

By the time Teddy's count reached to forty-five, Sophie stood, motioned for him to raise his arms, and swept the brown shepherd's robe over his head.

"Finished. See how quick and easy that was when you cooperate?"

Teddy had already jumped down from the table and turned to race outdoors.

"Don't forget to close the door when you go out," she called. "But don't slam it!"

Too late. The front door slammed shut.

That boy! "Excuse me a moment, Katie." Sophie caught up with Teddy at the front gate. He was writing in the little notebook where he recorded passing ships, airplanes, and anything else that caught his interest.

"Teddy, do you remember the consequences for ignoring the rule about slamming doors?" Joe and Moira had dreamed up 'the rule' as a way of teaching Sam which behaviors were non-negotiable and Sophie agreed to try it with Teddy. The rule also eliminated the useless 'Because I said so' reason that no child in their right mind ever took seriously.

"I didn't mean to! It slammed by itself!"

Sophie held out her hand. "Your notebook, please."

"But Miss Sophie!"

"You know the rule, Teddy. You may have your notebook back in one hour."

Grumbling, Teddy relinquished his notebook. Sophie bit back a smile as she returned to the house. The first twenty times he'd put up much more of an argument. Perhaps the days of slamming doors were almost behind them.

Pinning the hem on Katie's white angel tunic was easier since Katie didn't have an all-consuming passion for running outside to watch passing warships. She did, however, have an overriding interest in decorating a Christmas tree, which they didn't have yet.

"How big will the Christmas tree be?"

"Sweetheart, I don't know. Thomas will find the best one he can."

"Where will we put it?"

"I don't know that either. It will depend on the tree."

"We could move my reading corner." Katie loved her reading corner. Howard liked to curl up with her there while she read before bed. It was also a respite for him after Cora wore him out during the day.

"We may have to. Or we could put the tree in front of the windows."

"What will we put on top?"

That was easy. As a boy, Joe had made a little model of the Southern Cross from wire and tin stars that seemed to twinkle in the lamplight. "We have a star ornament that Joe made when he was about Teddy's age. I think you'll like it."

"My mumma made paper stars. Could we do that?"

Sophie stopped mid-pin. The girl had barely said a word about her mother in nearly ten months. Sensing this unexpected mention might be a breakthrough, she let Katie take the conversation wherever she wanted. "That's a wonderful idea."

"We can have a star for everyone. Me, Teddy, and Cora. You and Mr. Parker. Mrs. Kelly and Thomas. Marianne, Sam, and Jean-Luc. How many is that?"

"Let's see...one, two...ten."

"Mumma and daddy and baby Patrick. Your mumma and Aunt Flora. Where is your daddy?"

"He died about fifteen years ago. He's buried in England."

"Oh." Katie seemed to ponder that for a moment, and Sophie wondered if she shouldn't have spoken of death, but Katie surprised her. "We should have one for him too. 'Cause my mumma and the baby are buried and we'll make one for them."

Sophie placed the final pins in Katie's robe and vowed to make a star for all the other loved ones who weren't with them anymore.

Ben. Annie. Robbie. Jean-Luc's parents. Joe's parents. Her own baby. Michael, even though their marriage had ended in shambles and tragedy, she had loved him once.

She was mentally going through the boxes of ornaments in the attic, and whether she would have a place for them this year because of all the stars, when Thomas came in with the news that he had found a tree.

"It isn't tall enough to reach the ceiling in the drawing room," he said, placing a Norfolk Island pine, its root ball wrapped in burlap sacking, in a shady spot outside the kitchen door. "But we can put it on a couple of fruit crates to raise it up. We can plant it after the holiday."

Sophie examined the tree. "It's perfect. Wherever did you find it?"

"Ways and means, missus. Ways and means."

When Thomas answered a question with that response, Sophie knew better than to press the point. Thomas had friends and acquaintances who could procure almost anything. And who was she to question his means when his motives were the same as hers: to make three children happy?

———

Somewhere in the SWPA
30 December 1942

Dear Marianne,
Good to know the Yanks appreciate our efforts. The bombers we lead in are huge. I'd love to have a go flying one of them. It would take a bit of training, though.

It's always a shock to feel and hear things bumping the undercarriage, since you never want that to happen under normal circumstances. I admit there are times I

*feel claustrophobic when all I can see below me is green,
and I can't wait to turn my plane and get back to
the blue. Then there are the times we're flying over the
water and all I can think is I can't wait to see green
again. The ocean and skies out here are beautiful and
awe-inspiring, but sometimes it's terrifying how immense it all is. If you go down out there, you'll probably
never be found.*

*I promise I'm being as careful as I can be, but I have a
job to do, and every sortie I do my job as well as I can.
I have every intention of getting home when this is all
over, so chin up, and keep sewing straight, please!*

*Sam
P.S. I hope you had a happy Christmas, in spite of what
you've heard about Aussie pilots.*

PART 4: 1943 - 1946

AUSTRALIA, NEW GUINEA, BORNEO, FRANCE

God knows the grief they suffer,
So keep it in your mind,
They are the bravest soldiers,
The womenfolk we've left behind.

Author Unknown,
"The Womenfolk We Left Behind"

Sixty

Tampered Evidence

February 1943

Several weeks after the hot and sticky entrance of 1943, Sophie greeted Joe from the drawing room while the children swarmed around him in the entry hall, clamoring for his attention. Teddy with the latest pages in his notebook. Katie's pride in a perfect spelling test. Cora simply wanted to be picked up, which she demanded by latching on to Joe's leg. Howard's dash around Joe's ankles completed the minor chaos.

Joe took it all in stride, with an approving nod for Teddy and a "well done" for Katie's score, all the while hanging his hat on the coat tree's hook and scooping up a giggling Cora. Would their life have been like this if she and Joe had met earlier and had a family? A few months ago she had resented his ease with them. Now it amused her and occasionally triggered a powerful desire to drag him upstairs and make a child of their own. Not that she could bear one, but that didn't mean the urge wasn't there.

This evening he looked tired, so she poured him a drink. "You are a wonderful woman," he said when he spotted the glass in her hand. He ruffled Cora's curls after he put her back on her own feet and sent all three children to the kitchen for their supper.

"You're home at a reasonable hour, darling. How was your day?"

"Frustrating." Joe took his first sip and sank down on the sofa, tugging the knot of his tie down and undoing his collar button. "The evidence in a murder case has been compromised."

Sophie kicked off her shoes and sat sideways so she could put her feet in Joe's lap and still see his face.

"What do you mean, compromised?"

"Exactly what I said. Tainted." Joe took a big enough swallow of his drink that the ice cubes clinked against the side of his glass. Goodness. He was usually a sipper, not a guzzler.

He put his glass down. His left hand settled on her right ankle resting on his thigh. He rubbed above his eyebrows with the other hand long enough that his left hand matched the rhythm of his right.

"Tell me. Start from the beginning and tell me everything you can," Sophie said.

Joe blew out a breath. "All right. A middle-aged man, Locke, was found dead by his wife last month. He'd been bashed on the back of the head once with the business end of a crowbar. His wife found him in their sitting room when she came home from shopping. The fingerprints that were found on the weapon matched the victim's, his wife's, and their two sons. There was a fifth set of prints that were later identified as belonging to Woods, a neighbor."

"Sounds pretty straightforward so far."

"It seemed to be straightforward, at the beginning," Joe said. "The officer in charge of the investigation was a Sergeant Fletcher. I've never met him, but his reports were all in order."

"What's the problem, then?"

"I called that station this morning to speak to Fletcher," Joe said. "He hasn't come to work for several days so I had to speak with his senior constable."

"Is Fletcher on leave? Out sick?"

"The constable said Fletcher had resigned from the force and enlisted in the army."

"Couldn't he have waited until the case was over?" Sophie mused.

"Apparently his brother signed up too and they wanted to be in the same platoon. So, that's the first problem. I need to see if Fletcher can get leave from training and be present at the hearing. I doubt it though."

Sophie nudged Joe's leg with her other heel. "That felt wonderful, darling. Do the other one now, please?"

He released her left foot. She wiggled her toes while his warm hand moved to her right foot. She waited patiently while he took a sip of his drink—not guzzling this time. The ice was beginning to melt so he swirled the glass to mix the water and whisky.

"And the second problem?" Sophie prompted.

Joe stared across the room for a moment.

"The second problem," he said, still staring and absently rubbing, "is that when we received the crowbar, there were no fingerprints on it."

Sophie sat up. "What?" How could that happen?"

Joe shook his head. "I have no idea. The first rule of collecting evidence is to not tamper with it. You bag it, dust it for prints..."

Sophie knew the drill by heart. "The evidence is returned to the bag, and it's locked up in the evidence room and kept safe."

Joe raised a brow at her. "And you don't ever wipe the evidence clean before you have to present it in court."

"Gosh, you do have a problem, darling. What's the timing for the court case?"

"The hearing is on Monday. It's already Wednesday evening, I have a missing officer who might be able to explain why the crowbar was wiped clean, and I'm going to have to order a set of tests on the weapon to see if we can get any other clues from it, and..."

"Like what? Another person's blood?" Sophie's face brightened. "You can test for that, can't you? Could the crowbar have been used in another crime?"

"And," Joe continued, "the lab technician who's supposed to run the extra tests for me has come down with the mother of all colds. He was running a fever and sneezing all over the office today. I sent him home before he could infect the rest of us."

"What extra tests do you want to run?"

Joe's face brightened. "There's something on the crowbar that looks like a fleck of paint. Now, if we can prove that the paint on the crowbar is the same as the paint used on the dead man's railings, we have our prime suspect."

"So would that rule out the wife or the two sons?"

"Probably. If the paint is fresh, as in only a few days old, it rules out the wife and sons because they were off in the Blue Mountains for a wedding. According to Fletcher's report, even if she had been home, the wife doesn't seem to be the sort who would get anywhere near a paint can, much less a crowbar. Society-wannabe was what the constable called her. Fletcher's notes recommended questioning the neighbor, who was painting his railings a couple of weeks ago."

"Any indication why the neighbor would want to bash the victim on the head? Or kill him some other way?"

"Not that I can tell. It seems they had the usual spats over the years. Locke always complained that Woods didn't keep up his property as well as the rest of the neighborhood. He was bringing the rest of the block down. The ironwork on his—"

"Where's the house?"

"It's a terrace in Elizabeth Bay, your old suburb. One of several that were built by the same builder about seventy years ago."

"Hmmm. So if one resident doesn't keep their paintwork fresh, they all feel the effects."

"Something like that," Joe said. "I have to tell you love, I like the puzzle parts of this job, but it has its own set of frustrations."

"At least you aren't being shot at anymore."

"True," Joe sighed. "There's just such a push to make a difference with limited resources. If I can't prove that a dedicated forensics department is pulling its weight and producing results, there's a chance the budget will get cut. We need more and better equipment. I need a secretary who can take shorthand notes and type more than twenty words a minute."

"Miss Pringle is a dear but she's rather old school, isn't she?

"I'll never let her go," Joe said. "She's been working for the police for so long that she knows everyone and everything that's happened in Sydney in the past forty years. For a relative newcomer like me..."

"Is that what she calls you? Even though you've worked here since 1922?"

Joe chuckled. "My twenty years here are a drop in the bucket compared to her forty years."

"Well, darling, I'm sure you'll figure out something," Sophie said. "You always do."

The next day, Sophie decided to drive to collect Teddy and Katie from school, so she could pass by the terrace houses in Joe's case before she picked them up. She might notice something that could be useful. Such a discovery would be well worth using some of her hoarded petrol ration.

She pulled up to the curb across the street and studied the row of houses while still sitting in her car. They were all painted the same shade of warm grey, with curved metal roofs over the top balconies. The intricate ironwork on the balconies, painted a darker, glossy grey, was Victoriana at the height of the style. She'd never painted anything like it, but it looked like it would be an absolute bear of a job. It wasn't the sort of thing where you could load a brush with paint and slap it on. No, you'd have to carefully work the paint into all the curlicues, the tops and bottoms, and inside the curves and rosettes. Even for professional painters, it would be a time-consuming job.

The house on the end of the row was beautifully maintained. The windows sparkled. The paint on the ironwork was glossy. The high, end wall was crisscrossed with wire to form a trellis for flowering vines. Potted ferns flanked each side of the shaded front door, and baskets of them hung from the upstairs railing. Everything looked fresh and well-watered despite the stifling summer heat.

Sophie got out of her car and crossed the street to the corner. She walked the length of the block, peering through the ironwork that enclosed the little forecourts at the front of each house. All but one house was as well maintained as the corner house. The front door could use a new coat of paint. The walk needed sweeping. The plants desperately needed watering. The ironwork had been freshly painted but it wasn't quite the same deep grey as the other houses. Errant blobs of paint dotted the footpath.

Perhaps there was a way she could help Joe's department. She dropped her car keys so they would land close to the biggest blob she could see. When she stooped to pick them up, she used the blade of the little Swiss army knife Jean-Luc had given her as a gift years ago to pick at the blob of paint. To her delight, she was able to scrape off a fairly large chunk of it. She carefully picked it up, tucked it into her skirt pocket, and nonchalantly made her way back to her car. Once she was settled in the driver's seat, she rummaged through the glove box and found an old envelope. She felt around in her pocket for the little chunk of paint and placed it in the envelope for safekeeping.

She wrote down the address of the house on the envelope and the date. What else should she record? She thought for a moment, and added the time, the weather, and a note that she hadn't seen anyone either on the street or any signs of inhabitants.

She should have brought her camera. She could have taken a few photos. If anyone had questioned her presence, she could have made up a story about looking for a house to rent or she was writing a story about Sydney suburbs, or terrace houses from the 1860s. The possibilities were endless!

Sophie put her pen and the envelope in her handbag, and she drove, quickly, to Joe's office to give him her prize.

———

Several nights later, Sophie looked on as Joe poured a glass of wine for her and then for himself. She lifted her glass in a little salute to him and prepared to take her first sip.

"Not yet, if you don't mind," Joe said.

Frowning, Sophie stopped with the wineglass midway to her lips. "Why ever not?"

"Because," he said, lifting his own glass. "There's something I'd like to say first."

Mystified, Sophie placed her glass back on the tabletop and studied her husband's face. His eyes were twinkling and a half-smile tugged at the right side of his mouth.

"I'm all ears," she said.

"I heard from the university. They've done the analysis of the evidence, and the fleck of paint on the crowbar matches the paint you scraped up from the pavement."

Sophie's face brightened. Joe hadn't been particularly happy that she'd gone to the scene of the crime on her own, even though he'd been intrigued by the short little report she'd made on the back of the old envelope.

"I'm still not happy that you went to the scene of the crime, especially that you went there alone," he said. "And I couldn't rely on the blob you collected. I had to send a constable over there to get another sample."

"Following police procedures," she guessed.

"Following official police procedures," he corrected. "However, because you spotted the blobs of dried paint on the pavement, we will be able to make our case that Woods killed Locke."

Joe picked up his glass and tipped it towards Sophie. "So, on behalf of the New South Wales police force, please consider this a formal thank you for your assistance in bringing important evidence to our attention." Grinning, he eyed Sophie's glass. She picked it up and Joe tapped the rim of her glass with his.

"But Joe, surely the paint on the pavement is circumstantial evidence, isn't it? Anyone could have painted that ironwork. It's not proof that Woods did it."

"Ah," Joe said. "What you don't know is Woods confessed after spending the night in a cell with a Bible that Thompson slipped to him for reading material."

"You're joking!" Sophie set her glass down and twined her fingers together. "A cold-blooded murderer confesses because..."

Joe waggled his head back and forth. "He isn't really cold-blooded. He just got fed up with Locke hounding him when he knew he was down on his luck. Apparently, he spent nearly his last quid on a quart of paint to get Locke to get off his back and Locke came over and criticized the job he was doing. It wasn't premeditated. Woods said he saw red and couldn't stand it anymore."

"I'm almost sorry for him," Sophie said. "Will he hang?"

"I doubt it. He'll probably get life in prison. Although his solicitor may be able to get the sentence reduced to ten or twenty years."

"What a waste," Sophie said. "A man loses his life because he's obnoxious and another man will effectively lose his life because he couldn't take being hounded. We're all under such pressure because of the war. It seems things get blown out of proportion so easily now."

Joe swirled the ruby red wine in his glass. "That's as good a summary as any," he said, taking a sip. "Anyhow, I thought you'd like to know that once again you had a hand in solving a case."

"Thank you, darling. I do endeavor to be useful as well as decorative," Sophie teased. "You know, it was twelve years ago when I first showed you how helpful I can be in solving cases—remember the society murder when I first arrived in Sydney?"

Since then, Joe had often turned to her for her insights on members of the wealthy circles she was involved—the moneyed ranks displayed a shocking propensity for crimes of all sorts, usually when inheritances, gambling, and revenge were involved—as the lower classes did, although Joe tended to have less sympathy for the former than the latter. He treated everyone equally, though, regardless of their station in society.

"I'm happy to assist Sydney's finest" Sophie purred after Joe reeled off the remaining instances when she'd helped and had lifted his glass to her a second time.

Joe was glad to have some good news to share. They hadn't heard from Sam or Jean-Luc in several weeks and were at the point of being utterly disappointed every day a letter didn't appear in the day's post. Each knew the other thought about the boys often in the course of a day, and Joe was certain Sophie said a little prayer for both of them before she went to sleep every night.

He was good at compartmentalizing his thoughts and emotions. As a police officer he'd learned to do both and it was holding him in good stead now. Sophie was less practiced, nor did she want to suppress everything. Before the children came to them, she spent her considerable resources, both personal and financial, doing projects to help those who were left behind—the wives with too many mouths to feed, the elderly parents who relied on their sons to supplement their incomes, as well as the women whose men had fought in the last war but hadn't come home hale and healthy or at all.

Now she had the O'Brien children and Marianne Ryan to think about.

Sophie was also taking more than a passing interest in all of the cases he was working. That was a double-edged sword. Technically, he wasn't supposed to discuss the details of cases with anyone other than fellow police officers. But there weren't enough of them to go around, since half the force was off fighting. His colleagues were stretched just as thin as Joe was. He wondered how many wives were being used as sounding boards, and whether they enjoyed it as much as Sophie did.

Sophie and he had worked well together in Chamonix, when they'd had to work out how they'd come to be in possession of a German army insignia and trench knife from the first war. Every godawful memory that he had buried had come roaring back to the forefront of his consciousness.

A young German had died because of the edelweiss insignia and the trench knife. Joe had spent the rest of their time in France coming to terms with his part in the tragedy. Sophie had been there with him every step of the way. If letting her in on confidential details

could help them get through worrying about their boys, Joe would
tell her everything he knew.

SIXTY-ONE

RED CROSS, RED DRESS

MARCH – JULY 1943

Marianne tapped her pen against her chin, wondering whether she should mention she'd finally relented and accompanied Patricia and TJ to a dance sponsored by the Red Cross.

Why shouldn't she? Sam was dancing with Land Army girls. They both needed a break from their daily lives. He had grueling missions to fly, younger pilots to lead, and a ruthless enemy to fight. She had parachutes to make, dresses to sew, and her own family to worry about in addition to his.

Sydney
6 March 1943

Dear Sam,
Your father and Sophie are doing well. Sophie has be-
gun inviting American servicemen to Sunday dinner.
The Red Cross is always looking for ways to make the
Americans feel less lonely since they are so far from
home. I have enjoyed meeting new people and these
dinners may be Sophie's way of feeling closer to you and

Jean-Luc since you are both away.

I attended a dance last Saturday night with Patricia and TJ, her American beau. I met a lieutenant from New Orleans. His French sounded like nothing I had ever heard. He assured me that his people spoke the same French his ancestors spoke when they left France for Nova Scotia in the seventeenth century. I never would have guessed I would hear ancient French spoken at all, much less in Australia, of all places!

That conversation had resulted in both them laughing until their sides hurt. He really had been charming. She'd worn the red silk dress again and the lieutenant said she looked like a million bucks. He was a good dancer. And he smelled nice.

Not as nice as Sam...

Enough of that.

The dance was enjoyable, and a most welcome change from spending my evenings altering dresses for other girls.

She might go dancing with the lieutenant again. Why not? Patricia kept saying she deserved to have a little fun. It wasn't like she had to marry him.

Sophie suggested I bring him, Patricia, and TJ along to the house for dinner, so we did that on Sunday. Teddy likes to interrogate guests on their uniforms and insignia, but he developed a disturbing habit of asking how many of the enemy they have killed until your father put an end to that.

Still, I think the visitors like being around the children as they are reminded of their own brothers and sisters, or even children in some cases.

Fly safely,
Marianne

Somewhere in the SWPA
31 March 1943

Dear Marianne,
I assume your Yank is polite and respectful? Let me know if he ever tries to cross a line and I'll fly down and buzz him from 30 feet. That would remind him to watch himself.

Sew straight,
Sam

Sydney
15 April 1943

Dear Sam,
He is not my Yank, although I think he would like to be. I wish you and Jean-Luc could surprise your parents again on Easter this year. Sophie wanted to have a big gathering for American servicemen, but Easter Sunday and Anzac Day are the same day this year. So, we are going to attend the dawn service at the memorial instead and then have lunch with just the family. We will miss both of you.

Fly safely,

Marianne

Somewhere in the SWPA
25 May 1943

Dear Marianne,
The real question is whether you would like him to be,
isn't it?

Sew straight,
Sam

Sydney
27 June 1943

Dear Sam,
Truthfully, as much as I enjoyed spending time with
him, he is not the man for me. I have no desire to leave
Australia for America whenever this war is over.

Fly safely,
Marianne
P.S. Please excuse the ink spots on this letter. I am at
your parent's house and Cora and Howard are run-
ning rings around the table where I am writing. I
would love to send them outside to play, but it is raining
and the garden is muddy. I am not brave enough to face
Mrs Kelly when they come inside and make a mess.

Sam chuckled at the thought of Mrs. Kelly's reaction to Cora and Howard tracking mud on her kitchen floor. He and Marianne had been writing for the better part of two years and each exchange was better than the last. She was funny, thoughtful, independent, and forthright. He could imagine her expressions blazing, tender, or amused depending on the circumstances. He suspected she still had no idea how attractive she was, all golden coppery hair and jade eyes and long legs and lips whose kisses he would never forget.

Regardless of how much he appreciated her spirit and beauty, the fact remained that the most intriguing woman he'd ever met made him smile when there was nothing much to smile about. She made him think when he didn't particularly want to. She made him want to be better.

He had never purposely toyed with anyone's affections, and he had no intention of toying with Marianne's, but he was going to do his best to be on her mind when the next Yank came along.

Still somewhere in the SWPA
14 July 1943

Dear Marianne,
I'm relieved to hear a Yank isn't going to spirit you away to America at the first opportunity. It's selfish, I know, but there's an Aussie pilot who needs you to keep sewing straight so he can take you dancing when he gets home. Someone needs to give the Yanks a run for their money.

Sam
P.S. Is it Bastille Day today? I may be a bit off on the date, but bonne fête national.

SIXTY-TWO

YET ANOTHER YANK IN AUSTRALIA

AUGUST 1943

Sophie rushed to answer the telephone, barely missing Howard, who seemed to think she wanted to play chase with him.

"Hello Sophie? It's Edmund. Are you okay? You sound out of breath."

"Edmund! I'm fine. Just trying not to trip over the dog. You sound like you're on the other side of the world. Where are you?"

Edmund chuckled. "Not quite. I'm calling from Brisbane. Listen, I'll be back in Sydney in a few days and then I'm heading up to Mount Victoria to do an interview with an American sailor. He captained a patrol boat that was sliced in half by a Japanese destroyer. The US Navy gave the crew up for dead, but islanders found them and a coast watcher radioed for rescue. The sailor has been recuperating at a hotel in Mount Victoria."

"I thought the Americans took over the Hydro Majestic hotel in Medlow Bath as a field hospital and rehabilitation center."

"They did. Last year it was where the US military sent personnel who were injured in battle. Coral Sea, Solomon Islands, you name it. But the army moved on and this guy is at a smaller place in Mount Victoria. He's the son of the former ambassador to Great Britain.

Fellow by the name of John Kennedy. Would you like to run up there with me? I know it's practically impossible for civilians to travel anywhere right now. Might be a nice change of pace for you to get out of the city for the day. He'd probably be tickled pink to meet an American lady who isn't a military nurse. Interested?"

"I am absolutely interested." At this point, going anywhere would be a treat, and the long drive to the Blue Mountains, where Mount Victoria was located, would be a marvelous break. She would have to rearrange a few things. Perhaps Thomas could do the afternoon school run. Cleaning the upstairs bathrooms could wait a day. "If we leave Sydney early enough, we could stop in to visit my mother and aunt in Leura. When?"

"Not sure yet. I'll give you a call when I arrive in Sydney."

—

Four days later, Sophie was dressed and ready to go before Joe, Teddy, and Katie left for the day. Miraculously, Katie's hair co-operated with her efforts to get it into two braids and Joe dealt with herding Teddy through getting dressed and tying his shoes. Sophie gulped the toast and eggs Moira set at her place while Joe ate his breakfast and read the newspaper.

"If I didn't know better, I'd think you were impatient to get away from us," he said.

She'd been feeling a little guilty for shirking her responsibilities for the day, but relaxed when she saw Joe's amused glance. "I don't often get the chance to meet the hero son of a former ambassador," she said, playing along with him. "Who knows? He may mention me to his father and I could become the next American ambassador to Australia."

"Is there an American ambassador to Australia?"

"Isn't there? At any rate, someone has to be the first woman to do the job."

—

"This is exciting," Sophie enthused after Edmund helped her into the US Army staff car he had procured for the day. "I get the feeling there's more to this interview than you told me over the phone."

Edmund glanced over to her, his eyebrows wagging up and down. "*Life* magazine and the *New York Times* did huge spreads on the incident, with Kennedy emerging as a hero. I think there's more to the story."

"Such as?"

Without taking his eyes off the road, Edmund reached to the floor of the back seat, brought forth copies of the magazine and the newspaper, and handed them to Sophie.

"Because of these articles, Kennedy is the most famous PT boat captain there is. He's a 25-year-old navy lieutenant who saved eleven of his thirteen men and swam several miles with the strap of a badly burned man's lifejacket clamped between his teeth. When some islanders who work for a coast watcher found them, Kennedy carved a message on a coconut which they delivered to their watcher. The watcher then radioed the navy to rescue the sailors."

"Impressive," Sophie said, flipping through the pages until she came to the article.

Edmund nodded. "It's the stuff of legend. While I don't begrudge *Life* or the *Times* their stories, my guess is that Kennedy's father had a hand in crafting them. It's well-known in certain circles that he wants one of his sons to become president one day. The betting line has always been Joe Junior, but after this, I'd say John may have taken over that spot. It would be tough to elect a Catholic, but being a war hero could ease the way."

"And are you trying to debunk this story? Or heap more glory on John's head?"

"Neither. I'd like to know the bits and pieces the *Life* and *Times* articles don't delve into. After we win this war—"

"You're awfully confident of that. Honestly, there are days when I just don't see how it's possible. Gosh, I haven't even admitted that to Joe."

"Cars must make great confessionals," Edmund said. "Have no doubt, Sophie. We will win this, because the alternative is unacceptable. Anyhow, afterwards there will be so many stories to be told and not all of them will be about the big names. I want to tell the unsung hero stories. In this case, I don't think the islanders and the watcher are getting nearly enough credit."

"So this interview with Kennedy is for professional *and* private purposes?"

"I was a journalist before this war began and I'll be a journalist when it's over," Edmund said. "In this particular case, I'll do a short interview and take a couple photos for an article of my own, but I want to pick Kennedy's brain about the coast watcher and the natives who saved him and his crew."

"I'm not even sure I know what a coast watcher is, much less what they actually do, aside from the obvious. They watch coasts. Where are they? Who are they? How do they communicate what they see to the people who can use the information?"

"The short, non-classified answer is they're everywhere. Hidden away in strategic locations that overlook shipping lanes. The Slot through the center of the Solomon Islands, for example. They have contacts with the native people who don't like the Japanese any more than we do."

"Because the Japanese are trying to defeat them too and take over their islands."

"Yep. Native people are helping the allies every single day. Often at great risk to themselves." Edmund glanced over to the magazine Sophie still held. "The coast watchers are mostly Australian military guys, but some are European and British civilians who've lived on the islands for years. In many cases they've given up everything to hide in the hills and watch. They keep their radios secreted away in case they're discovered, but I would imagine a determined Japanese could get them to admit where it's hidden."

Sophie shuddered. "And then what?"

Edmund shrugged. "They're shot if they're lucky. Or they're tortured and left for the jungle ants to finish off if they aren't."

After that sobering comment, the conversation lulled for a few minutes until Edmund asked about life on the Sydney home front. They chatted about Marianne, Joe, and the children while they passed the small towns west of Sydney.

When they entered the more open country of the Blue Mountains, Edmund slowed to a crawl so they could watch a mob of kangaroos bounding across a field. Sophie rolled down her window and inhaled deeply. "Can you smell the gum trees? The Blue Mountains were named because oil in the eucalyptus leaves diffuses and adds a blue haze to the air."

"And the oil can cause bush fires in summer if lighting or an errant spark ignites it. Honestly, this country worries me sometimes. I thought the spiders were bad, but oil in the air causing fires?"

"That's during the summer. It's cool now, and there's nothing to worry about. The air just smells fresh and lovely."

As they passed through Leura and Katoomba, the land to the west dropped. "That's the Megalong Valley on our left," Sophie said. "We should arrive in Mount Victoria any minute."

"It's ten-forty-five," Edmund said, glancing at his watch. "Depending on how long Kennedy is available to speak with me, we should have plenty of time to enjoy the scenery before we have lunch with your mother and aunt. But first," he parked the car in front of the Victoria and Albert Hotel in Mount Victoria, "we speak with US Navy Lieutenant John Fitzgerald Kennedy, captain of Patrol Torpedo Boat-109, and quite possibly a future president of the United States."

—

Since Lieutenant Kennedy had been shipwrecked in the Solomon Islands, which consisted of hundreds of coral specks that straddled the border of the South West Pacific and the South Pacific areas delineated by Allied command, Sophie had a hard time grasping exactly where the tiny islands were that he and his crew had taken refuge on. Edmund knew the area, so she sat back and enjoyed watching a seasoned journalist conduct an interview.

Kennedy was complimentary of his crew during their travails. He was obviously still upset by the loss of two men, which he thought could have been avoided if they hadn't had orders to use only one engine to minimize their speed and wake. He loved patrol torpedo boats in general, but they were often unreliable and were usually tasked with missions that larger, better equipped craft should have undertaken.

"The problem as I see it," Edmund said, "is now the folks back home, and many of the brass, think they don't need to fund better ships because you Navy guys have done stellar jobs with the PT boats."

Kennedy agreed, his Boston accent becoming even more pronounced as he spoke of telling his father the dismal facts. His hope was that Joe Kennedy Senior would take that information to the people who needed to hear it.

She could see Kennedy had been under a great deal of strain. He'd been charming and polite, but to her former nurse's eye his wiry body looked far too thin, even after two weeks of rest and rehabilitation. He often winced when he moved. Edmund had told her Kennedy had back and intestinal problems that should have kept him at his desk job in Washington, not on active duty in the Pacific. She was inclined to agree. Swimming three miles from their crash site to Plum Pudding Island with a life vest strap clenched in his teeth so he could tow a severely burned crewman would not have helped his back, much less his stomach after swallowing gallons of seawater in the process.

Kennedy had the highest praise for the natives who had found them and delivered the coconut with his message with their identification and location to their Australian coast watcher. But it still rankled that the US Navy had given them up for dead and had even conducted a memorial service.

SIXTY-THREE

UNSUNG HEROES

AUGUST 1943

S ophie waited until she and Edmund were back in the car and heading to her Aunt Flora's house in Leura. "What other stories about unsung heroes do you have up your sleeve?"

"I intend to start a piece on Chamonix as soon as I know more about what's happening there."

"Gosh, I've been wondering how Georges and Monique are cop-ing with Nick in the alpine troops."

"I heard from Will and Hélène that Nick and Chris are together. I'm guessing most of the troops have scattered into the mountains where they can keep an eye on the Italians and the Germans."

"And Vanni?"

"Oh, knowing him, he's definitely working for whatever resistance groups are active in the area. No doubt he's wreaking havoc on the Italian and German armies somehow. I've already written about a farmer in England who had to give up his land so the Army Air Force could build an airfield. Acres of lush, fertile land that has been in his family since the days of the Domesday Book have been paved over. Effectively obliterated. He was furious at first. Fought the army tooth and nail. He couldn't win and now he's heartbroken."

"You could write a piece on every country and publish an anthology of short pieces after the war."

"That, Mrs. Parker, is a brilliant idea."

"Why thank you, Captain Stone." They exchanged broad grins. "What else can we think of?"

"I need to do one on New Zealand. If anything, their pilots are even more reckless...erm...enthusiastic than Australian pilots. Apparently, the Japanese consider New Zealand a much more habitable country to occupy than Australia. Smaller, more concentrated populations to conquer. The terrain and weather are more like Japan's. Wool, farmland, plenty of deep ports The Kiwi pilots are desperate to get as many of the enemy as possible.

"Then there are stories about German subs in US waters, including the Gulf of Mexico. No one talks about subs in US waters much. Don't want to cause a panic, although maybe we should. I don't know of any coastal cities that mandate blackouts, which is exactly why we've had so many shipping losses along the eastern seaboard. I just hope there are some old Cajun fellas watching the bayous and oil refineries from New Orleans to Galveston."

"What about Burma and China? We get some news from there but not a lot."

"You want to talk about reckless pilots? There are American boys flying over the Himalayas to drop food in China. They call the highest mountains in the world the Hump. I can't imagine the dangers of flying that route. Unpredictable winds, temps far below freezing. If you crash in those mountains, you won't be ever found. Then there are the ATA gals who fly new planes from factories to the aerodromes. The black fighter pilots from Tuskegee who're escorting our bombers over Italy. The—"

"Sorry to interrupt," Sophie said, "but Aunt Flora's house is coming up. Do you see that iron fence with the roses? Turn in here."

The front of Flora's country home appeared modest and unimposing. Sophie couldn't wait for Edmund to see the views from the huge back gardens overlooking the mountains in one direction and the Megalong Valley in the other.

Her mother and Aunt Flora were waiting for them on the front veranda. Both ladies wore straw sunhats, cardigans over their frocks, and their most sensible shoes, a far cry from their usual tailored elegance in Sydney.

Sophie jumped out as soon as Edmund brought the car to a full stop. "Mother! Aunt Flora!"

"Hello darling. So good to see you." Lily and Flora returned Sophie's hugs and kisses and she introduced them to Edmund.

"Come and see what we've been doing," Flora said, and led them into the house, down its central hallway, and out to the back verandah.

The perfectly manicured lawns had been replaced with rows and rows of vegetables.

"We thought we might as well do our bit here, too," Lily said. "When the Hydro was a hospital for the Americans, they needed fresh veg. Now old Mr. Griswold and his son at the farm down the road adds our harvests to his. Everything gets shipped to our troops now."

"But who did all the digging and planting?"

"Farming is a reserved occupation, so his son does ours too. They have a couple of Women's Land Army girls who help on their farm and Betty comes here once a week to do anything that needs doing. In fact, she's here today. That's her down at the edge of the potato patch."

A young woman clad in khaki coveralls, rubber boots, and an olive-green jumper stood, stretching her back and rolling her neck.

"Betty!" Flora called. "Come meet my niece and her friend."

"I think I'll add your mother and aunt to my list of unsung heroes," Edmund said on the drive back home.

"Their bartering abilities are truly admirable," Sophie replied while she mentally reviewed the items they'd carefully packed in a big wicker basket which was now ensconced in the back seat of the car. Rounds of farmer's cheese and jars of pickles. Mrs. Kelley would swoon at the pound of butter and the bottles of cream.

During lunch, which they'd shared with Betty on the shaded back verandah, Lily and Flora had regaled them with tales of trading eggs with the town baker in return for bread, and bartering fruit with another farmer in return for butter and cheese. They'd always been capable and conscientious, so Sophie wasn't surprised they were exactly the same in wartime conditions. If anything, they seemed more content here than they ever had in Sydney with its myriad activities, museums, and their busy social lives. They also looked healthy and hearty, all twinkling eyes and frequent smiles, especially when they indulged in sisterly teasing.

"Lily is terrible at making bread," Flora said. "She kneads it too long and too hard and it comes out like a stone."

"But I'm good at taking care of the chickens," Lily said. "Flora has been afraid of chickens ever since we were girls."

Flora had shuddered. "Horrible, pecky things, especially when you have to feel around for an egg. We both do the weeding, so Betty can do the things we can't."

Edmund's list of what people of all nationalities were doing for the war effort was really quite long. When she added her own mother and aunt into the equation, she came to realize how many people, everywhere, were giving their all in the fight against Germany and Japan. She wasn't alone, far from it. Could she loosen the tight grip she kept on her fears, at least a little bit?

SIXTY-FOUR

'CHUTE NOTES

AUGUST – DECEMBER 1943

Reading through Sam's last letter, Marianne couldn't help smiling again. *There's an Aussie pilot who needs you and wants to take you dancing?* And he remembered the most important day in her French history? Was he flirting with her?

Sydney
3 August 1943

Dear Sam,
Your date was correct. 14 July was Bastille Day. How did you remember? Jean-Luc's French friends invited me to a small celebration they held. I admit it was wonderful to speak French all day, although I slipped into English often. Living here must be taking a toll. I am joking of course. I loved Sydney since the first moment I saw it from the ship when I arrived.

Everyone here is well. How are you?
Marianne

*P.S. If you are selfish then I am too, because there is a
French-Australian parachute maker who needs you to
fly safely so she can go dancing with you. To compare
with the Yanks, of course.*

*Somewhere in the SWPA
27 August 1943*

*Dear Marianne,
I thought it was important to know France's most note-
worthy national holiday when I'm trying to impress a
lady who's half French.*

*Life here is a mix of sheer terror when we go out on
sorties and being utterly bored the rest of the time. Not
the best combination. The YMCA has a hut where we
can play cards and get a cuppa. The Yanks often show
pictures, so we usually attend, if only for something to
do.*

*Believe it or not, we have our own vegetable garden here.
Tending it isn't my cup of tea, but it's nice to have a few
fresh veg to break the monotony of wartime provisions,
so I take my turn with the weeding and watering.*

*Sew straight,
Sam*

*Sydney
19 October 1943*

*Dear Sam,
I finally received word about my brother. Well, Ed-*

mund had some news, which he passed on to me, plus there have been a few small newspaper articles. After Italy surrendered to the Allies last month, Germany turned its sights to the French Alps. There is a German garrison at Chamonix, and they also occupy towns in and around the valley. Edmund says there is a resistance force in Chamonix, plus volunteer corps in every town.

Of course, I am worried, but as Edmund likes to say, "So far, so good."

The post between you and Sydney seems very slow. Presumably you are also still safe and well?
Marianne

Somewhere in the SWPA
27 November 1943

Dear Marianne,
You're right. The post from Sydney has slowed considerably, although it could be because we move around so often. I think Edmund's sentiments are good ones.

I'm still safe and well,
Sam
P.S. Do you realize we now have a date to go dancing?

Sydney
15 December 1943

Dear Sam,
Christmas preparations here are well underway and

the children are beyond excited. Teddy confided he does not believe in Father Christmas anymore, that he knows it is your father and Sophie, but he promised he will not spoil it for Katie and Cora. I do not think they would believe him even if he did slip up! Sophie and Mrs. Kelly are planning a party for Christmas Eve. The house will be full of soldiers and airmen, plus all the neighbors too.

Please continue to fly safely and all my best wishes for a Joyeux Noël.

Marianne
P.S. I think I am more excited about our date to go dancing than the children are about Christmas!

SIXTY-FIVE

ATABRINE YELLOW

JANUARY – JUNE 1944

Sophie rifled through the day's post, dropping everything when she spied an envelope with Sam's handwriting. She tore open the flap and skimmed first, scanning for words that signaled death or disaster.

> *Somewhere in New Guinea*
> *21 January 1944*
>
> *Dear Dad and Sophie,*
> *I managed to get word of Jean-Luc's whereabouts a few*
> *days ago. With any luck, in a few weeks he'll be able to*
> *taste Mrs. Kelly's cottage pie and lemon cake. I'm sure*
> *he'll be especially glad he won't have to share with me.*
> *I'll leave you to puzzle it all out. I'm safe and well.*
>
> *Cheerio for now,*
> *Sam*

Thank God. Both boys were still alive. Her grip on the paper relaxed and she re-read the letter slowly enough to decipher Sam's cryptic note. If she guessed correctly, Jean-Luc would be sent back to Australia soon for a much-needed rest after five months in New Guinea.

—

Somewhere in New Guinea
30 January 1944

Dear Marianne,
I assume Dad and Sophie told you Jean-Luc will be home on leave soon. He's had nearly five months of intense fighting and from all accounts they've had a bloody hard time of it. At the lower elevations there's impenetrable jungle with the constant threat of malaria, dengue fever, and scrub typhus, plus beriberi, dysentery, and jungle rot. If they survived all that and the Nips, then there's what the Yanks call the Ghost Mountain. No birds, no insects, no sound at all from anything and if you step off the trail you sink into six feet of moss or tumble down the mountain. But the enemy is still everywhere.

If Jean-Luc looks as bad as some of the blokes I've seen, Sophie will be worried sick about him, and rightly so. You may need to look after her while she's looking after him.

Sew straight,
Sam
P.S. For J-L, it's been a slaughter just like our fathers ex-

perienced, only in a different part of the world. Whatever you do, don't let anyone tell him to buck up or that he'll get over it in time. It doesn't help.

Sydney
7 March 1944

Dear Sam,
You were right. Sophie told me she hardly recognized Jean-Luc descending to the platform at Central Station. She said he was as skinny as a rake (what does that mean?) and as yellow as wattle blossoms (I know what those are).

I could feel all of his ribs when I hugged him and Mrs. Kelly spent the next few days preparing dishes with as much fat and starch in them as she could. He has been home for two weeks now and looks a little better, if only less yellow and bony, but he is still shaky. Sophie and the children have taken him to the beach several times, and he has had a chance to see his French friends who are still here in Sydney. Patricia suggested taking him to one of the Red Cross dances, and we promised to dance with him, but he preferred the Anzac Buffet where he could meet up with friends in the forces who are also on leave.

We are all worried about him, but we try not to show it. How are you?

Fly safely,
Marianne

Somewhere in New Britain
22 April 1944

Dear Marianne,
Skinny as a rake means as thin as the handle of a rake.

We're all yellow – it's from the Atabrine tablets they make us take to ward off malaria. It leaves an awful metallic taste in your mouth and the rumor is it'll make you sterile but quinine doesn't work against the mozzies here. I've seen men who are so sick from malaria it's hard to believe they could possibly survive. I take my Atabrine religiously.

I don't know how Jean-Luc managed to come through it, but I know him and he won't shirk when it's time for him to go back. He's a better man than I'll ever be. He's met the enemy face-to-face. I can't imagine what that's like. Honestly, sometimes I feel guilty that all I do is look for signs of them from above.

Sew straight,
Sam
P.S. I just realized I've never thanked you for looking after my family. Mille mercis. *I honestly don't know what I'd do without you.*

Sydney
11 May 1944

Dear Sam,
You moved again! I added another pushpin to the map.

Please do not disparage yourself. You and Jean-Luc are two of the bravest men I have ever known.

Fly safely,
Marianne
P.S. Don't you know by now that I am happy to look after your family? After almost five years here in Sydney they are my family too!

Back to where we were before in the SWPA
22 June 1944

Dear Marianne,
As you can see, we've moved yet again. Does that merit two pushpins in the same place? All in all, I'd rather be back at work during the week and taking you up in the Moth at night to see the stars.

Keep sewing straight,
Sam

Sydney
16 July 1944

Dear Sam,
I would love to see the stars from the air! Now we have two dates.

Please keep flying safely,
Marianne
P.S. I think I would like to see the stars first.

SIXTY-SIX

GOOD NEWS FROM FRANCE

AUGUST – OCTOBER 1944

As Marianne read Sam's latest letter, she became aware of Patricia watching her with a knowing smile on her face.

> *Somewhere in the SWPA*
> *4 August 1944*
>
> *Dear Marianne,*
> *Stars first it is. Make a note in your diary about our dates, even though we have no idea when they will actually be.*
>
> *Sam*
> *P.S. Picnic on the beach afterwards? Coogee is close to Mascot.*

"Another letter from your pilot?"

"He—"

"Have you *seen* your face when you read his letters? Or when you write to him?" Patricia rummaged through her purse, flipped open her compact, and handed it to her. "Look at yourself, not me, when I speak the next sentence. Not only is Sam Parker your pilot, you're falling in love with him."

Marianne simply could not stop the smile she saw reflected in the compact's mirror. Nor could she hide it when she glanced up to her friend.

Patricia nodded. "I'm right, aren't I? He is and you are. How do you feel about that?"

"Terrified? Exhilarated? "

Patricia jumped up from the sofa and enveloped her in a huge hug. "I knew it!"

After Patricia released her from her hug, Marianne opened the newspaper on the coffee table. "Would you please hand me the scissors?"

Patricia rummaged in the desk drawer and withdrew the scissors they used to cut paper. She'd once suggested Marianne could use her sewing scissors, but had received a little lecture on why scissors that were meant for fine fabrics should never, ever be used on anything else.

"What have you found?"

"This," Marianne said, handing over the slip of newsprint before she began clipping again.

"Rapid advance inland in south France," Patricia read aloud, speaking only the most relevant words. "London, August 17. Allied forces...pushed inland...southern France...20 miles in places...within 10 miles of...Toulon and Cannes."

"And this."

"Allies capture Orleans, Chartres, Dreux. Tanks thrust to within 32 miles of Paris. Normandy, August 17. American armoured columns...have established a bridgehead over the Eure River, 32 miles from Paris. Another column...has captured Orleans."

"And this." With a flourish, Marianne waved a third clipping. "*La pièce de la resistance*. Allies free Bordeaux, Lyons, Marseilles.

Drive to Swiss frontier. London, August 24. French Forces...joined with an American column to capture Bordeaux...Lyons has been occupied...completing the liberation of France's four largest cities. In eastern France the American column...is reported to have freed Annecy—"

Patricia said, "Annecy! I know that one! It's close to where your brother Chris has been!"

Marianne nodded and continued reading. "—and reached the Swiss frontier, presumably near Geneva, 65 miles north of Grenoble. French troops have liberated Marseilles. An American column co-operated with 35,000 French partisans to take Lyons. Remnants of the German Seventh ArmyNormandy...rapid American drive down the left bank of the Seine...on the road to 130 miles from the German frontier. Widespread German collapse in France...complete German rout in western Europe cannot be long delayed."

Marianne breathed deeply. Collapse. Rout. Annecy freed. Please God, let Chris be alive. Let him be safe and unharmed. Her efforts to remain composed failed miserably, and Patricia sat beside her, holding on tightly until her sobs subsided to sniffs.

"Let me have that," Patricia said, taking hold of the article in one hand and giving her a handkerchief with the other. She placed the article in the album. "It's good news, isn't it? Let's do something cheerful to celebrate. Could we work on my trousseau?"

TJ, Patricia's beau, had proposed and Patricia had accepted. The couple had no idea when or where they could actually marry, but Patricia's ring with diamond chips proclaimed their promise.

Marianne nodded and rose to fetch a packet of the precious lace she had brought from France. Her friend deserved the finest trousseau that she could muster. "Hop up on the coffee table. I'll pin the lace to your nightgown."

Patricia chattered about weddings and bouquets and bridesmaids while Marianne pinned lace first to the hem and back of the gown. She finally quieted when she broached the subject of honeymoons.

"My mother hasn't told me anything," Patricia admitted. "All I know is what my married cousins have said and that's next to nothing."

Marianne carefully pinned lace to the silk covering her friend's breasts. "My mother hasn't really said anything to me either. But my family lives in the country, so I have a good idea of the... the basics."

"Have you ever...?"

Marianne shook her head. "No, never."

"I want to. When TJ kisses me I want to. More than anything."

"Pat, please don't. What if you..." Marianne only had to compare her birth year with the year of her parents' marriage to know they had been intimate months before the Great War ended and officially exchanged marriage vows. "You would be taking a huge chance."

A flush spread over Patricia's fair skin. "Haven't you ever wanted to? With Sam?"

Marianne felt a flush of her own beginning. She had wanted to at the beach with Sam, and afterwards when they kissed, and every time she thought of their kisses and how his body felt so close to hers. She wanted to, more than anything.

Sydney
23 August 1944

Dear Sam,
Do you get any newspapers? Have you seen the news
from France? The Americans have been so successful
there that almost all of the country has been liberated.
I cannot tell you how relieved and happy I am. Now all
I need to know is whether Chris is safe and well.

Fly safely,
Marianne

Somewhere in the SWPA
17 September 1944

Dear Marianne,
If your brother is half as brave and strong as you are,
he'll be right.

Keep sewing straight,
Sam

Sydney
22 September 1944

Dear Sam,
Thank you for the compliment. I confess I don't feel
brave and strong most of the time. Most days I simply
get up, go to work, and pray that everyone I love will
come home safely. I do my job just like you do yours.

Please continue to fly safely,
Marianne
P.S. Yes, please. Stars and then a picnic at the beach
afterwards. I cannot wait to see the stars with you.

Somewhere in the SWPA
15 October 1944

Dear Marianne,
It wasn't a compliment. It was the truth. I think you're
the bravest soldier I've ever met. Sailing all the way
to Australia, digging in when the world went balls up
(forgive the crude expression, it's all I can think of at the
moment), and putting aside your dressmaking dream

to do more than your bit so that I and every other Aussie pilot can fly confident of their parachute? All while you're thousands of miles away from your family? I'm in awe.

As my mate Bluey would say, you're a bonzer girl.

Sam
P.S. I've never taken anyone up to see the stars. I can't wait to show them to you.

SIXTY-SEVEN

CHRISTMAS GIFTS

24 DECEMBER 1944

On Christmas Eve, a knock on the front door after dinner sent Sophie into a panic. An unexpected visitor could only mean one thing—someone delivering a telegram with the most dreaded news of all.

Her knees nearly buckled with relief when she opened the door to a grinning airman holding a small parcel. And a coconut.

"Are you Mrs. Parker?"

"I am."

"Good-o. I found you," he said, handing over the parcel and the coconut. "I'm a mate of Sam's. He asked me to deliver these personally."

By now Joe had come up behind her. "Sophie? Is everything all right?"

"Yes," she said. "This is a friend of Sam's. I'm sorry, would you like to come in?"

"Thanks, but my missus is expecting me, so I'll be off. Sam said he'll explain everything in his letter." He nodded to her and Joe. "Happy Christmas."

She and Joe returned to the drawing room where the children had been hanging the paper stars on the tree and the Kellys and Marianne were partaking of a post-dinner holiday tipple.

"Everything is fine," Sophie said. The adults immediately let out relieved sighs. The children gathered around her to see what she held. "It was a friend of Sam's. Apparently, he has sent us something for Christmas. Children? Sit down, please while I open the parcel."

She found a letter inside, several pages of Sam's scrawl. She handed it to Joe for him to read it aloud.

"He's back in New Guinea," Joe announced before he began reading.

> *Somewhere in New Guinea*
> *15 December 1944*
>
> *Dear Dad, Sophie, Mrs Kelly, Thomas, Marianne, Teddy, Katie, Cora, and Jean-Luc (I know he's there in spirit even though he's here where I am),*
> *It just occurred to me I should have written "Dear family," and saved myself some ink. I hope you don't mind that I write one long letter rather than several separate ones. I'm sending this parcel via a mate who will be home on leave for a few weeks.*
>
> *Firstly, I'm safe and well. Still taking the Atabrine but it's worth the disgusting taste and skin turning yellow if it keeps malaria at bay. But on to the goodies. Would one person please distribute items as I mention them? I confess I have a sentimental image of Father Christmas handing out gifts.*
>
> *Mrs Kelly, thank you for the many treats you've baked and sent. I've no idea whether you can actually put this coconut to use, but if anyone can, it's you. Anzac biscuits*

*for your favourite pilot? Lamingtons for the home front
mob?*

Sophie handed the coconut to Moira, who accepted it with a
laugh and an affectionate, "That boy!" She let the children each have
a turn touching its textured surface until Sophie asked them to sit
down again.

*Thomas, there are times when we could use your skills
at fixing things. Our mechanics here remind me of you
because they can fix things using only bits and bobs at
hand. One of the mechanics gave me this cog he found
on a beach. It's a beautiful thing, isn't it? He thinks
it must have dropped from one of the big American
bombers because it isn't one of ours.*

Thomas, true to form, hefted the cog in his weathered palm and
examined it from all angles. "I hope the Yanks managed to finish
their run before this went missing," he said.

*Dad, I always give my plane a thorough check before I
get in it. I don't want any cogs falling off my bird. So...
I'm being careful, just like I promised I would be.*

*Sophie, some of our groundcrew fashion all sorts of
things from bits of perspex, sea shells and spent shells,
empty food tins, toothbrush handles, anything they can
get their hands on. I saw one of them making stars for
his kiddies. The stars reminded me of that Southern
Cross ornament Dad made when he was a kid, so I
asked him to make some for Teddy and the girls.*

There were three flat little items folded into notepaper each with a name on them which Sophie distributed to the children. Katie opened hers carefully. Teddy tore the paper off in one swipe. Cora managed something in between. Each child had a tin star with their name inscribed on the front and a wire to hang it. The edges were all smoothed and the points had been blunted. The man clearly had experience with children and sharp, pointy things.

> *Marianne, all the pilots send their thanks for your hard work sewing parachutes. When I told them to look for notes from your fellow stitchers, they all dug through the pockets like kiddies looking for lollies. No one found a note, but it was the funniest thing I've seen in a long time. I asked the same bloke who made the stars to make something for you, too.*

Sophie looked in the box, found a package smaller than the stars, and passed it to Marianne. A minor scuffle between Teddy and a Christmas tree branch distracted her, but she heard Marianne's surprised 'Oh' as she opened her gift from Sam.

> *Dad and Sophie, there's a chap here who's a wonderful artist. He mostly does really detailed stuff for the war department, but he also does quick sketches and gives them to us. He's responsible for the enclosed drawing of me gathering my gear before a flight. Sorry I had to roll it so it would fit in the parcel.*

Sophie passed the rolled piece of paper to Joe, who opened it and studied the drawing for a several long moments before he held it up so everyone could see Sam in tropical flight uniform: shorts and a short-sleeved shirt, tall, lambswool-lined flying boots, and a peaked hat with an RAAF badge instead of the forage cap he used to wear.

He held his communications headset in his right hand as he leaned down to lift his parachute with his left hand. The pencil drawing, far more detailed than a quick sketch, was all in shades of grey with a few splashes of yellow.

Katie peered at the drawing. "What's the yellow thing around his neck?"

"That's his life vest," Joe replied. "So he'll float if—"

Sophie gave Joe a look warning him not to explain why life vests were necessary, but Teddy's exclamation took everyone's attention away from the idea of Sam being downed in the sea.

"Cor, look at that knife!" Teddy said, admiring the sheathed knife on Sam's left hip. "It must be a foot long! I want one of those when I grow up."

"God forbid," Sophie mouthed to Joe, who must have had exactly the same thought because he mouthed 'Never' to her.

Scrambling to distract Teddy from the knife long enough for Joe to carry on reading Sam's letter, Sophie said, "Teddy, would you please put your new star on the Christmas tree and help Cora find a place for hers?"

> *We're being called in to a pre-flight briefing, so I'll have to sign off earlier than expected. I know I don't say it often enough, but I miss you and wish I could be home with you instead of here with the mozzies and jungle.*
>
> *Happy Christmas and all my love to everyone,*
> *Sam*

The adults were still for several long moments—Sophie, Marianne, and Moira sniffing back tears while Joe and Thomas cleared their throats. Even the children were quiet until Sophie realized it was long past their bedtime.

"Up to bed," she exclaimed. "Father Christmas can't possibly visit this house until everyone is sound asleep."

"I'll take them, Mrs. P," Moira said.

"I'll do it," Joe said. "I'm sure you and Thomas are ready for some quiet. Tomorrow morning is sure to be a noisy one."

—

Sophie followed the crowd to the entry hall, said goodnight to the Kellys, and kissed each child before she returned to the drawing room to tidy away the wrappings. She stopped short at the sight before her. Marianne was curled up in a corner of the sofa, absorbed in studying the drawing of Sam.

Sensing tidying could wait, she sat beside Marianne. "That's a wonderful likeness of Sam, don't you think? It's hard to believe we haven't seen him in over two years."

Marianne startled, and she quickly handed over the drawing. "I have never seen him in a uniform like that."

"Neither have I. It never occurred to me they would wear shorts on missions. I suppose it makes sense, since it's so hot there and they aren't flying high enough for it to be cold in the planes." She was dying to see what Sam sent to Marianne, but it seemed too intrusive to ask. She tried not to peek at what Marianne held in her hand, but failed miserably.

Marianne noticed her furtive glance and placed Sam's gift on her palm. Sophie examined a tiny parachute with an even tinier kangaroo dangling from it, the silver flashing against her skin.

"It's just like the emblem on the parachutes," Marianne explained. "You can see the kangaroo is wearing a harness."

"Oh, this is marvelous workmanship," she exclaimed. "Is the back as detailed as the front?"

The parachute was barely an inch high, and only the top half was solid. The maker had just enough room to engrave an entwined 'S M' on the back. Oh. *Oh*. She knew Marianne and Sam exchanged letters regularly, and had often wondered if they were growing fond of each other. Apparently, they had. Apparently, fondness had grown to something more. Much more if the entwined initials were anything to go by.

"I never meant to..." When Marianne finally met her eyes, her expression was so vulnerable and trusting that Sophie's heart clutched at sharing such a precious, intimate moment.

"I'm so happy you did." She hugged Marianne, holding the young woman close. "I know I'm biased, but Sam is a wonderful young man." After a few moments she felt Marianne's body shuddering.

"I'm nothing like the other women he..."

Sophie pulled back and slipped her fingers over Marianne's cheeks to wipe her tears away. "He has always needed someone strong and independent. Fierce even," she whispered as she stroked Marianne's hair. "That's you, my dear. Don't ever doubt it. I couldn't have found anyone better for him if I'd searched the world. You just need to be certain he's the best choice for you."

Marianne sniffed a huge sniff followed by an equally huge sigh. "I've been so worried about him. And then I feel guilty that I'm not worried enough about my brother or my parents or Jean-Luc."

Sophie shook her head. "I know you're concerned about all of them equally, but everything is different when you're in love. I understand. I really do." An idea bubbled up. "Don't go anywhere," she said. "I'll be right back."

Five minutes later she returned downstairs with a delicate silver chain, which she passed to Marianne with a conspiratorial smile. "You could use this, if you'd like."

—

That night, Joe lay in bed staring at the ceiling, the image of Sam playing in his mind. Something about it nagged and niggled, but he couldn't figure out what it was.

Sophie finished her bedtime rituals and scooted close to him, her head on his shoulder and her hand on his chest. "That was a wonderful thing for Sam to do, wasn't it? A parcel full of goodies and a long letter. It was the perfect Christmas gift. He was always such a lovely boy and now he's such a thoughtful man. I'm very proud of him."

Joe knew what had been niggling the moment Sophie said the word 'man.' The man in the drawing was focused, capable, and confident. He had been entrusted with training hundreds of inexperienced cadets to fly complicated aircraft. Now he was leading them in desperately difficult combat situations, guiding American bombers to camouflaged Japanese gun positions. Fully capable of using the knife at his side to cut himself free if his parachute became entangled or to defend himself and his fellow airmen. No doubt he was just as capable of using the sidearm that must be holstered on his right hip.

If the portrait had been of another man's son, Joe knew he would have automatically assumed he was looking at a strong, skilled pilot. A warrior, even, fully prepared to do his duty for his country and his loved ones.

It was high time that he recognized that his son possessed all those traits.

A burst of breath escaped hs lips. His greatest fear had always been that he had failed Sam somehow. In the heat of the child-rearing years, and especially the tumultuous teenaged years, one never knew how much or even whether they were listening. The truth was Sam had become a man who deserved his respect.

"I am too," he said, fighting the lump in his throat. "I am too."

———

Marianne read the note Sam had written on the paper her gift had been folded in for what seemed like the hundredth time.

Somewhere in New Guinea
15 December 1944

Dear Marianne,

Since I think of you every time I wear my parachute, I asked our bloke to make this for you. You deserve gold, but all he had was a bit of silver. He punched a hole in the top so, in his words, 'Your girl can wear it as a necklace.' I hope that isn't presumptuous.

Bisous pour un joyeux Noël,
Sam
P.S. I think of you almost all the time, not just when I wear my parachute.

Her fingers had trembled when she held the drawing of Sam earlier. The artist had captured him perfectly, so vibrant and dynamic compared to the posed studio photos in his formal RAAF uniform. She had kissed those lips, held the same hand that held his headset, felt the strength of his arms around her and the vitality of his body pressed to hers.

It no longer mattered that she hadn't meant to fall in love with Sam. She had, and she had no intention of stopping. Even if the worst happened, she always would, and he needed to know exactly how she felt. She touched the little parachute at the base of her throat and matched his declaration with her own.

Sydney
24 December 1944

Dear Sam,
Since I think of you every time I sew a parachute, and most of the other times too, your gift is perfect, not presumptuous. I love it. Sophie gave me a chain, so I can say I am wearing a parachute, just like my pilot.

Bisous pour une bonne année et pour la chance,
Marianne

Since Sam had written his closing, *kisses for a happy Christmas*, in French, he should be able to figure out hers—*kisses for a good new year and for luck.*

SIXTY-EIGHT

'CHUTE NOTES

JANUARY – MAY 1945

Sydney
17 January 1945

Dear Sam,
It has been a busy month so far since Christmas. There was a bush fire near Leura, where Sophie's mother and Aunt Flora live. Sophie was frantic until Flora called to let her know that the wind had finally shifted. She said the fire sent many kangaroos running from the fire through the town.

The same westerly (I think I have learnt all the major winds by now!) practically devastated Sophie's gardens. Every leaf wilted and started turning brown. Your father gave up rowing on the Sunday and I helped him and Sophie water all those rows of vegetables. Thomas gave up his day off to help Vern and Alf at Flora's Vaucluse gardens. Luckily the wind blew itself out by

*Sunday evening. We do not yet know how Flora's Leura
gardens fared.*

How are you? What do you need?

Bisous,
Marianne

Somewhere in the SWPA
10 February 1945

Dear Marianne,
*Good to hear Flora's place in Leura wasn't burnt. I
remember spending a week there with Jean-Luc right
after Dad and Sophie married. We spent the days exploring and climbing in the Megalong. It's beautiful
country. You were supposed to go when you first arrived
in Sydney, weren't you? Did you ever have the chance?*

*It's so humid here that a westerly to dry everything out
would be more than welcome. Barring that, I could use
more notepaper and sharpened pencils. My fountain
pen had been leaking and then the nib broke. I'm reduced to using stubby pencils like a primary schooler.*

Thinking of you,
Sam

Sydney
2 March 1945

Dear Sam,
A newspaper article reported good news about the

memorial in Villers-Bret. The local municipal council looked after it in my father's absence. It was struck by a few shell fragments and machine gun bullets, but is otherwise in good condition. Papa will be so relieved.

Sophie and I packed parcels for you and Jean-Luc. You will both receive paper, pencils, soap, toothpaste, foot powder, and some of Mrs. Kelly's Anzac biscuits. We also included an extra little surprise.

Sophie sends her love, and so do I,
Marianne
P.S. I helped with the baking on Sunday. None of the biscuits were burnt. M x

Somewhere in the SWPA
25 March 1945

Dear Marianne,
Parcel received as you can see from the new paper. You can't see that I smell better because of the toiletries, or that I've made good headway on the biscuits. The gum leaves were an excellent surprise. They smelt just like home. Whose idea was that?

Thinking of you always,
Sam
P.S. You and Mrs Kelly must love me if you both gave up your Sunday to bake.

Sydney
6 May 1945

Dear Sam,
The leaves were Sophie's idea. She said your father sent
some to her while she was in England when her father
was ill.

I have finally seen whales! Your father, Teddy, and
I took a walk along the cliffs towards Watson's Point
after breakfast today. We went mainly to let Teddy run
off some excess energy, but we spent most of our time
telling him to stay away from the edge. Your father
finally resorted to telling him there was a new rule that
he had to stay back at least three feet or he would lose
his notebook for the rest of the day. When you were 12
years old were you a daredevil like Teddy? I suspect you
were.

I wish you could have been there with us.

Thinking of you too,
Marianne
P.S. Silly man, of course we love you.

Somewhere in the SWPA, but not where we were
29 May 1945

Dear Marianne,
Find another pushpin for your map. We've moved to a
different island to the east and north of where we were.
Hopefully the censors won't black that out.

I was probably as energetic as Teddy is. I remember
Dad looking very tired when we returned home after
our Sunday afternoon jaunts. The rule for me was
always that I wouldn't be able to ride my bike with my

friends after school.

Isn't there a French expression that fits? Plus ça change... Sorry, I can't remember the rest of it. I don't have my dictionary close and I want to get this in today's post, so time is of the essence. In English it's the more things change, the more they stay the same. It sounds like Dad's doing the same thing with Teddy that he did with me. He never raised a hand, just tried to get me to realize there were consequences for my actions. All it took was a few times stuck in my bedroom when my friends were out exploring and I got the message. Dad was right, too. Those cliffs are dangerous.

Yours,
Sam
P.S. I have been for a very long time. Yours, that is.

SIXTY-NINE

VICTORY IN EUROPE

JUNE 1945

Within a few days of Victory in Europe day, there was a flurry of telephone calls and telegrams to, from, and within Sydney.

Joe's call was to Assistant Commissioner Davies. "Sir, I need a favor from your brother."

"Joe, you're not asking to get your commission reinstated again, are you? With everything winding up in Europe, it won't be long now before we finish off the Nips."

"No, it's something else. I need to know the whereabouts of Private Patrick O'Brien. 2/7th. He was wounded and taken prisoner by the Germans in Crete. Presumably he's in a camp somewhere in Germany. Or Poland."

Bobby Davies blew out a big enough breath mixed with a few choice words that Joe moved the receiver several inches from his ear.

"That's an impossible request, Joe. Do you any idea how many prisoners there are? It'll be months before that's all sorted out. Maybe longer."

"That may be true sir, but this is a special case. I don't need to know about all of the prisoners. Just the one. There are three children who deserve to know if or when their father is coming home."

Sydney
15 June 1945

Dear Sam,
I received a telegram from my parents! My brother
Chris is alive and my parents are returning home. I
am so relieved. I am still crying tears of joy every time
I think of them.

All my love,
Marianne
P.S. I am certain I will cry tears of joy when you tell me
you are coming home.

SEVENTY

NEWS FROM BORNEO

JULY 1945

Just when Sophie despaired of hearing from her sons, letters from both arrived at the house on the same day.

On another island somewhere in the SWPA
2 July 1945

Dear Sophie and Joe,
We've been on the move again, this time further north.
I've heard from Sam. He told me to be on the lookout
for a low-flying plane with a young woman writing a
letter painted on its nose. I'm certain I saw him over-
head.

Affectionately,
Jean-Luc

Somewhere in the SWPA
3 July 1945

Dear Dad and Sophie,
Quick note to let you know we're helping J-L and his
mates again. I'm flying a new B now instead of my old
W.

I'll leave you to puzzle all that out,
Sam

Joe turned to her after they'd read the letters. "Sam has a woman writing a letter painted on his plane?"

"It's news to me as well. We know who it is, though."

"Do we?"

"Darling, think about it. Easter three years ago? Jean-Luc saying Sam and Marianne have always been crazy about each other but they just didn't know it yet? They know it now."

"Does that mean Sam's choice in women is as good as his father's?"

Sophie fluttered her eyelashes at her husband. There were times when he said exactly the right thing. "It would seem so, although you mustn't breathe a word about it to either one of them. They'll announce it in their own time. What does he mean by flying a B now?"

"Boomerang, love. The RAAF is replacing the Wirraways with bigger planes."

Still on an island further west and a little north
4 July 1945

Bon jour Mlle Parachute Maker,
I have a new plane and I've been issued a new 'chute,
but alas, there was no note of encouragement in English
or Français. Could you send one to your favourite pilot
for luck?

Yours,
Sam

Marianne nearly shuddered at how lucky Sam had been so far, but she pushed that thought aside and let her heart dictate what she wrote.

Sydney
12 July 1945

Cher Sam,
Courage, mon amour. Reviens-moi, s'il te plaît.

Tous mes bisous pour la chance,
Marianne
P.S. Tu me manques.

Perhaps Sam's French was good enough to understand her words without using his dictionary. *Be strong, my love. Come back to me, please. All my kisses for luck. P. S. You are missing from me.*

SEVENTY-ONE

THE END OF THE DREAM

AUGUST 1945

Sydney
15 August 1945

Dearest Sam,
I cannot believe the war is finally over! We are all
counting the days until you are home, me most of all.
I cannot wait to see you again.

All my love,
Marianne
P.S. The post is extraordinarily slow. Neither I nor your
parents have received anything from you or Jean-Luc
since early July. I hope you received my parachute note.
It was in French, so have your dictionary close by! Love,
M x

VILLERS-BRETONNEUX 23 AUGUST 1945
TO M RYAN SYDNEY AUSTRALIA

MAMAN AND I BACK HOME
CHRIS VERY BAD SHAPE
NEED YOU HOME ASAP
SOONEST SAILING FROM SYDNEY

PAPA

Marianne drummed her fingers on a notepad while she waited for the operator to connect her call. After receiving her father's telegram, she and Sophie had investigated all the ways Marianne could return to France as quickly as possible and had come up empty. There were no passenger cruises to Europe yet because all of the steamships had been requisitioned for military use. Sophie's last hope was that Edmund, who had received orders to report to Berlin to write instructions for GIs in Germany during the post-war occupation by the Allies, might be able to find a solution.

She jumped when the phone rang. "Ryan-Lawson residence."

"Marianne, it's Edmund. I've managed to finagle you onto the flights with me. The only trouble is we have to leave Sydney on Saturday."

"That's the day after tomorrow!"

"Yep. Sorry for the short notice. Do you think you can be ready to go by then?"

Stunned, Marianne gently set the telephone receiver down and sank into her armchair, thoughts swirling after the conversation with Edmund. She couldn't leave without seeing Sam again, but passing up the opportunity to return to France now could be the only chance she had for months. Her parents needed her. Chris needed her. It was an impossible situation.

Her gaze swept around the flat she shared with Patricia. Maps punctuated with pushpins on the walls. An album filled with newspaper cuttings about the progress of the war in the Haute Savoie, where Chris had been fighting in and around Chamonix. She flipped through it, barely seeing the headlines until she reached the last article she had clipped one year ago, the one that confirmed Chamonix had been liberated:

Allies Free Bordeaux, Lyons, Marseilles. Drive To Swiss Frontier.

It had taken twelve months since that headline for the Allies to declare victory in Europe and two massively destructive atomic bomb strikes on Japanese cities for them to declare victory in the Pacific. After six long years she was going back to France. Her war was over.

Sydney
31 August 1945

Dearest Sam,
I am writing to tell you I am leaving Australia to-morrow. My parents have returned to France from England and need my help because my brother Chris was wounded during the fighting in Chamonix. I will fly with Edmund from Sydney to London. Then I will take a short flight from London to Paris and then the trains home.

As much as I look forward to seeing my family again, I am certain none of the flights will be able to compare with the first one I experienced. Thank you for taking me up. I loved it. You will always be my favourite pilot, and I will always treasure the tiny parachute you gave to me.

I wish we could have been more to each other. My

heart is breaking that we did not have the chance to see the stars or dance together. All I can do now is wish you every happiness in life. I hope you find someone who loves you as much as I do. She will be the luckiest woman.

Please always fly safely my love. I cannot imagine a world without you in it.
Marianne

P.S. You will always be welcome if you ever find yourself in Villers-Bret.

She slumped in her chair as the reality of what was happening sank in. Reuniting with her family. Leaving Australia. She would never see Sam again.

The tears started, great drops sliding down her cheeks faster than she could wipe them away. Marianne gave up trying and succumbed to them.

SEVENTY-TWO

MOPPING UP IN THE PACIFIC

OCTOBER 1945

Despite Allied victory on both sides of the planet, the barrage of prison camp atrocities that were being discovered in two hemispheres, German in the west and Japanese in the east, was unrelenting. Sophie reeled from the news until she finally had to admit she didn't have the capacity to process it all. She gave herself permission to stop reading and listening to everything except what was still happening in Sam and Jean-Luc's world.

But that news remained frustrating and demoralizing. Japanese troops, holed up and holding out, were still ambushing Australian troops. Australian and Allied planes were still being shot out of the sky or crashing into impenetrable jungle. Her sons were still in harm's way.

And the post between Sydney and wherever the boys were seemed to have stopped completely. They hadn't received anything from Sam or Jean-Luc since July. Three months with no word from them was too long.

Her frustration had reached its peak when Joe arrived home from work and caught her in the act of crumpling the newspaper in her fists. "Why aren't they home yet? Why haven't we heard from them?" she grumbled instead of her usual affectionate "hello, darling."

"Sophie, you know how long it takes at the end. Everyone doesn't simply stop what they were doing and rush home. I had to wait five months to be shipped home after the armistice. I never received the last letter you wrote to me."

She knew Joe wasn't trying to be patronizing. She knew he was simply trying to help, but his response sent her over the edge. "We've had victory parades and ticker tape and celebrations. All I can do is wait, wait, wait, and cry and worry and I'm sick of it!" Feeling like a petulant child, she threw the newspapers across the room as hard as she could. "I just want my boys back, Joe! How can you be so... so... detached?"

He retrieved the newspapers, his knuckles growing white as he squeezed them into even smaller balls. "Don't ever think I don't want them back just as much as you do."

After a few moments of fuming, she said, "I'm sorry. I'm tired and frustrated. I shouldn't have taken it out on you." She glanced at the crumpled newspapers he still held and offered him a contrite smile. "We have a rule about throwing things in the house, don't we?"

Joe's eyes had stopped blazing, so she knew her apology had been accepted. "We do. It's a good thing Teddy is nowhere in sight or you'd never hear the end of it."

"Oh Lord, where is he?"

"No idea, love. I just got home, remember?"

Sam climbed out of his plane and reached up to stroke the painted cheek of the letter writing young woman, just as he always did before and after a flight. Knowing Marianne loved him had kept him going through some truly brutal sorties in the months before the war ended, some boring days when he wasn't flying, and many long, lonely nights.

Pulling off his headset and unhooking his parachute harness, he spoke to the aircraftman who rushed over to inspect the plane for damage. "Probably just some scrapes on the undercarriage. I thought I saw something after I dropped the food and needed to get closer. Nothing to worry about."

"There's a coupla nicks taken out of your starboard wingtip, too," the man scolded. "This is no time to get sloppy."

Damn. He'd been so eager to get back to the airfield that he hadn't even noticed. He could have cartwheeled into the sea if his wing had dipped any lower. He'd seen it happen more than once—they flew so low that pilots could fail to gain enough height while banking to turn away from land. If a wingtip clipped a tree hard enough the plane could cartwheel—wing over wing over wing—and there would be no time to bail out, no chance of rescue when the plane exploded on impact with the water. He'd made it through another sortie, but he needed to make it through all of them. He had to be more careful.

He headed to the intelligence room, reported to Franklin, his squadron leader, for de-brief, and then stowed his gear in the cubby marked S Parker, F/L. All he wanted to do next was grab a cup of tea in the mess and write the letter he'd been thinking about all week.

He touched his talisman, Marianne's latest parachute note, where he kept it in his breast pocket since he received it nearly two months ago. A man would have to be insane to not take what she had written in that note seriously. You are missing from me. What a thought! He'd understood exactly what she meant because he'd been dreaming of her since before he knew her.

There was always the chance Marianne could change her mind. He didn't think that was the case, but best not to take any chances because he had a question he wanted to ask her, the most important question he would ever ask in his life. Not that he would ask in pencil on RAAF-issue notepaper. No, he would do it right. As soon as he got home, he would ask his father for his mother's engagement ring. As a boy he had been fascinated by the opals flashing different colors. If Marianne wanted something else, he would buy her whatever she liked, but he wanted to be prepared when the right moment arose. And he needed to make sure she knew how much she meant to him ahead of time.

> *Still somewhere in the SWPA*
> *28 October 1945*
>
> *Dear Marianne,*
> *The post between here and home has been nonexistent since the middle of July, so I hope this letter will get through.*
>
> *We're dropping food and looking for prisoners and will be here a while longer, but as soon as I get home, I want to take you out to celebrate. Dinner. Dancing. Champagne, even. Whatever you want. Wherever you want. I've lost some weight, but my dinner jacket should still fit. You could wear the dress you wore when Edmund took you to that dinner dance at the Australia Hotel.*

No sooner had he finished writing 'Hotel' with a well-chewed pencil, than his name echoed in the mess.

What did Franklin want and why was he carrying a file folder? Had he forgotten something during the de-brief? Franklin was new, and a stickler for details. Best to be all present and correct. Sam stood and waited for his squadron leader to sit on the bench opposite him. "Sir?"

"Have a seat. There's something I need to speak with you about."

"Of course."

"I hear you clipped a wing on your way back today. You don't make mistakes like that."

Bloody hell. He was thirty years old. He'd been flying for more than five years in the RAAF and another six before that. Did he really need a lecture on how to do it? He'd let Franklin have his say and get it over with. "Sir. It won't—"

"Steady on. I'm not here to reprimand you."

"It won't happen again."

"No. It won't. You're grounded."

Grounded? What the—?

Franklin flipped the folder open and scanned the contents. "Let's see... You trained hundreds of cadets, flew anti-submarine patrols off the coast at home, been on damn near every close-air support run this squadron flew out of Port Moresby, Tsili Tsili, Nadzab—"

"Just doing my job, like everyone else."

"Over to Cape Gloucester, back to New Guinea, and then to Moratai. Shot at too many times to count. Then there was the landing when your gear didn't descend. Now you're in Labuan dropping food to the 7th Division while they search for prisoners. Why are you still here? You passed the maximum number of hours and missions allowed weeks ago. You should be home already."

"But we aren't finished. My brother's here with the 7th. I want to see this through."

"I've had word the 7th thinks they've found everyone who needed to be found. We can manage a few more food drops without you. You're going home in three days." Franklin snapped the folder closed, lifted his chin at the letter, and grinned. He had never seen the man grin before. "I'm grounding you because your young woman would never forgive me if anything happened to you between now and then. You can tell her you'll see her soon."

After Franklin left, Sam's stunned gaze took in his surroundings. The mess, home of almost adequate meals and copious cups of tea. The intelligence hut, its task board too often bearing witness to pilots who didn't make it back. Planes arranged in ordered rows, ready to be wheeled onto the steel-mesh runways. Palm trees swaying wildly as Bluey's Boomerang came in for a landing.

His war was over. He picked up his pencil with shaking fingers.

My squadron leader has just informed me that I'm scheduled to leave here in three days. I have no idea how many days it will take to get home, but I'm counting them until I see you again.

Until then, don't forget I'm yours. Always.

All my love,
Sam

P.S. We could still see the stars first. Whatever you want. Anything you want. I want everything with you.

Seventy-Three

Home Is Not Where the Heart Is

Early November 1945

Before dinner, Sophie went in search of Jean-Luc and found him on the balcony, leaning on the railing. He was still tinged yellow, still too thin, his pre-war clothes too loose. His shirt billowed like a sail in the breeze. In spite of the heat, he wore trousers cinched at the waist, perhaps to hide the still-healing sores on his legs.

He had carried a bottle of white wine upstairs with him and held a glass of it while he stared out at the whitecapped ocean. He turned when she secured the French doors against slamming in the wind.

"I thought you would find me. Would you like some?" He didn't wait for her answer, pouring wine into a second glass and passing it to her.

"*Merci, chou chou.*" Sophie responded with the nickname she had always used when he was younger, hoping it would make him smile, if only for a moment. "This will go well with the chicken Mrs. Kelly is making for supper." They'd heard enough about bully beef and goldfish—sardines in tomato sauce—that fish and beef were off the menu for a while. "*Comment vas tu?*"

"I am as well as can be expected," he replied.

"But not as well as you would like to be?"

"For the last five months we were in Borneo, guarding Japanese prisoners and restoring law and order. There were three death marches in Borneo. When we arrived at the Sandakan camp we discovered twenty-four hundred British and Australian prisoners had been there. Only six survived." Jean-Luc drained the last of his wine and reached for the bottle. "Six."

His gaze flicked up to Sophie at her intake of breath. He was still displaying tremors when he was overtired or emotional, but these were nothing compared to the anguish in his dark eyes. This was the first time, she realized, that he had spoken of his experiences.

"They gave us the choice of leaving the army or staying and performing occupation duties in Japan. Knowing about the prisoners...and how brutally they were treated...I could not have gone to Japan and retained my sanity. Or my humanity."

"We had an inkling of how bad things were." Sophie let that thought hover in the air between them until she could speak again. "What will you do now that you're home? Go back to the winery? I remember they said they'd have a position for you when you returned."

"I am feeling restless. With the exception of you and Joe, no one cares about the war. They want to get on with their lives. I do too."

Even as she watched him struggle to articulate his thoughts, Sophie knew Jean-Luc was about to announce something momentous. Something that would change not only the trajectory of his life, but hers too.

"I need to go back to Lebanon."

She had no idea how to respond to that. Hadn't he established himself comfortably into adult life in Australia? Not in Sydney, or even New South Wales, but the state of Victoria was close enough that she could see him fairly often. She'd interpreted his letters praising the wonders of Lebanon as simply emotions of the moment. Uprooting himself from Australia hadn't ever crossed her mind.

"But you were at war in Lebanon, too."

"Yes, but we were fighting a different kind of enemy, with a more traditional code of conduct. One I could understand."

Sophie watched, mesmerized, as Jean-Luc trailed a shaky finger down his glass, wiping away condensation that had formed in the heat. As a boy he had done the same thing whenever his glass held a cold drink. Her heart ached for those easier days.

"There's a winery there," he said. "In the hills east of Beirut in the Bekka valley. It's hot and rocky. Dry as a bone. Nothing tropical in sight. The air smells clean and there are ancient vines hiding in the scrub. I became friendly with the old man who runs the place."

As Jean-Luc spoke, his expression softened to that of a lover gazing at his beloved. Sophie wondered if a woman was there too, a daughter of the old man, perhaps.

"He invited me to work for him if I ever found myself there after the war. I need to go see if his offer is still open."

Focusing on logistics seemed like the only way to let the enormity of his announcement sink in and settle. "How will you get there?"

"There are freighters leaving Sydney every two weeks. I will work on board to pay my passage so I can save my deferred pay."

"Oh." This wasn't something Jean-Luc could be talked out of. His plans were in place. His mind was made up. "When do you leave?"

"I will wait until Sam comes home, then I will make the final arrangements. *Tu peux comprendre, n'est-ce pas?*"

She knew the need to escape too well. She had bolted from England to Paris after Michael's suicide, and she and Jean-Luc had fled to Sydney after his mother's death. Only time and a different setting had eased their pain then.

She pulled Jean-Luc into a hug, her tears falling on his chest and his falling on her shoulder. She stroked his curly dark hair and held him close, just as she had when he was tiny. "Yes, my darling boy, I can understand. Of course, I can."

SEVENTY-FOUR

SAM'S HOMECOMING

MID-NOVEMBER 1945

Sam's homecoming had been noisy with everyone crowded in the entry hall. He hugged Sophie and his father, Jean-Luc and Mrs. Kelly, ruffled the children's hair, and shook Thomas' hand, all the while searching for the one person who wasn't there.

Sophie hadn't said anything, but waited until the welcoming clamor died down, and Moira and Thomas had shooed the children and Howard into the kitchen. Then she took his arm and led him into the drawing room, his father and Jean-Luc trailing after them.

"Is Marianne at work? Will she be here later?"

Why were they looking at him like he'd lost his mind?

"Sam," Sophie said. "She's back in France. She left Sydney at the beginning of September."

"What?" No. That wasn't possible. "It's the middle of November now. That's almost three months ago? Why?"

"She didn't have a choice," his father said. "Her brother had been badly wounded. Her mother needed her help."

He slumped in one of the armchairs, elbows on his knees, his forehead resting on the heels of his hands. "I can't believe... She can't be gone. Why didn't she tell me?"

Sophie's voice worked its way through his misery. "You didn't receive her last letter, did you? The one she wrote before she left?"

"No. The last time I received anything was in July, right after we flew up to Borneo."

"You need to read this." He sat up wearily as Sophie handed him an envelope, his brows knitting when he recognized Marianne's handwriting.

"The post between Sydney and wherever you were..."

"Borneo."

"Nothing was getting through from you, and Marianne was afraid you might never receive her letter or it would be lost. She gave this to me if that happened. She said it's an exact copy of the last one she sent."

He tore open the sealed envelope, scanned Marianne's letter quickly, and then went back to the beginning to read more carefully.

He looked up from the letter, his eyes wide and wondering. "Do you know what this says?"

Sophie shook her head. "I don't. But I do know she was absolutely heartbroken at having to leave before you came home."

He jumped up from the chair, running his hands through his hair. If Marianne hadn't received his last letter, then she didn't know he was in love with her too. What good was knowing half the pilots in Australia if he couldn't find a way to get to France so he could tell her? "I need to talk to... I could be there in..."

His father spoke the same words he had been thinking. "Do whatever you have to do to, son. You will always regret it if you don't."

Jean-Luc grinned and clapped him on the shoulder. "You two have finally realized you're crazy about each other, haven't you? You have to go after her, brother."

SEVENTY-FIVE

AUSTRALIAN EPILOGUE

SYDNEY, DECEMBER 1945

Sophie stood beside Joe while they read the telegram from AIF headquarters in London. Patrick O'Brien, the children's father, had died in a prison camp.

They quietly watched the ocean shimmering and shifting until squeals of laughter broke the twilight silence. Katie and Cora, followed closely by Teddy and Howard, dashed in their direction. Teddy slipped on fallen jacaranda blossoms carpeting the front walk. He hauled himself up and frowned at his sisters.

She tucked the telegram in her pocket. "What now? What are we going to tell them?"

Giggling and squirming, the girls burrowed into the space between her and Joe. Howard raced from Teddy to join them.

"You didn't catch us, Teddy!" Katie cried. "We're safe and home!"

Sophie gazed at her husband above the children's heads, tears shining as her brow raised in query. When Joe nodded, she responded with quick nods of her own.

She reached for Teddy, motioning for him to join their circle.

"You're home too, Teddy," she said. "You're all home now."

—

Joe gently set his scull in the water beside the dock and stepped into the craft, carefully balancing so he wouldn't tip the boat and fall like a novice into Blackwattle Bay.

He squatted until his bottom touched the molded wooden seat, wiggling back and forth a few times to get everything in the right place. When he felt the cutout portions of the seat align with his behind, he stretched his legs and fitted his sock-clad feet into the footholds. This morning he was rowing for himself, for a chance to let his mind wander while his body got some desperately needed exercise.

He pushed off from the dock and drifted to a point in the water where he could start slowly and get into the rhythm he needed. He rolled his head, rolled each shoulder, rotated each wrist, stretched his arms across his chest and behind his back, until all of his muscles loosened and relaxed before he put them through their paces.

Sunrise was thirty minutes ago, but along this bend of the bay wattle trees lining the banks still blocked the warmth of the new day and the air rising from the water was chilly. Joe repeated the entire warm up process until he could feel the blood coursing through his limbs. Then, gripping each oar in just the right place, the callouses on his palms and fingers hard against the smooth wood, he began rowing, slowly at first, settling in to a rhythm, before gaining momentum and pitting every ounce of his strength to conquer the water's resistance.

As he sliced through the water, Joe let each dreadful moment from his work rise to the top of the other thoughts. He would never unsee the woman curled around her baby in lifeless pallor or the two little girls huddled in a corner alternating their terrified stares between their mother and him. He would never unsee the garishly made-up women who had once been young and lovely before they used their bodies as the only escape from grinding poverty. He gave each memory a respectful moment and then filed each away. This was the only way he could cope with horror—by acknowledging its effect on his psyche, paying respects to the victims, then clearing those memories to give whatever came next its place.

His mind emptied. He let happier thoughts have their turn. He and Sophie had begun the process to formally adopt the children.

Joe still couldn't quite believe he was becoming a father again so late in life. The idea of raising daughters to adulthood was more than a little daunting. There would be boys and parties and a whole slew of things he'd never had to deal with when Sam and Jean-Luc were teenagers. He shook those thoughts off. There would be time enough to work through all that later. Katie was only ten years old. She had emerged from her shell, first asking him for help with words when she read Sam's childhood books and now checking over her math and Latin homework. At seven, Cora had become a chatterbox after she finally stopped sucking her fingers and that stuffed rabbit's ears. Teddy had settled into his first year of high school even though he still put off doing his homework as long as possible in favor of taking things apart and trying to put them together again. Thomas thought he showed signs of being a gifted mechanic. Sophie had hinted at university and engineering, like her father. Joe thought policing might be a good fit given Teddy's penchant for noticing and recording everything about whatever caught his interest.

They'd had letters from Marianne in France and Jean-Luc en-route to Lebanon. Sam was investigating his options to fly in the burgeoning post-war airline industry. Sophie was as fascinating and desirable as ever, even though sleep almost always claimed them as soon as their heads hit the pillows. He was a lucky man.

Satisfied he'd worked through the things that had been simmering, Joe looked over his shoulder. Sunlight pierced the Harbour Bridge's ironwork and warmed the air so the breeze coming from the ocean didn't chill him, only dried the sheen of sweat on his skin. Time to turn around and head home. Sundays were Mrs. Kelly's day off and his day to make breakfast. He'd had years of practice when Sam was growing up, and he'd continued the tradition after he and Sophie married. The only real difference between then and now was he made drop scones less often because flour was still rationed.

Then he saw Sophie, waving at him from the shore. Before the children had come to live with them, she had sometimes accompanied him on Sunday mornings to watch training or races. He sped up his strokes to get back as quickly as possible, not knowing what could have happened to bring her out here.

Sophie was smiling when he edged up to the dock, her eyes glinting with the same hint of mischief he'd seen when he met her by chance in Paris all those years ago.

"I've made an executive decision," she announced as he climbed up and stood before her. "And I thought I should tell you as soon as possible. From now on," she continued, moving close enough that the light cotton of her dress fluttered around his bare legs, "the children will be spending one Sunday afternoon a month with Mother and Aunt Flora. Thomas and Moira will take them there right after Mass. You and I can spend the day doing whatever we want."

As he worked through the possible scenarios, the rising delight he felt must have been evident because the corners of her mouth turned up even higher.

She nodded. "Today's the day. Put your scull away and come with me."

"I need to shower first—"

"I put a towel on the seat of the car. We can shower at home."

We? He was fifty-four years old, and his wife was still plotting ways to get his kit off? He linked his fingers with Sophie's and tugged her a little closer. "Have I ever told you how lucky I am to have you?"

She responded with a tug of her own. "Not lately that I can recall."

"What if I show you exactly how much I appreciate you?"

Her gaze flickered over his shoulders and down his body and then up to his lips, just as she'd done the night she suggested they didn't have to wait three more weeks before they got married. "Before or after breakfast?"

"Your choice. You said we could spend the day doing whatever we want."

"What are we waiting for? Let's go home."

SEVENTY-SIX

FRENCH EPILOGUE

VILLERS-BRETONNEUX, JANUARY 1946

Marianne trudged up the path to her family's home, rolling her head every few steps to work the kinks out of her neck. It had been a long week at Madame Delphine's dress shop in Amiens. Madame had been ill during the war, and Marianne had been taking over more and more of the shop's business. She had worked late every night sewing a wedding dress for a client, its long white skirt reminding her so much of parachutes that she often had to step away so her tears wouldn't spot the pristine fabric.

"*Maman, vous êtes là?*" she called as she opened the front door.

Her mother usually acknowledged her return with "I'm in the kitchen" but there was no response. A big pot of stew simmered on the stove. The table was set for five instead of the usual four. Her father must have invited someone home for dinner, but the house was quiet.

Puzzled, she passed through the living room and opened the French doors that led to the lawn and the river. Despite winter's chill, and the early twilight, the sky was turning that lovely shade of blue before the sun set. She could see figures down at the river's edge, all of them facing the water. Her father, still wearing his uniform and polished boots. Her mother, a full head shorter than her father, with her arm around his waist. Chris, bundled up against the cold, sat on the chaise longue where he spent sunny days drowsing while he continued to recover from a head injury suffered during the last days of fighting in Chamonix.

Murmurs of conversation and laughter carried across the lawn. Marianne strode down to greet her family, but stopped short when the breeze shifted drooping willow branches and revealed a tall man. Even from behind, even though it had been nearly four years since she had last seen him in person, she would know those broad shoulders and that head of fair hair anywhere.

She called his name and started running to him. He turned and met her halfway.

She felt rooted to the grass while she took in the sight of him. Eyes the color of Sydney's immense sky. A half-smile tugging at his lips. Then there was nothing she could do except throw her arms around his neck and cling to him, laughing and crying, while he lifted her and spun her around and around.

They pulled apart, but Sam kept hold of her hands. She linked her fingers with this. "You're here! How is this possible?"

His half-smile broadened to a grin. "Have you forgotten I'm your pilot?"

"You flew? All the way from Australia?"

"It was the fastest way to get here. And I seem to recall you said I would be welcome if I ever found myself in Villers-Bretonneux."

"You did get my letter!"

"Sophie gave me the letter you left with her. I never received the one you posted while I was still in Borneo, or I would have been here sooner."

"You're here now. That's all that matters." Still holding Sam's hands, she kissed his cheeks, three times, lingering on each to relish his warmth and familiar scent.

"Are you still sewing straight?"

"Of course. Are you still flying safely?"

He touched the tiny parachute nestled at the base of her throat by a delicate chain. "I made it to France, didn't I?"

She looped her arms around his neck, gently this time, and turned her face up to his. "You must tell me all about it."

He smiled and nudged the tip of his nose against hers. "It's a long story and I don't want to wait until it's finished to kiss you. If you want me to, that is."

"Sam Parker, I will always want you to kiss me."

His lips were as firm and warm and wonderful as she remembered. His arms around her, hers around him, their bodies pressed close. The missing part of her slid into place.

When Sam stopped kissing her long enough for them to catch their breath, she peeked around him. Three heads swiveled back to looking at the river. "I think should wait until my family aren't watching our every move."

"After dinner? Your mother invited me to stay."

"Did she? It's usually Papa who does the inviting."

"I like them." Sam began nuzzling her cheek, her earlobe, her jaw. Her knees were turning to jelly. She barely managed another peek at her family.

"Sam?"

"Mm hmm?"

"Hurry and kiss me again. They're coming our way."

*****

Did you miss Sophie and Joe's story in Book 1 of the Immense Sky Saga? Get *Dare Not Tell* to read it now!

Want to know what happens next in the Parker and Ryan families? Sign up for the latest news and updates about the Immense Sky Saga at
www.elaineschroller.com.

Afterword

Hundreds, possibly even thousands, of novels thoroughly cover the events of WWII as it unfolded throughout the world. Everyone knows about the Rats of Tobruk, D-Day, the incredible exploits of the RAF and the USAAF in Europe, the tragic loss of life in concentration and prison camps, huge battles in the Pacific, and so many other compelling topics.

As I planned out the content of *The Bravest Soldiers*, I discovered I wanted to tell the unsung hero stories in the WWII lives of the Australian, American, and French characters I created in my WWI novel *Dare Not Tell*, Book 1 in the Immense Sky Saga. Very few know about the battles in Syria and Lebanon, the midget submarine attacks in Sydney Harbour, the Sydney women who sewed thousands of miles of silk to create parachutes for the RAAF and the RAF, or the experienced Australian pilots who first trained raw cadets at home and then flew in the South West Pacific Area.

Sam's No 4 Squadron flew tactical air support and reconnaissance for the Australians and the Americans that was instrumental in driving the Japanese out of New Guinea and preventing them from invading Australia.

Jean-Luc's 7th Division was one of only three Australian divisions that fought in both the Middle East and New Guinea; however, the 7th received little credit for it in the face of more well-known divisions in Tobruk and North Africa. Because of this, the 7th was known as the Silent Seventh.

While they were deployed in the Pacific, close to one million US personnel passed through Australian cities and towns. Edmund Stone is a fictional character, but the booklet he wrote, Instructions for American Servicemen in Australia 1942, was a real publication produced by the US War Department.

Ten thousand young Australian women married American servicemen and left their homes to live in the United States. In most cases the women, often with babies in tow, had to wait until 1946 to finally make the journey.

Chamonix, in the French Alps, and the location of key events in *Dare Not Tell*, was occupied by German forces until the French Resistance liberated the town on August 17, 1944.

And finally, as much as Sophie Parker would have liked to be the first, I find it overwhelmingly fitting that Caroline Bouvier Kennedy, daughter of U.S. President John F. Kennedy, was appointed the first female American ambassador to Australia on July 25, 2022.

INVALUABLE RESOURCES

The Australian War Memorial, https://www.awm.gov.au, and its extensive online collections. The photographs of Jean-Luc's 7th Division—troops cooling their feet in a Roman irrigation canal, Sam's No 4 Squadron—planes, uniforms, vegetable gardens, gifts made using toothbrush handles, and Marianne's parachute work, were an incredible source of inspiration.

The National Library of Australia, https://trove.nla.gov.au/, and its digitized collection of every Australian newspaper ever published. I can't tell you how many hours I spent searching for and reading applicable articles and advertisements. Every article I've quoted in this book appeared in the *Sydney Morning Herald*.

SELECTED BIBLIOGRAPHY

Berti, Eric and Barko, Ivan. French Lives in Australia: A collection of biographical essays conceived and introduced by Eric Berti, Consul General of France in Sydney (2012–2015) and edited by Ivan Barko assisted by Edward Duyker and William Land. North Melbourne: Australian Scholarly Publishing Pty Ltd, 2015.

Dean, Peter J. MacArthur's Coalition: US and Australian Operations in the Southwest Pacific Area, 1942–1945. Lawrence: University Press of Kansas, 2018.

Dean, Peter J., Editor. Australia 1942: In the Shadow of War. Port Melbourne: Cambridge University Press, 2013.

Moremon, John. Royal Australian Air Force 1941–1945: Australians in the Pacific War. Canberra, Department of Veterans' Affairs, 2005.

Smith, Colin. England's Last War Against France: Fighting Vichy 1940–1942. London: Phoenix, an imprint of Orion Books, Ltd, 2010.

Ralph, Barry. They Passed This Way: The United States of America, The States of Australia and World War II. East Roseland: Kangaroo Press, an imprint of Simon & Schuster, 2000.

Rickard, J (23 August 2012), No. 4 Squadron (RAAF): Second World War,
http://www.historyofwar.org/air/units/RAAF/4_wwII.html

Special Service Division, Services of Supply, United States Army and issued by War and Navy Departments Washington D.C. Instructions for American Servicemen in Australia 1942.

Wells, Patricia. Bistro Cooking. Workman Publishing Company: New York, 1989.

Acknowledgements

Writing is a solitary endeavor, but so many people deserve my thanks for helping me bring *The Bravest Soldiers* to life:

My husband, Gary, who makes the best apple tarts, my mother Beth Aucoin, and my dearest friends Lyn Raffan and Cass Hall, for being with me from the very start of this adventure. Rae, Kimberly, Jan, Monica, Cass, and Suzi, for reading and critiquing early versions of the book. Lewis Poore for his patience while working with me to make a beautiful cover.

Finally, you, dear reader. Thank you for reading *The Bravest Soldiers*. It's my greatest hope that Sophie and Joe, Marianne and Sam, plus Jean-Luc and the O'Brien children touched your heart because I wrote them from mine.

All my best to each and every one of you,

Elaine

P.S. If you enjoyed this book, I would be very grateful if you would rate or review *The Bravest Soldiers* on Amazon. Ratings and reviews help other readers find this book. All it takes is a few words or even just a few stars. Thank you!

About the Author

I was a long-time technical writer who devoured historical fiction and historical mysteries on nights and weekends as a way to escape from writing about computer software during the workday. Now I write historical novels about love and loss, found families, and little-known pockets of history.

I grew up in Houston, Texas and southern California, and attended high schools in Algiers, Algeria, Northwood, England, Clear Lake City, Texas, Beirut, Lebanon, and Kingston-upon-Thames, England. For many years I've lived in Bellaire, Texas. My husband and I raised our son here. Now we have a rescue cocker spaniel underfoot and travel as often as we can convince our son and his wife to look after the dog for us.

I'm writing the next chapter in the Parker—Ryan story: it features characters from *Dare Not Tell* and *The Bravest Soldiers*, plus a few new additions. And yes, there will be a dog, too. Find free short stories and the latest news about the upcoming Book 3 in The Immense Sky Saga at www.elaineschroller.com.

Did you miss Sophie and Joe's story in Book 1 of the Immense Sky Saga? Get *Dare Not Tell* to read it now!